Hurricane of the Heart

Vinalhaven Island

Farley Dunn

●●● THREE SKILLET

VINALHAVEN ISLAND, Dunn, Farley L

First Edition

Hurricane of the Heart, Book 2

 THREE SKILLET

www.ThreeSkilletPublishing.com

Cover design by Farley L Dunn
Cover photograph by Farley L Dunn

ISBN: 978-1-943189-36-6

Hurricane of the Heart

Vinalhaven Island

Chapter 1

THE MELODY of the summer rain danced a steady beat on the Robert Hutchings Goddard Library roof, damp fingers tapping a mournful accompaniment on the plate glass windows. The building smelled of old books and cleaning supplies. Tables wore puddles of lamplight, and opened reference materials decorated the workspaces. Moisture clouded the inside of the windows, making the library and all its books seem cut off from the outside world that was prestigious Clark University.

Once, two years ago, Professor Jessica Johansen would have considered that a very good thing, the pattering on the roof overhead reminding her of how much her husband loved her. But then, she'd loved the rain then. She didn't love the rain any longer.

All around her, Professor Johansen's students murmured with the industrious nature of their assignments, giving her a moment of peace in a day that had gone on far too long to be tolerable anymore. She walked among them, glancing at their progress, pointing out an errant word or phrase here and there. A bright smile offered, and when the work was good, a word of praise as garnish. Each time she stepped away, however, she couldn't remember the student's work.

The rain pulled her to the windows, and her heart churned with sadness.

"It's wonderful, isn't it, Dr. Johansen?"

"Wonderful?" Jessica turned, and she forced a smile on her face.

"This old building. My grandfather went to Clark, you know. Are you related to the library's builder, John Johansen?" The girl, pretty with short hair and a flowered top over jeans, prattled on for a moment, then remembered she had come to Jessica with a question about a source she needed to reference. It was something simple to resolve, and the girl was once again at one of the library tables, immersed in her work.

The girl never gave Jessica a chance to disclaim any relation to John Johansen, for there was none, but at one time, Jessica had indeed considered this building to be the jewel of the university, the most intriguing structure on campus. In her first semester, she'd walked through the century-old grounds, and she had fallen in love with the library's windows. There were many repositories of academic knowledge on this hallowed campus, but to her, this one put all the rest to shame.

Today, however, nothing seemed wonderful to her. In her gray world, how could it? She rubbed her arms, the chill that she could never drive away raising goose bumps on her skin. The summer rain might bring humidity that would swell to unbearable levels when the sun slipped from behind the clouds, but Jessica hadn't felt really warm even once since the day of the accident.

She sighed, giving in to the glass's pleading, and she reached across the low bookshelf just under the massive window, leaning forward to place her hand against the glass. She had done this very thing then, too, reached and touched the glass of her living room window those two years ago. She'd pressed her skin there, felt the cold, and Jeffrey had been on the other side. The condensation on the window drew to her skin as if in empathy. The moisture remembered. It had wrapped her hand when Jeffrey was alive, and it had known her pain once he was gone.

Closing her eyes, she took a deep breath and stood as still as she could. She wished the dampness could wash her clean, but her sadness ran too deep to be so easily rinsed away. As her hand rested on that expansive library window, the previous two years were as if they had never been. Jeffrey was at her side telling her that the rain had prevented the regular sportscaster from arriving at the studio, and the station wanted him to fill in if he thought he could make it. He leaned over to kiss her as she lay in bed, trying to pull herself from the warmth of the night.

"The big time," he said. "It's the Early Morning Wake-up Show. Everyone will be watching. This might be my chance for getting my foot in the door." He sat on the edge of the bed, his suit already on, and a smile on his face.

9

"It's Saturday. It's our day, Jeffrey. You already give the studio so much of our lives." Her eyes burned with grogginess, and she didn't know why he had to give the station their weekend. It was her birthday tomorrow, and she'd thought they would spend the day in front of a fire. She'd been awakened several times during the night by the rain rippling on the skylights, and she'd seen the forecasts for the day. They came on right after Jeffrey at four minutes before noon.

"Nobody watches at lunch, Jessica. They're all at work. This is Saturday. The Wake-Up Show. *The Wake-Up Show!* I've got to go." He looked hopefully at her, pleading for her approval.

He would stay home if she insisted, but he wouldn't be the charming companion she hoped for. She loved him, but she knew him, too. He would give a stranger the shirt off his back, but he had big dreams in that head of his. He didn't turn loose of his dreams easily, either, not even for a rainy day in front of a cozy fire.

Finally, she smiled and waved him away. Especially not for a rainy day in front of a cozy fire, even with his wife. He would give in to that only if he knew all his other duties were sliced, diced, and in the oven. If she let him go, he would be happier. Besides, her birthday wasn't until tomorrow. She could give up this one Saturday for him.

She closed her eyes and worked her head back into the pillow as she felt him stand, the bed shifting with the release of his body. Then she smiled as she smelled his cologne growing stronger. He was going to kiss her, and probably on the side of her face just where her jaw turned up to meet her ear. She turned her head without looking, as if she were already asleep and just casually shifting her position. She inhaled deeply as she felt the softness of his lips gently brush her skin.

"I love you, Jessica." His breath ghosted her face, flooding her senses with the memory of the times he'd said those words to her during the middle of the previous night. Then, other things had been going on, and her birthday had been far from her mind.

"Hmm." She smiled and slowly opened her eyes. However, he was gone. She laughed and threw back the covers. She was fully awake now, and she wanted to repeat his words to him. Running to the front room, she looked for his keys and umbrella by the door and saw they were gone.

Pulling the curtains back, she searched through the glass. The window was fogged with moisture, and Jeffrey was running down the walk in the early morning dimness, his umbrella in hand. She smiled as he paused to push the remote on his key fob while holding the umbrella to keep the rain at bay. She'd have been soaked, but Jeffrey was managing it just fine.

Tenderness toward this man she loved welled up in her. She reached and pressed her hand to the glass separating her from the weather and from the man she adored as part of herself. As the moisture seemed to gather to her skin, she whispered, "I love you, Jeffrey. I tell you, but never enough. Know that I love you on this day. Always, always, I love you." She stood watching the rain long after he'd driven away, as if her hand on the glass was sending her love to him, as if he needed her today more than she needed him.

As she turned from the window, she pulled her hand

away and noticed her handprint. Just where her hand had been, the glass was perfectly clear, but all around it, the images coming through the condensation were fogged, as if the world around her had suddenly become something she could no longer see clearly.

The glass hadn't been especially cold, yet a chill had run down her spine just the same. She let the curtain fall, hoping the sensation would go away. She lit the fire even though Jeffrey was gone for the morning, and she pulled a chair close. It took a very long time for her to get warm, and she couldn't seem to feel Jeffrey near her at all.

"DR. JOHANSEN?"

A voice gently interrupted Jessica's reverie. Somewhere in her thoughts, buried under her sudden upwelling of memories, she had known her class was still gathered behind her, finishing up the assignment she'd brought them to the library to do. She had known she would be approached by her students at some point, but in her sudden, overwhelming self-pity, she had let herself become immersed in memories that were better left at home.

She turned, letting her hand drop from the window. It was a young girl of maybe nineteen. The girl's words continued, "The rain does that to me, too. I love to watch it, and sometimes I reach to touch the glass, just like you were doing."

Jessica smiled at the student, and then she let the forced cheer fade from her face. It was an excruciating struggle shifting back to the real world after thinking of Jeffrey.

"The rain matches my thoughts on days like this," Jessica admitted. "It takes me back."

The girl reached to where her teacher's hand had been, and in the moisture next to it, she drew a heart. "Rain makes me think of love and snuggling with someone I care about. What about you, Dr. Johansen?"

Jessica took a deep breath and sighed. She placed her hand back on the glass, and after a moment, wiped it all away. "That and other things, dear. That and many other things." She knew other things, however, weren't the same as pleasant things. Not by a far cry.

THE KNOCK on the door was jarringly loud, and Jessica jerked awake. She looked out the sliders at the pool, and a light rain still rippled on the water's surface. The knocking came again.

"Coming!" She stumbled to her feet, throwing her blanket back onto the chair. She did notice the fire hadn't burned down. Not much time could have passed. Perhaps Jeffrey had returned, and he'd forgotten his key. The day would be theirs, after all. Despite her anticipation, she rubbed her arms to fight the chill. She was suddenly cold again now that she was standing. The warmth of her blanket was left bundled up in the chair.

Before opening the door, she pulled the curtain back to see who it might be. At first glance, she noticed the handprint from earlier. Through it she could see the day had brightened, and her eyes caught the bumper of her car parked in the drive. There were other things there, too, blurred in the moisture still covering the rest of the glass. Other cars, she thought, and perhaps flashing lights. They had nothing to do with her, though, and she dropped the curtain.

"Yes?" Unable to see clearly through the leaded glass of the door, she called out her question before turning the knob. "Who's there?" With the answer to those words, she knew her world had changed forever.

"Worcester police, ma'am. May we come in?"

Her heart began to pound. She'd seen the news reports before, and she knew why policemen came unbidden to someone's door. She caught the reports sometimes when watching Jeffrey's station to view his Sports Shorts. *Car spins out of control. Driver injured in bad-weather incident.* Her stomach began to churn as she turned the doorknob. The flashing lights were just outside, and they were for her. For Jeffrey. The chill from earlier. That had been Jeffrey. She knew, now.

She opened the door to see two officers in their rain gear. Water poured from ponchos pulled over their uniforms, forming puddles on the walk underneath where they stood. Jessica could see two cruisers at the street, and their lights pulsed rhythmically in a silent parody of a police chase up and down her quiet suburban lane. As the nearer officer reached a hand to tip the hat he wore underneath the hood of his poncho, Jessica felt her vision narrow and her breath grow shallow. She didn't want to hear his words, and she knew they were coming, anyway. The world outside her door turned gray with despair.

"Ma'am, your husband is Jeffrey Johansen?"

Jessica managed to nod her head, and she replied with barely a whisper, "Is there a problem, officer?"

"Yes, ma'am." He reached to adjust his hat, and he ducked his head. Then he looked directly into her eyes. "I regret to inform you there's been an accident . . ."

14

At those words, she felt her head start to spin. As the officer at her door reached out to assist her, her world went dark. It had remained dark ever since.

"JESSICA, YOU cannot remain a lonely old stick-in-the-mud forever, you know, even if you did just refuse to celebrate another birthday." Mags Brier-Sheldon, Jessica's closest friend, licked her ice cream cone, content to let the midday heat torture those students who insisted on roaming the campus in direct sun. She was nice and cool on her bench underneath the tree. She continued, "You know, sweetie, Worcester has the highest percentage of males to females in all Massachusetts, and Clark University has even more." She paused as if considering something she just remembered. "Unless you count Assumption, and they have one percent more men than we do." She licked her frozen confection and looked at Jessica out of the corner of her eye. She smiled and pricked her again, "Men, Jessica. You know those two-legged things that grow that third leg . . ."

Jessica quickly stood up and turned her back to her friend. "My birthdays are not a topic of discussion." She crossed her arms and shook her head in disdain.

Mags grinned. At least her friend hadn't stomped off. She had to push Jessica, always had, even back in grade school. That time when they'd wanted to be cheerleaders, Jessica and she had practiced for weeks. "Go, Cats, Go! We're the best there is! They can't do no mo'! Let's show 'em our biz!" She had to laugh now, but it had been important to them as fifth graders. She could see now that the cheer they'd made up had been as corny as the day was long, but they'd been so proud of it.

Then, the day of the competition, Jessica had called in sick. Mags had known better, and she'd rushed home at lunch. Grabbing a sandwich, she'd run next door to Jessica's, and there she was, puking her guts out in the bathroom.

"It's just your nerves, you wimp!" Mags had made her go, practically dragged her to the competition after school. They'd won, too, corny cheer and all. They'd been cheerleaders for the next seven years. Jessica had been that good. Mags had ridden her coattails, and she wasn't sorry one tiny bit, either.

Now, Jessica needed to come out of her shell, and Mags intended to push her until she did. She didn't want to break her, though. After all, that awful death Jeffrey had died. Her friend had been a near basket case for a long time. She'd spent almost two months at Mags' little apartment, and her place barely had room for one. She'd been there since college, though, and it was rent controlled. Nearly sixteen years, and her rent had hardly gone up at all.

However, that was beside the point. The point was that Mags now knew things about Jessica that she'd never intended to know, and there were a few things she wished she'd never learned at all. She knew just how many tissues her friend used to blow her nose, and how often she polished her dress shoes. Never, was the answer to that question. She never polished them. "I can always buy new ones. Why bother?" Depression from Jeffrey's death? Maybe.

However, who wants to know what her best friend's

underwear looks like when it's drying over her head in the shower? Or that she always wears her pantyhose twice? Or that she could sit and look at a picture of her deceased husband in his wedding tuxedo for four hours a night for nine days in a row? Mags knew. She'd watched the clock to see if there would be even one night when the grief-drenched picture-holding would set a new record. Nope. Jessica was so organized, she even timed her grief.

It was real grief. Mags knew that. In an apartment as tiny as hers, she also knew Jessica cried three times each night. The first would be seven to nine minutes until she fell asleep, and the second would happen around midnight. That one would last about twenty minutes. The final time would be at six.

"Why six?" she'd asked her friend one morning.

"On our honeymoon, Jeffrey always woke me at six to make love in the early dawn light."

Jessica hadn't even cried when she'd told Mags that. She had looked at the picture in the tuxedo twice that day, though.

Mags watched several new teachers walk the far part of the quadrangle. A couple of them were certainly male, and one was walking all by himself. Good-looking, too. She tapped Jessica on the arm and pointed.

Suddenly, Mags' ice cream was snatched from her hand. She looked up to see her friend with the confection already to her mouth. Her jaw dropped when she saw her friend bite into it and then hand it back to her with a mouth-sized chunk missing.

"Why, Dr. Johansen! How dare you!" Mags' outrage was a stage-worthy act. She stood and held out her injured sweet treat as if the bite that had been taken was personally offensive to her. "Now I shall surely burn to a crisp in this torrid Worcester hell that this summer day has become." Then she sat and laughed, looking at Jessica. Licking the treat one more time, she raised her eyebrows and winked. "Was I good, there? I'm taking a class with the good Mr. Pearson, and he says I act very well."

Jessica crossed her arms and looked down at her friend, tapping one finger against her sleeve. "He's not a full professor, yet? Mags, he's been here almost as long as I have. Find you someone with potential."

Mags hooted and stood, flipping the rest of her treat into the waste bin. She reached and put her arm through Jessica's, and she pulled her into the sun, as they headed toward Jessica's office across the quadrangle. "He does have potential, my dear. Have you ever felt his arm when he's helping with an especially difficult acting position? Hmm. If that isn't potential, I don't know what is."

Jessica pulled away and turned to look at her friend, an expression of disgust on her face. "Mags! Surely you aren't taking that class just to be touched by Mr. Pearson?"

Mags moved to grab her friend's arm once again. "Is there a better reason, dear Jessica? That's why I worked so hard back in junior high to learn those splits. What better way to show off in those cheerleading outfits?" She giggled. "You did the same, except it was all for Jeffrey, wasn't it? He wasn't a sportscaster then, but I remember you telling me how good he was in speech class. 'He gives the best speeches ever. I could watch him all day. He has so much potential.' Remember that?"

Mags gave Jessica a syrupy smile, tugging her friend

faster across the quadrangle.

"I NEVER did say that, you scamp." Jessica laughed a little too brightly at Mags and her remembered version of those past events. She'd been irritated earlier by her friend's too-graphic description of the male anatomy, and she hadn't enjoyed being reminded of crying all through her last birthday. To get back, she prodded her, "Did you really learn those splits just to show off the underside of your wardrobe?"

She also hoped to get her friend onto a safer topic and off Jeffrey, because she wouldn't admit remembering it, but she did recall saying that very thing about him. Hearing her friend's words made her miss him, and she couldn't afford to cry on campus. When she got home, she could shed her tears in peace.

Without warning, she felt Mags fall against her. The unexpected weight knocked Jessica off balance, and she threw out her arms to try to maintain her dignity as well as her posture. It was hopeless, and as she fell, she realized she had fallen directly onto someone else.

Chapter 2

PETER CASSEL remembered none of it, but he had the newspaper clippings. There was even a story in *Medical Monthly*. "New, Untried Procedure Performs Miracles." The doctors had saved him a copy. When he went in for his six-month checkup, he walked into the outpatient clinic, and there they had been, with a cake filled with candles. Thirty-two of them, in fact. Candles, that was. There were only six doctors, along with several nurses.

"Hey, Doc. Is someone celebrating?"

It looked like a birthday party, and it wasn't his. He was just there for his checkup, and he wasn't even sure he needed it. He was in better shape than he'd been in for five years.

Doctor Rossi walked up and put her arm around his

waist, and she gave him a hug before pulling him to join the group. "It certainly is someone's birthday. Around here, we count them in six-month increments. That's all some of our patients get after traumatic heart surgery, although we expect you to live a very long time." She laughed, tiptoed, and gave him a peck on the cheek.

She'd told him the story of her grandson, and how his hair had been the exact same tawny color as Peter's, as tears had come to her eyes. Had been, because he'd died from heart disease at twenty-four, all because no one had been there to give him a compatible replacement. His death had motivated her to pioneer her new technique for substituting the ubiquitous but life-threatening endomyocardial biopsy with a more patient-friendly process. Her battery-powered device was implanted directly into the donor heart, and it performed a continual biopsy for possible rejection, even supplying doses of medications directly to the affected tissue. Her process allowed hearts that would otherwise be incompatible to be matched with a wider range of recipients' bodies. Peter had been her first, and he'd been a runaway success.

During the party, the doctors sang to him, and they even had him blow out the candles. They laughed when he could get only twenty-nine blown out before he ran out of breath. He heard one of the nurses murmur a surprising phrase when he paused to prepare for the final three.

"Twenty-nine. How appropriate."

He glanced at her, but she was already cheering for him to *huff* and *puff* and *blow out the rest.* He did, and he laughed with everyone else. Later, though, he found Doctor Rossi, and he held her hand in his. She looked at

21

him with a twinkle in her eyes as she waited for him to speak.

"You gave my life back, you know. You saved me, Doc." He sniffled, and then he tried unsuccessfully to blink back the moisture.

"No," the doctor replied. "I just used the opportunity. All our available donor hearts were either located too far away for viable transport, or they weren't similar enough to match your body type. You know that. You knew it then, too. Someone else saved you that morning." She looked at him as her eyes misted. She glanced around the room at the party-making doctors and shifted topics. "Over the past six months, the media has grabbed onto this new medical process as the greatest miracle of the new century. How do you like being a miracle?"

Peter took a deep breath as he took in the room and the people enjoying his cake. "Better than before the surgery. My wife left me, and all because of my illness." He looked at her, hoping she got his meaning.

"I know, Peter. That must have been difficult."

"Yeah. Was the donor twenty-nine?" He looked hard at her this time, knowing she would have this information. For months after the surgery, he'd been trapped in that hospital room, and he'd kept up with nothing outside of just staying alive. When he began to improve, he hadn't wanted to know. He just wanted to get home. Then there was the television movie—on hold until he proved he survived—to chronicle his amazing story of illness and miraculous recovery. He'd suggested it wouldn't do for him to be proclaimed a miracle, have a movie made, and then die before it could hit the cable channels. They'd seen his point and reluctantly agreed.

When he finally began to sort through the stories, the newspaper clippings he had were about him, and they told little about his donor, other than that he had been in the local media. Even the eyewitness reports about the events directly surrounding the accident hadn't mentioned names, just the horrifying details of the crash, giving the event a very human scale.

When he reentered the world, and his favorite sportscaster, Jeffrey Jay, was off the air, for one wild moment, he suspected he knew the donor. He was horrified and excited all at the same time. After he'd gotten a better grip on reality, he knew better. Now, though, he felt he was about ready, and he wanted to find out just what had happened.

Doctor Rossi stood very still and looked into his eyes. "Green with gold flecks, beautiful, but I've told you that. Just like my grandson's. You know the donor information is confidential. I thought you might have gotten the story from the papers and put two and two together. You'll have to do that on your own. I won't lie to you, but I cannot tell you more."

"Just this, right or wrong. Was he twenty-nine?" Peter hated to beg, but he would if she forced him.

"Good guess, my miracle patient. Don't ask me more, though."

She hugged him, and for a moment, Peter felt as if she were hugging her grandson. He smiled even though he knew she couldn't see it, and he returned her hug, as a good grandson should.

"You do my heart good," she whispered to him.

He laughed as he released her. "No, Doc. You do *my* heart good. I mean that, too." She stepped back and laughed, but Peter reached and gave her another hug. He'd seen the tears in her eyes, and he knew they weren't for him. They were for the grandson she could never hug again.

JESSICA WAS appalled. She looked up at the sky and the trees in the quadrangle; and she placed her hand down in an attempt to get up. When she shifted her weight, she realized her hand was directly on the person she'd fallen on. It was obvious he was a man, too. Yanking her hand away, she covered her face in embarrassment. She heard laughter from next to her, and she opened her eyes to see Mags also trying to stand. However, it seemed her friend's difficulty in standing was for another reason entirely.

"Jessica!" Mags was laughing so hard her eyes were flooded with tears, and she was holding her side, unable to control her mirth. "You were such a hoot when you went down!" She waved her hands wildly in the air, imitating her friend.

"A little help, Mags?" Jessica wanted up, but she wasn't sure just how to climb out of this mess. Her hand couldn't be allowed to return to the last place she'd put it, and *what* was Mags finding so funny? This was certainly not amusing at all to her.

She watched her friend stand and wipe the tears of laughter from her eyes as she reached her hand in Jessica's direction. Just as she was about to take it, another hand, a masculine one, reached from underneath her toward Mags' proffered help.

"I apologize." The words softly rumbled into Jessica's ear. "I guess I wasn't watching where I was going." A second hand wrapped her waist and gently adjusted her position. Then, with Mags' hand for assistance, the mystery man managed to quickly get them both up and on their feet.

Jessica attempted to stand on her own, and her foot slipped on a broken heel. She cried out as her foot twisted sideways underneath her. The man tightened his arm once again around her waist, and in her surprise, she inhaled a sharp breath, drawing in the scent of his cologne. It was a warm and musky smell, one that reminded her of Jeffrey. Her heart caught at the memory. Then, there was the feel of the man's arm around her waist, and the sound of his deep voice as he apologized once again. His words tumbled softly over her shoulder, and it sounded as if they were being whispered into her ear.

"I've got you. You won't fall again. Is your foot bothering you?"

As she stabilized her body, she felt him kneel to reach for her ankle. He grasped it gently in his hand as he checked it for damage. He looked at her until her eyes finally dropped to rest on his.

"No injury that I can see. Can I walk you to the first aid station? You can't tell, sometimes. I do think you broke the heel on your shoe, though."

Mags interrupted at just that time, and she grabbed the man's arm. With a smile she blurted, "This is my friend, Jessica. She's lucky you still had your arm around her. She might have fallen a second time, if you hadn't. She can be a bit clumsy at times. She's not married, either."

Jessica shot her a look of venom. She hissed under her breath, "Mags!"

"Are you new on campus?" Her friend grinned.

The man jerked, startled into action, and looked at his watch. "Ex-wives, heart doctors, and now beautiful women! Everything slows me down! I'm about to miss my appointment!" He gathered his things from the ground. "Please excuse me. I've got to go. You be sure to have that foot checked. I'm sorry I was so careless." In a quick motion, he was running away.

Mags couldn't keep the smile from her face. "Tawny hair and those gold-flecked eyes. Could they come any more handsome?"

Jessica took several deep breaths. She'd just been walking, and then this whirlwind of a disaster had hit. He reminded her of Jeffrey, too. His smell, anyway, and that was very disorienting. At least he had apologized.

Then she remembered. He hadn't bumped her first. Mags had! She grabbed her friend's arm, and she yanked her into the building as she limped on her one good shoe.

"You! You did that on purpose! Why?"

Mags raised her eyebrows. "Well, sweetie. I did point him out to you. You just wouldn't look, and you simply cannot let all the really good-looking ones get away. Well, maybe you can, but I can't."

Jessica snorted. "You can have him, then. He's all yours."

Mags flipped her hair with her hand, as she looked at her friend. "No, dear. I have the wonderful Mr. Pearson. This one's all yours," and she gave Jessica an impish grin that seemed to travel from ear-to-ear.

PETER'S STORY had made it into print. *Real Life Dramas* had run a special loosely based on him. "Sportscaster Gives Life Twice to Same Man." All the names had been changed, but the magazine had gotten all the medical details correct. He was being transported by ambulance to the best facility in the city, although they hadn't mentioned it was Worcester. The story also told of the doctors' hopes that he could be kept alive until a suitable donor heart could be located. A freak accident on rain-slicked roads had sent his ambulance careening into oncoming traffic, killing both the driver and the attending paramedic. The wreck crumpled the front of the vehicle, twisting its frame, and buckling the rear doors. Peter, hooked up to IVs and groggy from pain medication, was hardly aware of what had happened.

Then, the engine of the ambulance burst into flames. It was the heroic actions of his donor that had rescued Peter from the back of that ambulance. The man had seen him inside, and in a valiant and even senseless act of bravery, he stopped his car on the side of the road to run and give assistance.

As dozens of bystanders watched, Peter's rescuer had leaped inside, unstrapped him from the gurney, and lifted him out of the truck. Halfway across the road to safety, a searing ball of heat had blasted them, knocking the two men to the ground as the ambulance exploded.

That alone would have made a riveting note the local media could have added to enhance the nightly news, even used to promote their upcoming golden boy sportscaster. However, the angry road gods weren't finished. It was the

27

next series of events that truly made the story newsworthy. A tractor-trailer rig was barreling down the highway, and for whatever reason, the driver didn't see the accident. Hitting his brakes too late on the rain-slicked road caused his rig to jackknife.

Witnesses told how Peter's rescuer literally threw him to waiting arms on the side of the road. Two more feet, and Peter's angel of mercy would have made it to safety, too. The bumper of the rig caught him, and there was nothing anyone could do.

Both men were transported to UMass Memorial, the hospital Peter had been headed to before the accident. The injured man's wallet showed him to be an organ donor, and the rest was history. Peter's physician, Doctor Rossi, was on duty that morning, waiting for him. While the local hospital wasn't set up for a heart transplant procedure, luckily—for Peter, anyway—it did have the facilities to do the same procedure for livers and kidneys. Preeminent Dr. Rossi stepped in, and soon Peter had a new heart beating in his body, one from a man who had rescued him from a burning ambulance in the morning, and who, that after-noon, gave him his heart. Peter thanked God for Doctor Rossi and her confidence in both her skills and her new cutting edge heart procedure.

Peter always said he didn't remember any of what had happened, but there were flashes from time to time. The intensity of the heat from the exploding ambulance. He remembered that. At least he thought he did. It was a burn-ing sensation, rather like when his old heart would flare up, and he would suddenly have a hot flash so intense he knew he must be about to die.

Then there were images that sometimes flashed into his mind, none coherent, of course. One, though, a clean-cut man's face. Was the man his rescuer? He didn't know. Perhaps it was the paramedic who had ridden in the ambulance with him, or one of the bystanders who had helped pull him to safety when he'd been thrown free of the accident.

"Superman," he told the nurses. "You've saved Superman's life, you know." When they'd looked at him with puzzled expressions, he'd laughed. "I flew from that man's arms all the way to the side of the road. Luckily for me, someone was there to catch me. I was Superman for a moment, though. When you saved me, you saved Superman."

He usually got a laugh, and one or two of them had taken to calling him Superman after that. He didn't know more about the man who had given him back his life twice in one day, but he was grateful. One day he'd write his version of the story, and it would include all the details. He'd go to the paper, pull up all the articles. He was certain research would reveal the man who'd died to save him. He'd also tell of Doctor Rossi and her innovative procedure, and he'd describe his exhausting recovery. Doctor Rossi would have a prominent place in the story.

He knew he needed help, however. He was a writer, but mystery stories do not documentaries make. Besides, he hadn't sold even one of his novels to a major publisher. The story he needed to write had to be as good as any ever written, and he knew he needed professional advice.

Peter was going back to college.

Chapter 3

JESSICA FLIPPED on her monitor. Her campus office used to be spotless, and every student paper that came inside was immediately looked at and sorted to its proper place. She sighed as she listened to her computer run through its start-up process. At least it was coming alive, unlike her and the dull, gray world that continued to swirl around her each day.

She was aware that her friend thought she needed to get over her grief, but Jessica wasn't sure that was possible. Grief was either there, or it wasn't. Hadn't she learned that in her college psychology classes over a decade ago? Denial, anger, bargaining, depression and acceptance. Well, she certainly didn't see where she'd worked her way through that mess, and she didn't know she had the energy to do so.

Her office *was* part of the problem right then, and that was something she freely admitted. It was dusty, and she had papers crowded where there was no room to have them. Most days when she walked in, she felt overwhelmed and wanted to cry. Then, after she dealt with her immediate emotional trauma, she would flick some of the most obnoxious dust around, and she would find she just didn't care enough anymore. She would think of Jeffrey, and the mess around her would seem unimportant. The only item she could get her mind around was the next thing that had to happen, and for months, that hadn't been cleaning her office.

She reached down and rubbed her ankle. It hurt. Also, she'd have to get new shoes, for sure. She'd ruined hers when the heel came off. Or, maybe she'd just wear black shoes instead of these blue ones. The two weren't that far off in color, and she wasn't sure she could develop an interest in shopping anymore.

Then she took a deep breath. Wearing black when only blue would do? During high school and college, she'd been in too many beauty pageants to not care. She'd get new shoes before she wore anything tan or blue again. She just wouldn't shop for the best price. She'd pay whatever it cost and let the expense be like water off a duck's back. Her leg at least felt fine enough to walk on, and she thought perhaps she'd get by with just a day of stiff muscles.

However, she did need to check her class rosters. She had let this go until it *was* the next thing that needed to happen. The new session started in less than a week, and she did have classes to teach. It was one thing to live her life in a haze, and it was another to let it deteriorate until it became unbearable. She was too practical for that.

Out of the corner of her eye, she caught the flickering shift of information on her monitor that told her the computer was ready. When the school logo scrolled across her screen, she reached up to tap the enter key. It flashed a warning at her: *Logging on to a secured network. Do you wish to proceed?* Of course, she did. Why did these machines always ask? If she didn't want to log on, she wouldn't have started up the computer.

She reached to input her password. It was the one motion of her day that she looked forward to. She had kept her password the same for two years, even though the system wanted her to make a change every three months. When Jeffrey was first gone, she sought to be reminded of him all the time. She changed all her passwords to the letters in his name. Then, when the university's system popped up its first warning message telling her she had to change her password, her heart had dropped from her chest, as if Jeffrey were being taken from her all over again. Her hands had shaken, and her vision had narrowed. She hadn't been able to concentrate on anything except the injustice of the school taking those seven letters from her. Doing so seemed to contain an unprecedented level of malevolence that was intended to steal her Jeffrey from her once more.

Mags had come to her rescue that time, and her treasured password had been her comfort ever since. Jessica's fingers reached to her keyboard, and in a rapid fire of movement, she entered the correct letters: *Jeffrey8.* Then she ran her hands lovingly over the keyboard as she watched the display begin its chattering entrance into the world of the school's infrastructure. It was almost as if she could feel Jeffrey in the surging pulse of the electronics, as if he were somehow with her again. She knew it wasn't so, but that didn't stop her from feeling his presence.

Now, however, she had information to pull up, and it wouldn't get done if she just sat and watched the screen-saver come on, would it?

"YES, MR. CASSEL. I have your paperwork right here. You faxed these, let me see, on the twenty-sixth. You say you only want to audit a class?" The counselor pulled his glasses from his coat pocket and slipped them on the end of his nose to read the forms better. After a moment, he raised his eyes to look at Peter while still holding the papers in his hands. "No credit, this means. It isn't any cheaper. Whether for credit or just to audit, we still must pay the teacher and run the utilities. It's to your benefit to take the credits."

Peter cleared his throat, putting together an answer. After all, he'd sent his payment to the school's offices, and his forms did say he wanted to audit. He didn't need the credits. He needed the help, the experience that he could get from a teacher who did this for a living, someone who was better at it than he was.

Besides, he couldn't get his mind off that woman he'd run into on the way to this meeting. He'd dropped his dog off at the groomer's that morning, and he thought he had plenty of time. Then, when he'd gotten there, a woman with three Shih Tzu triplets had gotten out of her car and walked in the door just ahead of him. He had his eighty-pound retriever with him, and he'd been forced to wait for twenty minutes while she explained each and every peculiarity of each of her three pets to the groomer.

Then, he hit the three lights on Main, and they all turned red just as he was approaching. That was nine minutes right there. He still thought he had the timing covered, though. He'd driven a shortcut down an alley, and he only sort of ran that last red light just outside the college. After that, he'd checked his watch. He could barely do it, he'd thought, but he *could* still be on time.

He didn't know what had happened out there in the quadrangle. He didn't remember bumping into that woman. It had been more like she'd sailed into him, and in a tangle of arms and legs, they'd both been on the ground.

He found himself under her, very aware of her presence; and her perfume was very feminine. He hadn't forgotten women since he'd gotten divorced. Quite the opposite. Then, just as he felt the beginnings of a physical response to her sudden closeness, she had placed her hand on him, and God forbid, she'd tried to stand.

Now, his thoughts kept returning to how he'd wrapped his arm around her and held her as he helped her to her feet. He could kick himself because he hadn't gotten her last name or told her his. He would have, but he'd remembered this appointment, and, in desperation, knowing he was surely late, he'd vaulted from the scene of the crime.

Lateness hadn't been his only excuse, though. He'd also been embarrassed. His clumsiness. Knowing he'd felt aroused, and she must have been able to tell. Now this man wanted to know why he wished to audit the class. Peter didn't see the question as relevant at all. He turned his head

34

to look at the books lining the dark, wood shelves surrounding the room, and shaking his head to clear his mind, his answer seemed obvious when he finally said it.

"I already have a degree." He turned to rivet the man with his eyes, and he drummed his fingers on the arm of his chair. "A double master's, actually. However, engineering doesn't write documentaries. I need a professional to provide oversight. I thought I might find that here. Your school does have a reputation of the highest of literary standards."

The counselor cleared his throat, and by his expression, he was flattered by Peter's remark. "Thank you. I counsel the students who help keep those standards high, and I consider their success akin to my own. As a school, we certainly strive for the best. A double master's, you say. In engineering? A double?" He was clearly impressed by this new information.

Peter chuckled. He'd misled the man in his phrasing. He spread his hands wide and flexed his fingers as he explained his degree. "I was to be a divinity major, you see, at Harvard, and then I realized I'd have to be celibate." He felt his neck warm at the admission. "I already had the hours when I switched to a more practical vocation. Engineering; physics; computer science; Robert Goddard and all. I could make money and get married, too.

"Since Goddard was once on staff here, well, that decided me. My engineering portion was completed at the Thayer School, Dartmouth. I now have a physics degree from Clark, an engineering masters from Dartmouth, and with only a few more hours, I was able to go ahead and get my masters in divinity from Harvard. That gives me divinity-engineering double masters. You can check the school's records, if you wish. I'm in there."

He'd given up the Faith for a wife and a real income. It hadn't worked out. He'd married, gotten ill, and the engineering jobs had evaporated. At that point, he hadn't wanted to return to the Faith, and he wasn't sure he could have, not after having his beliefs shaken by impending death. He'd needed something he could do with his heart problems, and he'd tried his hand at writing. Apparently, publishers hadn't thought any more of his writing than the engineering firms had of his double masters' degrees. He had sent off and won a few contests, even had several short stories published, but nothing that paid any real money.

"I want to learn. What do you think? Can you find me a spot? Here at Clark? I know I'm down to the deadline, but surely, just to audit a class?"

The counselor cleared his throat. "To the deadline? Past it is more like it. I could certainly get you into one of the other schools in the Consortium, but our classes here at Clark fill pretty quickly." However, he smiled and mentioned how favorably it would reflect on the school to have a double masters returning to join in the academic pursuits of the school's English department. It would inspire the other students who were just starting out in their academic endeavors. How noble!

Peter smiled as the man turned to his computer and begun inputting his information. After a few moments, he turned back to Peter and announced, "We are just able to squeeze you in, Mr. Cassel. It seems our summer session is very full. However, just for an audit, I've been able to find you a spot. It's the only one available. A Dr. Johansen.

She's one of our very best, if I do say so myself." He slipped a blank sheet of paper and a pencil Peter's way. "You might write this down: Dr. Johansen."

The counselor turned back to his computer, and he pressed a few keys, his finger coming off the final one with a flourish. When he shifted his attention back to Peter, he smiled as if he had done him a very good turn, indeed.

Peter grinned. He knew how good his book was going to be, and all he needed was a little help. This Dr. Johansen would be just the person. She was probably very experienced, wise, and somewhat like his much-loved Doctor Rossi. She might even be the type of grandmother to him that Doctor Rossi had become. Peter looked forward to meeting the venerable Dr. Johansen very much.

JESSICA TACKLED one more layer of her university's information infrastructure. Even after logging into the main system, she still had to enter her password yet again to get access to her rosters for her summer school classes. As she did, the phone rang. She ignored it for a moment.

Then, the sun dappling through the narrow window high on one wall caught her attention. The building's architect had designed tall, asymmetrical ceilings throughout the facility, even in the individual faculty offices, and hers peaked on one side far overhead. She looked up, wondering as she had so many times in the past why the window had no blinds. It ran all the way across the room. She couldn't open it, and she really had no idea why it was there except to remind her when the sun was out.

She narrowed her eyes into a squint. Yes, she noted. The window was dirty, too, just like the rest of her office.

The good thing about that was there was no way she could be expected to clean up there. The bad thing about it was that she couldn't clean that window even if she wanted to. She couldn't reach it.

She looked at the phone as it settled into its customary silence, and just as she was about to go back to her computer, it startled her as it began to ring again. Her heart thumped in an old, vain hope. She was empty without Jeffrey, and she was desperate to have him back. She knew he was gone, but she somehow hoped that each time she picked up a ringing phone, it might be him. It never was, though.

With her mouth pressed into a tight line, she reached for the offending instrument. Pulling it from under a sheaf of papers, she held her hand on it for a moment as it jangled a few more times. Then she lifted it and put it to her ear. When it got tangled in her hair, she pulled it away, shook her hair back, and pressed the receiver to listen once again.

"Dr. Johansen speaking. How may I help you?" She pressed her shoulder to hold the phone and reached back to the keyboard with her hands.

"Did you find out, yet?" The words were barked loudly into her ear.

She dropped the receiver as it clumsily slipped from her shoulder. Quickly rescuing the fumbled phone, Jessica held it back to her head, shaking her hair out of the way.

"Mags, is that you?" Her heart pounded with the sudden, overbearing intrusion into her morning, and her words were harsher than she intended. However, it should have been Jeffrey on the phone, not Mags, and her irritation felt justified.

"Sweetie, does anyone else ever call you? I'm just outside. You can see me waving if you'll climb on your desk and look out those windows. You won't though, so I'll just come on in."

About that time, the door to her office clicked open, and Jessica looked up to see it swing wide. In walked Mags, and she reached out with a triumphant tap on her phone, turning it off and dropping it into her satchel of a purse. She grasped a pile of papers on a chair, picked them up, and dropped them wholesale onto the floor. Then, she let herself fall into the empty seat.

"Jess, we have to get you some help." Mags reached to run her fingers through her hair, letting it fall into a beautiful cascade of cinnamon curls.

"Mags," Jessica began. "I'm very busy. What do you need?"

Jessica's friend sat up very straight, and she put a look of mock despair on her face. "Why, you were my very first and best friend, Jessica Moritz Johansen. Now you shun me just because you're busy. You have torn my heart from me, and I shall never be the same." Then she collapsed into a bundle of giggles, slapping her leg. "That was right from our new play. I had to say that line, without your name of course, and I got to practice with Mr. Pearson. Now, I want to know about your man."

"Why are you here, Mags? If you're talking about that man you *pushed* me into out on the quadrangle, surely you cannot expect me to actually have the time to chase him down. That's more your style. You go find him. I've got work to do." She reached back to the keyboard.

Mags leaned forward and grabbed her arm. "Sweetie,

39

I know that you turn your underwear inside out to let them dry. That's why I told you I was waving at you, by the way." She let go of Jessica's arm and dropped back into the chair, pulling one foot up under her. Her eyes glistened with laughter, and a smirk hovered on her lips.

Jessica took a deep breath. "So, this is about my underwear? You waved at me because of my underwear?"

"No, silly. I waved because I know you, and if I'd given you any real warning, you would have been conveniently too busy to see me. You've got to get past all this grief. You're my best friend, and I can't let you just old maid and die. Besides . . ." Mags looked up at the ceiling and started whistling a haunting tune in a minor key. She didn't finish her thought, and she didn't look like she intended to.

Jessica's eyes had begun to burn at her friend's mention of her grief, but she wasn't crying. Sometimes Mags made her so angry that she wanted to kick her. Now, Jessica was frustrated that the woman wouldn't leave her in peace. She did have work to do, even if Mags could play all day. Jessica didn't have a trust fund to fall back on if she had short hours at work. She had to live on her paycheck, unlike some other people.

She also knew she didn't really have to live on her paycheck. The trucking company's insurance had paid out handsomely. She could quit work and still live quite nicely for the rest of her life. However, she was forever the practical one. She'd put the money away, refusing to touch it. She made herself work. It was her therapy. Her days might be laced with lingering grief, or even devastated by over-powering sorrow, but to be at home alone would be worse.

Even on her most self-pitying days, she could see that.

"Besides what, Mags? I'm listening." If Jessica knew one thing, there was a purpose to this charade of her friend's. She was her best girlfriend, and she'd been there for her in the days after Jeffrey's death. Jessica had been able to wail at her, and her friend had taken everything Jessica had been able to throw at her. She had loved her back. Jessica might not like the convoluted game she was playing, and she might appreciate it even less, but there was a point to it. She would be better to let her friend play it out.

Mags looked at her and stopped whistling for a moment. She pursed her lips to fight back a grin. "Are you, Jess? Really? This is especially good news, you know."

Jessica looked at her friend, and she let one hand slip to the keyboard. She began to tap its plastic case in hopes Mags would take the hint. Finally, she said, "The news. What is it?"

Mags held her hand up in front of her and bent her fingers over to look at her nails. She studied them for a moment before answering. With feigned focus, she continued to watch her fingertips as if uninterested in the words she was speaking. "He's not married."

Jessica rolled her eyes. "I could have told you that, Mags. It's on his school web page. Mr. Pearson has never been married."

Mags jumped up and grabbed a handful of her curly hair in each hand. She twirled around as she let out a screech of frustration. Finally, she stopped, giving Jessica a how-can-you-not-see-this glare. "You are so dense, Jess. I *know* Mr. Pearson's not married. Otherwise, I wouldn't be hanging all over him. I'm not a wanton woman, whatever you think. I'm talking about your new man."

This time Jessica laughed. Mags had that effect on her. Spend enough time in her presence, and the heaviness that had surrounded her the past two years would fade away. It would later return. Jessica knew that. However, it was nice just for a moment to feel what real life was like again.

"Mags, I don't have a man. Jeffrey hasn't been replaced, if you haven't noticed. I sleep alone."

Mags paused before answering, and then tapping a finger on her lips, she murmured cryptically, "We'll see about that." In a quick movement, brighter, she reached and touched Jessica on the nose with a fingertip. "The one you tripped over today. That's the man I mean." She pulled one leg up under her and plopped back onto the chair.

Jessica was no longer amused by her friend. She snorted and turned away from her. "The man you pushed me into. Besides, how do you know he's not married?" She reached to jiggle her mouse, and the screensaver blinked off.

"No ring, sweetie. I looked." Mags giggled.

Jessica sighed. "Like that means anything. Mags, I really have work to do. May I?" She glanced at her friend, ready for a little peace. She knew she loved Mags, but sometimes she needed a break from her, too.

Mags stood and picked up her purse. As she turned to the door, she looked back and said very casually, "Just thought you should know. Bye, sweetie." She blew her a kiss and was gone.

Jessica sighed and murmured her thoughts as she brought up her class rosters. "Who cares, Mags? I'll never meet him again. Besides, I want Jeffrey, and it's too late for that."

As the lists popped up, she noted that all her classes were completely filled. That gave her a certain amount of satisfaction. She prided herself on being a good teacher, and she judged how successful she was by the number of students who signed up for her courses.

Just then, her computer beeped at her. Jessica frowned as a message popped up in the middle of her screen. *A more current version of this page is now available. Would you like to access it at this time?* Jessica liked her classes full. Surely there were no dropouts this early in the semester. The first class hadn't even convened.

When she clicked yes, she looked at the page and at first couldn't see the difference. Then, there at the bottom, she saw it, and it didn't make her feel appreciative at all. Just below the list of her regular students was one more in a category of its own. *Audit only.* She didn't care for auditing students. They were usually older retirees who had nothing better to do. They didn't receive grades, so they usually didn't apply themselves, and auditing students quite often dropped the class when they tired of it. That hurt her professional pride, and the records reflected the drop as a drop, audit or not.

She looked at the name. Peter. Peter Cassel. He might be any age; she couldn't be sure. This roster didn't list specifics about her students. On the first day of class, she would just look for a very old person, one with white hair, probably, and maybe even a cane or a wheelchair. That would be Peter. She could take that to the bank.

She reached up and flipped the computer off without

even waiting for it to go through its shutdown procedures. She should have listened to Mags. She did work too hard, and now she was unhappy with one of her classes. That was her fault, she knew, but it didn't mean she had to like it.

She stood and grabbed her wallet and keys. Now she wished Mags had hung around. They could have gone out to eat or something. She didn't really want to go home. It would remind her too much of Jeffrey, and she was down enough already.

Stepping out of her office, a voice accosted her.

"Jess! It's about time. I thought I'd have to wait forever. I'm hungry. Let's go." Mags grabbed a purse sitting nearby, and her hand snatched up a set of keys and a pair of sunglasses.

Jessica just closed her eyes and smiled. Yes, she was very glad Mags was her friend. She was the best she had ever had.

Chapter 4

PETER WRAPPED Transplant in a warm hug before letting him out the door. He laughed to feel the big animal nudge the place where he could sense Peter's scar. Transplant seemed to know where the surgery had sliced through his master's chest, and he'd been a major boost to Peter during the early days of his recovery. That was one of the reasons he'd gotten the dog.

Transplant was nearly two now, and he'd grown to his full size. A golden retriever, he was full of life, and his boundless energy required Peter to get out of the house even on those days when he didn't feel like it. As a puppy, in the early days of Peter's recovery, Transplant had needed only the short walks his master's newly installed heart had allowed him to take. Then, as the puppy grew, the dog's walks needed to be longer and longer.

At the time, on some days, Peter had cursed Doctor Rossi. She was the one who'd suggested Peter get the dog. "It's not hospital policy, Peter. It's my own recommendation. Get a dog, one big enough it must be taken outside for walks. You won't regret it." Two years into his recovery and Peter understood what she meant. His growing pet had forced him to extend himself just that little bit farther each time they walked, and he had healed faster in the process.

"Classes start today, boy. I've got to stay pristine." Peter pushed the dog's nose away from his chest. He stood and opened the door. "Go, boy!" He snapped his fingers and pointed. Transplant looked at him for a moment and wagged his tail. Then, when Peter snapped his fingers a second time and jerked his head sideways, the big dog flew through the door with his tail wagging behind him.

Once he was in the yard, the big animal looked around and grabbed a Frisbee lying on the grass nearby. Holding it in his mouth, he dropped the front of his body to the ground, ready to start the morning's play. The dog jumped forward twice with the Frisbee still clenched tightly in his teeth.

"Sorry, boy!" Peter closed the door and looked at the dog through the glass. There the animal stood, just waiting for him to open back up. Taking a deep breath, Peter turned around and glanced at the clock on the wall. He knew why a dog was called a man's best friend and a woman could only be a lover. A dog couldn't be one, and no woman could be the other. He knew. He'd been married, and she'd run from Peter at the first sign of trouble. Transplant would never do that. If anything, he'd sit out there and wait for Peter all day with that Frisbee in his mouth.

"Sorry, boy." He whispered the words this time. He knew how it felt to be abandoned, and although he knew that big, wonderful animal in the yard was just a dog, and he wasn't being abandoned, it still tore at Peter to see him look so expectantly at his master and then to just close the door.

"Sorry, boy, but I have to do this. No one can write my story for me, and I need Old Lady Johansen's expertise to do it justice." He smiled at that, looking forward to Doctor Johansen becoming a second grandmother figure to him.

His eyes glanced at the clock again. Here he was on the first day of class, and he was cutting it close once more. He had to move, or he'd be the last one through the door. He snatched his keys and his wallet. Punching in his four-digit code on the alarm panel, he opened the door and stepped through, pulling it firmly shut behind him. Then he remembered. Laptop. The course syllabus said he had to provide his own laptop. It was in the house, still.

Cursing his foolishness, he took his keys and pushed the one for the front door into the lock. As he swung the door open and reached to code the alarm pad, he felt a twinge just where his surgical scar ran down his chest.

He paused and forced himself to slow down. His chest did that sometimes when he put himself under too much pressure. He'd try to cram too much into his day, like he'd done when he was carrying twenty-four-hour class loads a decade ago, and his body couldn't take it anymore. He might be late, but he wanted to at least get there alive.

He found his laptop bag on the table just where he'd

put it the night before. The instrument had cost over half his monthly allotment check. He'd have to be careful until he sold this book and had some real money rolling in. He didn't need his book to make him rich, but enough to pay the bills would be nice. That and a little bit left over for a few extras. That would be all right, too.

With his laptop in his hand, Peter tossed his keys up in the air and caught them as they came down. Then he felt of his pocket just to make sure his wallet was still there. As his hands brushed the fabric of his pants, he was reminded of the attractive woman he'd briefly held on the school's campus the other day. She was the first woman who had truly been in his arms since that improbable day two years ago, the day of the double miracle. He laughed at that. At least his teacher today wouldn't be grabbing him when he was lying down, not that he'd mind if she was as pretty as the woman who'd fallen on him.

He opened his car door and set the laptop beside him on the seat. He started up the engine, and he knew he desperately needed those red lights to stay green this morning. He could sure use that nine minutes, and he didn't want to run any of them. He looked through the windshield at the morning sky overhead, and he spoke to someone he couldn't see.

"God, I don't have my collar on, but You know I have the right to talk to You. Please, green lights this morning. Green lights all the way. Thanks in advance, God. I need to impress my new grandmother."

Peter had never been taught to pray for green lights in divinity school, but he'd never been taught to pray for a rescue from a burning ambulance, either. He'd gotten that, so he didn't think a few green lights were too much to ask. After all, there must be a God up there somewhere answering prayers. Just look in the mirror. Peter did every day, and he saw the answers to his prayers looking back at him. He was alive.

Peter looked at the clock on the dash. He whispered, "Green lights, God. Just three green lights. That's all I need."

JESSICA CLICKED the mouse pad on her notebook, and the school logo popped up on her screen. She felt her fingernails click on the keys as she typed in Jeffrey's name. Somehow, it always felt satisfying for the clicking of her nails to ring out as her fingers moved across the letters. The rest of the time, she could angle her nails to miss the keys, hitting with just the tips of her fingers, and she wouldn't disturb those around her. When she was typing in Jeffrey's name, though, she didn't care if the keys she clicked with her nails were a nuisance. Others could just live with it.

She looked up to see the first of her students walking in the door. She smiled at the hesitant look on the young face, and she called out, "Writing Development 201?" When the girl looked down at her book and then back to Jessica with a smile, Jessica motioned with her hand. "Take any seat. I'll need to see your student ID card to get your number after you put your things down."

Jessica looked back to her notebook and moved her finger on the mouse to click on her class roll for the morning. She would have these students for two hours, and then she'd have a break. Her second class would be after lunch. That would give her time for individual help with those that requested it. She always hoped some of the students would. Those were the ones she knew were going to shine. Success wasn't always about academic ability. The willingness to work hard was much more important. Students with mediocre academic ability who were willing to work long hours would often outshine those bright students who had learned to get by on their brilliance alone. Of course, the ideal was to combine brilliance and hard work, but how often did that happen? Not very, she knew.

As the students started to roll in, Jessica smiled at each one, directing him or her to a seat and requesting to see IDs. She dutifully typed in the number on each card, and the school's servers somewhere on the campus grabbed the information, matched it to carefully aggregated data somewhere else on some other server, and it sent her back a match showing that the student was enrolled on one of the campuses in the Consortium of Worcester colleges. Banded together for academic purposes, there had to be a method of letting the individual schools know which students had taken the class. In a summer session like this, it was not unusual to have students from as many as ten of the schools that made up the Consortium sitting together in one classroom.

After a bit, Jessica looked down at her computer to see her student roster was full of green dots beside each of the names, and that meant all the students had checked in with her. Then she noticed a scroll bar on the right side of the screen. That was unusual. Her rosters, even with her normally filled classes, never took more than just the one page on her notebook screen. She reached her finger to the touch pad, and she pulled the scroll bar down. She frowned to see a red dot separated a bit from the rest, and it jumped off the page at her. The clock blinking in the corner of her monitor told her the class was about to start, and she still had one student missing.

PETER SWORE under his breath as he slammed his car door shut and looked at the sky. "Thanks, God. They were all three red. How is that supposed to help me out? Just show me there was a point. Please. Just show me that." He stuffed his keys in his pocket and strode angrily toward where he thought his first class was located. Then he stopped in mid-stride when he remembered he'd left the laptop in the seat of the car. Turning around, he looked at his set of wheels. What he drove didn't really bother him, or so he tried to convince himself. Rather, it rarely bothered him, was more like it. He was usually focused on other things.

Now, though, he saw the old-style design of the fenders and the lack of simple accoutrements, such as a keyless remote, as a stamp of ugliness the car could never overcome. Never mind it had been very serviceable during all those long years of university course work, and it had even once been new during his high school years. He'd been very proud of it then.

Now, it was just a piece of metal to get him here and there. When he thought of it that way, it didn't matter what it looked like. Here on campus, though, every twenty-year-old student he had seen today seemed to be driving one of the newest models of whatever sports car was currently in vogue with advertisers.

He shouldn't be surprised, he knew. This was one of the most expensive schools in the Massachusetts area. If these kids' parents could afford to send them to this college, Peter guessed they could afford to throw in a new car to ice the cake.

His cake wasn't iced, however, and he needed his key to get his notebook out. He reached into his pocket and pulled, only to see his paperwork for class, his wallet, and a roll of cash notes flutter to the ground. Stunned at his ineptitude, and with a glance to his watch, he fell to his knees to snatch the items before they could get away. He was glad there wasn't much of a breeze, or he'd have to choose. Forget his money or forget the class. The university paperwork was paramount, though. He couldn't forget that.

His pockets bulging with their rapidly stuffed disorganization, Peter ran to the car. He stopped when he got there, out of breath. His chest had begun to burn. Since the surgery, it had never done that. He knew he had to slow down. He paused, and with a glance to his watch, he was certain he could still make it to class on time if he planned it just right. He could cut through the park and the Lasry Center to shave off a few moments. He'd done that a few times in his undergraduate days.

This time he checked to be sure he had everything, and he shut the car door and started off. A steady walk was what Doctor Rossi had suggested. Just visualize Transplant right in front of him. They were out for a walk. Steady, with even steps.

His imagined words came through in his head, *Trot, Transplant. Take it easy, and we'll cover our two miles.*

Right foot. Left foot. Repeat. Look down the street. Continue across.

Peter breathed in. The pain had faded, and his heart felt back to normal, beating at an even rate. Rather, someone's heart felt back to normal. It was keeping him alive, though, and he was thankful for that. As he thought of just how badly he'd felt before he received his new pump, he closed his eyes for a moment, and he knew he wasn't just thankful. He was truly grateful in his heart. Well, he was grateful in someone's heart.

Then, he opened his eyes again and glanced at his watch. "It's going to be close." He looked up to see a student exiting a dorm, and as the door swung wide, he could see another door at the back. Peter smiled, and he waved. "Hold the door, please." His destination was just on the other side. He glanced up at the sky once again. "You do love me, right? Keep that in mind, God. You do love me."

Stepping out the back door of his shortcut, he breathed in the summer air. He hoped God loved him, anyway. If so, anytime would be a good chance to show it.

JESSICA LEANED in, and she saw the hated words above the name. *Audit only.* She already had a drop, and the first day of class hadn't even started. It irritated her that it was the person she had known it would be.

A noise in the room rang out as a cell phone began to play the Sousa march, and Jessica looked up to see a boy in the back fumbling with his rucksack as he scrambled to turn it off. Across the aisle, she watched a young woman—no more than a girl, really—blow him a kiss when he glanced up to see if anyone had noticed his phone. Jessica required all phones to be turned off in class. It was in her syllabus. The boy knew. The girl grinned and waved, and the boy smiled back. Then, the door next to him began to open.

Jessica felt herself smile in anticipation and looked down at the name with the red dot. Only one person was missing from her roster, so maybe she wouldn't have a drop on her record after all. Not today, anyway. This was the moment of truth. She refused to look up as she considered the possibilities. Peter, young or old? She would find out soon.

PETER STEPPED to the classroom door. It was shut, and he groaned. If class had already started, he hated to go in and disturb the teacher. She was probably hard of hearing, and when he tried to explain, she would get it all wrong. He would become the butt of all the stupid jokes for the day. Then he realized his watch hadn't beeped at him yet, so at least his personal timepiece thought he was punctual. Glancing at the clock above the door, he saw he had two minutes. He smiled with relief and reached for the knob.

"Good job, God," he whispered, as he swung the door wide.

Stepping inside, he looked over the tiers of seats. They were full. He ran his eyes quickly over the dais at the front, and he was relieved the elderly Dr. Johansen hadn't arrived. Her wheelchair battery must have taken longer than expected to recharge. He glanced quickly at the trim assistant doing something on a notebook computer. Attendance, probably, and he had no place to sit, yet.

The urgency to find a seat yanked his eyes away after just a brief look, and Peter groaned once again. The front row was all that had any empty spaces, right in the middle of everything. At least the assistant would know he was present. He would earn credit for his attendance today. She wouldn't be able to miss him.

JESSICA BET herself about something else that had come to her mind on this first morning of class. Cane. This auditing student would be using a cane. Someone in a wheelchair would usually take the class online. They had learned that the frustrations of navigating the campus weren't worth the effort. A person using a walker often found it too cumbersome to carry the necessary items to class, and her class syllabus had requested a personal notebook computer. It would be a cane, because someone using a cane usually needed a walker, but wasn't ready to give in to old age. They were determined to show that by being out there to be seen, they were young and vibrant, still. Why, just look at them still taking college classes!

She didn't mean to make fun, but it was true. Besides, it was hard for her to be accommodating with others when God hadn't been very accommodating with her. Jeffrey was gone, and so was much of her compassion for other people. Well, maybe her concern for those who needed it wasn't entirely gone, but it had definitely been put on the back burner. When Jeffrey was stolen from her, so was her interest in, and sometimes her patience with, the problems that seemed to afflict so many of the people in the world around her.

PETER STARTED down the steps. "Excuse me." He reached and touched a shoulder to get a fellow student's attention. One young man's laptop case was in the aisle. "I'm sorry to bother you." He smiled, but it was as much from nervousness as from politeness. That chair right on the front row had him preoccupied. The front row! Just for him to audit the class!

The young man whispered to Peter as he stood his case up, "That's okay. I thought everyone was inside, since they closed the door." He waved away Peter's attempted apology with a grin, sending him on his way.

"Pardon." Moving forward again, Peter accidentally bumped a young woman's shoulder with his computer bag, and he paused to smile as he apologized. Inside, he cursed himself. He couldn't even walk to his seat without causing a scene.

She smiled back and just waved him on. "Hurry!" She pointed to the front two seats.

Peter took a deep breath and moved ahead.

JESSICA COUNTED to fifteen to give the cane a few moments to find an empty chair. She knew where it was, too. It was one of only two seats available, and both were on the front row. A smile grew on her face as she kept her eyes on her computer. It would be the cane. She hadn't heard it tap, but then these days they often had rubber tips on them. A walker would have elicited many apologies, and a wheelchair? There would have been a general hubbub as it couldn't have managed the steps. Someone at the back would have been forced to relocate. Even her class's behavior convinced her this elderly Peter would be using a cane.

TAKING THE last step, Peter slipped into one of the seats and placed his bag on the empty chair next to him. Reaching inside, he pulled out his laptop and opened it. He touched the power switch, and it hummed gently as the monitor began to glow. As the words *Welcome, Peter* appeared on the screen, he smiled. Just then a bell chimed, and he realized he had made it, literally at the last moment, too.

JESSICA RAISED her eyes, and when she did, her stomach turned over with a lurch. There, staring into his computer, was a man she clearly recognized. She didn't know him, but she did recognize him. He had that tawny hair, and as he looked from one thing to another on his monitor, she caught his green eyes. She thought she even saw gold flecks. What she really envisioned, though, was something no one else in the room could. She saw her hand, and it was firmly pressed into a strange lap, and that lap was now sitting in her classroom directly in front of her.

She quickly turned around and faced away from the students. Surely this wasn't Peter Cassel. She could feel her neck grow warm, and with that, the room was much too hot for a summer day that had just begun. She'd grabbed this man's crotch, and he had held her in his arms. Then, she'd run away.

Or, maybe she hadn't run away at all. Now that she thought about it, perhaps *he* had been the one to run away. He'd been late for an appointment. He said that. Was he a professor on campus? Mags had thought so. There must be something else going on, though. Surely he was no professor, not if he was in her class as an auditing student.

There was one additional detail that Jessica remembered from that fateful meeting on the quadrangle. His cologne. It had reminded her so much of Jeffrey's. She felt the warmth from her neck move up into her face. It was Mags pushing her into this man. It was that cologne. It was the memory of Jeffrey that this man had stirred in her. Had it been a fluke, or would it happen again? Would she smell Jeffrey on him today? She needed to find out.

With unexpected anticipation, she realized she planned to do something she had never done before with any of her students. She wouldn't ask him to bring her his ID card. She would go to him. When she did, she would to lean in very closely and find out just what this man smelled like. Maybe his smell wouldn't be so much like Jeffrey after all, or maybe it would. It was important that she know. Why? She didn't even ask herself that question. It just had to be done, and for a woman like her, doing the next thing that needed doing was just what one did.

PETER'S EYES were on his monitor, and he was suddenly aware of a person standing directly over him. Unsure of the reason and unwilling to look up, his eyes blinked with the aroma of a familiar perfume. He'd smelled it before, if he could just place it. He hesitated when the person didn't move away.

Then he, no, *she* leaned in to whisper into his ear, "Do you have your student ID ready? I need to see it to log you in."

Then, with those words, Peter knew. His hand on her

waist, and her hand on him. This woman had felt him in a way only one other woman ever had. He sank into his seat, and he knew his face was turning very, very red.

JESSICA INHALED deeply as she asked her question. She closed her eyes, and it didn't even occur to her that he wasn't answering. In her mind, it was Jeffrey who was sitting in the chair just in front of her, and the past two years had never happened. She moved her hand, and she knew she was going to place it at the nape of his neck, and then she would brush his ear with her lips. Jeffrey would run his hand along her ribcage and up under her breast, then he would turn his head, and their lips would meet.

"Dr. Johansen?"

A student on the second row called to her. Jessica recognized the voice. The young man had been in her class the previous spring, and this summer he wanted to get a jump on his sophomore year.

"Are you feeling okay, Dr. Johansen?" It was the boy, again, and she was yanked back into the classroom, with Jeffrey nowhere near.

PETER'S EYES sprang wide as the woman leaning over him suddenly jerked and moved away. He glanced up to see her chewing her lips as she looked across the classroom at nothing he could see there. She paused for a time and then held out her hand.

Peter glanced at it, and he didn't know what to do. This was Dr. Johansen. Jessica, if he remembered from their encounter yesterday. She was no wheelchair-bound senior citizen. She was his dancing partner, or rather, his falling-to-the-ground-and-crashing partner. They *had* danced on the way up, if he could call it that.

He also remembered she wasn't married.

SHE CLEARED her throat, and her words were hoarse. "Your ID, please." She looked down when she felt it in her hand, uncomfortably aware that her eyes had inadvertently moistened with the sudden breaking of her unexpected reunion with Jeffrey, and she laughed at the name to cover the tears that threatened. That moment of contact had been in her mind only, but it had felt very real.

"*You* are Peter Cassel. Somehow, I expected a cane." She laughed again and turned from him. She stepped back to the dais, and she reached to her computer.

HOWEVER, AS she paused to key in his number, Peter noticed that her face was pale, and she was chewing her lips once again. She was very pretty, though, and she was much better than a grandmother. She was probably seeing someone, despite what her friend had said. No woman so pretty would be alone. Her behavior today seemed just a touch odd, but that was okay to him. He thought maybe he liked that. It seemed to give her a more human scale.

When she finished with his number, she reached and carefully placed the card on the desk beside her computer. Then she looked up to catch his eye. When she saw him looking at her, she smiled and tapped the card under her fingers. She slid it his direction to remind him to take it with him when class was over, and she turned and began to speak.

Peter took a deep breath. After class. That way he

didn't have to stand just as the class was starting. He glanced at his computer to make sure it was ready, and then he looked up, just as Dr. Johansen began to speak.

"GOOD MORNING, class. This is Writing Development 201. Each of you should have a personal computer with you. It should now be opened and running. This should be the first thing you do each day when you arrive in my class. Do I have anyone here without a computer?"

Jessica glanced around the room, looking anywhere but at the man who reminded her so much of Jeffrey. She knew he had a computer. She had seen him with it out, and she knew no one would think anything of her surveying everywhere but his chair. She made a point to keep her eyes only on the other students. She would avoid this man at all costs.

When no hands went up, she reached to her own computer and tapped a few keys. Then she ran her hand across her mouse pad before tapping it one more time. She glanced up at the ceiling as the projector blinked on, and the screen on her notebook was duplicated on the Smart Wall behind her. She walked up the wall and tapped an icon. Suddenly the image changed, and the opening paragraphs of a story appeared. Below it was the image of a computer keyboard the size of an old-fashioned electric piano.

Jessica turned back to the students seated around the classroom's amphitheater. "In the class syllabus, a good beginning to a personal story was requested but not required. How many people brought that personal story with them on their laptops?" She paused to see most of the class raise their hands. She also noted, without looking at him, she assured herself, that this Peter had also brought a story. When she caught his hand out of the corner of her eye, she immediately imagined the story he had begun.

"I was walking across the school campus one day, and this inept member of the faculty ran right into me and knocked me flat . . ."

She felt her face grow warm at the memory, and she turned to hide the flush she knew went along with it from the class. An errant thought flashed through her mind that if these were the hot flashes her mother had endured in menopause, she wanted them over and done with. However, her mother had been nearly fifty. It had been a late menopause, and Jessica had no reason other than the repeated warmth on her face to think she was already there.

It was that man, Peter, and what Mags had done. Jessica knew that, but she also knew she had a class to teach. Thirty-one students were depending on her for their education, and she couldn't let them down. Thirty-one? No, that was a misnomer. Thirty students and one "audit only." Thirty students were depending on her to be the best teacher she could, and she wouldn't let them down, no matter that this man and the crotch she'd grabbed were sitting right in front of her.

She reached and tapped an icon on the wall. An overlay of red words flashed over the black ones she'd pulled up previously. She spoke as she touched one of the new words to explain what she wanted the students to look for in their stories.

"A hook." She turned to face the class as she said the word. Her touch had changed it to boldface, and as she spoke, the red letters that defined the term also turned bold. "A hook is something that grabs the reader's attention and *keeps them reading.* Your hook should be in the first paragraph. If you can't get it in the first one, stick it in as quickly as possible. Every word the reader looks at without seeing the hook is one more chance for him or her to grow bored and set your story aside. On your own computer, find the hook in your story and highlight it. Now, turn it bold, and save that."

Jessica reached up and ran her finger along a sentence in her own story, and highlighting jumped around the words. Then, she tapped another icon, and the words changed to bold type. She turned back to the class once again.

"Now, for those of you who haven't started a story yet, I'm giving you time to find something to write about. Just remember, you cannot edit what you haven't written. Put your fingers on the keyboard and type. If you don't like what you get, we will edit it, change it, rewrite it, and it will get better. Now, go!"

She began to walk around the room, going up the steps to the top tier, and then walking back down when she got across the room. She let her eyes play across the screens, and she caught a word or two. This was a time for the students to gather their thoughts, and she expected nothing more. Words on the computer, any words, would satisfy her right now.

She would have denied what she did next as she stepped to the front row, or she would have if anyone had asked her later. No one would, though. Everyone in the room except Jessica was typing furiously, and all their eyes were glued to their screens.

She hadn't tried to read any of the stories, and she never did. Not at this point. However, just this once, she looked down the row where Peter Cassel sat, and she let her eyes pause on his computer. Then, she snorted in disgust, causing two students just next to her to look up. She just smiled and waved them back to work.

She hadn't been able to see anything. Not a word, and she had tried. She'd been curious what this man would write, and he'd refused to let her see. Now she felt nosey, almost embarrassed. She knew she would read all the stories eventually, but it would be with the students' permission. Not sneakily. She felt her neck warm once again.

No, she amended to herself as she took a deep breath. He hadn't refused. His computer had one of those new privacy screens. He must have spent a fortune on his laptop. That told her something. This was a man who had money, and that made her wonder why he was here. He could probably hire a private tutor, a whole publishing company, in fact, to help him with his story. She didn't know why he needed her.

Oh, well. She would assist him, regardless. She wasn't prejudiced against those with money. After all, Mags had money. Her family even had that place she and Mags had summered at back in college. It was their old family estate out on their island off the coast of Maine. People there without money mingled just fine with those that did. If they could do that there, then in her classroom, Jessica could do the same.

She paused, recalling the name. Vinalhaven. It had

been a decade since they'd gone up there, but she hadn't forgotten the name for a moment. It was a lobstering island filled with ordinary working families, and it didn't all belong to Mags' family. Only the Point. Mags' family's place was out on the farthest point there was. She and Mags had been able to see the big, white farmhouse from the ferry when they'd ridden over. It was over a hundred years old and as sturdy as a rock. They had enjoyed such a great time that summer. Jessica didn't begrudge Mags her family's money, and she wouldn't do it to this man, either. At least she wouldn't if he'd pull his weight.

She turned to glance at him, and just for a moment she glared at the top of his tawny-haired head. Then, she began to smile again as she scanned across the room looking at the other students. They were all so clean cut and fresh. They were so *young*. She glanced at the tawny hair again. She'd give Mags her due. He was good looking. Not so excessively *young*, either. As the storybook character would say, "This one seems just right."

She was still angry at Mags, though. Jessica had grabbed this man's pants. That embarrassed her and made her hackles rise. It was Mags' fault. That rotten friend of hers would get an earful for this, and not even this man's good looks would change her mind.

Chapter 5

"MAGS!" Jessica hissed the word into her phone. She'd tossed her notebook computer onto a pile of papers on her desk, and now she squeezed the receiver as if doing so would make her friend suffer. "He's in my first class. Writing Development 201."

The receiver cackled back at her. "He's in your class? That's rich, Jess! Did you get his name?"

Jessica threw herself into her chair. "He's on my roll, you nit. Of course, I got his name. I was so embarrassed. You've cursed me the last time, you know. Next time you see a good-looking man, you take your cauldron and head into the next county. No, I take that back. You head into the next *state*. I want you nowhere near me." She pushed her desktop's keyboard aside and reached to her notebook.

She raised the top, and with the push of a button, she turned it on. Then she wedged the phone between her head and shoulder, reaching to rapidly type Jeffrey's name to bring up her university information.

Mags interrupted, "So, did I hear you correctly? The next time?" She snickered at her choice of words.

Jessica looked at the class roster opening on her screen. She shifted her position, and the phone slipped. She grabbed at it, and the computer slid sideways on its stack of papers. "Good heavens!" she exclaimed.

"He's heavenly? Did I actually hear Miss Grieving Widow say that?"

Jessica barked into the phone, "Are you just making up things to irritate me? Heavenly? I didn't say that, Mags. What's with you?"

Mags' end of the phone went eerily silent, and that in itself caught Jessica's attention. Mags didn't have the ability to stop talking, not without an ulterior motive. Jessica steadied the computer with one hand and held the phone with the other, watching as her screen came alive.

There was a small hiccup of a giggle in the silence, and Mags' voice whispered, "You said the next time I see a good-looking man. That means you thought this one was good-looking. Is my Clark University logic working properly, or should I demand six years of tuition and fees be reimbursed to my trust fund immediately?" The hiccup of laughter came again, and this time there was also a faint humming in the background. The tune was a familiar love song. It finally came to an end, and after a prolonged and uncomfortable silence, Mags asked, "Jess? Are you there?"

"Mags, how could I have done what I just did?" Jessica felt her gut wrench, and her torment bled into her words.

With Jessica's change in tone, her friend immediately sobered up, and her earnestness came pouring through the phone. "Sweetie, what do you mean? Is something wrong? I can drop everything and come right over. Sweetie?" Mags paused a minute, and then she broke the continued silence with a demand. "Jess? Talk to me. Are you there?"

"I typed Jeffrey's name, and I didn't even think of him. Not at all. Mags, I betrayed Jeffrey."

"HONEY," MAGS consoled, "you couldn't betray Jeffrey if you tried."

She could see where this was going. She didn't know the details, but just for a moment, her friend had pulled her feet out of the grief that had kept her in a quagmire the past two years, and when she realized she was free, she stuck her feet right back inside. Mags had loved Jeffrey, and she'd been broken-hearted when the reports of his death came in. She knew it was a hundred times worse for Jessica, but the woman needed to let go sometime. Two years was enough. Move on! That was what she wanted to say.

"But I did," Jessica wailed.

"Sweetie, your love for Jeffrey is written in everything you do. No, you didn't betray him. You did what Jeffrey would have wanted you to do. You lived for one bright moment during this beautiful day, and now you're taking time to remember that you had a wonderful man who was taken from you for no reason." Mags knew the grief was real, and she couldn't deny that. Nor would she try.

"No reason, Mags?" Jessica's voice was broken and on the edge of sobbing. "Another man somewhere lives because of Jeffrey. Don't take that from me. That was something Jeffrey would have wanted. His death helped someone else live."

Mags intentionally brightened her voice, "I'll tell you what, Jess. Once the summer session wraps up, let's go up to the Point. My grandmother's house just sits up there and waits for us to visit. Hey, no one's there after Labor Day, ever. We could take a month, take two. You remember back in college when we took the entire summer up there? We pulled the small skiff from the boathouse, and we dragged it to the high tide line. Then, when the tide was running, we rowed it to the float and tied it up. At night we went out into the cove, and we trailed our hands through the water. The phosphorescence glittered behind us as we floated along. Then we ran back up to the house in the dark and goofed around on the old apple tree's rope swing until it got too cold to stay out any longer. Remember, Jess?"

JESSICA SNIFFED, drawn back to that idyllic summer. Jeffrey had been taking classes at the university, and she'd called him every evening.

"I remember, Mags." She brushed her face. Those had been good times, ones she never wanted to let go of. She finally chuckled, unable to fight off her friend's entreaties. "Then we'd huddle on your grandfather's bench in front of the Franklin, poking at the last of the day's coals, trying to get enough warmth to knock off the chill we'd gotten outside. Do you remember that?" She actually laughed at the memory of what they'd do next. "We'd run upstairs and

69

fill the old claw foot tub with enough hot water to warm our feet. Then, we'd dry them off and jump into bed. The floors were so cold!"

"Promise we'll go, okay, Jessica? After Labor Day. It's been years, and it's so beautiful up there. I'd almost forgotten. My aunt still spends all summer at her place across the cove. She tries to get me up every year, and it just slips away."

Jessica was pulled to a better time by her friend's offer, and she knew why. That long-ago summer had been a time of no worries, best friends together, and everyone alive. Just the offer was a boost to her heart. Sure, she determined. She desperately needed a change of scenery. Being anywhere but Worcester would be good for her heart and soul. They would go, and she told her friend that. They would go, and there were no ifs, ands, or buts about it.

"Promise?" Mags insisted.

"A hurricane couldn't keep me away. I'll be there."

"Good," Mags replied brightly, teasing. "It *will* be hurricane season, you know."

Jessica just laughed. Hurricanes were for Texas and Florida and the Carolinas. The chances of a hurricane hitting New England were a thousand to one.

Mags laughed along with Jessica about that.

HOWEVER, THE chances were more along the line of ten to one, and it had been twenty years since the last hurricane made landfall. According to the record books, a hurricane hitting New England had become overdue about nine years earlier. That made the chances for a hurricane pretty good, indeed.

70

PETER TOSSED his Frisbee, and he cheered as Transplant jumped and caught it. Several kids were playing touch football off to one side, and one boy, wearing tangled hair and a neon orange shirt, probably about fifteen, tripped and tumbled into a flowerbed. A friend, close cut and lanky, with stylishly ragged jeans and a white tee, doubled over, laughing at him, then reached a hand to help him out.

Although the sun was bright, a breeze kept the heat at bay, and the scent of new mown grass was in the air. The park had become their second home, with the dog able to run and play his games. The big animal seemed to enjoy the open spaces, and he gladly took the little bit of freedom Peter gave him.

Peter whistled, and he smiled to see Transplant stop and lift his ears. The animal looked to find him, and as he did, his tail froze. The pair were stationary, statues in a moment of intense concentration, their eyes locked. Then, with a quick jerk of his head, Peter moved, and his pet did the same.

Released, the dog's head flicked from side to side, and then seeing nothing in his way, the animal bolted for Peter, dropping the Frisbee at his feet. Peter fell to his knees and grabbed the dog around his neck.

"Good boy, Transplant." He ruffled the dog's fur, and when the animal shook his shaggy body, Peter just laughed.

"Mister, is that your dog?" A small voice caused Peter to turn to look. "I have a dog at home. He's got long fur, too."

71

Peter chuckled. Next to him stood a small boy of about eight, and he winked at him. Then he spun back to Transplant. "Are you mine, boy?" He laughed as he jerked his hands back and forth over the dog's body, causing him to shake and bark twice. Without looking, he asked the boy, "What breed of dog do you have?"

When there was no answer, Peter grinned and wrestled with the big retriever. When he'd shared his choice of breeds with Doctor Rossi, she had told him to get the animal out. Walk the animal. Play with it. Give the dog some attention. She'd also congratulated him on a choice well made.

Peter had done as she asked, too. Even when he would have rather lain in bed, he'd gotten up and walked the puppy he'd brought home. As he'd grown, he had taken him to the park to throw the Frisbee or to play chase—anything to drain the animal's energy. Now, this boy was interested in his dog, and that made Peter interested in the boy—and in hearing about the boy's dog.

"Is your dog big like mine?" Peter stopped to look at the youngster, waiting for his response. He laughed when a big tongue caught him on the side of his face. He pushed the dog's head away.

"Nah," the boy replied, reaching his hand out to pet Transplant. "Mine's small, but he plays just like yours." He laughed when the big animal reached out to lick his fingers.

"Here," Peter said, reaching out to the boy to pull him closer. "You can pet him. His name is Transplant. He likes people." When the dog leaned over to the boy to lick his face, Peter laughed. "It looks like I'm not the only one he wants to lick. He likes you."

The boy grabbed Transplant with both hands, wrapping his arms around the dog's neck. He pressed his face into the dog's fur and held him. Peter sat back on his heels, and he watched the event unfurl. Transplant was serving as a channel for some very intense emotions.

"Hey." Peter reached out and put his hand on the boy's neck. "Is everything all right?" At one time, he wouldn't have known to ask. Since the heart surgery? Things like this got to him.

When the boy turned his face, Peter saw tears glistening. He listened as the boy sniffed. If he could get the youngster to talking, it would be better for him.

"My dog," the boy began. "When my dad left—"

Just then a voice called out, "Trent! Trenton! Get over here, now!"

The boy turned his head and looked, obviously compelled to obey. His eyes jerked back to lock on Peter's green ones. They were suddenly those of a boy who was determined to do what he was supposed to do, not what his heart demanded he do, and he whispered, "I like your dog, mister." Then, in a flurry, he was gone, running across the grass to a harried-looking young woman who must be his mother.

Peter pulled Transplant to his chest, and he wrapped his arms around the animal. The big dog resisted for a moment, and then he became limp and dropped into Peter's lap. Peter worked his fingers around the base of the dog's ears, and Transplant looked up at him with his big brown eyes.

"You're my best friend, Tee," Peter began, unexpected

emotions welling up in his chest as he thought of the boy and how he'd reacted to Transplant's friendly advances. He knew the dog had been the one to bring him back to life. He had been there for him when no one else was.

He looked up at the sky, and the blue was laced with wispy clouds. As he pressed his face against the dog's fur, he remembered a conversation with God where he'd insisted God take sides. "Heal me, God!" He'd demanded that. "Heal me, or let me die!" He'd been willing to die, too. He had hurt that much, and he hadn't understood why God let this happen to him. He'd had plans, things he wanted to do with his life.

Then he'd remembered a divinity professor's lecture in one of his classes. "If we have an agenda, God has no obligation to endorse our plans. He can follow through or not as He wishes. However, if God initiates something, He's bound by his Holy Word to follow it through to completion."

Peter knew he was very much still alive, so perhaps God had taken one side and not the other. A new heart had come to him, after all. Now, he expected God to follow through with all the rest, like taking care of an animal that meant a lot to him. Taking sides meant that.

Peter closed his eyes as he sat with Transplant, and a prayer escaped his lips. "God, please. You gave him to me. He's become my best friend. I don't have my collar on, but You know who I am, the one You gave a new heart to. Whatever You do, keep Transplant under Your care. He's been my lifeline, and he's been the reason for me to live these last two years. Please, God. That's all I ask."

Then Peter wiped his eyes, his emotional hiccup over,

and he laughed. What was he thinking? His own heart had been putrefying inside of him, and another man had died to provide him a new one. Hadn't God done that for him, set up that very unique set of circumstances? For God to let him down now? To not do something as simple as take care of a dog? The inexplicable feeling of dread was gone as quickly as it had come over him.

Peter jumped to his feet and grabbed the Frisbee. Transplant looked at him in surprise, and he barked. With an abrupt release of tensed muscles, his master released the flying disk, and with a thrash of animal energy, the dog was off after it. Peter called after him in encouragement.

"Get it, Transplant! Yes!" Peter pumped his arm in a victory sign as his dog went airborne and caught the disk in his teeth. "Good boy, Transplant!" He knelt as the animal came bounding back, waving the Frisbee in his mouth.

Peter reached for his dog, and in his heart, he hoped without words, the dark shadow of past pain not quite gone. His eyes burning, he knew Transplant was all he had. No woman would want a flawed man like him, and every man needed someone. Transplant was all he would ever have, and he hoped that would be enough.

Chapter 6

IT WAS Jessica's favorite song, one set on her alarm clock's playlist. However, at this particular moment, she was finding it especially offensive. It was trying to wake her up.

All night long she had dreamed of that man. She'd seen his tawny hair, and his green, gold-flecked eyes, and in her dream, he had taken her heart by storm.

Now, daylight was trying to steal him away, and she wasn't ready to give him up. With that admission to herself, she reached her hand to the alarm and flipped it to silence.

"Oh, my head," she moaned. "I need four more hours sleep."

She knew, however, that a class awaited her, and the

man who had tormented her dreams would be there. She might dream of him, and she might wish him away, but when she arrived in her classroom, he would be present. As his teacher, there would be times she would have to stand close to him, even if his cologne did initiate a flashback for her every time she was near. However, she would weather this, just as she'd weathered Jeffrey's death. It would happen, it would be over, and her life would go on.

In her more lucid moments, though, she was willing to admit she hadn't gone on. She'd become immersed in her grief, and her life had ground to a standstill. She wasn't moving anywhere. She was teaching her classes, and from time to time, she and Mags went out to grab a bite to eat. Despite their moments of frivolity, she was fixated on Jeffrey, and had been for the past two years. Sometimes when others said that to her, she would look at them and sink into the loss as if Jeffrey had just died. The feelings of grief were still immeasurably intense, and two years didn't seem nearly long enough. Other times, she saw what they meant, and she knew just what she was doing.

However, this man, Peter. He wasn't supposed to be at the forefront of her thoughts. He was a student in one of her classes, and her students were just that. Students. She never saw them as anything more. Oh, she gave of her time to them, and she found their stories interesting. Occasionally, she even had a bite to eat with one of them as they worked together reviewing a challenging assignment.

Yet, they were always her students and nothing more. Sometimes she really liked them, and other times she easily let them go. However, she never dreamed about them.

This man was obviously an exception to the rule. His hair, and those green, green eyes. Plus, there was one other fact she couldn't deny. She'd fallen on him, and she'd been made aware of something she hadn't fully admitted, even to herself. When she'd placed her hand on him to try to stand, she'd become unmercifully aware that he was all man, in every way.

Had he responded to her in the same way? She knew she'd definitely been responding to him, even as she'd railed at Mags for her ineptitude.

If he hadn't shown up in her class, though, she would have forgotten him as a momentary interlude in one crazy day. That would have been so much easier. She might have thought of him from time to time, and he even might have come to visit her at night during a dream or two. However, she also knew her grief for Jeffrey would have returned, and her aching sorrow would have driven the new man from her thoughts. He would have been banished forever, and only Jeffrey would have remained.

Jeffrey hadn't been with her during the previous night, though. Peter had come into her classroom. He had shown her his story. It had flashed on her Smart Wall, and that was how she'd known it was a dream even as it was happening. She never displayed her students' works for everyone else to see, and there his had been. It had started off just as she had expected that day he'd shown up in her class, but he had written more, so much more. She'd been touched by it, and the class had cheered.

Now, it was morning, and for some reason, Jessica began to cry with the memory. She didn't love this man. She didn't even know this man. Until he sat there, and she walked up to smell him, he had been old and in a wheel-chair. She smiled and reached to her eyes with the backs of her hands, pushing the tears aside. No, he'd walked with a cane, that she distinctly remembered. He *had* been very old, though.

He tricked her as he took his seat. He did the prince thing on her, although he certainly did it in reverse. Her old man frog turned into a prince right in front of her eyes, and no kiss had been needed. She'd seen it, and no matter what she dreamed, she knew she never dared kiss this prince. He would become a frog again, and the thought of that made her tears begin to seep once more.

As she threw back the covers and sat on the edge of the bed, she reached to run her fingers through her hair, closing her eyes and shaking her head to get her tousled mess to fall into some sort of order. She kept her eyes shut as she saw once again the dream words on her wall. They had been as big as life, too, and she smiled.

"I was walking across the school campus one day, and this inept member of the faculty ran right into me and knocked me flat. I held her in my arms, and then I let her go. I should have kissed her. I wish I'd done that. Then she'd be mine forever."

In her dream, the class cheered, and she blushed. With the prompting of her more idealistic, youthful students, the man who had written those words stepped to her. He was hesitant at first, and his face was red. He smiled, though, and he took her in his arms. His lips pressed against hers, and she was unable to stop her arms as they responded to him in kind.

However. With the morning had come reality, and she

79

was back in her bedroom once again. Her eyes opened, and she laughed aloud to her walls. It couldn't have happened, not with that man. He was an old man frog in a prince's body, and if she'd kissed him back, why, then, he'd be a frog once again, wouldn't he? How would that look to have a frog hopping into her classroom four days a week, all summer long? Well, half a summer, anyway, unless he was also taking part two of the class.

She would have to check later in the semester for his name on the list for her next class, although those wouldn't post until later in the session. She would have time then. Now, she had to get out of bed.

PETER HAD been up since four in the morning. Tee had come in and plopped at his feet, and he now seemed to be fast asleep. A lamp was on low, the pool of yellow light casting soft fingers of shadows far into the corners of the room. The window at his side was dark, still, and it seemed he was the only one awake in the world. Peter sat at his desk, the glowing screen on his computer lighting his face. He frowned in concentration.

Unable to let go of all the things he'd learned in his first class with Dr. Johansen, that old woman who wasn't old at all, he struggled with the idea of a hook. He had to get the reader's attention. Dr. Johansen also said to never erase. Dr. Jessica Johansen. He'd also thought about her all night. He'd gotten up early to work on his story before going to his class at the university. He hadn't been able to keep his mind on the issue at hand, though.

In fact, he was having a significant degree of trouble focusing, all because of that woman. His frown grew deeper, and he tapped the slash key idly, making a row of them, then two. Dr. Johansen had said to never erase. He was trying not to, and in fact knew he had just six weeks to finish his book if he wanted to have the good professor's advice. However, he saw her point. A hook. He had to hook the reader, and he could tell his words wouldn't. If he were to pick up what he had written so far, he didn't know if he would want to turn to page two.

Peter reached to the keyboard, and he grinned. How stupid could he make it? If Dr. Johansen wanted something to grab the reader's attention, he could go there. Deleting the slashes, in a moment of silliness, he typed the most outlandish words he could think of, and then he hit the enter key several times to put some space between his new hook and the body of the story he'd already started. He hadn't known just how to begin his tale before he signed up for his class, just that the syllabus had said he needed to start before the first day if possible. He hadn't been happy with his beginning, but it had been something. Now it *said* something. He had a hook.

"I am a man who died twice."

He sat back in his chair and looked at the words. He drummed his fingers on the edge of the notebook's keyboard and turned to look out the window. There was a streetlight on at the end of the block. At this time of year, it would get light very early. He wasn't worried about not making it to class.

At the movement of his head toward the window, the big dog on the floor at his side jerked his muzzle up as if in hopes that he'd just seen an interest in something other than simply sitting inside all morning. Peter reached to him

81

and let one hand scratch behind the animal's ears.

"No, boy," he said. "Stay." Then he turned back to the words he'd written and smiled. He liked what he saw. He liked it a lot.

AS SHE began to dress, whipping a black slip from her closet, Jessica remembered something about her frog prince. She stood in front of the mirror as she pulled the slippery fabric over her head, watching it fall gracefully around her slender body. Losing Jeffrey had certainly helped with her figure. She was back to her cheerleading weight. Still busty, though, Mags would say. "Give me just half of what you've got, girl, and I'd be satisfied." She'd huffily snapped that to her on one occasion, years ago in college.

Jessica thought about the prince who had waltzed into her life, and she knew she didn't have to worry about him hopping into her classroom if she kissed him. He would roll in on the wheels of a gleaming chrome chair, or, as she had bet herself, tap the light fantastic with his rubber-tipped cane. Jessica pictured a very old Fred Astaire waltzing down her classroom aisle, doing a little footwork number at each step, moving lower and lower down each level until he was at the front row. Then she imagined him twirling his cane in a very theatrical manner as he reached the seat Peter had been in the day before, and blowing her a kiss as his white-shod feet did a final little dance on the floor.

She reached to the closet, and she pulled out a black number just a bit dressier than she would normally wear to work. Donning it, she was very satisfied to see the edge of the black lace that trimmed the top of her slip just peeking through the dress's neckline where it plunged a little lower than was really appropriate for a college professor. She reached her hand to pat the exposed lace. It was just enough to keep this dress modest, and it looked very good. She even touched her lips with a shade deeper lipstick than she normally put on in the daytime.

She wouldn't have admitted it to herself, but there was a bit of a bounce to her step as she headed for her keys and purse, ready to exit out the door. She didn't even grab the keys to Jeffrey's old car as she did on most days. She paused for a moment at the small console that sat in the front hall, and she looked out the window to where she could see the two cars in the drive. Her eyes fell to the table at her side to see the two sets of keys there. She reached with her hand, and she placed one finger inside the ring that held the keys she usually took. Then she twirled them in a circle where they sat on top of the console.

Suddenly, with a laugh, she moved her hand and snatched up the set to her new car, the one she had bought to fend off the expense of rising fuel prices. "Thank you, Mr. President. My old clunker was worth all the cash you gave me for it." Her new vehicle was tiny, but it sipped fuel, and it suited her. She was tiny, except for this chest that Mags envied so, and she liked her little roller skate. She would drive it to work today.

She felt good about her choice. Changes were good, weren't they? Today, she felt it was true.

IT WASN'T until later that day that she would remember something she had forgotten to do. It was something she had done every day for two years, and this one morning it never crossed her mind. Mags would have cheered had she known. Jeffrey would have been pleased, too, although Jessica would have been appalled to think so. Who knew what Peter would have thought? He wasn't even part of the picture, except in Jessica's dreams.

Jeffrey's photograph sat beside the keys that remained on the console, and in the frame that had been rubbed to bare metal by Jessica's grieving hands, he grinned his hundred-watt smile. It was part of what had gotten him on the station's team. It gave him "TV good looks," they'd told him, and when he'd said his interest was in sports, they'd signed him on the spot. Give us some time, they'd also said. You must earn your creds. Just be patient.

That photograph sat there, unaware life had gone on without out it for just this one morning, and the face inside still smiled with all the energy it could muster. Jeffrey wasn't inside that frame, and he never had been. Jessica's memories of him were, though, and that was why she'd taken time every morning during the past two years to hold that frame to her, letting her tears wash it almost daily.

This morning was different, though. She reached to pick up her keys, and her eyes didn't even see Jeffrey's smile. She knew she looked good, and her lace was showing in just the right place. She was even taking her new little car with its new car smell. She felt a buzz from the inside out.

Later, she would assure herself that she'd skipped her daily ritual because she was tired, and she would blame it on her dreams of that man who had come to her classroom to spend the summer with her. She would be half right, too.

She was tired, but that wasn't why she did what she did. Blaming it on that man was the part that was closer to the truth.

His presence in her dreams had done something to her that her body hadn't felt since that last morning when Jeffrey had been alive. She felt strangely bold and vigorous. In her choice of clothing, she would have said she was asserting herself to show her new student she was strong and independent. Her black dress and darker lipstick would distance her from him, making her more professional looking.

Mags would have seen through that, and that was the reason Jessica did something else that morning. She took the long way to work. Her car was sipping gas, and she hadn't driven it in nearly a week. It needed a good workout, and if that meant she had to change her plans and miss meeting Mags for breakfast, then change her plans she would.

"I AM A MAN who died twice."

Peter glanced down to see Transplant's ears shift as he caught the sounds of his words. "I did, too, Transplant. I was dead if I didn't get a new heart, and then my ambulance crashed while I was in it. It was in flames, too. The driver was dead. The paramedic with me was dead. I was about to be dead, but it wasn't to be. The man who carried my heart died that day, too. I guess I could say I'm a man who died three times. However, I won't change it, now. That's my hook, and it's in the first sentence. I can't grab the reader's attention any faster than that."

He looked back to the screen, and he smiled. "Good

job, Dr. Jessica Johansen. I think that counselor of mine picked the right teacher, for sure. Yeah, the right one, for sure." His voice faded away as his attention slipped from his surroundings and back to the story he needed to write.

Without any warning, a noise from outside startled him. Peter looked up to see the sun filtering through his window, and old Lennie Cartwright from next door was firing up her ancient truck. He knew what time his class started, and he also knew to the minute when Lennie started that truck each morning. That meant he was already running late, and he knew it. He had no time to spare.

"Dear God," he muttered. "Let me be on time." He jumped up, and the chair he was in fell over backward. Transplant yelped and jumped out of the way.

Peter closed the top of the computer, trusting that the new laptop had the auto-save feature turned on, and that he wouldn't lose any of what he had just typed. His face broke into a sweat, not understanding how he could have missed the *sun*. It was his alarm clock this morning, and he'd been so engrossed in his writing he hadn't even seen it come up.

Peter let his eyes bounce around the room, and his heart pounded with the need to hurry. He knew he should slow down, or he would be back at Doctor Rossi's with more than just good news. He had no idea the time could melt away so quickly when he was writing. He'd done a lot, too, already completing the three thousand words he wanted to type each day.

Taking a deep breath, he dropped his sleeping pants and kicked them aside. Pausing, his heart still pounding, he stood still, giving his pulse a chance to slow. He reached a hand to rub his bare torso, noting where the hair on his body hadn't regrown in the area of his scars. He traced the rough skin where his old heart had been taken out and the new one put in.

He'd really tried not to think about it over the past two years, but he was damaged goods. When he was all buttoned up, he looked passable. However, it might be strange if he got married and only removed his shirt in the dark. He could see the conversation now.

"No, honey. I don't think you're ugly. I just like all the lights off when I get naked. Every time."

That'd go over like a lead weight. He guessed with his tortured chest, he was a loner from here on out. If he couldn't get this book written, that divinity degree might be looking pretty good, celibacy and all.

Peter finally felt his heart settle, or at least he felt the heart inside his chest settle, and he reached to his clean clothes on the chair. As he pulled them on, he whistled to get Transplant's attention. It was time to get him to the back yard and head out the door. Breakfast, playtime, and everything else would have to wait.

Chapter 7

WHEN JESSICA'S phone rang, she gripped the steering wheel firmly and reached into her bag. She had known Mags would call. She dreaded answering it, but she knew she might as well get it over with. She swiped it then set it aside to talk over the car's system.

"Jessica! I sat here, and you never showed. I thought you were my friend. We have breakfast every morning. What will Paul think?"

"Mags," Jessica explained tentatively, "I spent a long night tossing in bed." That was true, at least.

"Sweetie, are you ill? I don't remember you ever being sick, and I hope it isn't some wasting disease. After all, what with Jeffrey's death, you can never be sure. It seems like some people are determined to wallow forever."

"Mags, what an appalling thing to suggest! I'm running late. We'll meet for lunch." Her thoughts of this new student of hers had her distracted, and she couldn't focus on driving, a conversation with Mags, and thinking of Peter. She needed off the line. "It'll be a dinner date if I'm tied up for lunch. Gotta go!"

She waited until the dial tone started and the speakers went silent. Then, seeing brake lights just ahead of her, she tapped the radio on and began to slow for a traffic light that was still green.

ON MAGS' end of the line, Jessica's friend swiped her phone and placed it in front of her. She just looked at it as it sat on the table. This was not the Jessica she knew. Mags had intended to tell her friend her news at breakfast. She had been invited to spend the weekend at her parents' place in Upstate New York. They'd gotten a new horse, and it had been a while since she'd ridden. Would Jessica like to go with her?

However, running late? Jessica? That woman had never been late in her life, and in two years they'd never missed a scheduled breakfast. There was something going on, and the only thing Mags could see that was different with her friend was that man she had pushed her into the other day on campus.

She smiled and nodded in satisfaction at the phone. Then she looked at the empty seat in front of her and finally out the window at the parking lot. Her small Porsche was sitting there, and the top was down. Bright yellow. The dealer had tried to get her to buy one already on the lot. "Ms. Brier-Sheldon," he had insisted, "this red color is all the rage in these sporty little numbers. We have three in red."

No, Mags had insisted on her favorite color. The dealer had been forced to pull one in from three states away and deal with the shipping charges. After all, it had cost her trust fund an arm and a leg. She *should* get what she wanted.

Jessica or not, she intended to enjoy her breakfast, and when the day warmed, the top on her car would close to allow her to run the air. Then, and only then, she would see just what was going on with her friend. Perhaps indeed it was this man. It was time, too. Jeffrey would think so. Now, maybe Jessica could finally get her act together and move on.

Mags smiled when the waiter stepped to her table. Before she could speak, the young man's face grew perplexed at the empty chair across from her.

"Dr. Johansen's not here today. Are you breakfasting alone, Ms. Brier-Sheldon?" He poured water into the stemmed glass at her plate. The clear liquid caught the light, sending glittering shards of rainbows across the gleaming knife at its side.

Mags smiled, and then she turned it into a smirk at her memory of what she thought might have really pulled her friend from their regular rendezvous. Not what. Who. "Something more important than me required her attention. He, er, it caused her to run a bit behind schedule. *I* will have my usual, Paul. In fact, make it a double."

"Four Benedicts coming up." Paul Rizzo, a Clark University student who worked at Scortio's to help fund his education, reached and unfolded her napkin for her.

"Since you're alone, may I put a little zing in your orange juice this morning?"

"Paul, you are a dear. I love you, you know." She winked at him as she reached for her napkin. He would get an extra tip for his service, but he was just a boy. She'd seen him on campus and thought he might have been in one of Jessica's classes. If he was working, he was probably on scholarship, and he could use the money. Mags' trust fund could well afford a few extra dollars to make her waiter's life a little easier, and she could well afford that "special" orange juice with her double helping of breakfast eggs. With Jessica off chasing her man, or so Mags hoped, no one would ever know. She knew Paul would never tell, either. He was a good waiter, the finest, and the finest never, ever divulged what went on when best friends were away.

JESSICA PULLED her little car into her parking space. It fit with lots of room remaining. When she'd gotten it, some of her fellow professors had teased her, telling her she had enough room left over in her parking space to put a spare. Then, if she ever ran out of gas, she'd have a backup car. She'd laughed in return, telling them it used so little fuel, she carried an eyedropper of extra just in case. She could squirt that in the tank and drive an extra dozen miles or so to the station.

A few months later, they stopped laughing when fuel prices shot up. She had stopped by the station she usually used, and one of her colleagues was fueling his SUV. Jessica put the nozzle in her tank, and almost before she had her purse back in the car, the pump cut off. Her colleague laughed.

"Just topping off the toy, Dr. Johansen?" When she gave him a puzzled look, he prodded her, nodding at the pump. "You barely got it turned on, and it's already finished."

That was Jessica's cue to laugh. "No, it was empty. That's just all it holds." She pulled her receipt from the pump, and when she drove off, he was still there clicking up dollars in his SUV, filling his massive tank that would run dry long before hers.

She reached to the dash and flipped the air on high for a moment. For some reason, she just couldn't cool off this morning. It didn't seem any hotter than usual outside, and it was still early morning. Usually she didn't need to run her air at all on summer mornings.

Perhaps it was the dress she was wearing. It did have a full slip, and she guessed the fabric didn't breathe as well as she remembered. However, she was here, and she was wearing it. She certainly couldn't change now.

She reached to open the door, and that was when her phone rang for the second time. It had to be Mags, she knew. She looked at the key in her hand, and she was aware the car wouldn't stay cool with everything off and closed up. She breathed a sigh of relief when the ringing finally ended. Pulling the lever to open the door, she was reassured to find a breeze blowing. At least it would help her keep from overheating before she got to the building.

Prior to closing the door, she reached and triggered the rear hatch release. At a sudden, loud whistle, she turned to see what was going on. There was nothing that she could locate. She walked to the back of the car and waited for the

92

hatch to rise when she heard the whistle again. She ignored it and reached inside, pulling out her bag with her materials for her first session.

Just as she stretched to close the hatch, she saw a hand reach just above hers, and startled, she backed away. Then, her hatch was closing itself, and she didn't even know whose hand was doing that for her.

A muted whistle, one that matched the others she'd heard, came softly in her ear. A masculine voice followed it. "Pretty lady, this is a faculty spot. You'd better park on the other side of the building. It's a long walk back, but I'll be glad to keep you company." The speaker cleared his throat and spoke two additional words. "Sexy dress!"

Jessica turned to look at her chivalrous—and very forward—companion. It was obvious he'd run to catch her before she closed her car's hatch. The hair on his head was damp, and he was breathing heavily. She supposed she looked puzzled. Then, when the young man saw her face, his expression changed from interested to horrified. He immediately began to backpedal.

"Oh, Dr. Johansen, I'm so sorry. I didn't recognize you. You look so, so . . . pretty. No, not pretty . . . um . . ." The boy was truly speechless, and red began to flush up his neck.

He was one of her students. At least he had been in the spring. Now, he had gone on, and she didn't know why he was still here during the summer. Perhaps he'd encountered difficulty with some of his other classes. He'd done quite well in hers.

Despite that, she was pleasantly surprised at his schoolboy response. It had been a long time since she'd left someone speechless. Touching her hair with her free hand, she knew she had worn exactly the right clothes for this morning's class. She quickly smiled and patted him gently on the arm. "Robbie? No, Robert. I believe the word you're searching for is sexy." It was the very word he'd used earlier. She turned her head and smiled, not wanting him to see how amused she was at his embarrassment. He probably didn't even know what a faux pas was, but he had just committed a whopper.

Robert turned and caught the attention of several friends of his who were standing by a distant building. Out of the corner of her eye, Jessica saw them offer multiple thumbs up for his success in meeting the beautiful girl who was quite clearly new to campus, and all he did was shake his head in return, waving one hand to back them off. He turned to his teacher, working his hands nervously.

"Dr. Johansen, I should've known it was you. Your car. I've seen you in it before. However, I've just never seen a teacher dress like this for a summer school class. I didn't know you could look like this. It's good, um, the dress looks good on you. Your makeup is different, too."

She looked at him, a very serious expression on her face, quite flattered by his response. "Different how, Robert?"

He was already flustered, however, and her question threw him off. "What do you mean, Dr. Johansen?"

She pursed her lips. She would tug this from him. She felt very charmed by this boy's bumbling, even if he was only a student from last semester's class. This morning, she needed charm, and she intended to milk it for all she could get. "My makeup. How is it different?"

He paused and licked his lips, almost as if he was unsure how to say what he meant. He smiled hesitantly. "Do you really want to know?"

Jessica stood there holding her bag, shifting it from one arm to another. "Tell me, Robert, exactly the way you thought it when you first saw me. No grades. Anything you say gets an A." Her eyes twinkled with her promise. He wasn't in any of her classes anymore, and she could do nothing even if she didn't like what he said. Besides, she really wanted to know.

"Your lipstick. It's darker, like for night. It suits you, too." He paused and pressed his lips together, then he quickly licked them. "It makes you look . . . um . . ."

Jessica shifted her bag one more time. "One word, Robert. Can you do that, tell me about my lipstick in less than a complete sentence?"

He looked away, obviously discomfited, when he noticed her bag and how heavy it looked. "Can I get that, Dr. Johansen? I'll carry it to your classroom for you. I was there just two weeks ago. I know exactly where you're headed. May I?"

Jessica gladly let him take it, and she turned to walk beside him. She was not done with him yet, though. She pressed him to answer her. "My word, Robert? About my lipstick?"

He chuckled, his embarrassment less apparent than before. It helped, someone in the psychology department might have explained, that there was no possibility of failure here. She was a teacher, and therefore not a contender for his affections. If she was irritated, he could just laugh her off, and it wouldn't damage his ego at all.

95

He looked at her and caught her eye. "Kissable."

Then he looked away, and Jessica could see the red creeping back up his neck. She looked away herself and smiled. She hadn't expected that, but she wasn't displeased in the least.

"Thank you, Robert. A-plus." She said it very matter-of-factly, as if it counted. She knew he was probably nineteen, perhaps twenty if he'd failed a year of public school. Or private, if his parents were wealthy. No, she took that back. Wealthy parents' children never failed. They were simply tutored. He was nineteen, and to a nineteen-year-old, A-pluses mattered very much, indeed, even if they weren't real.

As Robert dropped off her things in her classroom, her phone rang once again. "Thank you, Robert," she called, and he waved to her as he exited the room. Reaching into her bag, Jessica grabbed the phone and turned it on.

"Dr. Johansen here."

"Jessica! Where are you?" A breathless voice burst over the airways.

"My word, Mags, is that you? Are you running a marathon? You're absolutely panting." Holding the phone with one hand, she began to sort her morning's materials with the other. "I'm in my classroom, and I was walked to class by a very handsome man. You should have seen him. He even told me I was kissable."

"Who cares about handsome or kissable? It wasn't your Peter from the quadrangle. I just saw him," Mags snorted. Then she giggled. She'd enjoyed two additional orange juices, one compliments of Paul at the restaurant. "Jessica, are you there?"

Jessica put her things down and turned, now irritated, to lean back against the desk to talk to her friend. She was a wild one this morning. Jessica needed Mags to see that she certainly was not interested in this Peter character, not after her sleepless night with that man haunting her every moment.

"All right, Mags. What's this all about? And, by the way, why would I care about Peter? Other men can walk me to class, you know. I'm sexy, and my lips are kissable. I have that on very good authority."

"I like you, Jess. No, I love you, and you know it. However, sometimes you're as dense as a rock. That man of yours just got a ticket."

Robert? A ticket? He'd just walked out of her classroom. There had been no time for him to get a ticket for any reason. Perhaps it had been before he carried her bag for her. She laughed lightly, determined to appear unconcerned at her friend's very unhelpful news.

"He didn't tell me about that, but then why would he? If you must know, he was just a student from last spring. Now you've taken the fun out of my flattery. He thought I was a college girl."

By this time a note of desperation had begun to creep into Mags' voice. She tried once again to get through. "Of course you're a college girl, Jess. You work there, for heaven's sake. If he was in your class last spring, why didn't you recognize him when you bumped into him?"

"Mags, have you been drinking?" Jessica finally understood what this was all about. "Did Paul serve you spiked juice again? Oh, my heavens, are you driving your Porsche drunk?" A note of hysteria found its way into

Jessica's voice as she pictured her friend piled into a tree. Desperately trying to think how best to get her friend off the road, she covered all Mags' points in one breath, her words thrown out in a rush. "Mags, when did I ever bump into Robert Whatever-His-Last-Name-Is from my spring class, and pull your car on the shoulder until I can get someone there to take you home! You cannot drive drunk."

"Robert? Robert, Jessica? Let's get on the same page. Peter. Peter from the quadrangle. The one who's not married. He just got a ticket on the way to class, to *your* class. He ran two red lights. He might be late." She giggled. "And I'm not a drunk driver, whatever you might think. I know perfectly well what's going on."

Jessica laughed, a sensation of relief flooding her limbs. "Now I get it. Did you stop to vouch for him? *People Magazine.* I can see it now. 'Wealthy Massachusetts Socialite Vouches for College Student. Officer Dismisses Ticket.' Fame and fortune, Mags."

The line was silent for a moment, then Mags snorted, "I am not rich, Jessica. You know that."

"That's debatable. Rich to you and rich to me are two different things."

"Jess, c'mon. All I have is that little-bitty trust fund. You're the one who has a real house in the suburbs and all. Rich is as rich does. Besides, what does that have to do with Peter?"

"Porsche. Don't call me rich. I have a mortgage. I also have a job."

"And I'm still in school. There. That's done. Now, this Peter. What are you going to do?"

"I am going to have class. I'm all dressed up and ready

for my students. By the way, how do you know he ran two red lights?"

Mags giggled the way a small girl might. This was funny to her. "I was right behind him, and when the light turned yellow, he must have really accelerated. He cleared the first one, but the next two he sailed through on red. Maybe his accelerator got stuck." More giggles came through over the phone. "Or, maybe he just couldn't wait to get to class to see you."

Jessica had heard enough. She thumbed her phone off without even saying goodbye. She turned and dropped it into her purse, and her eyes glanced to where this man would be sitting in about half an hour. Finally, she relaxed and smiled. He had run a red light, even two, if Mags was correct. He was human, despite everything. Maybe, just maybe one kiss wouldn't turn him into a frog after all.

Then the smile dropped away, and she turned to her things. This was her classroom, and he was a student. What was she thinking, anyway? Kissing a strange man. Good lands!

However, she took a deep breath, and she felt electrified. He wasn't entirely a strange man. She may not know him, but in a bizarre twist of events, she had come to *know* him, even if it was in the most glancing sort of way. Unconsciously, she flexed her hand, and it just happened to be the very one that had rested on that strange man's pants. She didn't notice that, but she did notice that she suddenly felt very warm once again, and she didn't have the key to adjust the thermostat on her classroom wall.

PETER HELD out his hand to the officer, and he leaned

his head back against the headrest. His eyes leaped to the clock on the dash. He could still make it. Two days in a row, and he was cutting it close both times.

He looked up as he felt his plastic license pressed back into his palm. The officer looked up and down his car. He smiled and opened conversationally, "Great car. Classic, isn't it? Never see these anymore."

Peter pursed his mouth, and he wondered at the tone of the man's voice. He'd just written him a ticket, two probably, one for each light, and now he wanted to discuss Peter's old car. *Just rub it in, officer.*

"It's not a classic yet, sir. Nine more years, and it will be."

The officer continued, "Runs good?"

Peter snorted. "Mechanically. Through red lights? Not so well." He wished the officer would just give him the ticket and let him get on his way. His class was waiting.

The officer held out the ticket and smiled. He thumped the paper with his free hand. "I thought I recognized this name. I was there, you know."

"There?" Peter looked up, not understanding this part of the ticketing process.

The officer continued, "Heart transplant, right? That was you, wasn't it?"

Peter grunted and just nodded. "I'm surprised you remember." Peter had never been commended publicly about it, and he'd never had a stranger ask him if he was "the man who received a new heart." He guessed it was the recovery time that had given fresh news the opportunity to overshadow him. He was happy with it that way, too.

"Buddy, I was following that tractor trailer rig that took

that other guy out. You know, the one who rescued you from that ambulance. Anyway, that rig started to slide, and I said, 'Oh, my God!' I knew you were both goners, and then that sportscaster *threw* you to the onlookers. Took him out, though. Say, I heard through the grapevine you got his heart. Hmm. How about that?"

Suddenly, Peter was interested. His book. This was an expert eyewitness that he could use for a source. Yes, he remembered he still needed to get to class, or the book would never get written. However, he needed this man. His excitement rising, he tried to explain.

"Officer, I'm on the way to a class at Clark, where I'm writing a book about that day. Can you just give me the ticket so I can be on time? I want to call you, though, to talk to you about what you saw. Please, if I can impose." Peter looked at him with pleading in his eyes.

The officer laughed. "There's no ticket. When I saw who you were, I downgraded it to a warning. You really need to watch those lights, though." He reached in the car as he handed Peter the paper and tapped his chest. "Gotta keep that ticker inside of you working. Otherwise, that sportscaster wasted one good life. He was the best, too. I used to watch him. My name's on the paper, Officer Craig. Jim Craig. The front desk will put you through to me."

Peter took the paper and smiled. "Thanks, officer. I appreciate it."

Then the officer slapped the top of Peter's car. "Hey, I can help you get to class. Follow me. I know Clark. Turn tight. We're taking a shortcut." He leaped back to his motorcycle, and in a moment, they were off with the lights flashing. He did turn tight, too, and Peter's car was just able to keep up.

As he arrived at the school, Peter glanced to the sky and said a silent prayer of thanks for the extra help. He still had to park, though, and he pulled into a lot where there were openings.

The officer waited until Peter was in a space, turning his lights off before he waved. "My name's on the paper," he called, reminding Peter he was willing to help. With a spinning tire catching in a patch of loose gravel, his bike roared, and he was gone.

This time Peter made sure he had his computer in his hand before closing the car door. He couldn't waste time to go back for it. Walking briskly but not wanting to stir up any chest pains, he stepped into the building where his class was located.

He had written quite a lot that morning, and he was excited about sharing it in class. He was also excited about having the chance to see just what his teacher, the good Dr. Johansen, would have to offer him today. If it was half as good as her hook idea from yesterday, it would be very beneficial, indeed.

JESSICA LET her eyes play across the students. Over the next few days, she would learn to recognize the early arrivers. They would be regular as clockwork. Occasionally one might be off, but punctuality was a big issue for those that were run by their internal clocks.

Others would be the skimmers. They would time their entrances to the last few moments before the bell chimed. Jessica had her issues with both. Those who were habitually early often came with other things to do, either that, or they had cell phones that disturbed her right up to the moment she started class. However, she was never sure she could trust the skimmers. When a student left no leeway for errors, then it didn't take much to delay his or her arrival. Those students didn't always make it to class on time, and disruptions during her opening remarks were just that, disrupting.

After the first day, she wouldn't take roll. All the students were logged in, and if they showed, they showed. If they turned in the work and received a passing grade, they got credit for the class. If they didn't meet the requirements, they failed. If they weren't here to ask for help, sometimes they managed to squeak by, but not always.

She looked in front of her. The seats were filled except where Peter had sat. *Auditing.* She still didn't like that, but she hated for this man to be the one to prove her right.

She realized she was actually looking for him this morning. It was certain he would sit in the same seat if he showed. In a full class like this one, it was rare for a student to move to a different position after the first day. After all, humans were very territorial, and people tended to give in to their perceived need for previously claimed private space, even if the private aspect of the space was all in the mind.

As she turned to her Smart Wall to tap an icon from her computer, she heard the door squeak. She smiled and glanced that direction. There he was, and she felt her pulse race. A full class, she told herself. That's all it was. He showed, her class was now full, and no one had dropped. Turning back to the wall-sized display, she reached her hand and tapped her icon.

"Class," she began. She turned, and there was her auditing student. His hand was up. He'd managed to be on time and avoid disrupting her opening remarks, and he wasn't content with that. He still intended to make her diverge from her planned lesson.

Jessica touched the lace at her neck, and she adjusted it as inconspicuously as she could. In that moment, she remembered what the student in the parking lot had said about her clothing. Her lipstick, too. Kissable. She wasn't sure why that thought came to her mind, but she was glad to know her choice of makeup had made an impression on someone. This man? Peter? He wouldn't care. He was disrupting her introduction. He wouldn't care at all.

She smiled at him. "Yes? Mr. . . . ." She made a point to pause and step to her computer, pulling up her class list in a sidebar as if she weren't sure just what his name was. "Mr. Cassel, I believe. Correct?" He smiled, and her heart jumped. She would have to be careful with this one. His looks made him dynamite on two legs.

"Yes, Jessica, er, Dr. Johansen." He stood and heard the class titter. He looked around to find the cause of the laughter among the other students, and not seeing anything, he continued. "You gave us a hook yesterday." He smiled as if very satisfied with himself, even as his hands brushed the legs of his pants, leaving damp streaks of nervous perspiration.

Jessica smiled, glad she had worn her black dress. It certainly separated her from her students. Most of them were dressed in their most casual clothing. Summer was on their minds, and they had no cause to wear anything other than jeans or shorts. This man would have to cave to her superiority. She knew that. Perhaps for her to put him in his place would be the thing. Gently, though. He *was* one of her students.

"Yes, Mr. Cassel, I did." She made sure to glance at her computer once again before calling his name to make it very clear she hadn't remembered what it was. "However, my hook was just an example. You were to use your own. I do hope you didn't write the beginning of your story using my words. That would be unfortunate. It would also be plagiarism. Do you know what that is, Mr. Cassel?" She smiled a very sweet smile, and she checked her records once again. "Good, it is Mr. Cassel, I see."

She waited on him to answer, pleased she'd handled this very precarious situation with such professional poise.

PETER STOOD there with a grin on his face. He had no idea what she was talking about. He just had two thoughts on his mind. The first had nothing to do with the paper he was writing, either.

He had walked in the classroom, and he'd been especially nervous. This woman. This teacher. She was doing something to him, and he knew it had started back on the day he'd been on campus for that first meeting with his counselor. He knew it would have never started if she hadn't tackled him, but now, there was nothing to be done. She'd distracted him all night, and then when he'd walked into her classroom just minutes ago, she'd been there dressed to the nines. Her black dress, and the new color on her lips. She was, what did all the college students say? Hot. That was it.

Now, he was standing in her class to tell her what she'd

given him. Finally, he just blurted it out.

"I am a man who died twice. That's my hook." He'd said it. He stood and grinned.

JESSICA GAVE him a mystified look. That didn't make any real sense to her. However, it was certainly an attention getter, and that was what she'd suggested.

She smiled.

When she did that, several students in the back began to chuckle. Jessica looked to find them, but by the time she did, the laughter had spread throughout the room. She watched Peter turn red and slowly slip into his chair. This was appalling, and she had to find a way to stop it.

"Very good, Peter," she called out in a very firm voice. "That's exactly what I was going for." She was satisfied to hear the laughter evaporate. She began to walk around the room as she strengthened her support of this man's belittled idea.

"A good hook should be exactly what Peter has given us. It should be bold and often unexplainable. The story will do that, tell us what the hook means. All it has to do on the first page is intrigue us." She looked at the man whose idea she was trying to rescue, and he looked at her with tear-filled eyes. Surely he wasn't going to cry! Then he winked and smiled. When he did, she doubled her efforts.

"How can a man die twice? Can anyone here in this room, except you, Peter, tell us that? Anyone? Any takers? No?" She was on a roll now, and she was just getting warmed up. Something had her interest in her job at a height it hadn't seen in the past two years. She didn't know what it was, but she knew this: She remembered being like this long ago, and she remembered how much she had enjoyed it.

"The Good Book, what many of you know as The Holy Bible, is chock full of hooks. The character Jesus, He used them prolifically. Look at His parables. Though seeing, they will not see. Though hearing, they will not hear or understand. I will utter things hidden since the creation of the world. The kingdom of God is like a king who prepared a wedding banquet for his son. How can Satan drive out Satan? I am the vine, and you are the branches. What good will it be for a man if he gains the whole world, yet forfeits his soul? No one can enter the kingdom of heaven unless he is born of water and the spirit." She paused expectantly before continuing, taking a moment to glance around at the now-attentive students. "Even the character Nicodemus asked of Jesus, 'Surely man cannot enter a second time into his mother's womb to be born.'

"Class, without the rest of The Holy Bible, none of these statements make sense. None. Without Peter's story being written, his hook won't make sense, either. When you laugh, you show me your shortcomings. You show me you're not willing to read beyond the surface of the words. People who cannot read beyond the surface cannot write an intriguing story that other people will want to read.

"Today, class, I expect each of you to do what Peter has already done. I expect each of you to come up with a hook so cryptic it makes no sense at all. However, before you start, I must tell you. There is one caveat. You must know your story when you start. You must have lived it, either in reality or in your mind. Only then will your story bear out the hidden meaning behind your hook."

Jessica paused to take a breath, and in that moment of silence realized what she'd said, and worse, why. She caught Peter's eyes, and panic flooded her chest. Then, unexpectedly and unintentionally, more words poured forth. They were words of desperation.

"Today, we will dismiss to the library to work on our hooks. You'll be free to come and go as you wish, but be aware. Tomorrow, we will all share our hooks. If anyone else in this room can understand yours, you haven't followed my instructions. Let's go."

Jessica turned to her Smart Wall, all her lessons for the day thrown out the window. This man had done that to her. He had fumbled, and yes, it had been because of enthusiasm, but it had been a fumble, still, and she'd forfeited her lesson to rescue him. Now, they would be spending three days on something she had planned for one. Was she ever stupid! She should have just let him drown. He wasn't getting credit for this course. He could have gone home today, cried into his evening whiskey, and given up on her class. She would have suffered a course drop on her record, but then she'd no longer have to think about him being in her class each day, sitting right there in front of her, drawing her attention away from her lessons, and messing up her entire summer syllabus.

She drew in a deep breath and reached a hand to her face to brush tears of frustration away. At last it grew quiet in the room. All the students had escaped to work on their hooks. Many, she knew, would go back to dorms to sleep, or they'd show up at the library and not find her there. Then, they'd decide they could work better elsewhere.

She needed a break, though. Two days into the session, and she already needed a break. She laughed and turned to the empty classroom, and to her surprise, the room wasn't empty at all.

She'd been so sure she was alone. She'd let her emotional guard down, and she'd let her tears run from her eyes. Then she turned, and there he was, quietly sitting in his seat. He could barely get here on time, and then he wouldn't leave when she told him he could. Was this man a crazy bleeding heart for suffering? Did he like to always do the wrong thing? That could get people killed, if he kept it up. Who would step in to rescue this man? Not her, and not her Jeffrey, she knew that. No, this man was useless.

As he looked at her patiently, waiting on her for something, Jessica knew another thing. In her moment of perceived security, she had indeed let her guard down, and when she'd seen him there, she'd felt something deep inside. She didn't like it, because it suddenly reminded her that she hadn't hugged Jeffrey that morning. In fact, she hadn't thought of him at all, not once this morning. She had thought only of this man, and she had enjoyed it very much. Even her frustration at him for all his perceived flaws had been her anxiety over that empty seat. It had been the thought of him not returning, and of never seeing him again.

With her sudden memories of having forgotten Jeffrey, shame for her neglect welled up inside of her, and with no method of regaining her composure in front of this man, it burst from her in great wracking sobs.

PETER STARTED to stand to go to her, but then he sat

back down, unsure of the proprieties of such a situation. He didn't want her to be reprimanded for contact with a student, and he did know that such actions could impact an educator very severely. When her sobs slowed, he tried another tactic.

"Was it that good or that bad?" He waited for her to respond. When she started searching for something in the drawers of her desk, he quickly realized it was for tissues, and he reached to hand her one of the boxes sitting on the small ledge at the end of each row. He prodded her to see if she would talk. "Well?"

Jessica took the tissue she pulled from the box, and she blew her nose. She looked at him, and she snorted a rough sort of chuckle. "Was *what* good or bad?"

"You know, you made quite a presentable speech just a few moments ago. I was very impressed. However, you have that wall on, and you didn't use anything up there. I doubt that you would have sent thirty students to the library for a playdate, if I hadn't up and interrupted your well-planned, organized lesson."

Jessica chuckled and looked down at her hand, this time with the beginnings of a smile. "No, this isn't exactly what I had planned. I was intending to tell the class to put interesting, meaningful events from their own lives into their stories. For example, take someone who runs two red lights in a row and gets ticketed. That would be great in a story, because it would show real emotion. The person who could tell that would have an emotional investment in the events, and that emotion would carry over into the minds of the readers. That was to be my lesson for the day."

Peter let out a laugh, causing Jessica to smile. "Now, who would be able to tell a story like that?"

JESSICA GLANCED up and found the face of the man who was sitting in the room with her. She looked into his eyes. They were crinkled with humor, and she could see he was quite charming in appearance when he smiled. If she were the romantic type, she might even say his eyes twinkled, but she knew that was no more than a figment of the storyteller's imagination. "Twinkled" was simply another word for the bouncing rays of light that catch on the moisture in a person's eyes. Storytellers could be romantic, or they could be factual. Romance had died two years ago for her. She had lived with grief ever since.

Even so, somewhere in the back of her mind, she admitted it wasn't her grief that had caused her to burst into tears as she stood in front of this man. It had been her shame. It had been the shame she felt for not enduring her daily allotment of misery, the crushing guilt of living her morning as if Jeffrey had never been there. Even now she knew she was pushing that shame from her. She was finding herself drawn to this man, and she was finding this fresh taste of life very invigorating. It had been a long time since she'd felt the sweet flavor of life on her tongue, and she was finding it had been way too long.

She answered Peter's question with an amused expression, one that she hoped didn't twinkle. "I know a person who might be able to tell that story. He's very near to me, also. You might have even met him."

Peter chuckled, and he reached one arm to stretch it across the back of the seat next to him. He casually ran his fingers through the hair at his temples and shifted one leg on the floor in front of him. He seemed to be enjoying himself.

Jessica thought nothing of it when he looked down to see his shirt gaping, and he reached his free hand to snug up the opening. Instead, she noticed how thick his hair was, and that his hand hadn't mussed it at all. Her heart raced, but that was the side effect of the story she was telling, she assured herself. It had nothing to do with that thick head of tawny hair.

He was her *student,* after all.

PETER GLANCED up to see her watching him. At least she was no longer crying. He ventured, "This person. Did this happen to him very long ago? Or to her?" He was definitely enjoying this. He didn't know just how she could be aware he'd been stopped on the way to her class, and because of that, he wasn't absolutely certain she was talking about him, but he liked the fact that she could be. That gave them a sort of connection, and it warmed him inside.

She laughed and reached to turn her computer off. "Oh, not so very long. You might even say recently. Very recently."

Now she had him really curious. The policeman, did he radio it in to the school? Were the students attending this campus monitored that closely?

He pressed her for more information. "Did this man actually get a ticket? Do you know that? Sometimes famous people get off with warnings. Perhaps this man was famous at one point in his life, and the officer giving him the ticket recognized him." Peter grinned as he watched this woman's face. He liked what he saw, and he also liked how it was making him feel.

Two years he'd been alone. No, it was closer to six. His ex had been distant for a long time before she left, and she hadn't stayed to the end. Nearly six years since being with a woman, and for the past two, he hadn't let himself get even close to one that was really attractive to him. He hadn't been able to afford that luxury. Now, one had jumped into his lap, literally, and he hadn't been able to avoid her. After only two days of being in her company, he didn't want to.

Quite the opposite, in fact.

JESSICA LAUGHED his question off. She felt this was getting too close to telling just how much she knew, or perhaps didn't know. "No, my dear Mr. Cassel. We have dedicated law officers in the good city of Worcester. If a man runs a light, he gets a ticket. That's the way it has to be."

"What if he gets a warning, though? Just what if? Would he get a reward for that? Like, maybe, a gold star? Or lunch?"

She stopped putting her things in her bag and looked at him. She thought she just heard an invitation for, dare she think it, a date.

"Lunch?"

Peter grinned. "In the syllabus, it says you're free to meet with students outside of class to discuss the merits of their work. I guess that means to offer suggestions for improvement. You see, I'm writing an entire novel. I guess

113

that's the right word. It's going to be a documentary. I'm aiming for a hundred thousand words, and I want to have it finished by the end of this session."

Jessica stepped to the chair next to Peter and sat on the edge. She looked at his face, and she could see he was serious. However, his plans were very ambitious. She wondered if he realized just what he was getting into.

"One hundred thousand words? You want your book, not a novel, by the way, to be one hundred thousand words? In six weeks? Less, actually, since the session is already started, but let's say six weeks." She paused, her eyes shifting as she did the math in her head. "Over three thousand words a day if you take weekends off. One thing you need to remember, no matter how perfect you think it is when you write it, you must allow time to rewrite, edit, and proof your work. All writers have to do that, even the best." She paused, putting her hand out to touch his arm. "You've done your research? My word, just the research alone could take two years, depending on what your topic is, of course."

She wondered if he was crazy, or if it was her realism forcing her to see the flaws in his plan. Whichever, his enthusiasm was engaging. She wanted to be engaged by him.

PETER SAT, electrified. His body roiled inside, and all he could think of was the touch of her skin on his arm. Finally, he coughed, and with the movement of his body, her hand fell away. He leaned forward and blinked to clear the fog from his eyes. He took a deep breath and tried his voice. It croaked, but it worked. That was a relief.

"I've researched this for eight years, the last two most intensely. This morning, I think I might have found my best material witness." He glanced up at the ceiling, afraid to look at the woman next to him. He still felt her touch on his arm, and he didn't trust the pull of his body toward her. All he wanted was for their skin to touch once again, and that was something he knew he couldn't allow. Instead, he returned to an earlier allusion of hers.

"Your scripture references. I found those most interesting. You knew so many, and you quoted them exactly, except for one. You were off a word or two on it, but I understood why when you had to pull it out of context. New International Version, I believe." He glanced at her, glad to once again be back on neutral ground.

She ducked her head, smiling, before looking directly at him. "My father was an ordained minister. Fundamentalist. I learned scripture from day one. I still remember a lot of it. I'm surprised I went into teaching. Anything to do with words was something I thought I would have run from, as hard as that scripture was ground into me." She laughed and then looked away. "Or, maybe that's why I became a teacher. I wanted to show people how it should be done. I like to think I'm good at it. Sometimes I don't know."

Peter looked at her until she caught his eyes. "You are. In two days, I've seen that. You're very good. Now, my hook. I read it in class, and I thought it was quite a piece of work. You had to rescue me from my own foolishness, though. Now, what was the foolishness that caused all the laughter? Was it my hook, or was it the timing? I wasn't absolutely sure you really loved the hook, or if you simply wanted to shame those who laughed at me."

He waited expectantly, thinking that no matter the answer she gave, just to hear her speak would be enough.

SHE STOOD. This man was seeing her too clearly, and in her moment of weakness, she had already let him get his hooks into her heart. How could she have done that? However, it was not something she could undo, not in the state she was in.

She turned briskly and looked at him, speaking in a torrent of words. "Both. No, not both. All of it, and lunch at eleven. Scortio's. Be on time, bring that computer, and you pay. This is not a date." Then, in a rustle of gathered things and flashes of movement, she was gone, her bag in her hand, leaving Peter alone in the room.

HE SMILED. He reached to turn his computer off, and he closed the lid. Then he leaned over and kissed it. He whispered his words of gratitude to the machine, "You are worth every penny." Then, he stood and picked up his things, slipping the machine into its bag as he walked out the door.

There was one thing he was reminded of as he walked to his car. When he had first stood, Dr. Johansen had looked three times to remind herself of his name. Three times. Then, when she rescued him from his blunder, she seemed to remember his name very well, several times, too. His first name, even, and she hadn't called his first name once from her roll. He liked that idea very much, and he hoped it meant something. He would like that very much, indeed.

Chapter 8

JESSICA THREW open her office door, and she jumped back in surprise. She looked around the space that was hers to do with as she pleased, and right now it was not as she pleased.

"Mags, are you in here?"

A head popped up from behind her desk. "You hung up on me, Jess. I hope you just lost your signal, but it sounded distinctly like you hung up on me." Her head disappeared behind the desk once again.

Jessica stepped to her desk and looked to see what her friend was doing. She leaned over. "Is that an extension cord? Whatever you're up to, I don't like it."

Mags sat up. "I don't care what you like. I'm doing this with or without you. See that garland around the ceiling?

Now, watch." She reached and flipped something on the floor, and the entire string lighted the room in flashing red, white, and blue lights.

Jessica fell into a chair, then jumped up when she realized she was sitting on a stack of papers. Dropping them to the floor, she returned to the chair.

"Mags, that's so ugly." She shook her head in dismay. "Why are you doing this to me?"

Mags got up from the floor and went to her. She placed her hand on one side of Jessica's face, and she gently kissed the other side. "Because I love you, Jess." Then she stood, and less gently, she continued, "And this place is a mess. I need some sort of distraction when I walk in here. Your housekeeping service keeps your home spotless, and I remember when this place used to be. I'm willing to help, but you have to give the word. Now? I'm here."

Jessica took a deep breath and sighed. "This is all Jeffrey, you know that."

Mags barked out a laugh. "This is not Jeffrey, and you know *that*. This was Jeffrey two years ago, and now it's just Jessica Johansen. It's time to move past this, and I want to help. Today? Today would be good."

"Mags, today would not be good. For your information, I have a date for lunch. Eleven O'clock. Scortio's. There. Satisfied?" Jessica smirked, looking aloof at her friend.

"A real date, or is this a teacher date to work on someone's paper?"

"Mags!" Jessica stood and turned away, pulling out her computer. She made sure Mags couldn't see her face. She needed to pull off indignant. "You amaze me. I finally do what you want, and you make fun of me. I thought you wanted me to move on. Well, if you're going to be that way, *you* can just move on. Go, now. Go! I won't even look your way until you do." She couldn't. She was certain Mags would see her lie written on her face.

"Well!" Mags grabbed her purse. "I hope you enjoy your lights. The way you keep this office, I expect they'll be there when you retire. Good morning!" Then the door slammed.

Jessica looked up at the ceiling. She had no idea how the woman had gotten the lights way up there, but she couldn't reach them to take them down. She also realized Mags was right. This office was a shame, and it needed to be cleaned. Mags' help would be appreciated, but it would have to wait. She hated what she'd done to get her to leave her office, but she just couldn't let her know she'd lied to her. This *was* a working lunch, and it *was* with a student. However, he was paying, and that sort of made it a date. Sort of.

Anyway, her comeback to Mags had been one of frustration. If she'd been forced to tell who she was meeting, her charade would have been exposed, and that would have spoiled Jessica's pretense.

Jessica knew the deeper truth. It wasn't the pretense she'd played out with Mags that she didn't want exposed. It was the pretense of a date with this man, one she'd allowed into her heart, into her very soul. That was the pretense she needed to hold onto, even if it was just for a few hours. They would meet, and lunch would be served, and they would talk of small things to occupy the silences. In a moment of breathlessness, he would reach and take her hand. Then . . .

Jessica shook her head. Then he would drag out his laptop, and he would ask her advice on his story. She would say to cut this or rearrange that, and he would laugh and choose to ignore her every word. Then she would go home, and Jeffrey would be there, and she would be stricken with guilt that she had spent the day chasing a man who was not hers, could never be hers, and moreover was a student in one of her classes.

She sat in her chair and looked up at Mags' lights blinking around the perimeter of her ceiling. She closed her eyes as she felt shame overwhelm her. One of her *students*, for land's sakes!

However, he was her age or even older, and he was only auditing her class. That wasn't like a real student. He didn't really attend the college. He had a job and money and one of the most advanced computers she had ever seen. He could own his own company, for all she knew. He even had gold flecks in those green eyes. Gold flecks. Now, that was something she'd never wanted before. Still . . . gold flecks. Gold flecks and tawny hair.

Mags! Curse that woman and her wicked ways! She had brought this on her, and now, here she was falling for him, hook, line, and sinker.

She stood and began dumping papers in the trash bin. She didn't care anymore. Besides, she'd lost track of whose they were, and if she'd lost track, she knew her students had. She needed a clean slate, and it wouldn't come to her all by itself. She would have to do that on her own.

Her trash bins finally full, she knew she'd done enough

for the day. Besides, she had her date with Peter. She looked at the clock, and it was ten-thirty. She had time to visit the ladies' room and head off to Scortio's. She hoped he showed up. That's all she needed, to betray Jeffrey for a no-show. That would be the end-all to a really rotten two years, and this man had better not let her down.

JESSICA SAT in her car outside Scortio's, and she studied the building in front of her. It was quite a nice place, and it had been handsomely redone several years ago. Historic, she believed. There was a plaque there somewhere, if she remembered just where to look.

However, her eyes were searching for tawny hair and broad shoulders that spoke of something that she couldn't quite name. She would feel herself called out if someone suggested it was other than a simple desire to help an eager student, but she knew there were more layers to this rotten onion she was letting grow around her than she wanted exposed.

One thing she was feeling was fear, that was for sure. She wanted to trust this man to be here, to not let her newly exposed feelings down. In addition, she wanted these feelings and this man to be very private, to keep him for herself.

She also wanted to grieve for Jeffrey, but she'd grieved for two years. She was now acknowledging that she hadn't died along with him. She wanted to live again, and she didn't know if perhaps that was what she was looking for as she sat in her car. She hoped to see life walking across the parking lot, and it just might be embodied in one tawny-haired, green-eyed man.

She glanced at her watch, then at the clock on the car's dash. Nearly eleven, and she didn't see him anywhere. Her eyes scanned the cars in the lot. Which one was his? There were several exotic models, one similar to Mags', even, and she tried to picture him in one of those. No, she couldn't do that. He wouldn't drive a low-slung sports car. The truck? It was unusual to see a truck here, but he might be the truck sort. Then, there was that old classic. Well, maybe just old, but it did sort of have a vintage look. Perhaps he might drive that.

She knew it didn't matter. She drove her little gas sipper, and other times she was in Jeffrey's car. Both were very different, and yet she was exactly the same. The car didn't change her into what the car wanted her to be. What Peter drove was unimportant.

Besides, she knew rich people were often exotic in their tastes, and she didn't mean to suggest him only in an exotic car. Rich people often drove cars that appealed to something other than vanity. It might be a connection to an event in their past, or because it was Gramps's old car, or that it fit in the garage. Sometimes they just didn't care, or they kept their good cars at the house in the country. A city car was one for getting around town, not for show.

She glanced down at her dress. This was an item of clothing for show. She was beginning to wish she hadn't worn it. It was very out of place for a college professor out to lunch with a student.

She reached her hand to open the door, and as she glanced up, she caught her eyes in the mirror. Tilting it a bit, she looked at her lipstick. It was too dark, too *kissable,* as Robert had said this morning. However, she had no more with her, and she would have to live with it. She reached up and worked her fingers into her hair just at the roots. Drawing them out, she let the mass fall to her shoulders. She took a deep breath and sighed. She would have to do this. She could have backed out when he first asked, but that time had come and gone. This had to be done.

She pushed the door wide and stepped out. The day had warmed, and the sun on her black outfit was toasty. She wrapped her key ring in one finger and pushed the door shut. She took nothing else with her. This man must be here, or she wouldn't stay. She had told him it was his job to pay. She must also see his computer at the table, or he would dine alone. She wouldn't stay for anything that appeared to be a date, no matter how much she wanted to.

As she approached the door, she was surprised to find it opening for her. Scortio's was very elegant, even though it catered to the breakfast, lunch, and dinner crowd, but there was no doorman. That would have been something she would expect at an evening-only establishment.

At first thought, she wondered if the man she had come to meet was greeting her with a flourish. She prepared a smile on her face, and she wracked her brain to find a suitable quip to start the lunch on neutral terms. *Heard any new hooks, lately?* How trite! She could do better than that. Perhaps she could level the playing field with, *I bring all my students here.* Oh, heavens! She couldn't say that! Her heart was in her throat, and she had no idea what she would say to him. She wished she could see through the smoky glass door, but that wasn't possible, even in the bright, midday sun.

Then, the door swung wide, and she saw the white jacket. It was one of the waiters. Her thudding heart sank. It wasn't him. He hadn't come to the door. When she'd thought it might be him, she'd prepared herself, and she'd imagined the nuisance it would be to deal with him as they were taken to a table. She had imagined irritation at the inconvenience.

Now, she knew she'd been frightened. She tried to push aside how strongly she was feeling this, how much she wanted this contact with life again; she wanted to fend it off as long as possible. She wanted to play at this game, and then when her taste of emotion had sated her sensations, she would go home to her mausoleum of a suburban home, and Jeffrey would be there once again. Her betrayal could be forgotten, and she could hold his picture and cry for his forgiveness.

However, at this moment, she didn't want to cry over Jeffrey's picture. She wanted contact with this man, and she couldn't keep her guilt pushed aside. If she had seen him approach the restaurant, she could have waited until she was sure he was seated already. That would have given her more time to prepare herself, to place him as a fixture in the building, just someone who happened to be at the table they shared. She would have lunch, look at his story, and she would leave him here when she was done. She smiled at the knowledge that she could claim indigestion and run for the door. That way he would still be sitting at the table when she drove away. That would be a fine ending, and then he sure enough would stay away from her class at the school. She would be free of this hedonistic foray of hers into life, this misadventure she was letting herself get embroiled in.

"Good morning, Dr. Johansen." The white jacket held the door wide for her. "I saw you pull up, and you look stunning today. This must be a very special lunch date."

Jessica looked to see this wasn't just any waiter. This was Paul, and she relaxed. She knew Paul. Very well, in fact. Oh, she didn't know where he lived, or if he owned a car. However, he was a student at the university, and he had been in one of her classes. He was Mags and her usual waiter for breakfast. During the regular semester sessions, he took afternoon classes at the school, she thought. Or, maybe it was evening. Anyway, he was always here in the mornings, and he was safe.

"Good morning, Paul. This is a treat to have someone greet me at the door." It was, too. It gave her the chance to reorient her thoughts away from this man she had come to have lunch with. "I'm meeting someone, Paul."

"Ms. Brier-Sheldon?" He made as if to lead her to a table, and she put her hand on his arm to redirect him.

"Not today, Paul. There's a man, a student I'm meeting. He should have a computer, a laptop, with him. Tawny hair, green eyes, and a nice smile. Very charming." Jessica froze, horrified at what she was doing. She was describing this man in emotional terms, and this was not to be an emotional meeting. Oh, she knew it was very emotional for her, but he was a student, and she would remember that. She would play with the emotional side, because her heart—and her body, she had to admit—would force that from her. However, it would all be very proper. A valued Clark University professor and one of her struggling students would sit on opposite sides of the table, and the student's

125

portable computer would be opened between them. Both diners would have serious expressions on their faces, and everyone would see that this was a working lunch. Then, she would get ill and run from the building, and she wouldn't think about falling on him in the quadrangle, not ever again.

Paul paused, and he pursed his lips. "Charming, you say. Hmm."

Jessica looked away. She was now embarrassed at how she had handled her description of this man. When she'd agreed to this back in her classroom, Scortio's was the first place that had come to her mind. It was public, very public. Students frequented it, and so did Clark faculty members. No one would see a lunch date here as an assignation. She winced. Date. This was not a date, and she must stop thinking of it that way. This was a session. Ah, she liked that word. A session. She looked back to Paul to see him smiling at the series of emotions she knew must have played out across her face.

"Yes, Paul. Charming." She couldn't take it back, after all. She might as well admit to it. "He probably charmed you when he was seated. He does that with everyone, and it drives us crazy. He's shameless. Do you know the man I'm describing?" She was rambling, but at this point, she just wanted to be seated. *Please, Paul, just take me there.*

PAUL LAUGHED. He was finding this woman amusing. He had sat through her classes, and he knew the story of her husband. It had happened before Paul came to Clark, but everyone knew. She was a good teacher, but she had been distant. Her smiles had been bright, but they had faded when she thought no one was looking. It was only when she was with her friend, Ms. Brier-Sheldon, that she seemed to come to life. Now, even he, Paul, the harried waiter who was a student with no life outside of school and work, could see that someone else had gotten through to this woman. She liked this man, student or not.

She had also described him well. Charming. He *had* charmed the staff here. It was strange, too. He gave them his name—Peter, Paul remembered—and told them he was meeting someone. His voice was animated, and his eyes looked at everything almost as if he was soaking up the world, as if he had been given a second chance at life. Yes, this woman was good in her word choices. Paul remembered that from her class, and he saw it again this morning. *Charming.*

"I know exactly who you mean, Dr. Johansen. He's in the back. He requested a table where he wouldn't be disturbed."

She gave a wry grin. "Oh, he did, did he?"

Paul glanced at her and caught her look. He grinned back. "He didn't say who he was meeting, but he did say it was a working lunch. He told us that several times, and very forcefully. You would almost think he was trying to convince himself. He does have a computer out, and I believe he's using it already."

AT THAT revelation, Jessica was both relieved and disappointed. She needed to interact with this man, and although she must keep this very aboveboard, she wanted to experience more than just a discussion of his story. This would be a very safe place to do that. However, it seemed he would be all business. In fact, he might not want to talk to her at all unless it was about that story.

However, if she got the chance, she would ask him about one thing. It had to do with his story, too, so it would be perfectly acceptable. Died twice? What did that mean, anyway?

PETER LOOKED up from his laptop to see a waiter with Jessica, and he smiled. He lowered the top to his computer, letting it drift into hibernation mode. It would save everything he had opened and operating on the computer, and it would all be the same when he turned it back on.

The waiter winked at him, and with a smile, he asked, "Mr. Shamelessly Charming, I presume? I trust you won't drive our dear Dr. Johansen crazy. She has a best friend that seems to have that job cornered." He pulled out a chair to allow her to be seated. The young man continued, "Dr. Johansen is one of our very best patrons, and we do want her to come back again."

After the boy left, Peter looked at his lunch guest. "Mr. Shamelessly Charming?" Then he leaned in to her, and in a serious tone, he asked, "A character? Jesus is a *character* in The Bible? C'mon, Doc. A *character*?" He leaned back and smiled. This could easily be the best lunch of his life. He intended to make the most of it.

JESSICA WASN'T happy with this table in any way, or with Paul's introduction as he seated her. This spot was certainly in the back, and, no, they wouldn't be disturbed. However, it was wedged into a corner. Two sides of the table were against the wall, and the other two were right next to each other. She couldn't sit across from this man, treat him as a fixture in the restaurant, and then run from him when the meal was done. They were brushing elbows. She would be sitting practically shoulder-to-shoulder with this man who *was* shamelessly charming. Paul didn't have to tell him that, though. She wasn't happy at all.

At least she saw he had his computer out, just as Paul had said. It was on the table. It was out, and it was closed. Did that mean they were going to have a conversation, or did it mean they were going to work?

She looked at her keys in her hand. She had nothing to put them in, and they certainly could not go in the pockets inside this dress. There was barely room for her, and none for keys. She looked at his computer already out, and she sighed. She dropped her keys alongside it.

"So, Jesus is a character in The Book?" Peter grinned. He proceeded to cover other ground that seemed interesting to him, also. "That boy back there seems to know you pretty well."

She glanced behind her to see Paul seating another couple at the far side of the building. "Yes, he was in one of my lit classes last year. He's a sweet boy. Perhaps too literate these days." *Shamelessly charming! How had Paul had the nerve?* "My friend and I come here, and he always waits on us."

"So, he was in your class, and now he works for a living. He dropped out? Failed? Couldn't take the pressure?" Peter's eyes teased her, and he reached up to tap his computer. "What about me? Should I just call it quits now? I do have a dog at home. He would love me regardless."

Jessica felt her control of this situation slipping out of

her grasp. This man was truly shameless. He was charming her, or perhaps disarming her would be a better choice of words. Paul was a neutral topic, though.

"Our waiter was in my class, and he's still in school. He takes afternoon classes on campus. This is his morning job."

"So, he has an evening job, too? I know it cost me an arm and a leg to get into your class. Do you think all his are fake? What do they call those? Prosthetics? By the way, I still don't know if I should continue or call it quits."

Jessica looked at him, and she worked her mouth, unsure of where this conversation would take them next. It seemed that anything she said was just a jumping off spot for this man to leap a new direction.

"Well, I cannot actually fail you." She reached to place her hand on her keys, and then she quickly pulled it back again.

"You can't? Now, tell me why not." Peter watched her hand, then he looked into her face. He smiled.

Jessica had an epiphany. God help her if he didn't know he was throwing her off balance. That must be his intent. However, she was a very strong woman, and he wouldn't get through her shell by knocking her off balance.

"You're an auditing student. You don't get a grade."

"Ah! I remember. I'm there solely for the purpose of an education. I'm not showing up for a grade. I have no degree plans in mind. I don't even need to be there, and yet I've shown up for two days. I guess that means something. What do you think?"

A smile cracked Jessica's face. She was starting to see

an element of humor in this man's convoluted logic. She could put together a strong comeback to this. After all, words were what she did all day. She propped her elbow on the table, and she flipped her hair to get it back from her face. Then she rested her chin on her hand. With a smile, she tried to best him.

"Most of the students who share that class with you would sum up your behavior from this morning in one word." She waited on him. He had to ask her for it. She wouldn't tell him without that.

After a few moments, Peter broke. "And that word is?"

Jessica smiled, and it was sweet. Her reply came in the most genteel manner she could command. "Stupid."

"Stupid? Did I hear you correctly?" He watched her face intently.

Jessica paused as Paul approached, and taking each of their glasses, he poured water for them. "Your lunch will be here in a moment." He smiled and stepped away, leaving them in peace.

"You ordered already?" That surprised her.

Instead of answering her question, Peter smiled and asked, "Stupid?"

"And deaf. Yes, Mr. Cassel. Stupid and deaf." She raised her eyebrows and smirked at him.

He put both his arms on the table, and he leaned in to her. "However, what if I'm writing a story so good it's worth one summer sitting in a classroom?" He chuckled. "Would I still be stupid?"

Jessica pulled her hand from under her chin and touched his nose, pushing him back from her. "I did not call you stupid, Mr. Cassel. I said my students would. My students think they are smarter than God, anyway, and all this schooling is just an obstacle in the way of the better pursuits of life. Partying. Sleeping in. Chasing the opposite sex, or the same if they're so inclined."

Peter laughed at that. "I like that last one. Of course, I am not so inclined, thank you. I find your type more interesting."

Jessica looked at him, wondering at that last statement. This morning he had asked her for a date, or at least she thought he had. At lunch, he was telling her he found her interesting. Would they be married by nightfall?

Just then a cart rolled up, and Paul was there. "Pardon me, Dr. Johansen, Mr. Charming. Your food is served."

Jessica rolled her eyes as the waiter took her plate and transferred the food from the cart for her. As he placed her order in front of her, she was surprised to find it was her usual lunch of baked tofu with grilled vegetables. She glanced at Peter then at Paul.

Paul winked at her. In a stage whisper, he told her, "He is certainly very charming, Dr. Johansen. However, I insisted he order your favorite. It took some doing, but he finally acquiesced."

Jessica looked back at Peter. He chuckled.

"The boy's right, Dr. Johansen. I wanted heart healthy food, and he recommended the bacon grease and butter of a rich meal. Well, here we are. At least someone gets what they want."

"Heart healthy? Bacon grease? Are you sure you don't have that backward?" Jessica looked to see what he was being served, and she covered her mouth with her hand and laughed to see it was the same as what she had. "Where's the bacon grease?"

Paul reached to the covered platters on his cart, and then he paused dramatically. "Bacon grease, coming up!" With a flourish, he pulled a simple hamburger patty out. It was topped with crisp bacon, and a bun was on the side. As soon as it was placed on the table, he pulled out a fresh napkin. "To keep your computer grease-free." He smiled, covering the machine. He bowed, backing away, and was gone.

Jessica looked at the table, then at Peter. "The burger? I don't get that."

He just shook his head, studying the tofu in disbelief. "When the young man insisted you would rather have the tofu and veggies, I hardly believed him. However, if you were willing, I was going to be game. Despite that, I was certain we needed a backup plan. If the tofu wouldn't go down, there needed to be something else on this table to eat."

She smiled at his logic. "What was that about heart healthy? The tofu, yes. I suppose it could be classified as heart healthy. That burger? I doubt it very much."

Peter looked at the meat longingly. "The burger, not at all. However, I can eat it and still be heart healthy. It just covers my meat allowance for the next two weeks. They don't serve ground turkey."

Jessica looked at him as he picked up a fork to tackle his tofu. It was an acquired taste. She had to give him that. It was also interesting that he would try it because of her. He should just eat the burger. She assumed he was teasing about the heart healthy and ground turkey. That sounded like someone with heart concerns. This man looked healthy as a horse. She doubted he'd been sick a day in his life.

She did note that after he consumed his tofu with much face making, he did reach for a slice of the bacon. He seemed to relish it more than the rest of his meal combined.

When Paul returned to clear the table, he looked at Mr. Charming to see if he wanted the burger left behind.

"Take it," Peter said resignedly. "Take it, or I might actually eat it."

Jessica reached to the plate before he did, and she took one slice of bacon. "For you, Mr. Cassel. You shared my food, and now I'll return the favor." However, she did hand the plate with the burger to Paul to remove with all the rest.

Just then, Jessica heard a voice she couldn't mistake, and she reached a hand to cover her eyes. *Dear God, no,* she prayed. However, that didn't stop Mags from walking right up to their table.

"WELL, WELL, well. What's this I see?"

Jessica cringed as Mags' voice penetrated the well-bred silence of the restaurant. Her friend boldly stood behind Peter with her arms crossed. Jessica took a deep breath and tried to prepare herself. She'd led Mags to believe this was a date, and she felt her stomach churn. She was ready to die with embarrassment.

"Jess," Mags started, "you must see who I've been having lunch with. I won't leave you alone until you do. Look this way, sweetie." She reached to pull Jessica's hand from her face. "Come, my sweets. You can do this."

Jessica dropped her hand to see Peter glancing away.

She also saw his mouth fighting a grin. She glanced at Mags to find an impish smile on her face. Behind her was the good Mr. Pearson. Jessica sighed, now regretting this impromptu lunch more than ever. However, Mags was here, and the best way to handle this was to go at it head on.

"Why, Mags. You're dining with your Mr. Pearson. Peter, let me introduce you." She reached to touch his arm, and he turned with an embarrassed smile. "Mr. Cassel, this is my best friend, Mags. You must remember. She's the one who pushed me into you out on the quadrangle."

She smirked at Mags. That would get even if anything would.

PETER TURNED to glance at the other woman and back to Jessica. That was news. He had a pretty good idea he hadn't stumbled, that it had seemed to be a flying tackle. He hadn't fallen into her after all.

Jessica continued the introductions, "Behind Mags, you must meet her drama teacher. He works at the university. Positioning, isn't that right, Mags? The good Mr. Pearson helps you with positioning?"

Mr. Pearson reached over to shake Peter's hand, and Peter gave him a nod and returned the shake. "Pleased to meet you," Mr. Pearson said with a quick smile.

Peter just nodded without saying anything. Jessica and her friend were fencing like mad, and he didn't want the sabre to swing his way. A fiery look flashed from Mags' eyes, aimed directly at the good professor.

"Why, Jessica," Mags purred silkily. "You do look beautiful today. Is that why you missed our breakfast appointment? You must have been making plans for this wonderful gentleman. What did you tell me in your office? It seems you said you had a date. Yes, that was it. A date. For lunch. At Scortio's. Eleven. I'd hoped we would see each other." She turned to Mr. Pearson to put her hand beside his face and gaze with exaggerated adoration into his eyes.

Peter jumped when he felt a foot kick him under the table. He looked in surprise to see an expression of desperation on Jessica's face. Her eyes flicked to the computer, and then she jerked her head sideways. He glanced at it, and then he felt her kick his leg again. Understanding what she wanted but not exactly why, he leaned far over the table and fiddled with her keys. As he drew back, he pulled the computer from underneath the napkin Paul had draped over it and slipped it neatly into his lap, and just in time.

Mags released her date, and her eyes focused on Peter, as if seeing him for the first time. Her face lit up in mock surprise. "Why, Jess, this is that new student of yours, isn't it? Peter, did you say?" She nodded to Peter and smiled engagingly. "My friend here, that's Jessica, you know, or Dr. Johansen, possibly, as you *are* one of her students, talks of you constantly. Peter this, or Peter that. I'm so relieved to see there's no work going on here." She leaned between them and placed her elbows on the corner of the table. She pursed her lips, then proceeded to whisper loudly as if revealing a secret, "You see, she brings all her best students here for educational purposes." She stood. "Don't you, Jess?"

Jessica was red with embarrassment, but her words came back with a bite, "Thank you, Mags Brier-Sheldon, for that fine professional rendition of my perceived academic activities. I have enjoyed seeing you once again, Mr. Pearson."

Mags wasn't through, however. She leaned in to look closely at Jessica's face. Then, she stood as if shocked. "Why, Jess! That lipstick! I do believe you're wearing that new shade we saw at the store last time out. What was it called? Oh, yes. I remember. Kissable Red. That was certainly it. *Kissable* Red." With those words, she turned and took Mr. Pearson's arm in hers. As they walked off, she raised her hand over her shoulder and wiggled her fingers in farewell.

Peter and Jessica sat in silence for a time. Then, Peter spoke. "She's your best friend?"

Jessica laughed at that. "Well, I don't have many. We've known each other since grade school. She's more like a sister."

He smiled and dropped his head. "I can see that. Um, can my laptop come out and play?"

Jessica touched his arm in thanks. "Of course. Let me explain."

However, Peter was aware only of her skin against his, and in that touch, time ground to a standstill for him. When she'd touched him earlier, there had been a crowd, and it had been a jarring of his arm. This, however, was no jarring. They were alone once again, and this was an electric jolt. He could see nothing, and he knew only the place on his arm where her fingers rested against him.

Then, she shook the arm she'd touched. "Peter, are you all right?" She released him to wave at the waiter. "You need that burger back. I'm so sorry. Feeding you just tofu

137

was a big mistake. A man like you needs meat and lots of it." She motioned again, unable to find Paul, and she stood.

Peter shook his head, and he took a deep breath. "Jessica, you needn't bother." When she started to step away from the table, he called her name to get her attention. "Dr. Johansen. Jessica!" When she paused and looked at him, he explained, "I'm fine. Just give me a moment. I need to get this computer on the table, that's all. They call them laptops, but they aren't really."

She peered at him with concern on her face "Are you sure? I saw the looks when the tofu went down. It could be preparing to come back up."

He took a deep breath and nodded. Then, with one hand, he motioned her back to the table. She smiled and sat, an expression of relief on her face, but whether it was at his proclaimed well-being or his gallant handling of Mag's attack, he couldn't have said.

"Thank you for moving that, by the way. My friend and I had a disagreement earlier, and she accused me of only meeting students for lunch. She thinks I need to date. I didn't exactly tell her we wouldn't be discussing the assignment, but I sure suggested it. I'm sorry. I had no idea she would be here. You must be so humiliated."

Peter pushed the computer to the back of the table. "I've had worse things happen to me. Let's talk of something more neutral. Jesus. Why do you call Him a character in The Bible?"

Surprise jumped onto her face. "Jesus? He's neutral? I'd hate to think what you consider a volatile topic. More wars have been fought over that man than anything else in history."

"No, that's not what I mean. You called Him a character. I don't see Him in The Bible that way. Why did you use that term?"

"Oh," she said, "I see what you mean. Character." She paused to think about it, and finally, she smiled. "He's such a small part of the whole story, and there are lots of other people in there. That's the reason, I guess."

Peter looked at her. "So, take Him out. What then?"

Jessica looked at him hard. Then she smiled and shook her head. "You can't, Peter. I can call you that, can't I?"

He smiled. He liked that question. "You have been. May I call you Jessica?" He had definitely used her first name several times. Asking was at least proper, if a little late.

"Okay. Fair's fair. Jessica, it is. However, back to your premise. If you take the character of Jesus out of The Bible, the whole story falls apart. You're back to the Old Testament, and we should all go to Israel and sign up to convert. The Protestant denominations would just evaporate. They'd have no point."

"Catholicism?"

"No point. Gone."

"So, Jesus is a character in a story, but if we take Him out, half the world loses its religious foundations. Just a character, huh?" Peter smiled at his logic.

Jessica waved her hands between them to show she meant no offense. "I grew up in the strictest faith there is, barring runaway Islamic separatism. I still believe, but life has dumped on me the past two years. I've become a bit of a cynic. God needs to show me He's there before I can find any of it again."

"Been there; done that. I understand you, Jessica."
Peter let out a soft, warm laugh. He reached to his water
glass and picked it up, swirling the clear liquid inside
before setting it back down again. He picked the glass back
up and took a sip. "I think He's there, though."

"A faith lesson? I thought we were neutral."

Peter leaned back and touched his chest. "Here. That's
how I know. He gave me a new heart." He looked at her,
prepared for some strange reason to share his secret. In the
circumstance of the moment, it seemed oddly appropriate.

Jessica chuckled. "Now I see. Peter, it's my turn to say
your words. I've been there and done that. I grew up
Fundamentalist. Remember? God gave me a new heart
twenty times before I was eight."

"Okay," and Peter nodded. He looked at her and
smiled, with a taste of disappointment floating in the back
of his mouth. "I give in on that track. My heart is *my* story,
and I'll have to tell it on my own. However, you still get to
help me edit it. Well, plan it, or come up with techniques,
anyway. Isn't that what this class is about?"

"You're a man who's died more than once." Jessica
smiled. "I get it now, Peter. Religious overtones, right?
This is a conversion story."

"No," and he smiled. "It's a hook, cryptic until the
story tells the meaning behind the mystery, or something
like that. You'll understand when you read my book."

As they stood to exit the restaurant, Peter pressed a
hundred note into Paul's hand. He walked Jessica to her
car, and just before she drove off, he motioned for her to
roll her window down. When she did, he called out with a
smile, "By the way, you have my hook wrong. I am a man

who died twice." Then he waved and turned away.

All in all, he thought the day had gone pretty well, and he wasn't unhappy with it in any way.

Chapter 9

TRANSPLANT ROLLED over in the grass. He lifted his head and snatched at the Frisbee next to him, and he flopped it back and forth in his mouth. With a growl, he jumped to his feet and leaped several times, bouncing higher and higher, as if he were flying through the air and catching the toy disk each time.

Then, with a twist of his head, the dog flung the Frisbee wide and stood as it caught the air. In amazement, he watched it spin for a moment, and then catching on a shift in the breeze, it began to return his direction.

With a yelp of excitement, he bolted for it, and he leaped. With a gentle snap of his jaws, the disk was snatched out of its flight, and it was his.

The dog fell to the ground with the Frisbee still in his

mouth. He tossed it back and forth, his throat growling in mock attack on the plastic trying to get free from his grip. Rolling onto his back, his legs held high in the air, he looked around. The world was upside down to him, and that was just fine. He growled a few more times as he twisted his head back and forth in an attempt to wrestle the disk for right of possession.

Finally, in a sudden movement, the big dog rolled to his side and let the Frisbee fall to the grass. His eyes jumped to the back door and then to the gate. There was no Peter. He was alone in the yard.

He grabbed one more time at the Frisbee, but his attempt was half-hearted. When it didn't come easily, he left it alone and laid his head down. With a shivering shake of fur, the big dog closed his eyes, and his chest rose and fell as he took in and exhaled a deep breath of air. After a moment, he was still. The only telltale sign of life was an occasional flicker of the skin around the dog's mouth and the periodic quiver of his legs. Every now and then, one of his ears seemed to flick away a gnat, or maybe he was hearing something no human could.

Transplant was dreaming.

In the yard, the sun was warm, and it washed over the big, golden dog. His ears twitched to the cheers only he could hear, and his legs quivered as he jumped. Then, with the smallest movement of skin around the dog's mouth, the Frisbee was the prize he claimed for his own.

In his dream, his master was there with him all day long.

DOCTOR ROSSI tapped her charts. Peter Cassel was her

success story, the one that had vaulted her new surgical technique to success. He had survived two years without a hitch, and there was a good chance he would have a full life from here on out. It was her implant that was doing it, she knew.

However, he did need to come in to have it checked. For the rest of his life, it would be a two-year repeat. He would come in, the batteries would be replaced, and the medicines inside the implant's chambers would be refilled. They were what kept the rejection of his new heart at bay.

In her time with Peter, she'd grown to love this man who carried someone else's heart inside his chest. He was kind and generous, the sort of person that made the time, effort, and money invested seem worth every bit. It would be good for him to find someone to share that new heart with. Happily married men lived longer, because love truly eases physical stress. His dog was a start—and it was plain he loved his dog—but a woman would be especially beneficial for his transplanted heart.

She had included the image of a heart as part of her medical letterhead. Love would do his heart good, she sometimes wanted to tell him, but his private life was his, and his heart had to be in love for him to go down that road. Still, she thought, as she tapped the heart-shaped image on the paper once more. Love is a good thing.

The good doctor knew from experience about the heart as a symbol of love. She remembered a tree on her old family place that had one carved into it. Inside were the letters DG + AT. She paused as she remembered over half a century before. Her love had been a tall thirteen, nearly fourteen, and she had just turned, herself. They had eyes only for each other. Chores could wait, and heaven forbid they had to return to school in the fall.

It had been hot that summer, and they had run in the woods. They were kids, and they did the things kids did: chased each other through the dried leaves of the previous fall, jumped in the creek in their skivvies, and climbed the tallest of the trees. They had been able to see for miles up in the branches. The river bottom had stretched into the distance, and they had been the lords of the world.

That boy had carved their initials into the tallest tree that year. It took him three days. When he was finished, she begged him, a heart! It had to have a heart!

He did that for her, and five days later he was dead. A freak storm, and a tree had come down. He had been trying to save a raccoon. A raccoon!

Doctor Rossi reached in the drawer of her desk and pulled out a tissue. She looked out the window at the city that flowed around her, and she smiled as she wiped her eyes. It wasn't a smile of happiness. It was a smile that told of the sweetness of memories that had softened with age. For the rest of that summer, she hadn't been able to smile at all. Her heart had been carved into that tree by that boy, and her heart had been ripped from her by his death.

That old tree still stood, she guessed. The home place had gone long ago. There were probably houses there. Of course, no one would know the initials as hers. She had finally gotten over her grief, and she had married. Her children were grown, and one of her grandchildren had died under her care. Through all that, however, she had never forgotten that summer, and how that boy had worked to carve that heart into that tree.

Was the heart the organ in the body, or was it the memory in the mind? Did this young man whom she had saved with her revolutionary process have his heart taken from him? Oh, she knew the pump had been removed. She'd done that herself. However, all the loves of his youth, were they still there? She looked at his photo in her files. Of course, they were. They were there in his eyes and in his skin. His loves were in the cut of his hair and the touch of his fingertips. His heart was the collection of who he was. She'd taken out nothing more than muscle. Nothing else.

However, how much had she put back? She reached to place her hands on the picture as if she could touch the man within, feel his hair, and know the memories inside his mind. Had she given him a pulsing organ built of cells, or had she given him more?

The man whose heart this had been was here in her files, also. She had pictures and his medical history. He had been married, and he had loved others with that heart, or with his mind, anyway. All that information was here, including the wife he had left behind.

What about those people? Did love carry over in the heart? Or did love die with the mind?

Doctor Rossi knew that boy from long ago had died that summer day, but he had lived, too. Each time she remembered him, he was still alive for her. She carried him in her heart, or in her mind, to be more accurate. His body had died, but he hadn't, not as long as she lived.

Back to this Peter, though. He had received another man's heart, and he was still Peter. His body must live, whatever it took. If he died, then two men died with him, and Doctor Rossi didn't want that.

She wanted to keep them both alive.

OFFICER JIM Craig flicked on the power switch at his computer. It was an old-fashioned model. The monitor was CRT, still. He looked around the department. His might be the only one still in the building. When the upgrade had come, and all the flat panel monitors had been delivered, he had requested they leave his old one. He'd claimed to like the image better. He did, too. Besides, he'd said, he rarely used it. Spend the money on something important.

He ran the search feature on the police files. Cassel. He might not have remembered the name, if he hadn't stopped the man that morning. Now, Cassel was writing a book about the accident. That was what Jim thought, anyway. The accident, sure. Or, and it was possible, maybe it was about the transplant, too.

There they were, a whole list. Most of the paper reports had been scanned into the computer. Other files were those that had been typed directly in. There were pictures, too. There were lots of pictures.

Jim remembered the accident had been big news then. People had talked about it for weeks. The driver of that rig had lost his job. He was drunk, or on the phone. Something. Not paying attention, perhaps. Jim didn't remember. When they got together, Cassel would want to talk about that day, and for now Jim just needed to refresh his memory on what was in the police reports about the original accident and the people who died.

He clicked on one thumbnail, and there was a photo of Cassel. Jim chuckled. Boy, the guy had improved since then. That new heart must be working pretty well. If Jim hadn't known about this and recognized the name from the accident, he would have never guessed the man he met today had been given a heart transplant, and probably wouldn't have believed him if the he'd claimed it.

Jim saw another thumbnail. He sighed. Jeffrey Jay, sportscaster extraordinaire. He seemed to recall that hadn't been his real name. He'd used a TV pseudonym. It had been two years, though, and Jim couldn't remember whether he'd kept one name and changed the other, or if he'd taken two brand new names. It had been to make his broadcast catchier. *"Jeffrey Jay, coming to you play by play."* It had just sounded good. Even two years later, it still sounded good.

Jim missed seeing Jeffrey Jay on the sports reports every day at noon. He skimmed the report on his monitor. Every reference had the man listed as Jeffrey Jay, and there was no suggestion of his original name. Oh, well. He couldn't help there, but he did know that Jeffrey had been married. The file didn't mention that, but word had gone around the department that the trucking company had paid handsomely to the widow. Hundreds of thousands, so it was said. Hundreds. Of. Thousands. Not the way he'd want to get rich, but still, there it was.

He pulled two other thumbnails with accompanying information. An ambulance driver killed instantly. A paramedic riding in the back decapitated. The whole series of events that day had been horrific.

Jim looked up from his monitor, and he glanced around the room. Some of the officers were at their desks. Most were not. Several people were walking in and out. One young woman was showing attitude to an officer who wouldn't remove her handcuffs.

This accident was coming back to Jim, and the memory of the events washed over him. He remembered the explosion when the ambulance went. The tractor rig had just started to slide, and then the noise of the pressurized fuel igniting and tearing the morning apart had drawn Jim's attention. He could still see the pressure wave as it rolled out from the ambulance. Then, billowing smoke had surged into the sky, and the ambulance had become a ball of flames.

Looking back at his monitor, he wondered how they decided whether the two men left in the ambulance were already dead or not. He'd seen that fire, and if they weren't dead when it started, they sure were by the time the explosion ripped everything apart.

That was what most of the police reports were about. Later, Jim knew, he could run more reports from the newspapers. He could access those from his desk here at the station, and he would if that Cassel guy got back with him. Otherwise, this would do.

He reached into a drawer, and he pulled a flash drive from a box. He popped it open and plugged it into his computer. He highlighted all the reports and right-clicked on the lot. With a few additional clicks, all the information was soon downloaded and safely ready to carry anywhere he wanted to take it.

Chapter 10

"TRANSPLANT!" Peter threw the back door open. "Come here, boy! Transplant!"

When there was no response, he walked to the fence and peered over, looking for the missing animal. The fence was as sturdy as they came, designed to contain a very large dog. He didn't see anything that made him think Transplant had gotten out. No holes under the boards, no scratch marks. None of the wooden slats were missing or anything. The gate was still latched.

He stepped outside the gate, saw old Lennie's truck in her drive, and headed that direction. If anyone knew anything about Transplant, it'd be her. He knocked on her door, looking up and down the street as he waited, hoping to catch a glimpse of the animal darting from behind one of the neighboring houses. He whistled once in the off chance his dog would come running. At sound of the door, he turned to face the house.

"Yes? Oh, oh, it's you, Peter." Lennie gave him a look, and she reached to unlock the storm door. As soon as she swung the house door wide, Peter let out a sigh of relief. The big mutt was sitting behind her, chewing on a short length of rope.

"Lennie. You have him. I was starting to panic. He was out of the yard."

She snorted. "Obviously. He came to me, although not by any choice of mine." She reached down and rubbed Transplant's ears while he just sat and looked at Peter.

Peter glanced at Lennie with surprise on his face. He'd expected the dog to leap forward, jumping all over him, knocking her aside as soon as he realized who was at the door. He hadn't, though.

Then, Lennie looked directly at the dog. "Go, boy." In a burst of energy and unwinding muscles, the dog flew at Peter, nearly pushing him off his feet. Lennie growled, "That's why he's like he is, you know. No discipline." She turned to walk into her kitchen. She called back, "Come on in. Got some cake I just made. The dog can come, too."

Peter followed her to the back room with Transplant trotting alongside. As she pulled out a chair to sit, Peter quizzed her.

"Lennie, how come Transplant's here?"

"Came home from work early. My back. It's bad, you know. Thought you were out playing with the dog." At the bemused expression on Peter's face, she relented and explained. "Saw the Frisbee. It was flying through the air,

151

and then the dog here would jump up and catch it."

Peter interrupted her, "Someone was there? In my yard?" He could see a twinkle in her eyes, although he wasn't sure what for.

Lennie laughed out loud, breaking her somber mood. Anticipation lit her features as she rocked her chair back on two legs. "Just you wait, boy. I'm not through with the story, yet." She winked at him, her amusement now unleashed. "Anyway, there he was jumping and catching that Frisbee. He was getting closer and closer to the fence, and I thought, That Peter had better watch out, or that Frisbee will be right in my yard." She stopped her story and laughed again, now so involved in her memory of the events that she held her stomach, grabbing the edge of the table for support. "Oh, my back hurts so much!" However, she couldn't get the smile off her face.

"Can I help?" Peter, concerned despite her obvious enjoyment in the telling of her story, didn't want his neighbor to be in pain.

"Yes, sir," she said, looking at him and pointing her finger. "You just listen. Anyway, there that dog was, jumping to the sky and catching that Frisbee, and that last time it sailed right into my yard.

"Now, I thought that after a minute, I'd see you over the fence after that Frisbee. You might have come to the door and you might not, and it wouldn't have bothered me either way. You didn't, though, and I thought I'd throw the Frisbee back next time I was outside.

"Well, I'll be danged if the next thing I saw wasn't that dog of yours in my own yard throwing that Frisbee to himself. Yep!"

By this time, her story had Peter imagining Transplant doing just that, and he was laughing so hard, he was also grabbing the edge of the table for support. He held Transplant with the other hand, as the dog seemed determined to be in the center of the exchange, and eighty pounds was too large to be in the center of anything other than a back yard.

Peter gasped for breath as he repeated, "He was throwing the Frisbee to himself?"

Lennie slapped the table. "You should'a seen him. He'd grab that Frisbee, and he'd flip his head. That Frisbee'd go flying, and then that dog'd be chasing it like nobody's business. He'd catch it every time, too. He's good."

She paused, chuckling a time or two as the story wound itself down in her mind. Then she reached out to pat his arm. "Let me get you some cake. Fresh. Warm, probably, still. I like it that way." She cut Peter a slice and put it on a plate, carrying it to the table and setting it in front of him, along with a fork and a folded paper napkin.

"Wow, this smells good." He cut a small bite and worked it into his mouth, soaking up the flavor. "You having some, also?"

"Already did, a bigger slice than that. You just enjoy, while I wrap you some to take home. I like seeing you enjoy what I cook up." She was already at the counter, pulling out a roll of foil, and packaging up a portion of the remaining cake.

Even Transplant got a small piece to enjoy on the kitchen floor. He didn't leave even a crumb. Peter offered to wipe the floor, but Lennie wouldn't hear of it, insisting that it was time to mop the entire thing as it was, and there was no need in doing it twice.

Later, as Peter walked Transplant out the door, she came running roughly after him with the cake wrapped in foil. "You keep that Frisbee put away when you're gone, you hear? That's a good dog, and you don't want to lose him. And here, don't forget this." With a thrust of her arms, she forced the package into his hands.

When he got inside and opened it, he smiled. It was the rest of the cake. All of it. She'd baked it for him. He looked out the window to see her toss Transplant's Frisbee back across the fence. She was a good one, Lennie was. He couldn't ask for a better neighbor, not even if his book was a success, and he made a million dollars.

JESSICA HAD been forced to return to the campus. Her morning class had been summarily dismissed with her change of assignments, but her afternoon class was still fully on track. After dealing with Mr. Peter Cassel during lunch, she knew it would make for a very long afternoon, and she hadn't looked forward to it.

It was the getting home that she was anticipating, now. There she would be able to forget about all that had happened, and she'd have peace for the rest of the night. It was when she pulled onto her street that she discovered she was very wrong, for there, sitting in her driveway, was one very bright yellow Porsche Boxster with the top all the way down.

When she opened her door, she wasn't surprised to find evidence that Mags was inside. She'd given her a key many years ago. It was her old one, the one Jessica had

154

carried for years. Jeffrey's was the one she carried now. What did surprise her was the pleasant scent that wafted throughout the house.

"Mags?" Jessica stepped inside. After their words today, she'd been surprised to find her friend's car anywhere near. In fact, she had been expecting at least three days of peace before her life was invaded once again. Obviously, that wasn't to be.

"Ah, Jess. You're finally home. Come in and see what I've done." Mags' face popped around the corner, and then it was gone again. Jessica took a deep breath and held it for a moment. She knew the extra oxygen would give her an emotional boost for at least a few minutes, and she might need it. She remembered what her friend had done to her office that morning.

"Jess, are you coming? Can you smell it?"

She could smell it, all right. It was nice, too. She stepped into the back room, and she was amazed. It had been transformed. The furniture was still hers, that was certain, but nothing else was. The sofa had been moved directly in front of the fireplace, and the wingbacks had been set off at the back corners of the room. A new rug had been placed in the center of the hardwood floor. All the pictures on the walls were new, and there were candles everywhere. The pool sparkled through the broad expanse of windows, sending flickering light onto the ceiling. The room glowed.

"My word, Mags. You did all this?" Jessica stood with one hand at her mouth, and her eyes filled with tears.

"Sweetie, was my top up on my car?" She walked up beside Jessica, and she put her arm around her. "Was it?"

155

"No, Mags. I just saw it in the driveway."

"Good! That means I did this all by myself. Well, almost. At the store, they put the rug inside. It hung out all the way here, too. I wedged all these pictures in the front seat, and I waved at everyone I saw. Girl, it was a blast!"

"Why, Mags? It's beautiful, but why? After lunch today, I didn't think I'd see you for a while. I was awful to you. Your poor Mr. Pearson."

Mags laughed. "Oh, you don't worry about him. He was in on it."

Jessica looked around to see if he was in the house. "Here? He's here?"

"No, sweetie. He was in on lunch. I dragged him there and told him to play along. Come sit on the sofa with me. I'm not too bright sometimes, if I believe what my daddy tells me, but I know my best friend. By the way, I would have gotten you a new sofa, too, except we couldn't find a way to get it into the Porsche."

"Oh, Mags. You're so good to me." As Jessica walked around the sofa, she noticed the fireplace. "Candles, Mags. It looks like a real fire. Better, even. Oh, this is gorgeous."

Mags plopped down, grabbing her friend's hands and pulling Jessica after her. "Let me tell you what I know. Jess, you are in love."

"Mags! You cannot say that!" Jessica immediately jerked her hands back. That touched a nerve. She'd wondered the same thing herself, and she was already filled with guilt about it.

Her friend just smiled. "I can and I did." Despite Jessica's protest, she grabbed her friend's hands again and held them tightly. "Now, all you have to do is listen. I came to spend the night with you, but if you want me to leave, I will. My parents want me to come home at least one weekend this summer—this one to be specific—but I told them I have an emergency. My emergency is you. Now, let me talk."

Jessica pulled her hands free, but she did give Mags the answer she wanted to hear. "You talk, Mags. You're obviously trying to do something here, and I'm not sure just what. However, I'll listen, for a while at least."

"Good!" Mags settled in. "You know, my good friend, I've known you forever. I've seen you fall in and out of love, and one day you fell and never came out again." She looked at Jessica and watched her until Jessica's eyes began to burn and she looked away. Mags continued, "That was Jeffrey, Jess. You fell so hard, and nothing ever shook that from you, not even his death."

"No, Mags. Don't say that word. You know I can't stand it."

"Yes, Jess. I'll say it, because it's true. Jeffrey died, and you're still in love with him."

"I know. God help me, I know. Every night and every day." She did feel a twinge of guilt. That would have been true yesterday. However, today it hadn't been true at all.

Mags reached and touched Jessica's chin, pulling her face to look her in the eyes. "Jess, I've seen that again. I've watched you do the falling thing all over again, and God as my witness, you've fallen as hard as you ever did with Jeffrey. Can you see it?"

Jessica sat without answering. As long as she denied it, it couldn't be true. She could continue to grieve for Jeffrey, and her life would return to normal. In fact, she could just call the school. She was a trusted member of the faculty, and they would understand. Someone else could take her classes for the summer, and when the fall session started up, this man would be gone.

"Jess, can you see it, or do you enjoy being blind?"

Jessica jerked up from the sofa, and she went to stand in front of the fireplace. After a moment, she knelt and reached to the candles. She moved her hand to run her fingers through the flames. "This is so beautiful, Mags. Jeffrey loved building fires during the winter. We would sit here and snuggle." She turned to look at her friend. "At least I think he loved doing that. I'm not sure, anymore. Do you know, the day he died, it was rainy?"

Mags nodded, "I remember that, Jess." She'd heard her friend tell it a hundred times in that two months she was at Mags' apartment.

"We were planning to stay in that day, and Jeffrey said he'd build a fire. We intended to snuggle, and the day would have been perfect. Then, the station called, and he was gone. I didn't even get to tell him I loved him." She turned back to look at the candles. She reached and picked up one, holding it in front of her.

"This I haven't heard before." Mags sniffled, and tears were in her eyes.

"Mags, there hasn't been a fire in this fireplace since then. I never wanted one. Now, today, I see these candles, and I want one desperately. I want one every day." She returned the candle to the brick opening, and she stood. "Mags, I wanted to believe I was being strong and independent when I on put this dress today. I was running from you when I missed breakfast. I was hiding, because I was betraying Jeffrey."

"Oh, Jess," Mags cried. She stood to hug her friend, but Jessica pushed her away.

"No, Mags. Wait. I'm not finished. You've pushed me, and you've pushed me hard. I've pushed back as well. Yet, here you are rearranging my home and making my life fresh and new. I think I know why, too." This time she hugged Mags, and she pulled her back to the sofa. "Tell me, though. Let me see if I know you as well as you claim to know me."

MAGS WAS relieved. She *had* pushed her friend, and today at lunch, she wasn't sure she hadn't pushed too hard. All this she had done around Jess's house had been a two-fold project. She'd wanted to make amends, and she'd also felt Jess needed to see her life, her surroundings, without Jeffrey. Jessica hadn't said anything yet about all of Jeffrey's photos being stored away. That had been a major part of the plan. Mags was making room for Peter, because she had seen them at lunch, and love *was* in the air.

Her actual words to her friend were less bold, although they said the same thing. When she finished, she was still welcome in Jessica's house. After dinner, when they had talked and worn themselves out, they headed off to bed. Mags got a big kick out of Jessica's second exclamation of surprise, because she had done her bathroom up with one hundred white roses. Only God knew how she had gotten them in her car, but she had, and listening to her friend's excited response made it all worthwhile.

"DOCTOR ROSSI, will I still be able to write?" Peter's

brow knitted in anxiety. He accepted that taking care of his heart had to take precedence in his life, but he also knew this was a major inconvenience. He'd been in class for two weeks, and his book was coming along smartly. He'd just stepped back into the world of the living, and now the good doctor was asking him to crawl back under the knife.

Doctor Rossi sat behind her desk, allowing the meeting to have a more formal feel than she liked. If any tough decisions had to be made, sometimes it was easier this way. She reached and tapped a pencil on a stack of papers, and in a quick movement, she swiveled the thin, oversized monitor on her desk to face her patient.

"My dear Peter, you do realize you've been an unqualified success, don't you?" She pointed to a list of names on the monitor. "All these people died." She looked at him, and she looked hard. "Every one. See that name there? Louis Washkansky. He was the first, back in the sixties. About two weeks. He got about two weeks of extra time because of his transplant, and it wasn't quality time, either. You've had two years, and it's been quality for you. How many symptoms have you reported? None? A little tiredness? A twinge or two? You've been the golden goose. You should feel lucky. You just don't have any baseline with which to compare. Well, look at this information. This is a baseline for you. Compare yourself."

Peter stood and walked to the window. He took a deep breath. The sky was brilliant, and the trees blocked much of the city buildings. If he could reach his hand through this window and pull a fistful of air inside, he knew it would smell as clean and fresh as it looked.

He had a girl, now. Oh, he knew he really didn't, but

he was finding himself very attracted to one. She was only his teacher, but in the two weeks he'd been in her class, she *had* warmed up to him. Her smile had brightened, and she had joked with him. She had joked with the class, too, he supposed. His brain was so wrapped up in her presence that he wasn't sure just what else was going on in that room. He had tunnel vision. He could see only her, even when he was interacting with those around him.

The best of all had been their conference lunches. Thank the stars they had been able to visit cheaper places than Scortio's, because he'd quickly learned he would run out of money in a hurry going there. He had surprised her with a picnic in University Park one day. She had laughed, telling him she'd never picnicked there, ever.

He had shown up first, and he had the blanket spread out before she arrived. There were ducks from the pond, and they had come over to beg for food. He tried to run them off before she arrived, and she caught him in the act. He was embarrassed, but she grabbed his arm as she laughed, and she told him how much she appreciated his efforts.

She hadn't actually seen any of his work. He asked her for tips, and he applied her lessons from class. He had done that. He just hadn't let her see his story. After the debacle about his hook, he was determined to turn her lesson back on her. He found it funny that she misread his cues. He even thought he would tell her in that one trusting moment he had touched his chest. If she understood, he would have bared all. As he looked out Doctor Rossi's window, he smiled at his memory of that first day in Scortio's. She would've known him better than anyone except the good doctor.

Then the moment had passed with her quip about his hook. She hadn't gotten it. It hadn't been about a conversion experience, not unless receiving his transplant had been a conversion from death to life. He guessed that could apply. In all those years of coursework earning his divinity degree, he'd learned all about conversion. Man walks down a path of destruction, and the eventual destination is eternal death in the burning lake of fire. Get converted, and the destination changes. The converted Christian gets eternal life inside the pearly gates of Heaven. So, in that context, he guessed the death and life part applied, although that was a parallel he wasn't using in his story.

He was amazed as the weeks passed at just how much progress he made on his book. It poured from him into his computer, and the words piled up in the thousands. When he called the number of his contact at the studios, they jumped at his news that the book was finally in development. They immediately gave him the publishing house he was to use and told him not to worry about rewrites and edits. The publisher had people who could do that. They wanted this story, and they wanted his name on a contract yesterday. Could he come out?

He was writing, he said. He had classes. He couldn't come out. They hadn't liked that, but they had accepted it. After all, it was his story, and he did have the rights to it.

Now, it was all going on hold, anyway. His classes would grind to a halt, at least for him. Dr. Johansen— Jessica—would go on teaching, and the actual students in her class would show up as usual. However, he wouldn't be there. He would be stuck in a hospital somewhere recovering.

He turned to Doctor Rossi. "You're putting a kink in my plans, you know. I'm in the middle of a university course, trying to write my book. Trying? I'm halfway there. I've had some help, I admit. And yes, I also know that after I finish my first draft, it will be edited and rewritten. I'm sure proofs will have to be done, but my basic words are halfway complete."

She looked at him and took a deep breath. "You are so much like my grandson. Saving you has been so very much like a second chance with my own tawny-haired boy. However, you aren't over all the bumps along your road just yet. You need to be aware of that." Doctor Rossi pursed her lips.

"It's the timing, Doc. I know it's important, but this class is happening right now." He tried to smile at her.

"We have a little leeway, but to wait another month until your class is over?" She shook her head, tapping her pencil on her pad of paper; and then, with a quick and warm smile, her words shifted focus, surprising him. "Let's set that aside for a moment and talk about your book. Tell me this, who's helping you, and also, I want to know if it's been hard for you to tell your story."

He laughed and looked back out the window. "Hard? I've written this story in my head, been preparing to write it, anyway, for eight years. For over two, now, I've read and reread the news articles, memorizing most of them. I have the eyewitness accounts." He turned to walk to her desk, and he stood looking at her in earnest, wanting her to see how important it was that the book continue. "My professor's name is Jessica, and she has this crazy friend named Mags. They've dragged me back into life with this book. I've scheduled a meeting with the police officer who watched the accident happen. He was there, Doctor Rossi. Do you know what that will do for my book? It'll make it real for people." He turned his head back to the scene outside. "I want it to be real. I want people to know."

Doctor Rossi paused at the names Peter had given her. "You're attending Clark, correct? I know the provost, there. The name Mags I don't recognize. It's distinctive, and I would have remembered. However, the other name. There's something about it. It seems familiar, somehow. Yet, I can't place it. I'm sorry." She picked up a pen and jotted the names in her files, as she did during all her patient discussions.

"Dr. Johansen. She's been the best thing for me. I couldn't have made the progress I have without her."

She encouraged him with a smile. "People will read your story and be amazed, Peter. Be patient. You'll be able to write. I don't think you'll be back in your classes, though, not right away. Will this police officer be willing to come to the hospital to see you? If so, I see no reason why he won't be able to visit you here." She smiled again for reassurance. "We'll try to make sure you're awake and alert when he's with you."

Peter stood and watched the world go on outside the window. Over the past two years, life had become real again, his. The last two weeks had been even more amazing. This girl, this woman he had met, had been a taste of his youth back, and he'd dreamed of her at night, dreamed of her when he walked his dog, and dreamed of her when he was writing his book. He didn't know if the relationship would ever go further, but he wanted it to.

Still, his chest pains. Despite his dreams of Jessica and his enjoyment of her class, he could no longer hide something that might impact the doctor's decisions concerning him. He'd felt that if he didn't share this with anyone, it wasn't real, and he could chase this dream. Once he told, though, he could no longer pretend, and the new direction his life would take might not be one he was happy to follow. Without turning to face the good doctor, Peter shared the revelation she didn't know.

"I've had twinges, Doctor. In my chest." Suddenly, he wanted to see her response to his words, and he turned his eyes to catch hers. "Severe, once or twice. It always goes away, though."

Doctor Rossi's face remained calm, but Peter had learned her expressions over the years. In her eyes, he could read some of what she must be thinking. Her face seemed unconcerned, but there had been a momentary tightening of the skin around her eyes, and then she had let it relax. She hadn't thought his news to be good at all.

"So, tell me, Peter. When do these pains come?" She became all business, allowing the meeting to take a more serious tone, as if this man and she might have to make some very tough decisions today.

He moved to sit in front of her. "When I run. No, that's not it, really. Stress. When I get in a situation where stress makes my heart pound. If I stop and breathe, it goes away. Once, it was bad, and I was frightened. I stood still for a bit, though, and it eased." He laughed, and even he could hear the nervousness in the sound. "Am I going to live, Doc?"

He couldn't maintain the pretense of cheer, though. Now that he had told, he couldn't undo his words and pretend the pain was only that of a stumped toe. He was a man with another man's heart beating inside his body. It was only working because of a revolutionary device that the good doctor had implanted into his new heart, and if that failed, his body would divest itself of the intrusive organ he'd been given, and it would do it summarily. Painfully, too, it had been explained to him.

Doctor Rossi swiveled the monitor to face her once again. She reached to her keyboard and typed a rapid series of strokes. Then with a flourish, one that was not unusual for someone who worked on computers daily, she tapped one final key.

She turned to Peter. "You'll live. However, this new information of yours is something I wish you'd told me sooner." She stood from her desk, moving closer, perhaps to make this part of the meeting easier for the man in front of her. "You were the first, you know. Of course, you know that." Doctor Rossi studied the man's eyes, boring into those gold-flecked green irises. "The device we put into your body has worked well, but the symptoms you just described to me say my assessments are precisely on the money. To be functional, the device must have power, and for that there's a battery. The battery must be maintained properly. There's also a series of reservoirs that hold certain medicines that must be replenished. I won't try to make this easy for you, my boy. Every two years, this must be done. You will never escape this. You can live a good life, however, and this technique you've helped me pioneer has already helped others to do the same. You must understand, though, that you are not as good as new. You will always be two people in one body, even if one of you is unaware of just who he is."

Peter looked at her with deflated hopes. Not return to class? Surely nothing could be that vital. He didn't feel that bad, not really. He remembered hearing this speech just after the surgery, but he'd pushed it aside. Life was too good to let this become a shadow he had to crawl out from under every morning. Now, it was that and more.

"When does this need to happen? I'd like to finish my class." His eyes burned with the thought of facing this. It seemed too much like it was two years ago, all over again. He drew in a deep breath. He was breathing, and he felt good. Then he felt a twinge in his chest. He grimaced at the sudden intrusion of pain. It went away quickly, but it had been there, and he couldn't deny it.

Doctor Rossi stood, watching him. "It just happened again, yes?" When he nodded, she continued, "As the medicines carried in the device implanted within your heart begin to run low, you'll find it will take less and less to bring these reminders of your mortality. If you hadn't told me of this, I would say next week, or even the next could be considered. However, watching you, I refuse to let you walk out that door. I want to check you in today."

Peter coughed. "Today? Now? May I at least go home to get my things? I have my dog, you remember. It was your suggestion, and a good one, too. My computer's there. I'll need it to write."

Doctor Rossi knelt in front of him. She reached and placed a hand on his knee. "I've grown very attached to you, more so than perhaps a doctor should with a patient.

I'm asking this with utmost seriousness. Peter, do you want to live?"

"That bad, huh?" He grew somber. She was serious. He'd thought he was home free, and now this.

"The pains. Only because you didn't tell me is it this bad. You might be fine if you go home. You might not make it back. I want you to live. Can we make that the priority? I want to replace your device. We've made improvements. Yours is good, but the new ones have a longer viable life." She stood and smiled. "Once replaced, we won't need to cut our margins so close the next time."

Doctor Rossi returned to her desk. Looking at her monitor, she murmured, "At three. We can work you in at three." She raised her eyes to him. "You have time to call anyone you wish. Plan to stay with us for several days, at least. Thank you for your cooperation, my boy. I'm looking forward to keeping you alive for a very long time."

He reached his hand and ran it through his hair. He was dealing with this. He knew he had to. He just hated walking out on his class. No, he hated walking out on Dr. Johansen, on their lunches, and their discussions about his progress on his book. No, it was more, and his eyes misted. It wasn't his book at all. He could work on that anywhere. It would be Dr. Johansen he would miss. Jessica.

His eyes caught the old woman's across the desk. He put a smile on his face. He really was grateful.

"I'm glad to be alive. Thank you, Doctor." Reaching up and running his hand over his neck, he turned and walked toward the door.

"Peter!" Doctor Rossi spoke his name perhaps more sharply than needed.

Before she could continue, he called back, "I know the process. I won't leave. I just have those calls to make."

Then the door was open, and he was gone.

Chapter 11

"YOU'RE A braver woman than I am," Jessica called to Mags. Her friend was high on a ladder, and she was removing the ugly garland that had flashed its red, white, and blue lights over her office ceiling. Jessica didn't know why she never thought of that. A ladder! How simple!

It felt good to see her campus office returning to a functional state. She didn't know how she could have let it deteriorate into the chaos it had become. She'd been depressed. She could see that now. She remembered the times she'd see a misted window, and she would place her hand there just to reconnect with her last morning with Jeffrey. She had been unable to let go.

She still wasn't completely finished grieving. She could see that, too. However, she could also see it was no longer all-consuming to her. She knew why, in addition.

Peter. This man and their long lunches. That picnic where he'd chased those ducks. He hadn't known she was watching far longer than he thought, and he had run wildly at them flapping his arms. In his desperation to rid the party of the intruding birds, he turned himself into a larger version of the squawking animals.

They never talked of his book, not really. She was surprised at that. Just to talk to him, though, to hear the deep rumble of his voice, and to see his eyes crinkle when he teased her. For that, she would have talked of anything he wanted.

He would ask her for advice, and sometimes he would mention small things he had written. None of it made sense to her. When she told him that at his picnic, he laughed. His eyes twinkled in the sun, and he told her it wasn't supposed to. It was because of his hook. She would have to read his book to know what it was all about. She'd like it, though. He assured her of that.

She did remember one thing he said he'd written. It puzzled her, and she thought about it that night. Then she let it go. It was his book, after all, and he said he would let her read it, would insist, in fact.

An ambulance. He'd ridden in an ambulance beside his heart. That hadn't made sense to her, not in the least. She remembered her guess about his hook being a conversion experience. She had been sure her revelation was on the nail, but he'd smiled and steered her away. Why he tapped his chest, she didn't know, but she remembered his words that day.

His book was about his heart.

How could a man ride in an ambulance beside his heart? Perhaps it was a love story, and his heart was a euphemism for the love of his life. She hoped not, because she was finding this man to be very attractive, and she didn't want there to be another love in his life. She also didn't want his loved one to have died. She had experienced that, and she wouldn't wish it on another.

"Jessica, are you planning to hold this ladder or not?" Mags called to her from near the ceiling. "You know, these windows are a mess. Have you ever cleaned them?" Her voice echoed from the peak of the room.

Jessica looked up and dodged as a section of garland came crashing down on her desk, shedding its parts as it fell. She brushed the fluttering remnants from her hair and looked back up. "I can get maintenance to bring up a towel and some spray. Do you want me to call?" She would love for her friend to take care of this. The idea of climbing up the ladder didn't appeal to her.

"Nah, let it go. I'm tired of being up here." Mags turned and grabbed the next section of the offending garland, and she yanked it hard. With a series of snapping sounds, the rest of the clips holding it turned loose. Releasing a flurry of additional shedding parts, it came flying to the floor.

"Aim it at me, if you don't mind." Jessica blinked her eyes rapidly, brushing at her face.

"Well," Mags said from her vantage point, "it looks better on the floor than it did up here. Thank goodness for that!"

Jessica bantered back, "You didn't have to live through the hail storm. My word, Mags, were you trying to kill me?"

"Being up here is killing *me*. It was a tradeoff, Jess. You lost. Sorry. I'm coming down, now. Hold me!" She began to climb down, and the ladder wobbled unevenly with each step. Without looking, she called to her friend, "Are you still holding on?"

"Got you, girl. Come on down. Just be careful."

When Mags got to the bottom, she rested her hand on the office phone sitting on her friend's desk. Recently, the phone might have been buried under a mound of paperwork, invisible. However, the space had been cleaned to quite a degree. The mess in the office would still take some time yet to organize, but with her new lease on life, Jessica was making quick progress. Mags' daily push was helping, too, as the newly visible phone could testify.

"You've got mail!" Mags grinned. "Oops, that was a movie, wasn't it? I guess I should say you've got a message."

Jessica looked at the blinking light. It surprised her. Rarely did anyone leave a message on her office phone. Email. That was the way she kept in touch. Not phone messages. She rarely used the office phone, anyway. All her contacts were in her cell phone.

She looked at Mags and frowned. "Who?"

Mags reached to the phone and picked it up. "You'll never know if you don't check it." She winked. "It might be your beau."

"My beau? My *beau?* This is not the Fifties, Mags."

"You know what I mean."

"I know *who* you mean, and he is not my beau. We didn't even have lunch today. He had an appointment."

She heard the disappointment in her voice, and she didn't want this matter pushed. It was still too fragile a time for her. She was trying to release Jeffrey, and this man pulling her away was making no commitments. She would have rebuffed him if he had, too. It was too early in the game.

Mags just held out the phone, and she whispered, "I know you, Jess. He could be."

Jessica took a deep breath, and tears filled her eyes. She did take the phone, but her words told what was in her heart. "Don't, Mags. Please don't. You're right, but life offers no assurances, does it? He's a student of mine, and the class is only for a few weeks of the summer." Then she smiled, determined to make light of her friend's suggestion. "Maybe he's just a summer thing."

Mags laughed, but she also gave her friend a look that clearly said she didn't think so. She didn't say it aloud, but then she didn't have to. She'd already made it plain how she felt.

After Mags watched her set the phone down, Jessica placed a stack of papers right on top of it. Mags snorted in derision, but Jessica just laughed.

"Later, Mags. I can't deal with whoever it is just now."

"You can't deal with *him* just now, is what you really mean."

Jessica sighed and reached to wipe one eye. "If you want. Right now, we have this mess to work on, and your garland isn't helping."

"Not even when it was hanging on the ceiling, huh?" Mags snickered.

"Especially not when it was on the ceiling."

Even with the disaster her office was in, Jessica knew

her friend was her stalwart rock, and she leaned to give her a quick hug. Still, Mags was Mags, and the garland did need to be gone. She grabbed one section from the floor, holding it out on the tip of one finger. "Mags?"

Mags looked at it, then she snorted. "For me?"

"For you."

She reached to take it. "It *is* ugly, isn't it?" Then they both laughed.

"LENNIE, THIS is Peter from next door. With Transplant?"

"Boy, I'm old, but I don't forget that quick." The voice crackled over the phone. "I know who you are, and I know how to make a cake you like. Is there a problem? You don't sound all that good. Is it your dog? Is he out?"

Peter laughed. He was glad he could do so. Old Lennie was quite the card, and he knew he could trust her to watch over his dog. She had once before.

"Lennie, I have to be in town for a few days. I can't get back, and good old Tee needs some attention. Food and water, too. I can pay you for your time when I get back."

Lennie's voice was quick to snap back at him. "Forget paying me! Neighbors do for each other, otherwise, what's the point? You got food and water out already?"

"Some. There's a key under his bowl. It fits the back door. The alarm code is written on the porch underneath the mat. You might have to reach over to unlatch the gate, though, to get in the back yard. That's where the key is."

"I can do that, boy. I can climb over if I must. I used to be quite the tomboy, even if you can't tell it now. Age takes those things from you, but I can still climb a fence.

I'll take care of your dog."

Peter chuckled. He was glad he'd remembered where Lennie worked. That was one less thing he had to worry about. However, he needed her to do something else for him, also. His laptop was in the house, and he needed it to work on his story. His *book*. Not his novel, but his *book*. Jessica had called it that. He let out a long breath at the thought of her. He'd left her a message at her office, at least.

Lennie interrupted his thoughts, "Peter? Are you still there?"

He chuckled. "Yeah, Lennie. I'm here. I have a computer inside the house. I need it. Can you bring it to me?"

Lennie paused, and the line was silent for a time. Then she asked, "You can't get it yourself?"

Peter replied, "That's why I'm asking."

The old woman reprimanded herself. "I'm sorry. I'm a stupid old woman. If you could, you wouldn't have asked. Is it heavy? Computers are big."

"No, Lennie. It's small, picture album size." He chuckled.

"I can do that. What's it look like?" She sounded relieved.

He described it to her, and he explained what else he needed her to bring. There was a case and the cord. She assured him she was writing it all down.

"You know I'm at work, Peter. When do you need this? I don't get off until three."

Peter was relieved that she would actually do all he'd asked. "Tonight, maybe. Tomorrow would be fine, though."

Lennie took a deep breath, one Peter could hear over the phone, and he also picked up sounds of a pen scribbling on paper. "Now, where do I take it? You're not in any kind of trouble, are you? I know where the police station is. I can find that with no problem."

"No," he reassured her. "I'm not in any kind of trouble. However, taking my computer to the police station might not be a bad idea. There's an officer named Craig. He can get it to me, I think. Write his name down. Officer Jim Craig. He knows me. You can trust him, Lennie. Thank you. I really appreciate it."

Peter breathed a sigh of relief. That was one more thing he didn't have to worry about. He listened for a moment to see if Lennie needed anything else.

"I CAN FIND the police station all right. I'll take it there, Peter." Lennie hung up the phone, and she took a deep breath. She hoped this boy wasn't in trouble. She didn't have any family left, and she was just learning what types of sweets he liked. She missed baking for her own sons, both of them gone. Two sons and her husband, too. It was that unfair Afghanistan war that had done it, all her family lost over there in the mountains.

She stopped before returning to work, and she touched her head and her chest. Then, quickly, she reached to touch both her shoulders. "Father, keep this one safe. I need him. Otherwise, I've got no one."

Then, with her eyes moist, she stepped back to the factory floor, and by the clock on the wall, she noticed it was still four hours until time for the workday to end. Four more hours. Now that she had a neighbor who needed her help, it was four hours too long. Still, it wouldn't get over until it was over, and she got back to work, just as she had every weekday of her adult life. It wasn't fun, but it was a paycheck on Fridays. Sometimes, life didn't offer more than that. No, it sure didn't. Not Lennie's life, anyway.

OFFICER JIM Craig picked up the phone. He'd just walked in from his duty shift, and he was anxious to get away. He still had a couple of forms to fill out first, and that would eat into some of his off-duty time. He sighed as he put the receiver to his ear.

"Officer Craig here. How may I help you?"

"Jim, this is Sally at the front desk. I'm glad to catch you. There's this man that's been calling for you, probably every five minutes. Says he's going under the knife, and he needs to talk to you before he does." She sounded puzzled at the situation.

"Under the knife? Suicide? Don't tell me, Sally, but does this mean that I'm going back out? I'm off in thirty minutes."

"I don't know, Jim. He's on the line now. Can I put him through?"

He took a deep breath. "Did he give you a name? That might help."

She laughed. "I'm so sorry, Jim. Yes, he did. It's a Mr. Cassel. Peter Cassel. Is this the one from that wreck two years ago? Or was it three? I lose track after a while. Is he the same?"

Jim sighed with relief. "The same. I want to take this call, Sally. Thanks for putting him through."

"You're very welcome, Jim. Anytime." She was

pleased with his response. That came through clearly in her voice.

He heard the line click over. "This is Jim. Peter?"

"Thank goodness, Officer Craig. Finally. I was afraid I was going to miss you, and I didn't want to just leave a message. Our appointment? It's still on, if you can make it."

Jim chuckled. "Okay. Is that all?" Not many people called up just to confirm an already firmed up appointment. He pulled out a pen to note any changes in time or location, just in case.

"Sorry, that wasn't clear. I'm heading into surgery in about thirty minutes. The nurses are here giving me dirty looks even now because I insisted on calling you one last time. I need you to meet me here at the hospital."

"Not serious, is it?" Jim knew transplant recipients sometimes lived, and sometimes not. He'd looked healthy a couple of weeks ago. Transplant recipients could go downhill fast, though, if their new organ went south.

Peter downplayed his situation. "Routine. It just crept up on me. I got a call in to my neighbor. She offered to drop my computer by the station. Bring it up, will you? I may be here a few days, and I'm well into that story we talked about. I don't want it to lag, not now, not when I'm on a roll."

"Sure," Jim replied with a chuckle. He liked this man, and he liked the idea that Jeffrey Jay's heart was still ticking along in someone else's body. God, but he'd liked that Jeffrey Jay. "That's easy enough. Anything else I can do?"

"No, I'm good. I've been told I might be out in a couple

of days, hopefully not missing any of my classes, depending on how things go. Think of that, in on Thursday, and out by Sunday, if I keep the medical staff here happy. My doctor gets the final word." He chuckled. "I left a message at the university for my professor, so I can't do more there. Everything else I've got taken care of. You just show up here, and bring me any information you've got. Those files, reports, whatever you have. I want to see it all. There might be something I missed, and I want it all in my book. I especially want to talk to you. Bring yourself." In the background, a monitor could be heard beeping, and a voice called to him to come lie down. "They want me. Be here. I'll be waiting."

As he hung up, Jim rested his hand on the phone. He still had to fill out his forms, but just for a moment, he paused. This Cassel certainly sounded upbeat, but a routine procedure that was so urgent this man couldn't take time to cover his own bases? That didn't sound good. He suddenly remembered he didn't get the name of the hospital. He rang back to Sally.

"Sally, Jim here."

"Jim! You called me this time! Is Friday good?"

He chuckled. He hadn't expected that. However, his kids were with their mother this weekend, and he did enjoy Sally's company.

"Sure, Sally. Friday's good. Five-thirty, your place. That man, Cassel. Where'd he call from?"

"Oh, that's all you wanted. Tomorrow's Friday, isn't it? We don't have to do tomorrow if you don't want."

"No, Sally. I want. I just also want the name of the hospital he called from."

"Let me check. I can pull it up on the system . . . let me see . . . there it is. Mass General, Boston."

"All the way in, huh?"

"You got it. Anything else?"

He paused, thinking about Friday. "Yeah. Wear something warm tomorrow. We're going to be on the water."

"Oh, Jim! Your new boat?"

"Maybe. Just be warm."

"I can't wait, Jim. Thank you!"

Jim hung up with a smile. He couldn't wait, either. He was glad Cassel hadn't told him the name of the hospital. This was a bonus he hadn't thought to wish for.

CRAYONS LITTERED the table. A small hand reached to grab a green one, and for a moment it seemed the right choice. Then, in a moment of clarity, the green crayon dropped back to the table, and one a slightly different color was snatched up. With determination, the hand scribbled away as fast as it could.

"Trent? Are you working on something?" A thin woman wearing a waitress outfit walked up behind him and looked over his shoulder.

He looked up and smiled. "It's the dog. From the park. See?" He pointed to the tan shape that wasn't quite colored in yet, and he turned back to his mother. "There's me." He pointed to something wrapped around the dog's neck.

His mother smiled. "That's nice, Trent. I've got to head to work, now. You'll be here by yourself all day. I've got to work a double. Junie's sick. There's pasta in the fridge, and don't turn the TV up loud. You know how it bothers Mr. Crakston down below."

Trent dropped his head on the table as he began to color once again. He muttered, "Mr. Crabby."

His mother corrected him, but she did smile where he couldn't see it. "Mr. Crakston. You respect your elders like they teach in your Sunday lessons. Be good today, and don't open that door. I'll be at the place in Boston this week. Remember, Jesus loves you. He'll be here with you while I'm gone." She leaned over and kissed his face. "I might be late. Mummy loves you, too."

Trent frowned as he reached and brushed his face where she'd kissed him, and he called in a wail, "Boston!" Then, in a quieter voice, he said, "Bye. I love you more."

"Don't forget Jesus."

He looked at her and sighed. "Love Jesus, too." His eyes followed her every motion as he whispered his next words. "I'll miss you."

"Me, too, baby." Then she was through the door, one hand pushing her hair behind an ear as she grabbed the knob to pull it to.

When he heard the door close, he stopped and listened for the sound of three locks. Then he knew he was safe, and he reached for a brown crayon. He held it to the shape of the dog as if considering its appropriateness. Then, in a quick motion, he dropped it and grabbed another. His teacher said he had an eye for color. He wasn't sure just what that meant, but he knew it meant he liked to drop his crayons when he found a color he liked more. He did that a lot. Some of the kids at school just chose brown or red or yellow. He wanted umber or vermilion or chartreuse. He didn't know the names of those colors, of course, but he knew them, anyway. They were in his mind, and for

Christmas last year, he'd asked for the biggest box of crayons his mother could find. She said she got him the biggest she could afford, and that was all right. He could get umber, vermilion, and chartreuse at school.

He had, too. He suddenly jumped up and ran to his room. He dug in his rucksack, and he pulled out a rolled piece of paper. The last day of school, the teacher threw them away. He dug in the waste bin, and he found them. The other kids were gone, and his teacher, too, but the colors weren't. They were his, now.

He unrolled the paper, and he pulled out umber, vermilion, and chartreuse. Running to the table, he plopped them down with the others. They weren't like the rest, though. The paper that wrapped them was the same, and just at a glance, his mother might think these colors had come with the Christmas crayons. Trent knew better, though. These were his special colors.

He took his umber, and he added a little color in the grass, just enough to show there was dirt in between the blades. Then he grabbed the vermilion and made a few short strokes just where the wind might have blown the dog's fur on end. He would color over those, and no one would be able to see them. They would change the color on top, though, just enough to make the dog look real. He set the chartreuse aside for the time being. When he finished the dog, he would use his chartreuse to touch the tips of its fur, just where the sun was shining its brightest. Then, in a quick motion, he grabbed the chartreuse and drew in a sun. He would put another color on top, but this would make it real, just like the dog would be real when he finished.

As Trent colored, he smiled. He thought of what his mother had said about Mr. Crakston. He had also seen her smile. The toaster was shiny, and he'd been able to see her face. He thought that was funny. Mr. Crakston *was* crabby, too.

"Hmm, hmm." Trent hummed a senseless tune as he worked on his picture. If he couldn't have his real dog, at least he could have this one, and he hummed some more.

"PUSH THE button, Jessica." Mags had finally uncovered the phone again, and she handed her friend the receiver. Even now, Jessica threatened to cover it back up. She said she had no intention of dealing with anything other than her office.

Mags was growing exasperated. It might be Peter. It was already afternoon. Surely his appointment would be over by now. Maybe he wanted to have dinner. Jessica needed to know.

Jessica took the receiver and placed it back in its cradle. "It's Thursday, Mags. There's a whole weekend before our next class together. He said he wrote furiously all last weekend, not even getting out for groceries. His only breaks were to take his dog for a walk."

Mags' eyes grew wide. "There's your hook, Jess. His dog. I don't mean one of your literary hooks, either. Men love their dogs. What breed is it? A name? Do you have a name?"

Jessica groaned. "I don't know the breed. A big breed, maybe? He just sort of refers to it as he talks. Tee, he calls it."

"Tee. He likes to golf, then. Male or female?"

Jessica made a face. "Golf? He's never said anything about that. And you want to know if the dog is male or female?"

Mags put her hand to her head in frustration. "No, Jess. Is Peter male or female? Of course, I'm talking about the dog. Does this man own a boy or a girl dog?"

Jessica thought. "Male, maybe. It seems he talks of it as a he. Yes, I'm sure. He has a male dog, and it's big. Very big, I think. The breed? That, I can't say." She looked up at the ladder and turned to her friend. "You can use that phone to call maintenance. They'll need to come get this ladder out of my office." She reached to pick up the remaining lighted garland, and she began to drop it into the waste bin. Then, seeing she'd filled it, she turned to Mags.

"We can do nothing else. More trash will go away next week. However, my can is full for now. You were invited to your parents' last weekend. How about this one? Is the invite open for a friend, as well?" She was tired of this summer, and she knew Peter wouldn't be here for the weekend. She needed to be somewhere else, someplace that didn't remind her either of the man she would be missing, or the man she had lost two years ago.

Mags beamed, and she reached to hug her friend. "Sweetie, you've asked the wrong question. Instead, you should ask if the invitation is open for a *sister*. The answer is always, absolutely yes. Going today will give us all day Friday and all day Saturday. How outstandingly glorious!" She grabbed the clock on the desk and she looked at it. "However, it's a very long drive. Honey, is there anything you need from your house?"

Jessica laughed. "No, Mags. Just clothes, personal

items, and a few odds and ends like that."

"Do you have a credit card?"

Jessica sighed. "You know I don't carry one. They're all locked up in the safe at home."

Mags grabbed for her purse, and with a smile on her face, she dug inside. With a whoop, she pulled out a small, plastic card. "Look at this! I have one! Well, not exactly credit. Better, in fact. This debits directly out of my trust fund. Girl, there's a little outlet just down the highway from my parents. We can give my trust fund a tiny work-out. Your car or mine?"

Jessica grabbed the card and looked at it. "When did you get this? I thought you had to beg your trustees to access that money."

Mags reached slowly and dramatically to the card, and when her hand was close, she snatched it from Jessica and twirled it slowly in the air. "At thirty, they had to give me this. At thirty-five, I get it all. There's something to be said for being an older, single woman. If I'm married, I can't touch it until I'm forty." She put her hand on her hip and looked up at the ceiling. She kissed the card and held it high in the air. "Thanks, Grandmother, for watching over your money." Then she burst into giggles at the very idea of her old, elegant grandmother watching her as she spent every penny.

Jessica laughed with Mags. "At least you can access your funds, now."

Mags suddenly grew pensive and pursed her lips. She slipped the card back into her purse and sighed. "Only up to ten a month. If I go over that, they hound me to cut back the next."

"Ten thousand?" Jessica's eyebrows jumped.

Mags huffed at her, "No, Jess. Ten million. Of course, ten thousand. What do you think I am? Rich?"

IT WAS cold in the room. Doctor Rossi was overseeing this operation, but she wouldn't be in the theater. She knew she'd gotten too close to her patient, and she didn't trust herself, anymore. That was acceptable, she knew, if she backed off and allowed someone else to make the decisions for him. It just couldn't be her. She wanted this boy to live, and at all costs. If there was a mishap, she wouldn't know when to pull the plug. Someone else would.

This was fairly routine, though, even considering it was the first heart implant they'd had to change out. The heart wouldn't even be stopped. The surgeon would slice through Peter's chest, go under the breastbone, unclip the center unit of the implant, and pop the new one in. That was something she had insisted on in the design. She didn't want a person's heart stopped every two years just to perform maintenance on a simple implant device. The breastbone, too. The surgery had to be manageable without sawing the breastbone in half each time they did this. It was what she would have wanted for her grandson. It was what she wanted for Peter.

She looked at the shape draped on the table, and she saw the scars on the exposed chest. She saw her grandson in the shock of tawny hair exposed at one end. His eyes were closed, and a breathing tube was inserted in his mouth. She was unaccountably frightened. They always looked so dead when they were like this. The difference was that this one mattered to her. She couldn't be objective.

She watched the nurse come in with the tray of instruments, and she sucked in her breath as she saw them gleam in the bright lights of the operating theater. She'd stood there before, and she'd held those instruments in her hand. She had done that with confidence and the knowledge that if something went wrong, she had given it her best, and also with the knowledge that when it was time, some people were going to die, and nothing could be done about that.

She watched the surgeon come in, and he chose one of the instruments. He was the best, and she had selected him specifically. On the tray was the fully prepared insert that would slip into the patient's exposed implant. When the surgeon made the first slice, that was when Doctor Rossi held her breath. She didn't remember breathing the entire time he worked in Peter's chest. It was when he was closing the wound with his final stitches that she felt herself breathe, and she finally let herself smile.

That was when all the alarms in the operating room went off. Immediately, the nurses scrambled to read the instruments, and the surgeon reached to pick a fresh scalpel from the tray of gleaming tools. He rapidly leaned forward once more toward Peter's chest, and the scalpel flashed in the brilliance of the lamps.

That was when Doctor Rossi began to cry.

Chapter 12

MAGS LAUGHED in the wind. She turned her head to look at Jessica. One of her hands shot through the open window into the air, and the wind flinging itself along the outside of the car jerked it backwards.

"Mags! That's dangerous, especially when you're riding in my car," yelled her friend over the noise of the rushing air. "It's unsanitary, too. What if a bug hit your hand, and at eighty, too?"

"Won't happen, Jess. They only come out at night." She laughed brightly, and then she made a face, yanking her hand back into the car. "Ouch! Something bit me!" She looked at her skin to see what it was. There was a big, yellow smear across her palm.

Jessica grinned. "Nothing bit you, silly. You just

slapped a flying bug at eighty-two. It says so on the speed-ometer."

"Well," Mags sulked, "it deserved to die for getting in the way. Don't those things know they're only to be out at night?" She looked at her friend. "Got a tissue?"

"See, Mags? You tempt them, and they fight back." With a look of sympathy, Jessica reached into the console, and she took out a travel-size box of tissues. She let her friend pull one out before putting it away.

Mags finished cleaning her hand, and she held up the tissue. "Can I throw this bug back to where he came from?

"The bug, yes." Jessica glanced at the tissue in Mags' hand. "The tissue, no. There's a bag in the rear floorboard. Put it there."

Glancing behind her, she did put the tissue inside the bag. Then, reaching down, Mags picked up her soda, and she took a drink. She turned to Jessica, "I really like your car, you know. I should drive it, sometime. I cannot believe we've come all this way, and you still have almost half a tank. How do cars go so far on so little gas?"

"You're just out of the loop. We should be about to your parents' place, soon. Do they still have that wooden horse sign at the road?"

Mags sank down into the seat. "I guess. I've lost track of where we are. I count by tanks of gas. By that measure, we're not even half there."

"Ha!" Jessica cried out in exaltation. "I think I see it. I recognize that red-roofed barn just off the road. That's on your parents' property, isn't it? Look there, down the road. The horse sign must be just past it."

Stretching her fingers just a bit to catch the wind out

the window, afraid now to stick them out too far, Mags glanced around. "I guess."

"What's wrong, now? You've been so excited this entire trip, and suddenly you're a lifeless lump. Give, girl. Why the long face?"

"I'm a bad girl, and I make bad choices."

Laughing, Jessica pressed her to explain that statement. She didn't know of any bad choices her friend had made. What was this little mood swing about?

"You can drive here on half a tank of gas." She turned to look at her friend. "My car would take two. That's not fair. Yours probably cost half as much, also."

Jessica chuckled. "A third, Mags. I could buy three of these and give two away for the cost of yours."

"I like this, though. Will you trade?" Mags ran her hand across the dash. As she let her fingers slide down the console, she kicked her shoes off and worked her feet comfortably into the carpet.

Jessica grabbed her hand. "No, I like it. You can go buy your own." She moved Mag's hand back to her own side of the car.

"You don't like mine? I really like this one." She reached and adjusted the radio controls.

Jessica laughed at her friend's melancholy attitude. "I can't afford the gas. This one suits me fine."

Mags drooped farther into her seat. "Fine. Keep it, then. Just don't be surprised when I drive up in one just like it." She glanced up to see a gated entrance recessed into the fence just by the red barn. "Turn here."

Jessica hit the brakes sharply. The horse sign where she had turned on her last trip here had to be farther ahead.

"Mags, are you sure?"

"Yeah." Mags sat up. "It's the stables' entrance. I want to see the new horse. Pull up here." When Jessica did, she jumped out of the car and turned to her friend. "Come on, Jess."

Climbing out, Jessica searched for the enormous horse-shaped sign she remembered but didn't see it anywhere. She called, "The sign is being replaced with a new horse?"

She must have misunderstood Mags earlier. She really liked the old one from when they were here last time, but Mags' parents did what they wanted. She remembered that from when they lived next door to her own childhood home. They must have had money even then, but Jessica had been unaware of it. She did remember times when they'd talked of moving to their "farm." That hadn't seemed rich to a teenage girl. In fact, she'd felt sorry for Mags when those words were said. Then, when their daughter went to college and got her own place, they'd moved to that country "farm," and now they lived in true style.

"Sign? You thought they were replacing the sign? No, they like that. It's still at the main entrance. This is a real horse, the sort you can race, except she's all raced out. She's just here for fun. I thought we might ride this weekend. Your boyfriend has abandoned you for his book, and look at the options I give you, instead. Horses on the open range. One horse, at least, and the range is safely fenced."

Jessica snickered. "It seems like I'm the one who wanted to come. Besides, there's no boyfriend."

"Oh? And how would you feel if he never showed up

in class again? Tell me that? You'd be sad, and you'd cry on my shoulder, and I'd have to take you to Grandmother's place on Crockett Point for a whole month."

"Maybe," Jessica conceded. "However, that's not very likely."

"Still, you've got to admit," Mags grinned mischievously, "that sounds like a boyfriend to me."

TRENT'S MOTHER unlocked three locks. Then she quietly opened the door. The apartment was dark. Stepping with as little noise as possible, she moved her bag in, and she pushed the door closed, turning the knob as she did so to keep it from making noise. She took the time to bolt all three locks.

Making her way through the house, she came to Trent's door. It was closed, and when she tried to open it, it seemed sluggish. She got her head in and realized he had piled all the sofa cushions in front of it. Her eyes teared up. He only did that when he was frightened.

"Trent, honey. I'm home," she called softly. She shoved on the door until it opened, and she walked to his bed. Sitting, she reached in the dark and found him huddled where she knew he would be. She slipped her hand under the blanket to rub her fingers along his back.

"Baby, I'm here. Everything's safe, now." She felt him stir and turn to her.

"You were gone so long, Mummy." His voice was groggy, but he knew she was with him. She was glad for that. "What took so long?"

As he rolled over, she felt his sunken little tummy. She would have to check to see whether any of the pasta was gone. Sometimes he got to coloring or watching TV, and he forgot to eat.

She tried to explain why she was so late as simply as possible. "Trent, remember when Grandpa got sick? Jesus was busy, and the doctors stayed a long time to help him out. Remember?" She felt his little body move, and she knew he was nodding his head. "Well, today a man got really sick in his heart. All the doctors had to stay to get him well. They asked me to stay so they could eat in the cafeteria afterward."

"Mummy, you don't work in the hospital."

She could hear him yawn, and he reached his hand to wrap his fingers into hers. She took a deep breath, keeping her tiredness pushed aside, and began to explain, "Trent, honey, you know my store where we serve all the food?"

"The cafeteria, Mummy?"

"Yes, Trent. The cafeteria. We have another one in Boston at the hospital. That's where I worked today."

She felt him roll over, satisfied with her answers. He pulled her hand with him, holding onto it quietly, tucking it into the ball he had made of his body.

"I'm glad you're home, Mummy." Trent's final whisper was almost unheard. "I left my drawing on the table for you to see."

Trent's mother smiled. He was such a good boy. She sat quietly until she felt his breathing grow shallow and even, and then she disengaged her hand.

Back in the kitchen, she turned on the light over the stove. She took the paper from the table, and she carried it over to where she could see it. She smiled. This one was really good. There was a brown dog, more gold than

194

brown, and a boy was holding it around the neck. She moved the paper farther up under the light, and she was surprised to see the boy resembled Trent. Then she saw a man with hair the color of the dog. His face was very clear, but it wasn't one she recognized. Over it all was a deep yellow sun. What surprised her most was the word written across the bottom. Transplant.

She sat down at the table and held the paper in the darkness. The man at the hospital with the emergency. She heard the doctors talking afterward. He had been given a heart transplant several years ago, or maybe it was only two. Then, today something had gone wrong with it. It had taken them a long time to discover the new machine they'd placed inside of him was faulty. He nearly died. Again.

Transplant. How could Trent have known? His mother put her hand to her eyes to wipe away the moisture that tiredness, a special little boy, and too much love can sometimes bring. However, the events at the hospital were now lodged in her mind, and before she went to sleep, the word crossed her thoughts once again.

Transplant.

OFFICER JIM Craig was taken aback when he looked inside the door to Peter's hospital room. It had surprised him enough when he was told Peter Cassel was in the cardiac wing. No, actually, that hadn't surprised him. He was in the critical care unit. That had surprised him. Thursday he had been on the phone with him, and Friday he looked like death in his bed.

He stepped forward when he saw Peter's eyes open. "Hey, man! Did they take Jeffrey back out? You look wasted." He grinned to show he was being upbeat and teasing. "The nurses didn't want to let me in. Some doctor here must really like you, because she took responsibility for my visit, insisted, in fact. Said she'd promised you, and there was no way she was letting you down, even if it was breaking hospital policy." He stepped to the window and peered out. "You're missing a nice day."

"Doctor?" Peter blinked to clear his eyes. "Was her name Rossi?"

"Yeah, that was her. Older, gruff, but I like her. Now, about Jeffrey—" He had a whole gamut of stuff to say, and he was surprised when Cassel cut him off.

"JEFFREY?" PETER repeated, as he turned his head to look at Officer Craig. His energy reserves were low, and he concentrated to focus. Doctor Rossi had come by and told him he would have bursts of strength, but expect to tire quickly. She'd also told him she wanted him monitored 24/7, and the best place for that was the critical care unit. She'd pulled some strings to keep him there, so enjoy the attention. Then she'd winked and let him know the appointment he'd scheduled was something she'd allow, if only he'd not exert himself. Keeping that in mind, Peter had rested all day for Officer Craig. This was important to him, and he refused to sleep through his visit.

"That's what I've come to tell you." Officer Craig stepped to the door and picked up a case he'd slipped to the floor. "That woman you told me about came by and said to bring you this. It's your computer. I'll leave it on the chair."

"Here." Peter put more effort into his voice, and he

motioned with his hands to the wheeled table at his side. "I want it turned on."

"Are you sure, man? You look like you've been beat with an ugly stick."

Peter smiled. "I just need a moment to get my strength up. What's this about a Jeffrey?"

A big grin jumped on Jim's face, and he pulled up the chair. "Jeffrey Jay. If they left that heart inside your body, you're part Jeffrey Jay." As he talked, he pulled out the laptop for Peter and began hooking it up. Then he turned it on.

Peter's eyes grew wide with surprise. "Seriously? The sportscaster from Worcester?" Once, he'd thought his heart might have come from the man. He couldn't imagine it might really be true, though.

Jim adjusted the screen for Peter and reached into his pocket. He pulled out a flash drive, holding it up for him to see. "Cassel, you are certified part sportscaster. The very same. Mr. Peter 'Jeffrey Jay' Cassel." He reached and tapped Peter's chest gently, apologizing when Peter winced. "Sorry, Peter 'Jay' Cassel." He grinned.

Peter closed his eyes for a moment, thinking, and then opened them again. "I should have figured it out. Jeffrey Jay. He was off the air when I was well enough to get around. I suspected at one time, but I never really put it together until now. The only information I had said it was a media personality who had given me his heart. How could I not know it was Jeffrey Jay? I'm so stupid."

Jim leaned over and plugged the flash drive into Peter's computer. "Not stupid. Just uninformed. No longer, though. This has all the information I dug up, mostly police reports and a few articles from the news-paper. I remember you saying you had most of those. Any-way, it's all here for you to dig through at your pleasure." He touched a key, then another, and a list of documents pulled up. "There. Keep the flash drive. I buy them by the box. We aren't permitted to reuse them once they touch another person's computer."

He stood and walked to the door. He leaned out to one of the nurses. "Can I close this?"

She nodded with the caution, "Just leave the blinds on the windows open. I must be able to see in. Don't wear my patient out, either." She winked, though.

He waved, and he held the door until it clicked shut. "Privacy! Can you type?" When Peter reached his hands to the keyboard and showed he could move his fingers, Jim smiled. "Good. You want to know what I remember about that morning two years ago? Let me tell you what I saw that day . . ."

Two hours, three nurses' interruptions, and one short rest later, Officer Craig paused and asked a question that he said had been plaguing him ever since Lennie had dropped off the computer at the station. "I know you've had a transplant, and yesterday there was some sort of complication here at the hospital, but who is Transplant?"

Peter smiled, the question bringing a burst of fresh energy. "Was my neighbor talking about him?" He felt his head spin for a moment, and he leaned it back to rest on the pillow.

Jim nodded. "Like he was her best friend. Then, I guess, with your transplant . . ." He shrugged. "Would you like me to call the nurse? You look like you took a spell there for a moment."

Peter answered in an upbeat voice, "I'm fine, just wearing down, I think. My neighbor doesn't know about my heart. No one does, except you. It's my dog. I got him when I received the new heart. He answers to Tee, sometimes. Tee for Transplant."

Jim chuckled. "Ah, that makes sense now. Your neighbor, you said her name was Lennie, right? Anyway, she kept telling me how he was catching something over and over. 'Catching it himself. Tell Peter. Transplant's catching it himself.' "

Peter rolled his eyes. "A Frisbee. Tee's learned to throw his Frisbee up and let it catch the wind. Then, he jumps and snatches it on the way down."

"What is he? Part clown?"

"I think." Peter took a breath, and he held it for a minute. His head had truly begun to swim, and he felt himself break into a sweat. The excitement of the day evaporated as sudden exhaustion overtook him, and he leaned back and closed his computer. His remaining reserves of energy faded just as quickly as his excitement had pulled them up. "Will you put this away? I've grown very tired." He pushed at the computer and closed his eyes for a moment.

Jim stood, putting his clenched hand to his mouth and giving an embarrassed cough. "I've stayed too long. Sorry, Cassel."

"No. Don't apologize." Peter's protest was weak, though. When his energy left him, he had few reserves.

Jim stepped to the window and looked to see the nurse at her station, silhouetted against racks of monitors blinking their life-giving information behind her. He turned back to the very sick man lying in the bed. He shook his head.

"I'm heading out, now, and thanks." Jim stepped to his bedside. "You've been good to spend time with. Believe it or not, sharing this has really helped me get all that from two years ago off my mind. I never talked about it much after the initial buzz in the media wore off. I didn't realize how much it still weighed on me. I'm glad I came." He moved toward the door, then turned as he heard Peter clear his throat.

"Thanks, Officer Craig. I needed the company. What you told me means a lot. By the way, he's a retriever."

"A retriever?"

"Yeah," Peter said as he closed his eyes, chuckling. "Tee's a golden retriever." He took a deep breath, and then his breathing evened into a smooth rhythm.

JIM LISTENED for a moment, and then he propped the door open. When the nurse looked at him, he whispered, "He's asleep."

The nurse smiled. "Good. Thank you. I guess he needed to be worn out." She winked a second time, then she looked down, and she was back at work.

Jim pushed the button for the elevator, and he glanced at his watch. Five. He could just make it. Sally would be waiting.

As he stood there, a grin spread across his face. Suddenly, he couldn't wait.

JESSICA LOOKED at the empty seat in the front row. It

was Monday, and class was back in session. The last of the students had come in, and the doors had closed. As the bell chimed, she took a deep breath to steady herself and turned away from the class. That empty chair. It couldn't be empty. He couldn't fail to show. She couldn't bear it.

Trembling with anxiety, she reached behind her desk and inside her purse. Grabbing her phone and palming it, she put a fierce smile on her face and strode to the door. Before opening it, she paused and turned to the class. She spoke forcefully and with authority.

"Good morning, class. Welcome back to the third week of the summer session. For our opening activity, we will be peer editing. Please trade laptops with someone around you. Highlight at least five areas you feel could possibly be improved on, and be prepared to make changes when your computer comes back to you. I'll be stepping outside to give you complete privacy during this process. Are there any questions?" Jessica paused for a moment, but not long enough to let any hands go up. "Good. Please start now."

With a burst of energy, she flung the door open and had her phone out. Punching in Mags' number, she leaned against the wall and threw her head back. Holding the phone to her ear, she stood as the instrument rang over and over. She groaned as Mags' voicemail clicked on.

"Good morning, golden gods and goddesses. Please leave your name. Heaven will wait, but you cannot. So, I will call you back. Toots!"

When the phone beeped, Jessica wailed, "He didn't come to class. Mags, pick up!"

Just then a voice on the other end interrupted, "Jess? I'm having orange juice at Scortio's. Excuse me for a moment. Paul? I'll have another. Thanks. Okay, Jess." Her voice sounded a bit slurred, but then, according to Mags, her phone didn't always pick up her words clearly, no matter how diligently she enunciated. Finally, after a moment's hesitation, Mags said, "Hey, shouldn't you be in class by now?"

Jessica held the phone to her ear as one of her colleagues walked by, and she waved and smiled. She also let it fade as he turned the corner. "Mags," she hissed. "He's not here. He's bailed on me. What am I going to do?"

Mags was preoccupied, though. Jessica could hear her speaking to a third person. "Thank you, Paul. I will. Thank you. Now, Jess. Who?"

Jessica's panic was now irritation. She had stepped from class to share her desperation with her best friend, and she was being ignored. Jessica barked over the phone, "Are you drinking again? Mags! You wait there until class is over. Do not get in that Porsche. It has too much power for you to drive drunk. Do you hear me?"

Just then another colleague stepped down the hall and waved to Jessica. Jessica smiled and pointed at the phone. "A friend. She's drunk and needs help getting home." The professor smiled at her, giving her a thumbs up sign.

"Mags," Jessica hissed into the phone. "Tell that Paul no more. Absolutely no more." She looked in the classroom to see the students were still busy, and she breathed back into her phone, "How do I contact Peter? Do you know that?" Over the phone, she could hear Mags laughing. "Mags, what's going on there?"

The phone became silent, and then without warning, her friend's voice came on. "This is so cute! Jess, Paul just

202

brought me a little umbrella to go in my juice. He's so absolutely sweet. I'm going to leave him a double tip. After all, it's all trust fund money, anyway."

"Mags! Please! Can I have some help here?" Jessica peered into the classroom to see some of the students trading back to the original owners. "Mags!"

"Check your roster, silly. I did that one time when you had your computer up. Double click on his name. How do you think I got Mr. Pearson's address? All the university lists are like that. Double click, and all the contact information just pops right up."

"Mags, you're a godsend. I didn't think of that. Bye." She snapped the phone shut, and she looked through the door. Her computer was at her desk, and she would have to go back inside to access it. Oh, she hated to do that. She took a deep breath and opened the door.

"Class. I can see most of us are finished with our peer highlighting. I wonder if anyone has a question." Again, she waited, but not long enough to allow a hand to actually go up. "Good. Now, after you have finished making the changes that were suggested to you, go back and add five adjectives to every sentence. Remember, we can and will edit later. You don't have to like your adjectives. You have to add them. Look for the simple subjects. That's where to add your adjectives. Please turn each new adjective red." She knew that should keep them busy for a time. Heaven knew what this would do to the papers. Oh, well. She could fix it later.

She pulled the roster back up, and double clicking on Peter's name, she saw all his contact information pop up. Hiding her phone in her hand, she typed in his home number. Then she walked to the door, smiling at students who looked at her, and even taking a moment to look at one screen as if checking the student's progress.

Exiting the classroom, Jessica punched the send button. Holding the phone to her ear, she heard it ring until it clicked to a message.

"Hey. Peter, here. Tell me what you need." Then the phone beeped.

Jessica hung up. She felt her world closing in on her, and she knew she could not do this class today. She looked around in desperation, and finally she opened the door. She took a deep breath, and she threw everything to the wind.

"Great job, class. You're dismissed for the day." With those words, her eyes welled up, and she turned to run. She would return for her things when the room was empty, but she couldn't face anyone now. A spare office on the next floor up became her refuge, and there she let the tears flow. She'd known this man for two weeks, she had let her friend convince her to trust him, and she had enjoyed his company. Now, he had let her down. She was devastated, and she couldn't find herself anywhere in this mess.

Jessica knew one thing for sure, though, and it wrenched through her like fire. She hated Mags. She hated her with all her heart, and she would never speak with her again.

Chapter 13

PETER LOOKED up from his computer. "Lennie? What are you doing here?"

His weekend stay that had now become multiple weeks in the hospital had been a boon for his book. He'd been engrossed. Consumed, he might say, and his word count was adding up. He'd hardly had time to consider that he'd maintained no contact with the outside world. The few times it occurred to him, he'd begun writing again, and that was that. Now, it seemed, the world was coming to him.

"Transplant is missing you, boy. You didn't tell me you were sick." Lennie stepped into the room, and she reached to place her hand on Peter's arm.

Peter laid his head back and closed his eyes. "Oh, Lennie, I didn't call you." He looked up. "I haven't called anyone. I'm so stupid. No one knows. The first time I was in two years ago, no one cared, and I've forgotten anyone would. You're a jewel to come see me all the way in Boston."

She looked at him, a look of betrayal in her eyes. "Did you hear me? Your dog needs you."

"I'm sorry, Lennie. I can't come home today. Two weeks I'm required to be here. How's Tee?"

She clicked her tongue at him. "Chewing my rugs. I can't run him like you." She looked at him as if just now seeing the monitors attached to him. "They've got you stuck here? Been nearly those two weeks. What's it for, boy?"

Peter tapped his chest. "Love, Lennie. My heart. A girl ripped it out, and they had to put it back in." He pulled his shirt up to show the scars. "They said I almost didn't make it."

Lennie's eyes were watery with emotion. "Thought you were in trouble. Police station, and all. You didn't come home. I got cakes piling up, Peter."

He laughed. "Oh, I love you, Lennie. Bring them to me. I miss your truck starting up in the mornings. I really do. If my two weeks are up, then maybe one more day before I can take Tee off your hands. I'm writing a book. It's almost finished."

He stopped and looked at the old woman. There were tears in her eyes. He realized she'd been worried. He hadn't thought about that. When he awoke from the surgery, he'd been groggy, then in pain. Afterward, Officer Craig had come, and he'd been absorbed in the information he'd brought. Some days, he'd been exhausted from additional medical procedures, and on those when he was able, he had written ferociously. He had been painfully aware he might not have tomorrow.

Now he knew his fears were premature, but they had felt real, nonetheless. The first few days he'd thought Jessica might call the hospital, but then he'd become engrossed in his writing. Life outside of the hospital had vanished, and he had thought of nothing else but his book. He watched Lennie's eyes, and he knew that had been irresponsible of him.

"Lennie, I think I'd like to have dinner with you. I can't take you out, but I can walk you to the cafeteria. It will be my inaugural visit, both to the Eat Street Café as well as the Ellison Building. That's where it's located. The nurses have all chided me for not getting out, telling me that's a place I should visit, since I'm ambulatory. Will you go with me?"

She looked at him long and hard. "You're coming home?" Her face was stern, leaving no room for compromise.

He laughed. "Of course, Lennie. Dinner, please? The Eat Street Café begs for our company."

She nodded. "This isn't a date, Peter. I want you to understand that. I have my own money."

He set his computer aside, and he threw his covers back, carefully unclipping several monitoring devices. He looked at his neighbor, and he grinned. "You may have money, Lennie, but I'm paying."

She snorted. "Oh, well. If you insist. I don't have to like it, you know, but if you insist."

"I do, Lennie. I would enjoy treating you very much."

Lennie just snorted again, but she did seem very pleased as he walked beside her to the elevator.

TRENT'S MOTHER sat on the bus and fingered the drawing in her pocket. He had told her about the dog and the man in the park. She remembered, too. She had seen Trent, and he had been with the man. She hadn't seen the man's face, but her son had held his arms wrapped around the dog, and she'd been frightened.

She loved her son, and she knew he loved his dog. When Trent's father walked out, she knew she didn't have the money to take care of the animal, and she insisted his father take it. Trent was devastated, and it had broken her heart.

When she saw him holding the big dog, she'd suddenly been very afraid. What if he left her? He might do that, want to live with someone else, someone with a dog. She called him back, insisted, even calling him by his full name.

When she asked him about the picture he'd drawn, it broke her heart once again.

"He's my dog. I know he's not really mine, but he's real. I met him in the park, and I might see him again. He's mine as long as I have my picture of him."

She'd been the one to take his dog from him, and he didn't know what she'd done. Now, she carried this picture each day, and it tore at her each time she thought of it. She would continue to carry it. When Trent saw her bringing it home from work one day, he was so excited. He wanted her to love his pictures, and she rarely had time to care. She wasn't sure she loved this one. It was very good; even she could see that, but it ached in her heart more than it inspired love.

Today, she was back in Boston. It was a hard commute into the city, and she usually had a double shift on her Boston days. Afterwards, it was a long ride home. She'd been present the night the heart transplant patient nearly died, and she'd been making a point to keep track of him when she had to be in the city. It gave her an imagined purpose for coming in. She'd never gotten the chance to see him, though, because he never seemed to eat in the cafeteria.

Trent's mother noted just how warm the day was as she walked from the bus station. Of course, the entire summer had been entirely too warm, as if a great fist held all Massachusetts in its grip. That meant it would be a warm night, too. At least she had air conditioning in the hospital. She would be cool during the hottest part of the afternoon. Maybe it would begin to cool down before she left to return home.

Inside was very busy. It seemed that everyone in Boston was visiting someone in the hospital, and they were eating in her cafeteria. It also seemed there were more tables to wipe than people going through the line. People must be bringing in their own meals.

Leaning to wipe down a table, she turned, and her heart caught in her throat. She watched two people carrying their trays to be seated at a table in her section. One, a woman, was very old, and the other was a youngish man with a head full of tawny gold hair. He was wearing hospital garb.

When she finally managed to free one of her hands, she reached into her pocket and pulled out the picture. She knew that hair, and she knew that face. Her Trent was very good. Then, she understood. Transplant. That was the man. Trent had known, but she couldn't imagine how.

"HE MISSED that first day, Jess, and you were all ready to give up on him, even then. Maybe he had the stomach flu."

Jessica tried to relax as Mags rubbed her shoulder with one hand. They had been through this daily for entirely too many missed classes. Paul's latest breakfast ministrations at the restaurant hadn't completely worn off, and Mags seemed to find too much humor in Jessica's traumatic situation.

"Stomach flu for two weeks? With no call?" Jessica turned to her, whitened in anger. "Do you actually think that man has had the stomach flu for two weeks? People with the stomach flu can still use the phone, Mags."

She felt pricked with guilt, though, and she hid it away under her hurt and anger. That flashing light that had been on her machine in her office. Mags and she had argued about whether she should listen to it. Now she couldn't. After returning to her office the next Monday, she had seen the flashing light, and without thinking, her finger had hit the erase button, clearing her phone for a new week. It wouldn't have been him, anyway. He had just been in class with her. Anyway, if it had been him, in two weeks, he could have called again.

At least the tears had stopped for a time. She glanced away again and looked around. She hadn't known where else to run that first day when Peter hadn't shown up for class. She had finally gathered her things and left the building. She had come to the park, and it had felt safe. Now, two weeks later, she was here again on a bench with Mags, and the park felt very exposed to her. She could even see where they had eaten that long-ago picnic. The ducks had chased him there, and he had run, or maybe they had run from him as he chased them.

She felt her eyes welling up again at the thought of the man she had allowed to seep into her emotionally tender world. Looking up at the sky, she choked out, "It's going to be hot today."

Mags laughed. "Hot today? Is that all you can think about? Hot today?"

"No, Mags." Jessica turned to her friend, glowering. She pressed her lips into a determined line, and she looked back to the trees and the pond. "Let me explain it to a drunk."

"I only had two today," Mags wailed in dismay at the accusation.

Jessica's eyes cut to Mags and away again. "For two years I was walled away in my grief, and over two weeks, I let that wall come down. Now, I'm exposed. I have no defenses, and I must *know* this man cares, or I'm devastated. He's *auditing,* Mags, and audits always bail. *Always!*"

Mags took her friend's hand and leaned to whisper, "Not always. I'm auditing Mr. Pearson's class."

Jessica yanked her hand away and curled it into her lap. She closed her eyes and then snorted a derisive laugh. "That's different, and you know it, Mags. You're trying to start something, and you imagine Mr. Pearson might be interested, too."

Reaching to rub her friend's arm, Mags cooed, "And you don't feel the same way about Mr. Cassel? Peter, I believe."

"You believe?" Jessica looked at her and quickly stood, facing the pond and pointedly away from Mags. Turning back, she chided, "You're not sober, yet? You know his name. After two weeks, you know him better than I do."

Mags slumped back on the bench, and she looked at her nails. She focused her eyes on one in particular, and she returned the barb, "Only because I love you, Jess. I watched you sinking into that pit of grief, and you weren't climbing out. I had to give you someone. Your Peter just happened to be the one who came crashing into your life at just the right time." She looked up and smiled.

"So," Jessica snorted, looking for the ducks again. For a moment, she felt that if she could find them, Peter might just be there, too. She knew better, though. "You're not as drunk as you seem."

Let her chew on that, she thought, with no sympathy in the least.

MAGS KNEW Jessica was in pain and fragile. Her friend needed to be handled with kid gloves. She had to be prodded and coerced, but it would do no one any good to allow her to be broken. Mags didn't need a Humpty Dumpty shattered at her feet. She cringed inside as Jessica went on.

"I'm emotionally an open wound." Wiping the corner of one eye with the ball of her thumb, Jessica continued, "I cannot chase this man, and I cannot control what he does or doesn't do. For two weeks, I've hoped each morning,

212

and I've endured two hours of torment when his seat was once again empty. I've gone to Scortio's at eleven and left without ordering when he wasn't there. He won't answer his phone, either. I'm so embarrassed each time I call, yet I can't stop myself."

"Messages? Do you leave messages?" Even with Jessica's devastated condition, Mags couldn't resist. It's what she would have done.

Jessica turned and glared. "Are you a dolt? Of course not! What would I say? This is your college professor, and I think I might be falling for you. Please dial the letters L. O. V. E. at the beep."

Mags chuckled. "It might be worth a try. Have you driven by his house?"

Jessica sat again, and she crossed her legs, leaning forward and resting one elbow on her knee. Across the clearing, a student had parked on the grass and pulled out several books. She spoke in a hushed voice.

"We have company, Mags, and there are no secrets among students. I don't want to become a spectacle, no matter how badly I feel. Keep your voice down."

"Well, have you?" Mags leaned in conspiratorially.

"I will not stoop that low, Mags. You can drive by if you want, but my car stays in my driveway."

"Well, I stoop very well." Mags poked her arm, a look of superiority on her face. "I looked him up on your computer, and I have driven by. It was night, and there were no lights on. None at all. If he were home, he should have turned on some lights."

That last statement piqued Jessica, and she turned to the woman beside her. "He should have turned on lights for you. Did you also go up and knock, maybe shout my name?"

"No, Jess. A big dog barked and barked. Lights came on in the houses on either side. If he were home, he would have gotten up to check."

"So, he's moved." Jessica's eyes reddened again. "He's just gone."

"No, Jess. That's not what I meant."

Jessica reached into her bag and pulled out her phone. She opened it and pressed a key, holding it until a number scrolled across the display. "Derek? Okay, Bill. This is Jessica Johansen. I would like that sub for my summer classes. Second session, too." She paused for a few moments. Then, she continued once again with additional instructions, "Sure. Donna Lambasky will do just fine. Tell her thank you for me, and no, I will not be calling her to fill her in. I have an emergency and must leave immediately. I'm sorry, Bill." After a moment during which Mags could hear someone on the other end speaking, Jessica finished up with, "I know you will, Bill. I will take care."

She hung up her phone and turned to Mags. "I tried to tell you I cannot go back. Is your grandmother's house still free?"

"Vinalhaven?" Mags made a last-ditch effort to rein her friend in. This bailing out of her duties was something she had never done before. Even with Jeffrey's death, she had taken a few days and then been right back in her classroom. She hadn't *bailed.* "Sweetie, your house payment. The school won't pay you if you let Lambasky teach your classes. Are you sure?"

Jessica laughed carelessly and humorlessly. "I have enough money in the bank, Mags. Jeffrey's money. I haven't spent a dime of it. Now, I shall. I shall spend it wantonly, and I shall wallow in the grief that he's no longer with me. I shall wallow shamelessly, and I shall forget this Peter Cassel. Obviously, he's forgotten me, so what else can I do?"

Mags watched her friend's face, and while the words were arrogant and strong, the expression of the woman saying them was anything but. She was about to crack.

"Sweetie," Mags said, "no one's there for July. That's my month, and I usually give it away. No one's asked this year, so the place is waiting with open arms. Now, you're sure you want to just run away up there?" She watched Jessica intently as she nodded. All the liquor was gone from Mags' system, and she was as sober as the broken-hearted woman next to her. She would help, even if she didn't agree with the running away. "So," she continued, playing this out a bit at a time, "first we must plan. When do you want to go?"

Jessica just sighed. "Now. Today. This very minute."

"It's a six-hour drive, maybe more, to Rockland. That's Maine, you know. We have to make it in time for the last ferry." While she was talking, Mags pulled out a pamphlet from her purse. "Here's the ferry schedule." She grinned at Jessica's look of surprise. "I always carry one of these. Old habits die hard, although this one apparently hasn't died at all." She ran her finger down the page. "Good. They're running the extended schedule this month." She turned to see sudden tears streaming down Jessica's face.

"I don't want to have to figure out any of this, Mags. I don't care about ferry schedules or how many hours it is to Rockland. I just want away. Anywhere. Just away."

Mags reached to give her a hug. "We will. We have to take clothes, though. There are no outlets on Vinalhaven. Anything we buy in town there is full price." Then she paused as if remembering. "Is this the third?"

"Of July? I guess. I don't know." Jessica glanced at her, frowning. "I don't care about the date. I want *away.*"

Mags laughed. "We have to rush, then. If we leave now, we can make the parade tomorrow."

"Parade?" Jessica took a deep breath. "I have no idea what you're talking about."

Mags was filled with anticipation. "That's right, we didn't go that summer we were there." She slapped her leg and shook her head in disbelief. Then she grabbed Jessica's arm, explaining, "It's a tradition. Every Fourth of July, there's a big parade down Main Street. They have a duck race, plastic ducks, and when the tide rushes into Carver's Pond in the center of town, everyone cheers for theirs to win. It's wonderful. We'll get to see it. We can be in it, if we want. Not the duck race, of course. We can only watch that. But we can be in the parade. We can take my car, and I can drive it, show it off." Her face brightened. "We can get a string of lights and make it a birthday car. Yours was only last month. Wouldn't that be fun? We could make a sign to hold up, and it would be just for you. You have to say yes immediately, because I'll need to call Lynn or Sarah today and get my car registered for the parade. Otherwise, they might tell me no."

Jessica snorted. "Can't we just take my car?"

Mags was appalled. "I like your car, sweets, but it won't look the same for the parade. It's not a convertible." She pursed her lips, wondering how best to convince her friend. "I'll let you drive, and I'll hold the sign, if you want."

"I don't care, Mags." Her tears were flowing again, and they flooded her cheeks. "I just want away. Can we do that? Just go?"

A caring hand reached to rub Jessica's shoulder. "Sure, Jess. Will you go to the parade with me, though?" Jessica nodded, and then Mags reached to give her a big hug.

As she did, she couldn't help but think, *Money? I didn't know Jeffrey had money. Who's rich, now?*

"SO, TEE misses me." Peter grinned at Lennie as they sat at the table in the Eat Street Café. He couldn't believe he had stepped into the hospital for a checkup, and he had checked out of his life for two weeks. He'd forgotten the world outside existed until it came to see him. He was missing his dog, now.

"Before work I rub his ears, and I bring him to my house at night." Peter raised his eyebrows at that. Lennie saw the look and smiled. "He barks when he thinks you're coming home, Peter. One night a car drove by very slowly. Transplant barked and barked. I looked to see if it was bad people, but it was an ugly yellow car. They went away, though. After that, I let your dog sleep in my house."

A movement across the room caught Peter's attention, and he looked up to see a slight, harried woman at the far side of the cafeteria. She was wearing a waitress's uniform and holding a sheet of paper in her hand. The way she stood looked vaguely familiar to Peter, but he didn't recognize her. About then, Lennie touched his hand, drawing his attention back.

"I brought you something." She reached into a bag at her side, and she brought out a stack of mail. "I've been getting it from your box. I didn't know if you might need it." She laid it on the table between them.

Peter looked at it, appalled with his carelessness. "I forgot all about that. I should've had it stopped. I'm sorry, Lennie."

She smiled at him. "There's nothing to be sorry for. I'm your neighbor. If I cannot take the time to collect your mail, what's the point? Besides, I like you, and I want to do this." She patted the stack. "Take it."

Peter stood and reached to give the old woman a hug. She tried to push him off, but when he sat back down, there was a flush to her skin and a smile on her face. Then, she looked at him, and her eyes jumped to something he couldn't see.

Peter turned to find the waitress from across the room who had looked familiar. She was walking their direction. He smiled at her and glanced at the paper in her hand. He watched her eyes shift to his face and then to the paper. She looked away as if unsure of herself, and then she moved to stand beside the table.

"I work here." She paused and looked at her clothes. With the realization of what she was wearing, she laughed at herself. "Obviously. You can see that. I'm not from Boston, though. I really work in Worcester. That's where I live. I'm here because Junie's been sick, and I'm filling in." She held the paper and turned as if to leave, then she held it out to him. "Is this you?"

Peter took it and glanced at Lennie, unsure of the strange request. If she had handed him a newspaper clipping, he might have understood. He also would have been surprised. He'd received no recognition from his heart transplant, other than from Officer Craig. However, he would've expected the clipping was about him. This was obviously not from a newspaper, though. She reached a hand and motioned for him to look at what was on the paper. When he glanced at it, he was amazed.

He looked up at the woman. "This is my dog." Emotion burned in his eyes as he turned to see Lennie reaching for the paper. He handed it to her and turned back to the woman standing beside him. "Where did you get this?"

TRENT'S MOTHER hesitated. She didn't know the whole story, just that the man in the picture was the same as the one in front of her, and that Trent had said the dog was from the park. When she saw this man, she suspected he must be the one her son had drawn, and now she was certain.

"My son," she started, and her eyes misted with the memory of Trent's dog and why he no longer had it. "He had a dog, and his father left us. He says this dog is now his. It was in the park one day, he said. Are you the man who had the, uh . . ." She hesitated and pointed to her chest where her heart would be.

"That's me." Peter smiled.

"My son. He put that on the paper. I don't know how he knew." She shrugged and reached to wipe a tear from her face with the back of her hand. "He's a smart boy, but not that smart."

She laughed and looked away at the ceiling for a moment, blinking her eyes to clear the teeming moisture. Then she glanced around the room to see if there was anything she should be doing, noticing a couple exiting at the far end of her section. They were leaving wrappings from a local take-out. She felt a sudden pressure to go and clear that table. She needed the money, and she couldn't afford to be reprimanded. The paycheck she earned was stretched too thinly already. However, this with the picture. It seemed it must be very important.

She turned her eyes back to the man and his companion and waited for a response.

PETER GLANCED at the paper as Lennie handed it back to him. He was puzzled by the woman's comment for a moment, but then he understood.

"Transplant." He looked at her and smiled. This was starting to make sense to him. "That's my dog's name. Tee for short."

"Ah. My son wrote the dog's name. I see." It was obvious she really didn't.

Peter chuckled. He recalled a boy, a thin youngster who had wrapped his arms around Transplant's neck just like the one in the picture was doing. "What's your son's name?"

"Trent." His mother smiled.

"Trenton?"

She looked at him, puzzled. "Yes, Trenton. However, he goes by Trent. How did you know?"

Peter glanced at Lennie, and he chuckled once again.

"I live in Worcester. I had my dog, Tee, that's Transplant, the one in the picture, at the park one day. A small boy, about eight, right? Anyway, he came up and told me he had a dog, too. Then you called him away. You called him Trenton."

TRENT'S MOTHER felt her energy drain from her. The remembered emotions of that event washed over her in a torrent of fear, fear that was wrapped up in what she had done with his dog. She remembered her sudden panic from that day, a terror that had convinced her that her son would leave her because of losing his dog. As her lungs struggled for air, she suddenly wished she hadn't come to this table. However. The picture. Her son had drawn a picture of his man, and that made it important. She reached and rubbed a thumb under one burning eye. It came away wet. "I remember. He wouldn't come, and I was afraid."

"I wouldn't have hurt him. He was just asking about my dog."

"He misses his dog. When his father left, there wasn't enough money. The dog couldn't stay. I think he loved his dog more than me. I was afraid he would go with you, and I'd never see him again." She smiled through her tears, and she wrapped her arms around her torso. She knew she couldn't be sorry for showing this man her paper. Trent had come back, after all.

Peter smiled and reached to put his hand on her arm. "I would've brought him home again. He's your son."

Trent's mother smiled and turned her eyes to the ceiling once again. "I know that. Here." She tapped her head. Then she tapped her chest. "I don't know it here."

221

At that, Lennie stood and wrapped her arms around the woman. "My dear, dear woman. You're afraid you'll lose your son. You still have him. Love him. He won't leave you." Lennie paused as if considering whether to tell more, and then she nodded to herself and continued. "Both my boys and my man are gone. Yours isn't. You're very lucky, so just love him. That's all you can do."

The woman nodded, still blinking her tears away, and Lennie patted her arm before stepping away.

"May I keep this?" Peter held up the paper.

Trent's mother smiled. "He can draw another. I'll tell him where it is, and he'll be glad I found you. Will you be back in the park someday?" When Peter smiled and nodded, she continued, "I'll tell him to look for you. Next time, I won't call him away. Thank you, but I must get to work. I need the money, and I can't afford any problems." Without giving either of the two at the table time to respond, she quickly moved away without looking back and busied herself at another location across the room.

PETER LOOKED at the drawing, noticing the underlying colors beneath the colors that gave it life. It was really very good, and he could see the likenesses in both Transplant and himself.

"You like it, Peter?" Lennie pointed to the paper.

He smiled. "Very much, Lennie. I like it very much, indeed."

She just smiled, her face falling into laugh lines she hadn't used much in a very long time.

Chapter 14

"OOH, THE tide's low. Be careful, Jess. Don't wreck your car. The ramp's almost straight down." Mags grabbed her friend's arm while craning her neck to see over the hood.

Jessica laughed. "It is not. Let me drive." She shook Mags' hand off, and she watched the car in front of her as it disappeared into the incline she must drive down. They had waited in the ferry line for nearly an hour and a half. For a while they had walked to the small park adjacent to the landing and watched the birds along the wharf. Mags had said they could go get something to eat in town, but all Jessica had wanted was crackers. "I'm not hungry," she assured her friend. "I just want to get there."

Now, they were pulling onto the ferry. It was very small. Twenty cars? Jessica wasn't sure, but it would be full. There was a long line behind them, and most would have to wait for the next boat.

When she got her car on the deck, she was directed to drive forward. The attendant signaled her to put her car in reverse and back up into a small space to the side. Locking her parking brake, the two women climbed out to smell the sea air.

"Jess, make sure your windows are up. A big wave might douse it." Mags chortled. "Remember that time in college when that woman had her newspaper drenched? She was sitting in her truck with the glass down, and a big wave hit the side of the ferry. It went right inside her window and completely soaked everything. She got out mad as a hornet. You remember how we laughed over that?"

The waves didn't seem bad today. Still, safe was better than sorry.

Mags turned to look at everything around her, grabbing the metal half wall that surrounded the ferry's car deck. "See the breakwater out there?" She grinned and pointed. "It's got a lighthouse on the end. We'll go right by it. I loved this as a child. I cannot believe I hardly ever come back." She leaned against the rail and closed her eyes for a moment, taking in a deep breath of the fresh sea air.

The ferry rocked as more cars drove on. Jessica pointed to the right. "That other light house on the cliff. What's it called?"

Just being on the ferry, the feeling of escape, had already lifted her mood, and she wanted to interact, to hear about all of this all over again. It had been a very long time since experiencing the sea air and the ferry, and it seemed wonderfully fresh and unknown to her. Distracted would have been the word, if she'd said it about someone else. Invigorated was how she felt, though.

"Owl's Head. The Coast Guard maintains it. You should see it at night when the fog rolls in." Mags gazed at it and laughed. The white building was perched on the top of the cliff. "I don't really think it looks like an owl's head, do you? The name of the one the ferry goes by is more sensible."

"Oh?" Jessica caught the sea breeze and drew it in. The afternoon sun, the moist air, and the sounds of the sea. Even Mags' voice was soothing. "More sensible, how?"

Mags giggled, giving her friend a quick, one-armed hug. "This is Rockland, sweetie. That's the breakwater. They call it the Rockland Breakwater Light. You'll get good views of both. You might even see some tall ships. Remember those from college?"

Jessica laughed. She didn't, really, but it was good to be out of Worcester. She felt like a real person again, even if she had been forced to throw off the trappings of who she was to get here. "I thought all ships were tall. It seems that way when I'm next to them."

Mags threaded her arm through Jessica's and walked with her to the back of the boat just as the ferry's horn blew to signal its exit from the landing. They both ducked and looked up in startled surprise.

"I always forget to hold my ears." Mags grinned. They felt the vibration as the engine revved, and the shore began to recede. "Tall ships are the ones with all the sails. There are several based here, right in Rockland." She drew in a deep breath, the excitement in the renewed memories energizing her. "Every summer, all sorts of big sailing vessels, new and old, come to the islands. You should see the Around the Island Race. Then, when the race is over, some of them hang around afterwards, and they sail all over."

"They just sail?" That sounded less than interesting to Jessica.

"They race. People get in their powerboats and zip around snapping photos. It's a real race, though, every summer. It's fun. However, tomorrow, we'll be at the parade."

"Point out your grandmother's house when we go by. I've forgotten so much I doubt I could find it." Jessica was enjoying the wind in her hair, and she was glad she had come.

"I will, Jess. My cousin's island, too. We go right by it. It's an hour away, though."

"Your cousin owns an *island?*" Jessica laughed at the grandiosity of Mags' cousin owning an island, not remembering anything about a cousin. Surely, she would have been told that when she was here in college. What else had she forgotten?

"Oh, Jess. There are dozens of islands out here, all sizes. Lots of people own them. I even have a cousin who owns a Coast Guard cutter." She glanced over and laughed. "Well, not exactly owns it. It really belongs to the Coast Guard. It's his, though. What I mean is, I have cousins all over the place, and they own all sorts of things. Grandmother just owned the point. See, we're not rich at all."

"Mags," Jessica began, now curious. She knew Mags' grandmother was dead. That was where the trust fund had come from. "Who owns it now?"

However, Mags was distracted, pulling her friend to the front of the ferry. "There, Jess. It's the Breakwater Light. It comes so close you can almost touch it. I love it every time I see it." She closed her eyes and sighed, then opened them with a laugh. "This is my home, Jess. I love it so. Look! Look, there. It's the Samoset. I threw my deb party there! I was only nineteen, and it was so glamorous!"

"Who does it belong to now?" Jessica didn't care about the Samoset and debutante parties. She wanted to know who owned the grandmother's house.

Mags looked at her, puzzled. "The Samoset? Probably Hilton. I don't know."

Exasperated, Jessica stomped her foot. "Mags! Focus. This is a real question. Who owns your grandmother's house now?"

The look on her friend's face was one of surprise, as if the answer should be obvious. "Why, Jess, it's mine. *I* own it, of course. Except the trust controls it, and I'm required to share my time there with the family. The deed, though? It's says Magenta Carlaina Brier-Sheldon." She laughed. "Grandmother loved me very much. She gave the entire farm to me."

"Farm? Estate is more like it. There are three houses there, if I remember." She lifted an eyebrow and turned to her friend. "How have I never heard your full first name?"

"I like Mags so much better, so that's the only name I use. That was another of Grandmother's gifts to me. She always called me Mags, and for that reason, so did every-one else in the family, except my aunt. Auntie always said my real name was too beautiful to butcher." Mags lifted a hand to catch the breeze in her fist, and she laughed. "And no, Jess. There's only one house. Murphy's is a chicken coop, was a chicken coop, anyway, even if it does have three bedrooms now, and the others are boathouses and sleeping cabins. Be sensible. We don't even have the studio any longer. It burned to the ground before I was born."

Jessica closed her eyes and let the sun play across her face. The day felt good, and Mags could explain everything thoroughly once they got there. She replied, "Okay, Mags 'I-Never-Knew-Your-Name-Was-Magenta' Brier-Sheldon. I'll be sensible. It's a farm."

The voice next to her returned its own barbed witticism. "Thank you, Jessica 'I-Never-Knew-You-Were-Rich' Johansen."

Jessica just let it go. She loved Mags, but she was from a different world than everyone else. It was a rarified world. Mags just didn't know it. She thought she was ordinary, and she was anything but. That was the very reason why Jessica was so glad to have her for a friend.

"HOW ABOUT tomorrow?"

Peter looked up from his bed to see Doctor Rossi speaking to him as she came through the door.

"Hey, Doc!" He set his computer to the side, and he dropped his feet to the floor to sit up. "Let me give you a hug."

"How do you feel, Peter?" Doctor Rossi walked across the room to put her arms around him.

He smiled. "Great! I've gotten lots of rest, and best of all, my book's just about wrapped up. I've even got the cover art."

"Cover art?" Doctor Rossi hadn't thought about him needing that. She'd assumed the publishing house would take care of the cover design just before they put out the book. "So, you've been speaking with your publisher?"

"Yesterday. They were here, even. Look." He pulled out a leather portfolio they had given him, and inside was a drawing of a dog. "That's the pet you told me to get. Transplant. Tee, I call him. A kid back in Worcester drew this. The publisher even plans to pay him, or his mother, I guess. They have to work that out. I just told them he gets a share of the money."

The doctor reached and hugged him again. That was something her grandson would have done, and she was glad to see Peter being so generous. When she backed away, she asked, "They left it with you, though? They'll rework the drawing, surely."

Peter grinned. "No. I argued that, and they had to give in. They really want my book, see. I said the cover needed to be a tawny gold, and the picture should be a photograph of the drawing. I want it to look like someone gave me the kid's drawing, I unfolded it, and there it is, fold lines and all. When I explained it that way, they seemed to understand. They even took a copy of the book with them."

"You printed it?" Doctor Rossi was very competent with computers, but this seemed too quick and easy to her, especially here in the hospital. She was quite aware the hospital had its share of commercial printers, but patients usually didn't have access to them.

He laughed. "Not a paper copy. Flash drive. They had one, and I just popped it in. I've got a contract signed, an advance on the way, and they said they'd have so many people on this, it'd be out in a month. Pre-release copies, anyway. I've done it, Doc. My story's out there."

"You pushed yourself, didn't you? I waited too long to give you my secret news, I guess." She smiled at her confession. She had wrestled with whether to reveal her information, and now it was too late.

"Secret news? What's that, Doc?"

"Remember at your birthday party, you asked me a question. Do you recall that?"

Peter thought for a moment. "A year and a half ago? The party with the cake and candles?"

"Yes, Peter. Your six-month party. A nurse let some-thing slip, and you asked me about it later."

He looked puzzled for a minute, and then he smiled. "You didn't want to tell me directly, either. I remember. Twenty-nine. That sportscaster was twenty-nine when he died."

Doctor Rossi paused and pursed her lips. "I came to tell you something confidential, today. His name." She wasn't supposed to, but somehow it seemed appropriate. Anyway, it wasn't like it was a real secret. Anyone with any sense could have figured it out.

Peter laughed, interrupting. "Thanks, Doc. I appreciate that. However, I met the officer who was at the accident. He told me already, although I appreciate your willingness to share that information with me. I already knew he was in the media from the news reports I'd collected. Then the officer told me he was one I'd seen on TV before." He chuckled, embarrassed for not having put it together years ago. "I'd suspected at first then refused to believe it."

"You know who he was, then." Doctor Rossi sighed and gently placed her hand on Peter's chest.

Peter smiled and punched out the line as it had once sounded on the news station, his voice deep and filled with drama. "Jeffrey Jay, coming to you play by play." After a pause, he went on, "It was a catchy byline, too. I missed him when he was gone, but I never made the real connection until that officer pointed it out to me." He smiled, and as he took her hand, he changed direction with his words. "I'll miss you, but not this hospital room. Two weeks are enough. Tomorrow, I'm ready to be free."

"Then, we'll make sure you are. Noon. I'll tell the staff to aim for noon. How does that sound?"

He smiled. "You take good care of me. Do you know that, Doc? You take really good care of me."

She waved as she walked out the door. His last statement made her feel guilty. She knew it wouldn't have mattered who was behind that knife. It had been the new insert that had been put in his implant that had been the culprit. However, she couldn't shake the feeling she had shirked her responsibility to this boy by giving that surgery away.

It wasn't until she was halfway down the hall that she remembered Jeffrey Jay's real name wasn't Jeffrey Jay at all. It was Jeffrey Johansen, and his widow taught at the university. Her first name escaped her for the moment, but Johansen had been the last. Oh, well. If he knew as much as he claimed, he knew that, too. That police officer would have shared that with him, she was certain.

She paused and stood for a moment, debating on going back to make certain, then she moved on. She had other patients in the hospital, and she needed to tend to them as well.

She looked up at a clock on the wall, and she remembered she also had a meeting scheduled. She hurried along, and Jeffrey Jay was pushed behind all the other expedient things that had to be taken care of that day.

TRENT'S MOTHER sat on her sofa. A man in a business suit perched across from her. She signed her name on the piece of paper in front of her, and he handed her a check. She looked at it, and tears came to her eyes.

She reached her arm over and hugged her son. "You have money, Trent. You can have new crayons, now."

"Is it from Jesus?" Where else could real money come from, at least the kind that was enough to pay the rent, the electric, and buy new crayons, too?

"This is for your picture, Trent." She smiled. "It's money, a check."

"For my dog picture? Is it a lot?" He had known the picture looked real. He had used his special colors, and with his mother gone, no one had disturbed him as he worked. He'd worked all day on it, too.

"A lot, Trent. More than Mummy makes in months and months." She looked up at the man in the suit to see him smiling.

"Will you stay home with me, now?" Trent's eyes jumped to the man and back to his mother.

She looked at it wistfully and smiled. "I don't know, Trent. This isn't Mummy's money. It's yours. It should go in the bank, but I'm sure the bank won't mind if we keep enough for crayons."

Trent reached and wrapped both arms around her neck.

He hugged her tightly, and his voice was intimate. "I'll share, Mummy. As much as you need. I'll share it all with you."

The publishing company representative across from them smiled. The papers in his briefcase included a download from Peter Cassel's computer, and with the literary and movie rights, the book was going to be a big money-maker. With the contract this woman had just signed, the one Cassel had insisted on for her, she would soon be very rich, indeed, and she didn't even know it.

It wouldn't have mattered to her if she had known. Rich was relative, after all. For some people, it meant the electric bill would be paid, and there would be money left for new shoes. Or for new crayons. Umber, vermilion, and chartreuse. If that was how rich was determined, then she was already the richest woman in the world, and the money hadn't even started to flow.

MAGS SAT on a granite pedestal and leaned back against an enormous stone eagle, a landmark of Vinalhaven's bygone quarrying days. They had gotten to town early. She told her friend she always watched the parade from the pedestal. It provided the best view around.

The streets were crowded, too. Everyone on the island, it seemed, had come out. Jessica looked around at all the people laughing and bumping into each other. Merry-makers were crossing the street, jockeying for the best positions for viewing their favorite exhibitions.

There was a feeling of warmth among the islanders; Jessica could feel that. She knew part of it was having Mags here, hearing her greeting people she had known all her life, the little things she could talk about, explaining them casually, things that only an island intimate would know.

What tugged most at the barbs in Jessica's heart were the small, intimate vignettes of love-infused life that were happening all around them. She saw a wizened man reach to the hand of an equally lined woman next to him. The woman smiled and pressed her fingers into his. Two teenagers ran by, and the boy grabbed the girl's arm. They laughed together in a way that made them more than just casual friends. A family huddled together, and then they rang with laughter at a private joke.

Jessica knew what she wanted, and she kept putting it aside, as if doing so would make it go away. For a long time, it would have been Jeffrey she desired as she sat there in her loneliness. However, it had been over two years, and she could no longer remember just exactly what his touch felt like.

She knew that what was bothering her was more than just the two years he'd been gone. She'd encountered no difficulty remembering his touch just a month ago. Something had come between them, and now that it was there, it couldn't be easily shaken away.

It was another man that was eating at her. She'd only touched him, really touched him, that one crazy time when Mags had shoved them together. Her hand had pressed against him, and that moment had been forever frozen in her mind. They had never spoken of it. His story was what had drawn them together. Laughter and each other's company had kept them together, or so Jessica had thought.

He had disappeared, though. She returned from her weekend with Mags, and when she stepped into her classroom, he was gone. She didn't know where, and she hadn't been able to find him.

Jessica glanced up as she heard music playing. Down the street just where it curved out of sight, a horn was sounding repetitive notes. It sounded like a tuba or a baritone horn. She smiled as she saw an older gentleman with a long beard step into view. Mags cheered and leaned over to tell her it was old Kellerman from Green's Island. He played every year. Then a series of children came by flinging wild rose petals into the crowd that lined the street.

Jessica smiled at the sight. Yet, her expression felt empty even to her. The thoughts that were crowding her mind were those of the first two weeks of the summer session. They had been spent in the daily hope that he would continue to show up in class the next day. He had for those two weeks, too, and she'd come to trust that. Then, she also remembered two additional weeks of despair while she was putting on her brightest smile to make it through her classes. His seat had been empty the final two.

She didn't know why he had run away, what she had done to cause that. She didn't even know if she'd done anything at all. Perhaps he had run because she'd done nothing. He was a student, though, and years of ingrained propriety could not be easily thrown away. Once the course was completed, and he was no longer a student, things might have been very different. However, that was now a moot point, as he had disappeared, and not even Mags had been able to locate where he had gone.

She sat in a daze, and she watched as a car decorated like a rabbit drove by. A man walking inside a ten-foot tall book was next. Children dressed as characters from the book were running in and out of the pages. Even a flatbed trailer drove by filled with flowers. The ladies from the local garden club sat atop metal buckets, wearing their most outlandish gardening gear.

The parade was humorous, and it was fun for those watching. It dealt with environmental issues and the local lobstering industry. It displayed art that decorated automobiles, and people who just wanted to once again play band instruments they had learned in their high school days. People in the crowd laughed and enjoyed the displays as they passed. When it was over, Jessica was exhausted and ready to go. Mags was just getting started, though. "Come on, Jess. The duck race is here. Then I want a lobster roll at the Harbor Gawker. They have the best ever! Afterward, we have to prowl the main street bookstore, if it's still open." She pointed to a sign just down the street. The simple frame building abutted Main Street on the front, and overhung Carver's Pond on the side. It was covered with weathered shingles, and the trim work was painted red. Wooden piers slathered with barnacles held it aloft. "They always carry the most fascinating merchandise. We'll buy you a souvenir, maybe a piece of stained glass to hang out by the pool." Mags laughed, and she was off. These were the remembered things from her childhood, and to not do them was unthinkable.

Jessica gave in, and she followed along, but her heart wasn't in it. Her heart wanted more. Her heart wanted love. That would be found in a man, not in a parade or a plastic duck race decided by the rushing tide. Jessica wanted Peter, and she was all alone. That's why she gave in to Mags' demands. She was all alone, and she always would be. Jeffrey had died, Peter had run away, and she thought she was about to cry. Without Mags, she would, and that was why she stayed next to her friend the rest of the afternoon.

Chapter 15

PETER WAS early, and he stepped eagerly into the class-room. One or two students were seated, their laptops opened. Another one on a back row was on his cell phone. He looked up as Peter entered, and catching his eye, he jerked his head up in greeting. Then he looked away to his desk, engrossed in the person on the other end of the line.

It had been two weeks, more now with the weekend, and Peter wished he had made a bigger effort to contact Jessica. *Dr. Johansen*, he reminded himself. He would have to call her that in class. He had left a message the day he'd gone in the hospital, thinking it would be overnight or a few days he'd be away. The complications during surgery had thrown him off, though, the thought he might actually die with his book unfinished, and the world had slipped right by him. Two weeks of it.

Now, he was back, and he hoped to talk to her before everyone else arrived, to make sure she understood. He also wanted to let her know he'd finished the book. Two weeks and sixteen hours a day can do that for a project. She'd laugh and congratulate him. He was certain of that. She'd want to know if he was planning to continue in the class, and he'd laugh and assure her he was. Why would he do that, she'd inquire. He'd make up something about follow-through or getting his money's worth. What he would really mean would be to spend the time with her.

Peter saw an unfamiliar woman walk in the room and up on the dais. It puzzled him for a moment, and then he realized that classes sometimes had guest speakers. He set his computer on his old desk and moved up to question her.

"Pardon me, but I'm a student in Dr. Johansen's class. I need to speak with her before the lesson. Can you help me?" He smiled.

"This is my first day. I'm Donna Lambasky. No need to call me professor or doctor. Just Donna." She reached to shake his hand, easily navigating with a neutral rudder the sometimes treacherous waters of a new instructor taking over the classes of a well-liked professor.

"Peter Cassel. I've had to be out a few days. I'd like to talk to Dr. Johansen, if you don't mind."

She smiled. "I understand. You must have gotten the message, though. Have you checked your student email?"

Peter was puzzled. "Student email? Um, I guess I don't have that."

Donna glanced at his desk and saw his computer, and she looked back at him. She didn't seem to know just how to take that in. Every student was given an email account and could freely access the school's wireless Internet. However, neutral rudder and all.

"I don't guess you got the update, then. I'm so sorry for the inconvenience. Dr. Johansen was called out of town for an emergency. She'll be gone the rest of the summer. I'll be finishing out her classes." She pulled her computer out and turned it on. "I'll be glad to arrange a time with you to get caught up."

Peter's was devastated, though, and he had nothing more to say. His book was already finished, and there was no reason for him to be in this class except to be with Jessica. Now, she was gone. He questioned the new teacher hopefully.

"Can you tell me where she's at?"

She looked at him with surprise. She offered a pat answer that the university faculty were told to give out whenever the need arose.

"I'm sorry. That's privileged information." She paused, then continued, "The time you wish to schedule our session?"

Peter turned and picked up his bag. He didn't even answer her. He walked to the door and out of the classroom that had suddenly become dull and lifeless for him. He had no need of Donna Lambasky's services. He knew, now. He needed Jessica. When he'd thought he could find her and it would be convenient, it had been easy to let other things get in the way. Now, he wanted to run back, grab Donna Lambasky by the collar, and shake the answer out of her. He wouldn't, though. He would . . . he didn't know what he would do, but he would do something.

When he got to his car, he stood and looked at the *For Sale* sign he'd placed in the window after getting out of the hospital. In a sudden burst of emotion, he kicked one of the tires. He hated his old car, and he hated his life. He hated this heart that had taken him away from Jessica, and he wished Jeffrey Jay had lived, and he had died. That was what should have happened. Peter leaned and placed his forehead against the roof of his car, and he stood there, wishing the world would go away.

Finally, when he lifted his head, and the air and the trees and the grass were all still there, he took a deep breath and sighed. He looked up at the sky and didn't care who heard.

"The point, God? There is a *point*, right? Is it because I don't wear my collar? Is that it? You took her away because I don't wear my collar?"

He stuck his key in the door and tossed his things into the seat, climbing in to sit behind the wheel. He knew it had nothing to do with the collar he never wore. It had to do with him, with Peter Cassel. It had to do with him being damaged goods, with him having someone else's heart in his body. It had to do with him not being good enough. That's all it was. It was him, and he wasn't good enough for anyone, especially not Dr. Jessica Johansen.

He slipped his key in the ignition, and when he turned it, the engine fired right up. He gave a snort of disgust. "You work better than I do, and no one wants you, either." He hit the steering wheel with his hand, then he put it into gear and drove off.

"SCORTIO'S. This is Paul speaking. Our special of the

day is lobster tail with red sauce. How may I schedule your reservation?"

"Paul! Thank goodness. This is Ms. Brier-Sheldon. I'm at my place in Maine, and I won't be in for several weeks. However, I have a special request of you."

"Good morning, Ms. Brier-Sheldon. I hope you enjoy your time away from the city. How have your morning orange juices been?" The humor was obvious in his voice. "Zingy, I trust. How may I help you?"

"Paul, Paul. Thank you. You know my friend, Dr. Johansen?"

"Certainly, Ms. Brier-Sheldon. She was my lit teacher last session. Is she still in town? I'll be glad to look out for her when she comes into the restaurant."

"No, Paul. She's here with me. I need you to keep an eye out for someone else, for you to call me when you see him."

"Certainly, Ms. Brier-Sheldon." He chuckled. He'd been asked to do stranger things. "If you could describe this person for me, I'll make a note of it and get back to you if he comes in."

Mags let out a sigh that carried over the phone. "Paul, you are so sweet. When I get back, you must still be there. You cannot quit or get fired. I'll double my tips to you forever."

He chuckled again. "That's very generous of you, Ms. Brier-Sheldon. The standard gratuity is perfectly fine. This person you spoke of?"

"Do you remember that man Dr. Johansen was in with several weeks ago? The man with the green eyes?"

For the third time, Paul found cause to chuckle. "Ms.

Brier-Sheldon, I rarely study men's eyes, but I do believe you're speaking of Mr. Shamelessly Charming. I do remember him quite well. He tips nicely, too. That I never forget."

"Good, Paul. If you see him, call me. At this number. Do I need to write it down for you?"

He quelled his fourth chuckle, as he didn't want to offend his best tipper ever. He did suggest that if she wrote it down, it would do him no good in any case. She was in Maine, after all. However, he had it on the restaurant's phone display. He would also program it into his personal cell phone. He would call her as soon as the dashing Mr. Shamelessly Charming showed his tawny hair.

"Paul, you keep track of hair color but not eyes? Now you tell me why that is."

"Of course, Ms. Brier-Sheldon. Even when I can't see faces, I can always see the hair. That's how I keep track of my orders."

"Then, Paul," she pressed him, "you tell me without thinking about it. What color is mine?"

He immediately snapped out, "A beautiful cinnamon gold. I've always been especially fond of that color, if I may say so, Ms. Brier-Sheldon."

Finally, it was Mags' turn to laugh.

"IS THE CONTRACT for the cover art signed?" Peter had refused to budge past that. He'd seen the look of desperation in that mother's eyes, and he wouldn't move past this part of the deal. If they wouldn't come through, they would get no signature from him.

Peter held the phone with one hand as he reached to

243

rub Transplant's ears. He smiled. The dog had been glued to his leg ever since his return. "Good boy, Tee," he whispered. The big animal turned his head to look up at Peter. He opened his mouth and began to pant with anticipation. Then, when no more attention was aimed his way, he dropped his head back to the floor.

"At the terms we agreed?" He no longer had any patience with these people since Jessica had disappeared. His demands had taken on a sharper, more forceful tone, and they could come through without negotiation. It all seemed rather pointless without her.

"Fine. Then I'm ready." His tone softened. He'd pushed them enough, and they had done as he asked. "What's the schedule? This does seem awfully quick, you understand. I would prefer several days to both sort out things here as well as get ready to be on the road."

The voice on the other end of the line assured him it was possible to give him that. "Remember, Mr. Cassel. You gave us the manuscript a week ago. However, we've been working with you on this for over eighteen months, two years if we go back to the actual wreck and heart transplant. An upcoming sportscaster died, and the circumstances under which you received his heart are gripping."

The voice also chided him, "This story should have been out within two months of the accident. Understand, we would have spoken to you about your story even earlier than six months into this but were not allowed to contact you until you were considered stable. Six months, and then you had concerns of your own at that point. You put *us* off. You were able to do that only because there were certain legal and contractual issues, you understand."

No, he didn't understand, but he was glad things were moving along now that his book was completed. There was a promotional tour scheduled before the book actually went on the shelves, and that would happen immediately. The publishing house would have just enough of the manuscript rewritten and proofed to give out teasers for the finished product. Then, when the studio put the movie into production, it could legally state that the book was already out, even though they would be released together.

"Three days, Mr. Cassel. I'll be able to give you that much time, then I am afraid we'll need you for at least a month."

Peter sighed. "I'll do my best."

The voice on the line chuckled. "Better than your best, I hope. You're officially under contract. Your cooperation with us has now become a legal and contractual issue, you see."

JESSICA HUDDLED on the porch of Crockett House, Mags' ancestral home, named after Crockett Point, the mile-long spit of land thrusting into Penobscot Bay off Mid-Coast Maine. She was wrapped in a quilt, and she idly rubbed the stitching. Someone's grandmother had made this, she could tell.

She had asked Mags, who said it hadn't been her grandmother. Her grandmother hadn't sewed a stitch in her life. Perhaps it was from a cousin who had been to the house.

There was a tag on the back. *Made with Love by A.P.E.* She smiled and dropped the corner back down. Someone's grandmother had those initials. Addie or Ada. The last name was probably something elegant. Perhaps Edwards or Ellison. She could imagine a petite, white-haired woman in her living room with the quilt stretched on a frame, sewing one tiny stitch at a time, all by hand. She smiled at that. She would like to have such a grandmother.

The fog had moved in. Tall spruce trees covered Crockett Point, and on three sides of the grand old farmhouse, courses down to the water had been cleared to provide views to the ocean. The sightline from the porch revealed vistas to Crockett Cove and the dock.

Mags kept a boat in the cove tied to a mooring, although it was missing, now. It was always ready, Mags told her, waiting for someone to use it. It even had *Crockett Cove* scrawled across the stern in loopy letters. The property's caretaker, John, put it out every June and took it in every September. It wintered in a boathouse back in town. It was too big for the property's private boathouse down by the dock.

Across the mouth of the cove was her aunt's place. Jessica couldn't see any of that now, just some of the trees poking through the fog as it swirled across the landscape. The day after the parade, they'd walked down the other two concourses. The tides had been low, and there had been gravel beaches at each one. Mags had reminded her of much Jessica had forgotten from her one summer here. There was Mussel Beach, known for the mussels that sometimes washed up there. The other was Flat Rocks, where the receding tide left shallow pools of water that warmed in the midday sun. Mags had played there as a girl, and she and Jessica waded the warm water for a while. Then, the tide had come rushing in, and it was soon covered by twelve feet of cold Atlantic current.

That day had been sunny and bright. This day fit Jessica's mood better. This one was closed in, and the world was far away. She could reach in front of her, and if she brushed her hand through the air, she could see the fog swirl in the movement of her fingers.

She heard the sputtering of a boat motor, and then it died. She'd already seen in her short time here how the fog distorted sound. The boat she was hearing could be at the dock, or it could be at a dock three islands over, although it was probably Mags. She'd taken her boat to her aunt's place across the cove. She could motor over in a few minutes, but it was three miles to drive there. It was a mile up the peninsula the Point was on, and then across and back down the other side of the cove. It was easier to motor. Row, Jessica had murmured, remembering the small skiff from their college days. Motor, Mags had corrected, knowing her boat was waiting at the mooring just out from the dock.

It would take a while to know if it was truly Mags. The boat had to be tied to the mooring. Then Mags had to untie and row the skiff to the float. Once it was secured, the walk to the house was mostly uphill. If it were Mags that Jessica had heard, she would see her emerge from the fog, a ghostly creature that would slowly gain substance as she moved closer to the porch.

On the day they'd arrived, Jessica had asked her how much land she owned. Mags had laughed. The whole Point, she'd said. All of Crockett Point was hers. When pressed, she'd guessed thirty to forty acres. It was enough to ensure a long walk underneath the towering spruce trees to get anywhere on the Point, and yet there were still acres of grassy area around the house. That way, if a tree came down in a hurricane, the house wasn't damaged, Mags assured her with firmness. It happened sometimes, she declared, trees coming down. The island was solid granite, and the trees' roots were shallow. There were a few that had come down over the years, just blown over in storms. Her man, John, kept them cleared, so it was hard to keep track of them all. However, she knew where one was on its side, and she could take Jessica there if she wanted. The roots went twenty feet in the air.

Jessica waved as she saw Mags emerge out of the mist. She called to her, "How could you see to get back?"

Mags laughed. "GPS. Never leave home without it."

"So, what was so important that you risked life and limb taking the boat in this fog?"

Mags walked up on the porch, and she reached to tap her friend on the nose. "I had a phone call to make, and my aunt has a land line. Have you noticed your cell never rings up here? No service. Anyway, I needed to talk to Paul."

Jessica shook her head and smiled, amused despite her melancholy mood. "Paul? From Scortio's? I thought you were attracted to Mr. Pearson."

Mags plopped on the porch swing beside her friend. She tugged on the edge of the quilt to cover herself. "Mr. Pearson doesn't know the recipe for orange juice. By the way, I asked my aunt about the quilt. Her daughter's husband. See. It was my cousin, sort of."

Jessica shot her an incredulous look. "Your cousin's husband sews quilts and signs them *Made with Love*?"

"No, silly." Mags stood and tossed her end of the quilt

down on the swing. "His grandmother does. She's from Texas. Fort Worth, if you can believe that. See? Poor people can come up here, also." She paused, no rancor or condescension intended, and looked out at the fog-shrouded landscape. "It's cold out here. I'm going where it's warm. Come inside later, and we'll build a fire." She walked away, and after a moment, a door opened and closed.

After she went inside, Jessica pulled the rest of the quilt around her, and it felt just a bit like she was being held by a grandmother's love. Not the rich kind that gives houses and trust funds, but the ordinary kind that gives quilts and hugs. She responded to Mags' pronouncement, too, even though she knew she couldn't hear her.

"Yeah, I'm one of them, Mags. If you count love, they don't come any poorer than me."

"TWO DAYS until I leave, boy. Do you think Lennie will want to keep you for a while?" They were at the park, and Peter reached down to unsnap the dog's leash. "Ready, Tee? Gotta go get it!" Then he stood and slung the disk as hard as he could.

He was relieved that he could still do this, and except where the small incision had been made to go into his chest, there was no discomfort at all. Doctor Rossi had told him his pain had been from the depleted medicines in his implant. Now he believed her.

Just then a boy's voice rang out. Like lightning, a small shape ran into the field after Peter's dog. About that time, another voice, a woman's, came over his shoulder.

"Thank you."

Peter turned to see Trent's mother at his side.

"He's been looking for the two of you every day. I told him you were the man who got sick, and that's why you hadn't been back to the park. Are you well, now?"

Peter chuckled. "As well as possible. All that means is that I'm not dead. I'll never be well, though. However, thank you for asking. Most people don't know about my heart. I don't tell them."

"I understand," she said. "I'll be quiet about it. Thank you, again."

"For?" Peter's eyes were on the boy. He was rolling about in the grass with his dog. Tee was having a marvelous time.

She looked at him, and when Peter glanced back at her, he noticed that she didn't seem so worn as she had in the hospital in Boston.

She pressed him, "You don't know?"

With her question, he remembered, and he chuckled. The contract. He had so much on his own plate, it was hard to keep up with all the things that didn't directly affect him. "The drawing. I understand. I wanted you to get more. If the book sells well, you will."

"I'd like to read it when you're ready. May I?"

She looked out to where the dog and her boy were playing, as if not wanting to take her eyes from them. Peter could see that she was very protective, and he appreciated that about her. If he ever had a son, he'd feel the same way. He already did with his dog.

"The publishers will have me a proof copy within the next few days. Even today, perhaps, if things have gone smoothly, or maybe tomorrow. I don't think the cover art will be ready, though. I can try to get an extra copy, if you wish."

She laughed. "When it's finished, then. I can wait. However, Trent cannot. His father is to pick him up early in the morning." She watched him for a moment. "I should call him in. Will you be back? Trent likes to play with your dog. Transplant, I believe you called him."

"Tee, if you don't mind." Peter chuckled. "I'm out of town in two days. There's a book promotion and the spectacle that goes along with it. I'll be back, though."

Trent's mother nodded and called for her son. Then, with a frown on her face, she pointed another direction. "Do you know that man?"

"Who?" Peter frowned, puzzled. He'd not been paying attention to anyone except Trent and Tee.

"He's been looking this way, at you, it seems. Now he's headed over here. Do you want me to wait, just in case? If you're not well and alone . . ."

He smiled and thanked her. He didn't sense any trouble. No one knew him well enough to want to bother him. He didn't say that. Instead, he threw out a more generic assurance.

"Students often cut through here to get to classes. He looks friendly enough." Besides, now that he could see his face, Peter didn't think this man was a stranger. He explained, "He looks familiar to me. He's probably an old acquaintance who's heard about my book. Don't know how, though, unless it's been leaked by the publisher." He laughed at that. He'd be disappointed if it had.

Trent's mother called for her son a second time, and Peter turned and waved to the boy as he ran up. He knelt

251

as he reached to shake.

"How's Trent?" He smiled at him as Transplant ran up to nuzzle Peter's chest. Trent shook hands and smiled shyly in the embarrassed way of an eight-year-old who is suddenly put on the spot.

"Say something, Trent," his mother encouraged. When the boy refused to speak, she looked at Peter and apologized. "He can be painfully shy."'

Peter reached and brushed his hand across the small head, remembering the boy's words from weeks ago. Then he stood and laughed. "I was that way as a boy. I understand." He looked at Trent, suddenly serious. "Until next time, Trent," he quipped, and was glad to see the boy break into a smile.

Trent's mother touched Peter's arm. "Thank you once more. I honestly cannot thank you enough for what you did." With a quick motion, she grabbed Trent's hand, and then she led him off.

Transplant plopped down at his master's side, panting. Peter turned to greet his visitor, and he remembered where he'd seen him. It had been over a month ago, but the situation had been memorable, that embarrassing first lunch with Jessica.

"From the restaurant, I believe." Peter grinned as he reached to shake.

PAUL SMILED, returning the handclasp. "Scortio's, yes. Beautiful dog. You're Mr. Shamelessly Charming, if I remember." He chuckled and looked at Transplant. "Your dog is also charming, I see. That boy seemed to enjoy him very much. The animal's name?"

"Tee." Peter knelt and rubbed the dog's fur. The big baby immediately rolled on his back, wanting all the attention his master could dish out.

"You're a golfer, then?"

"If a hole-in-one counts," Peter replied, reaching and touching his chest.

Paul laughed softly. "Did I overhear you're going out of town? Are you playing in a tournament?" This wasn't something he would normally inquire of such a casual acquaintance, but this was for Ms. Brier-Sheldon, someone who seemed to know this man without question.

"In a manner of speaking. I've got a book to promote."

"Ah! A writer. Taking your dog with you on the road?"

"No. I'm hoping my neighbor might keep him. I haven't asked, though. Why? You know a place I can board him?" He glanced at Paul hopefully. "He was with my neighbor for two weeks, recently, and she'd probably be grateful if someone else could board him this time. It would save her rugs. It'd be for a month. I'll be glad to pay."

Paul didn't know any kennel services. He might do it himself for the money, he told Peter, but it would be tough to manage with school and his job. He'd be glad to check around to see who else might be able to help. Could he have a number to call him back? He had an evening class, and he was on his way now. Paul pulled out his cell phone and typed in the information. Then, with a friendly wave, he was gone.

PETER BENT to rub Transplant's stomach. He looked at the young man running to his class, before he turned back to his dog. "Well, that was odd, Tee. That was odd, indeed. We might get you a good place to stay, after all. You've probably already worn out your welcome at Lennie's, and a kennel just doesn't appeal to me. Let's give this Paul a day and see what he comes up with."

They tossed the Frisbee a few more times, but they were both tired. The sun was getting low in the sky, and it was a bit of a walk home. They called it quits for the evening and let the park take care of itself for the rest of the night.

Chapter 16

JESSICA AWAKENED to the clanging of a bell. She swung her legs out of the bed, and she stepped down the hall, knocking on Mags' door. "Mags," she called with some humor, "I think there's an earthquake."

She heard a groggy voice moan from the other side, "Earthquake? Here?"

Jessica called back, "The bell. The one on the bell rock. It's ringing. Either it's an earthquake, or we have company."

There was a pause, and then the door suddenly swung open. Out flew Mags in her flannel gown. She raced down the stairs and through the front door. Jessica's eyes crinkled in amusement. She hadn't known her friend even owned any flannel.

Following her outside, she found her at the edge of the clearing with a pair of binoculars peering across the cove. Then she went to the granite outcrop beside the house and swung the old bell until it rang out into the chill morning air. As soon as it did, Jessica knew it wasn't this one that had given her that wake-up call.

"Mags, what's going on?" she called as her friend flew back into the house. She rubbed her arms. It was still cold outside, unlike the heat they'd left behind in Massachusetts.

"Phone call," Mags yelled back. "I've got to go over, and now!"

Jessica followed her upstairs where she was already pulling on pants and a heavy shirt. "How do you know?" she questioned.

"Auntie rings the bell. I use the binoculars to see. If she's on the porch and waves twice, I need to come to the phone."

"Wouldn't it be easier to get phone service here?"

"I have it, a party line. Well, I would, except for falling trees. My aunt's the other party on the line. The tree that fell is back up the road off my grandmother's property. I have to wait for the county to repair it."

Jessica went to pick up the phone by the bed to check that it was plugged in. The display lighted when she picked it up. She put it to her ear.

"See," Mags said. "No dial tone. I still get a bill, though."

"How long's it been like this?"

Mags pulled on her shoes, then she grinned. "Three years."

"Three years?" Jessica's jaw dropped. "You've been paying the bill for three years, and it doesn't work?"

Mags stood to leave, and she paused as she stepped to Jessica and touched her gently on the nose. She smiled. "The trust fund's paid the bill for three years. It won't get fixed ever, if the trust fund doesn't keep the bill up."

"Mags, the trust fund is your money."

She laughed as she ran down the stairs. "Not until I'm thirty-five. That's all the difference in the world."

After a moment, she heard the boat start up, and it roared away. She figured Mags must have run the entire way. At least it was clear out today, even if it was still cold and entirely too early in the day to be out of bed.

Jessica walked down the hall and threw back the covers on her bed. She crawled in and lay there in the quiet of the early morning, with only an occasional buoy bell ringing across the ocean to disturb the quiet. All this solitude wasn't quite what she needed to heal her damaged heart, but it was better than being home. If she were there, she would have Peter on her mind all the time, and that would be very depressing. Here, he was only on her mind most of the time. That was better, even if she didn't really know how much. At least here, she didn't have to put on any false happiness. She could grovel in her misery, even if she couldn't spend any of Jeffrey's money to do it. She had left her checkbook at home.

"SCORTIO'S. This is Paul. We open at six. May I make a reservation for you at this time?"

"Paul!" The excitement in Mag's voice was palpable. She had been waiting for this call. "You found him?"

257

"Ah, good morning, Ms. Brier-Sheldon. I don't suppose you would be interested in a breakfast reservation." He chuckled. "We have excellent orange juice."

"Paul," she hissed. "Have you found him? This is important. Mr. Cassel."

Paul wasn't through, yet. "I didn't find a Mr. Cassel." He paused for dramatic effect. "I found a Mr. Tee."

"Mr. T? From the TV show? Paul! I had to motor across the cove to get to a phone. Tell me you have good news." Mags glared at her aunt when she stepped into the room, causing her to retreat very quickly. She loved her aunt, but this was private business.

Paul laughed. "Mr. Tee's the dog that goes with Mr. Shamelessly Charming. It seems Mr. Charming is going on a book tour in two days. Mr. Tee needs a home for a month. Everyone looked well and healthy."

Mags stood and walked to the kitchen door, covering the phone's mouthpiece with her hand. She wanted to make sure was no one listening. A slip of the tongue by her aunt wouldn't do, and she and Jessica were to be over for lunch later in the day.

"Auntie, I'll be off in a minute," she called, as she stepped back into the kitchen. "Paul, where did you find him?"

"He was in the park with his dog. He was talking with a young woman, and a small boy was entertaining the pet."

Mags gasped. "He's married? Is the boy his? Could you tell?"

Paul cautioned, "I don't know, Ms. Brier-Sheldon. The boy didn't look like him, and the woman and the boy walked off together as I came up. He did tell me he needs a sitter for his dog. A whole month, too, and he hasn't yet asked his neighbor."

"Paul! We'll take the dog. Can you find him again?" This was a perfect opportunity to get Jessica and her man back in contact with each other. Now, if Paul could just work his magic.

"Ms. Brier-Sheldon, I did take his number. I told him I'd ask around. I could use the money, I told him, but it would be difficult for me to manage. I *do* work and attend school, both at the same time."

Mags' brain was already clicking, and she was now one step ahead of her beloved waiter. "Paul, you get that dog. I'll pay you to keep him, but he'll stay here. I've got at least thirty acres on my property. This is perfect."

"There's one problem, Ms. Brier-Sheldon. How do we get the animal there? The dog is quite large."

"I'm thinking, Paul. Give me a minute. I know! Mr. Pearson. You know him, Paul."

"Yes. He comes in with you from time to time."

Mags trembled with excitement. "I'll call him and set it up. He'll contact you. Thank you so very much, Paul."

"You're very welcome, Ms. Brier-Sheldon."

PAUL FOUND the arrangements for dog sitting tempting. To earn the cash and not have to actually keep the dog? That could cushion a whole semester of expenses on campus. However, it could still fall apart. Since Ms. Brier-Sheldon's place was in Maine, anywhere in Maine, the animal had a long way to travel. If he would work this out, it would be the easiest money he ever made. He needed it, too. Fall tuition was just around the corner.

"MICHAEL, FOR me. You absolutely have to do this," Mags pleaded. "You can borrow my car. It's sitting outside my apartment. I can call the dealership, and they can make you a new key."

Mr. Pearson hesitated. He'd have to miss a class, and that meant a substitute. However, he'd heard about Mags' summer home. In the past, he'd spent time on the island, tutoring children in the summers. Often, he'd stayed in the town of Vinalhaven, where rent was cheaper, then he'd motored to North Haven for his tutoring jobs where the families were wealthier.

He came to a decision and said, "I can drive my own car. Am I ferrying the dog all the way to your place, or will you pick up the animal in town?"

"Well, I can't meet you in town, unless I come in my boat. My car's in Worcester, remember. I'd appreciate it if you *could* drive out. Michael, will you please do this? It's about twenty minutes from town. I'll buy your lunch for a year."

He chuckled. "Can I stay the night? I'll have to cancel two days of classes."

"No, you won't. You can come up on Thursday, and that'll give you the whole weekend. By the way, you get to sleep in the chicken coop."

He moaned. "A chicken coop? Mags! I want a real bed to stay in."

She laughed. That meant he planned to make the trip. "Here's what you need to do . . ."

THE DOORBELL rang, interrupting Peter's attempt to

finish packing. He was holding the proof copy of his book in one hand. It had just arrived minutes earlier, and he'd been attempting to glance through it while continuing to pack. He hadn't been very successful at either. He closed it and glanced at the cover. He gave Transplant a pat on the head and headed to the entry.

Peter's job was to read over the proof copy for accuracy. This was still a draft, they had stressed. Let them know if anything didn't meet his approval. Peter had panicked at the thought of hundreds of loose pages. What if he dropped it? He wanted it held together somehow. So, for him, the printer had bound this particular copy.

It had a cover, also in draft form. *Transplant* was splashed boldly across the front in a block print, with a simple outline drawing of a golden retriever underneath. Trent's full color drawing would go on the final version.

Peter already had Transplant's things by the front door. He had some food and a few toys the dog especially liked: a Frisbee; a blanket, too. He'd put the things in a small case, and it was next to a chair. As he opened the door, he was surprised to see someone besides Paul.

"You're, um, Mr. Pearson. I met you at the restaurant with Jessica's friend, Mags. I remember you." When Mr. Pearson reached a hand to shake, Peter laid the draft copy of his book on the chair just by Transplant's case. He grabbed Mr. Pearson's hand in a firm grip. "What can I do for you?"

"I'm here to pick up Tee. Your dog?" Mr. Pearson smiled. "For a month, right?"

Peter hesitated. "I thought Paul was keeping him."

Mr. Pearson looked down, and when he raised his

head, there was a sheen of perspiration on his skin. "Paul had to go in to the restaurant. You can call him there if you want." His smile started to waver.

Peter glanced at the clock. "If I had the time. I'm in a bit of a rush." He invited the man in. "Don't worry about Tee. He's really well-behaved. He'll be just fine until you can drop him off."

"Thank you." Mr. Pearson set his keys and sunglasses on Peter's manuscript, and he followed Peter into the living room.

"He's in here." Peter walked into the back room, and Transplant jumped up to stand at his side, wagging his tail. "He's a golden retriever. He'll friendly you to death, so be careful. Tell Paul to be cautious, please. Try to let him run at least once a day. Oh, and I've left instructions with his things. It's all in his case by the front door. I'll pay when I get back, if that's all right with Paul."

"I don't think Paul will mind." Mr. Pearson knelt down to run his hands through the fur on Transplant's head. The dog twisted his head in pleasure as he stepped forward to lean against this new source of attention. Mr. Pearson laughed as he steadied himself.

Peter worked Transplant's collar around and hooked on a leash. "I think he already knows you're his friend. My taxi will be here any time, and I need to close down the house. Can you find your way out?"

Mr. Pearson laughed. "I can see the door. I guess so."

Peter knelt and rubbed Transplant's fur, and then he stood. He looked at the man taking his dog and handed him the leash. "It's easier if I don't make a fuss. I'll walk to the back room, and you just exit." He reached to shake.

"Thanks for doing this. I appreciate it."

MR. PEARSON smiled. As he answered, he felt his voice break. "You're welcome."

He *really* didn't like doing this. There was an element of deception in it. He'd told Mags that, but she'd been very convincing, and he did want to see her place on the island. Besides, he knew Mags wouldn't do the animal any harm.

When he got to the door, he saw the case, and there in the chair next to it was a thick book with a picture of a dog on it. He looked at it and then at the animal. He knew he'd seen Peter place it there as he walked in. It said Transplant, not Tee, but they could be the same, he guessed. It must be the instruction book. He knelt and opened the case to slip the book inside. Then he latched it, and he led the dog out the door.

He laughed as he approached his vehicle. It was one just like Dr. Johansen's, very small, and the dog was very large. He looked at the animal, and he realized it would barely fit, if it even did. Mags hadn't told him just how big his companion would be. Oh, well, he decided. What was done was done, and he'd have to work out how to fit him in.

He opened the door, leaned the front seat forward, and called, "Tee!" When the dog didn't move, he tried the name he'd seen on the front of the book. "Transplant!" He was pleased when the dog jumped right in. He placed the case in the floor and closed the door. He was sleeping in Maine tonight. He didn't like that it would be in a chicken coop, but Maine was Maine.

Mr. Pearson whistled as he walked around the car, not

considering that Maine was six hours away, and he was transporting an eighty-pound dog in a very small car.

MAGS WALKED into the house. Something smelled delicious. Stepping into the kitchen, she looked for Jessica, only finding a covered pot off to the side on the old-fashioned cook stove.

"Jess!" she called.

"In here, Mags!"

Mags moved into the living room to see a pair of legs sticking out from behind the sofa. She knelt and grabbed one ankle.

Jessica yelped, "Mags! Stop that!" She scooted out a few inches at a time. "I found your phone company's problem."

Mags rolled her eyes and turned to flop on a chair. The phone problem was three years old. She didn't care about it, anymore. "The fire's not lit. It's going to be cold to-night. You want one? It really needs to warm all day to build up good, hot coals."

"Mags," Jessica insisted, "did you hear me?"

"I heard you, and I just don't deal with that, anymore. The phone company says it's repaired, and I still don't have service. I can't fight them any longer. I simply go to Auntie's place and use hers."

Jessica reached for the phone on the end table. She flipped it to her friend, forcing her to catch it. "Turn it on." Mags made to toss it back, but Jessica held up her hands to block its return. "Turn it on, Mags."

Mags reached to press the button, and she was surprised to hear a dial tone. She pressed it to her ear. Then she pulled it away and looked at her friend. "Are you sure this is my phone?"

"Mags," and Jessica laughed, sitting down on the sofa, "your extensions were all plugged into the power outlets, but the base unit wasn't plugged into the phone line. You could have had a phone any time during the past three years."

Mags just held the phone in her hand as if it were a foreign object she'd never seen before. Then she laughed. "Technology should be easy, Jess. Then I'd have it figured out."

"But," Jessica said, "you'd still have to plug it in first."

"Jess, I smelled food." Mags said, changing the topic of discussion.

"Oh!" Jessica jumped up to run to the kitchen. "I almost forgot. I'm cooking on wood."

"Wood?" Mags was appalled. She knew it could be done, that the kitchen stove would operate on wood, but who would want to? "We have gas, you know."

Jessica laughed. "Wood seemed more novel. I've never done it, cooked with wood. I've had fun. Now, let's see what we've got." She pulled the lid off the pot on top, and a meaty stew bubbled. "Nice."

Her friend leaned in. "I thought I smelled sugar, though. Where's the sugar?"

Jessica opened the oven, and inside was a pie. "I found a can of peaches in the pantry. The label looked old, but the can was in good condition, and they were still fresh when I opened them."

Mags snickered as she bent over and closed the oven. "Still. Wood, Jess. You're cooking on wood. If you leave the door open, the pie won't get done. The heat escapes and doesn't build back up very fast. I'm glad you're enjoying this, but trust me. Gas is better." She paused, then studied each element of the old-fashioned kitchen. "Take-out is even better still. But then, I wouldn't be here with you."

Jessica laughed. "We can take this out to the porch when it's done. Will that do?"

"We've got company coming." Mags cringed when Jessica looked her direction with interest. "For the whole weekend." She picked up the empty peach can from the table and ran her finger inside. Then she licked it clean and smiled.

"Your parents?" Jessica liked Mags' parents, but they never talked of coming here.

"Bite your tongue, Jess. They hate this place. They want fields and dirt, not spruce trees and granite. They also detest the ferry ride." She turned to lean on the counter. "Mr. Pearson."

Jessica looked aghast. "Mr. Pearson? Mags, you can't be serious. You assured me in these very words, 'Jess, I'm not a bad girl.' If you have Mr. Pearson here, shame on you." Jessica turned her back on her friend. She lifted a cover on the top of the stove, exposing real flames, and one at a time, she began dropping small slivers of wood into the stove's fire box.

Mags grabbed her friend's face in her hands, and she kissed her on the cheek. "I love you too, sweetie. He'll stay in Murphy's. We'll keep this place. We also get the dog." She leaned back to see the effect that would have on her friend.

"Dog?" Jessica quit fiddling with her wood fire, and she turned to Mags. "I don't know Mr. Pearson all that well, but I do know he doesn't have a dog. Whose dog in this?"

"Peter Cassel's." Mags immediately turned away and flounced into the room-sized pantry where she stood looking intently out the window to the cove and her boat moored just off the dock's float.

Jessica walked to the door and leaned against it with one shoulder. She worked her mouth, and not one part of what she did could be construed as a smile. Mags glanced at her to see the glare in her eyes and looked quickly back out the window.

"Did I go too far?" Mags asked in a very small voice.

JESSICA HAD come up here to get away from anything to do with that man. Now, she had this thrown at her. Her words were forged with iron.

"You tell me what's going on, and I'll let you know."

"Jess, I found him." Mags turned to her, grabbing her arm, and pulling her to the kitchen table before she could resist. "He's finished his book, and he's going on the road, probably a signing tour. He had a dog, you remember, and he needs it boarded for a month. Please, Jess. I offered. It can run the whole Point. Run free, little dog! Crockett Point is yours! A month of freedom!" She smiled. "Am I forgiven?"

"Not yet. Why did he talk to you and not ask to see me, or at least talk to me?" Jessica felt her eyes begin to burn, and she knew she would cry if she sat here too long. She stood and marched to the front door, then she opened it and stepped to the porch.

Mags followed her and sat on the porch railing to face her. She had a very contrite look on her face. "Here's where it gets sticky, sweetie." She looked away to where she could see the ocean through the mouth of the cove, and then she cut her eyes back to her friend. "I didn't actually talk to him. You see, *Paul* talked to him, and Peter thinks *Paul* is keeping his dog. Paul has to work, you see, and he has classes, too. Peter was desperate, and Paul wanted to help."

"How did *Paul* find out Peter's dog needed boarding? Tell me that."

"Ooh, girl. You ask the hardest questions. Can't you just accept it as a baby-sitting job? I'll pay you."

Jessica felt ready to sling fire at her friend, and she barked, "Just answer the question, Mags!"

"Okie, dokie. This is the *really* sticky part, though. You see, I called Paul, and he's been my lookout." When she saw Jessica turn her head away to look off down the porch, Mags leaned in and spoke really fast. "I had to find out what was going on, sweetie. You had just come out of your shell, and you and Peter were so good together. Now you're not giving him a chance, and you're all sad and teary. I've got to see if I can fix this before it all becomes broken."

Jessica felt her anger drain away. At least Peter hadn't intentionally ignored her feelings *again.* She would've been crushed too low to ever recover.

"Jess? Are you all right?"

She laughed, and it was sour. "It's already broken. My life was broken two years ago, Mags. It's been broken ever since. I can live with this dog. As long as Peter doesn't know it's here, I can let it curl up in my lap, sleep at the foot of my bed, and it can run free, free, free!" She finished dramatically.

"I'm sorry?" Mags pleaded contritely.

Jessica looked at her friend with a smile, and it was real this time. "You have a good heart, Mags. Mine is just broken. How about we let it be broken, let me learn to live with it, and leave it at that? Okay?"

MAGS REACHED and hugged her friend. "Sure, sweetie. We can do that."

But behind her back, she held her fingers crossed, and she smiled as she told her well-intentioned lie.

Chapter 17

PETER LIFTED his arm and flipped the overhead air nozzle one direction and then the other. Either way, it was obnoxious. It was loud, and it was one little spot of cool in a very warm airplane.

Still bored—disinterested, he would have said in his book—he reached up and spun the nozzle until it turned completely off. Suddenly too warm, entirely too warm, he reached to spin it the other direction. For a moment, he breathed the air of a spring day coming through the small vent. Then he could smell it as it really was, the canned aroma of the airplane's recycled interior.

He didn't want to be here. That was the real problem. He'd wanted to sell his book, that was for certain, but he *had* sold it. He'd received an advance. It was not a lot compared to what some authors got, but it was enough for him to live on carefully for a very long time. Now he had other things on his mind, places he wanted, no, *needed* to go. He needed to visit Scortio's at lunch, or at least drive through the lot each day at eleven. He might one day find walking across the lot the petite shape of a beautiful woman he'd once taken on a picnic. He needed to wander the halls of Clark University in the hope that a class might let out, and she would be standing on the other side of the door. He might even take Transplant and just walk the campus. People were allowed to do that. He might carry a Frisbee and throw it from time to time. Students would talk about the man who threw Frisbees to his dog, the fact that they flew farther, and his dog jumped higher than any other. Finally, her interest would be piqued, and she would feel compelled to step outside to see what the hubbub was about. She would find him, and she would run to him. They would know that they should have been together all the time.

That was what Peter needed, but instead, he was here on this airplane, and they were flying far from Worcester, and far from his wonderful professor, Dr. Jessica Johansen.

"Here. They had to fax the whole thing." Frank Auvenshine was the publisher's representative accompanying Peter. "You're one lucky guy that this airport has a fax machine I could access. Even after I found it, I wasn't sure they would let the fax through. The man said it was too much paper. I just laughed and gave him a fifty. That shut him up quick as a wink. Where'd you say you lost your copy?"

Peter picked up the sheets of paper. They were loose, and he wasn't good with loose papers. They tended to slip, and if he dropped them, he'd have to reorder them. He looked to see if they at least had page numbers, and he was relieved to see they did.

"I didn't. I left it home. I know right where it is. I answered the door, and I placed it on the chair in the entryway. It'll still be there when I get back."

Frank snorted. "I hope so. The big guys make us account for each one of these. You lose it, and it comes out of my hide. I may have pursued you, chasing this contract from the beginning, but don't make me begin to wonder why."

Peter glanced at him. He was surprised at how the veneer of cordiality had seemed to wear thin once the contract was signed. Yes, Peter. Of course, Peter. We can do that, Peter. Now it was more like, Sit, boy. Beg, boy. Heel, boy.

He leaned his head back and closed his eyes. Maybe he was being too testy. However, they could have driven to New York. No, they had to fly. New York was the kingpin. If it went big, it started there.

New York wasn't where Jessica was, that was certain. He needed Jessica. He didn't need New York. He didn't need to be on this airplane. He didn't need this at all.

MR. PEARSON looked in his rearview mirror. If he lifted his head just right, he could see the dog he was transporting sprawled in the seat. He crinkled his nose. It kept passing gas, and he didn't know why. He'd looked in the case that came with it, and all he could find to feed the animal was some dry stuff. He'd taken heart and shared his hot dog with it. The dog had seemed to enjoy it so much, he'd bought it an extra. He'd forgotten to have the vendor leave the onions off the second one, but the dog hadn't seemed to mind.

He looked at his gas gauge, thinking this was taking a long time. He still had plenty, thank goodness. Mags had said to be there two hours early, that lines were long this time of year, and she'd insisted he write the ferry schedule down. He hadn't seen that as a problem. If he missed one, he'd just catch the next. How hard could it be? However, he hadn't actually considered the drive could really take six full hours. That's why he'd taken the time to stop and walk the dog a few times. He'd even thrown the Frisbee once. The dog had been exceptionally playful. He was exhausted now, though, and just wanted to get there.

Onions, Mr. Pearson realized. He realized the smell must be the onions. They affected him that way, and that was why he always had his hot dogs without. He groaned as he understood what that meant. It'd be like this the entire way.

He glanced out the front window and pulled his sunglasses off. It seemed the sky was cloudier than it had been earlier. It was getting breezy, too. With a push, he slipped the glasses into a compartment in the dash. The clock said four, and in summer in Maine, the sun would go down close to nine. At least he had plenty of daylight left.

At any rate, the glare was gone, and the wind would keep the mosquitoes away. All in all, it seemed like a start to a pretty good weekend. He glanced up to see a sign telling the name of the approaching town.

"Wiscasset." He murmured the name to himself, placing his location on the map winding itself out in his head. "If this is Wiscasset, not much longer." He drove through the middle of town as the road wrapped around the houses and the hills, and when the city dropped away, he could see the water. Ocean! Stopping at a red light, he glanced at the clock and realized he would be cutting the ferry departure time close. Awfully close.

The light changed, and he hurried across a bridge, cutting a sharp left as the blacktop pulled out of town. He looked in the mirror and spoke to the sleeping dog, "You missed it, Tee. Transplant. Whatever your name is. That was the prettiest little town I've ever seen, and you missed it."

He turned his eyes ahead. Rockland. He needed Rockland. Mags had reminded him that if he drove directly into Rockland, the ferry landing would be right there. He'd remember when he saw it; the town hadn't changed at all. Just follow the signs. All he had to do was drive to the red light and take a left. Well, for Mags' information, he was following the signs, and his ferry time was growing dangerously close. He heard a noise from the back seat and glanced in the mirror a third time. It would be nice to be there already and away from the smell. Gads, that was a bad one!

"YOU SHOULD have seen Magenta when she was a girl! On her first day here each summer, she would fly down the ramp, stand on the float, and strip her clothes off. Then she would jump into the water to make the biggest splash she could." Auntie looked at her niece, and her eyes sparkled.

Jessica wasn't sure if the sparkle was from the memory or the bottle of wine sitting on the table, but the elderly woman was certainly enlivening the day. She was glad they'd motored over for this lunch date. They had been doing this almost every day, and Mags' aunt seemed to really appreciate it. Later, Mags also wanted to motor into town to try to catch Mr. Pearson. Perhaps they could shop a bit at the bookstore, maybe even catch a lobster sandwich at the Harbor Gawker.

"Wasn't the water cold?" Jessica remembered Flat Rocks. It was only when the sun warmed the water that they'd been able to get their feet in it.

Auntie laughed. "Freezing! She'd come right back out, blue as you can be. It was the only time she would jump in all summer. I always watched with my binoculars. I missed it one summer, and I begged my mother, that's Magenta's grandmother, to make her do it again. My niece refused, though, and I had to live without seeing her jump that year."

Auntie reached to her glass and brought it to her lips. Taking a sip, she set it back down, catching the edge of her plate. "Oops!" she called out, readjusting it to sit firmly on the top of the table. "Nearly spilled that one."

Mags reached, pulled the glass back a bit from her plate, and said, "That's enough, Auntie. It's only lunch, you know." She glanced at Jessica with a smile. It was clear she loved her aunt, but it was also clear she was aware of her foibles, too.

"Sweetie," Auntie reached and placed her hand on Mags', "I never have company up here. That bottle is from the first of the season, and I start the season early." She glanced at Jessica. "April. I come in April. Sometimes there's still snow on the ground. Most people wait 'til June when it's crowded. June fifteenth. That's the magic date for them. Not for me. I want my peace and quiet."

Her eyes blinked a few times and misted. The glistening was brighter, now, and her voice was more private. "Eldridge is gone, and I never took the time to find anyone else. I just ran up here, and I hid away." She looked up, and she brightened her face. "Then, this summer, you two showed up. I'm having the best time." She reached for her glass. When Mags reached it first and put her fingers on the stem, Auntie grabbed the bowl and pulled it loose. She put it to her mouth and finished it off.

"Auntie," Mags started.

Auntie's old, weathered eyes looked at her niece, and there was no smile. There was no anger, either. There was something there that Jessica recognized, because she was going through it, also. There was regret for something that had been done, or perhaps left undone. There was a knowledge that a choice had been made, and it hadn't been the correct one. There was a lingering grief that a man had been taken from her, unfairly perhaps, but taken anyway, and his death had been allowed to push all other men from her. There was regret that she hadn't done things differently.

Then, Mags' aunt braved a smile, and she stood to lean over and kiss her niece's face. "Sweet Magenta. Find you a man. Don't wait too long. I think I'll go lie down. After all these years, I've no head for wine, anymore. The phone's there if you need it." She turned to Jessica. "You, dear. You're sweet. I hope that man of yours comes to see you while you're here." Then she was gone through the door, her hand touching it as she walked through, the brush of her fingertips just enough to steady her legs.

Jessica cut her eyes to Mags, a bit peeved over her aunt's remark. She hadn't told her friend's aunt about Peter. Then, she remembered the dog, and she let the feelings of irritation go. That was probably how she knew. Probably. She smiled as she picked up a slice of apple and bit off a small amount. Finally, she turned to look at Mags. "She's sweet. She's lucky to have you."

"Auntie never did learn to call me Mags." Her eyes misted, as if that was important in some way. "She's lonely. That's why she always wants me to come up. Look at this place. It's a simple farmhouse on the wild Atlantic shore, and it's the same as when my Uncle Eldridge died. Oh, the painters come, and repairs get made. Yet, I remember these same decorations from when I was ten. Even the pictures on the wall are the same."

Jessica remembered what Mags had done in her own home. She'd come in, and she'd wiped the slate clean. She looked at the pictures here in this old farmhouse, and she remembered all the new ones that had been hung in her living room. She now understood more of the reason why Mags had done that.

"Mags," Jessica began, feeling pensive. She was putting things together: their time together on this remote island; the dog that was coming to stay with them; the aunt's obvious loneliness. "This is all about Peter, isn't it? Oh, I shouldn't even have to ask, but I'm finally seeing it. All this visiting with your aunt every day. I've enjoyed spending time with her, but is this why we're having lunch here again?"

Her friend shook her head. Reaching to her own wine glass, she picked it up and swirled the dregs, then placed it down again. "Sweetie," she started, and she paused. "I get that from Auntie. Sweetie. My own mum never says that. Anyway, we came today because I love my aunt, and she needs my attention. You see, my parents have each other, and they love me, but I'm not the core of their lives. Auntie has no one up here. No one. That's why we're here for lunch." Then she winked. "What she said earlier, why, that was just icing on the cake."

Jessica stood and carried her plate to the sink. She placed it inside and looked out at the view across the mouth of the cove. Mags' place, her grandmother's home, was beautiful. Crockett Point reared out of the ocean, and great spruce trees stretched their mighty fingers to the sky. In a clearing near the top stood the expansive white farmhouse where she and Mags were staying. The porch swing swayed in the breeze that had kicked up that morning, and there was a tendril of smoke from the morning's fire rising from one of the chimneys.

She could see Murphy's off to the side down the hill. It was where Mr. Pearson would stay. It was wedged in a bit, and with its gray shingle siding, it nearly disappeared into the landscape. Above Murphy's, a grand promontory reared defiantly to the sky. A small cabin could be seen poking through the trees. Mags' grandfather had spent hours there, she said, writing novels.

On the other side of the big white house known as Crockett's was a flat area where an old foundation stood. Mags' grandfather had been a painter, portraits and landscapes, and in a disastrous fire one year, it was all lost. Only the stones that made up the basement walls remained. She glanced around Auntie's kitchen and saw a pair of binoculars on an open shelf. She picked them up and looked at Mag's float down on the water. She tried to imagine a ten-year-old girl out for her first day of summer, running to the box that formed the end of the dock and yelling in triumph. She would run down the ramp, jumping into water so cold it would drive her right back onto the float to dry off and try to warm her skin in the Maine sun.

She turned to gaze at Mags, to find her sitting with her chin resting in her hand and her elbow on the table. Her eyes were on Jessica.

"Mags, what should I do?" She set the binoculars on the window ledge, took in a deep breath, and turned to run water over her plate. Then she rested her hands on the edge of the counter and stared out the window. "I'm your aunt, aren't I? I've run up here to be safe, and I'm not safe at all."

Suddenly she felt Mags' arms around her. Mags' chin rested on her shoulder, and her words were soft and comforting. "This is a storm, Jess, one that you have to live through. We'll weather it together, you know. I'll be here for you every step of the way."

Jessica reached her hands and grasped her friend's arms where they wrapped around her. She whispered, "I have to do it alone, Mags. I have to figure this out on my own." Looking out across the view, she continued, "How can anything be so beautiful? Your place. You're so lucky."

Mags squeezed her friend, whispering in her ear. "I

know. I have you for a friend. That's why I'm lucky. Crockett's is just icing on the cake."

TRENT'S MOTHER reached beside her. A small book rested on the table at the end of the sofa. She touched it, and then she turned to look at her son drawing at the kitchen table. She wanted to move, find a better area for them, but this was at least familiar, even if she did keep three locks on the door. Worcester was safe, a college town, one that provided steady employment. College students always needed food, and they always visited cafeterias.

At least now she didn't need to go to Boston to work double shifts. The money in the book saw to that. It was so much, too. She'd been nervous taking it to the bank. What if they had told her the check wasn't any good, that she couldn't have the money?

Even when she'd put it in, and the numbers were in her book, she'd still been nervous. What if she went to take it out, and it wasn't really there? The first time she walked up to the desk, and she told the man she wanted some money out of her account, he had smiled and taken her book. When he opened it, he smiled even wider.

She walked away with some of her money, Trent's money, really, and only then had it been real. Sort of real. If she never had to pay it back. If that man's book really sold. If Trent's picture were really on the cover. If. If. If.

She pushed the book aside and picked up the remote to the small TV across the room. It had been hers from before she married Trent's father, and he hadn't been able to take it from her. She clicked the button and turned it on.

At first she was irritated to see the weather forecasts scrolling across the screen. Then she remembered the weekend coming up. She wanted to take Trent to the park. She knew the man with the dog had said he would be gone, but she would take Trent anyway. Perhaps the man and his dog would be there. If not, it would be good for her indoor boy to get out of the house a while.

The man on the screen was pointing to something out in the ocean, a storm, she thought, and there were arrows showing the direction it was headed. She pushed the buttons on the remote to bring up the sound. She saw Trent look her direction when she did, and she smiled at him.

"It's okay, baby. I just want to see the weather this weekend. We might go to the park. How would you like that?"

He sat up in interest. "Will Transplant be there?"

She laughed. That was all he was interested in, anymore. Transplant. Tee, the man had called the big animal. "Probably not, baby. We can look for him, though."

"Okay, Mummy. Look for pretty weather." He laid his head back down.

She called, "I will, Trent. I'll look for the best there is."

"I love you."

"Love you more," she whispered.

"I heard that."

She just laughed and pushed the volume up button.

"It's unusual to have a storm move into the New England area this early in the season. However, records show similar strikes in 1954, 1960, and 1991. The earliest ever recorded occurred in 1635 in early August. So, this is not totally unprecedented.

"In fact, one meteorologist with the Center for Global Climate Change actually suggests that with global warming, this may be a harbinger of the future.

"The current track suggests it will miss the Cape with a possible strike somewhere in the Mid-Coast region of Maine. We will keep you updated as the storm progresses."

Trent had been listening, and he called for his mother's simpler assessment. "Rain, Mummy?"

"Maybe not. We'll hope for the best. How about that?" She smiled as she turned the channel, dropping the volume and watching the images dance on the screen. She had a few minutes yet before she had to get ready for work, and she couldn't bring herself to get up before she needed to.

"Okay. I'm almost finished with my picture. Want to see it?"

"In a minute, Trent. Give me just a bit."

She touched the volume button, and a new voice filled the room.

"When preparing your spring bulbs, wrap them in newspaper and store them in a cool place. If they are favorites you've pulled from the ground, simply snip any growth off, and rinse the dirt from the roots. Towel them dry, and add them to the others. I find it easier in the spring if I write the type and color directly on the paper. Use a permanent marker—a Sharpie works well—and you'll know just what you have when you plant them next season."

Trent's mother flipped the TV off. She muttered, "Some of us have to work."

"What was that, Mummy?"

"Nothing, Trent. I just have to get ready for work."

"Okay, Mummy. I love you."

"I love you, too, baby."

"More."

She couldn't help thinking, *I don't think so, Trent. You're everything to me.*

He was, too.

MR. PEARSON started his car. Even after arriving at the landing, the ferry was still rocking, but nothing like it had been out on the open water. At least he didn't have to hang on, anymore. The dog hadn't liked it, either.

It had been a while since he'd been here, but as he remembered, he could see the town out across the harbor. It seemed the same. They'd improved the ferry landing. Now it looked like it could weather a real storm.

When the attendant pointed to Mr. Pearson, he shifted into gear and pulled ahead. At the ramp, he gunned the engine, and his small car surged up the incline and onto the shore. He looked behind him to see Tee sitting up and smearing his nose all over the glass.

Turning right, Mr. Pearson drove past the docks piled with lobster crates, and he decided he'd take a few out to the house. Mags hadn't asked, but he knew she would enjoy them. She often ordered that at Scortio's.

Stopping on the side of the road, he turned the engine off. Cracking the windows, he left Tee in the car and walked down and onto the dock. Crates and lobster pots were piled all around. The island smells and sounds brought a smile to his face. He had enjoyed it all those years ago, and he had forgotten how much. It was the smell of the sea, and the sounds of boats and buoy bells, all the things that made up lobstering.

"Can I help you?" A man in fishing clothes, wearing a billed cap, and sporting a scraggly beard, stepped out of a door. He wiped his hands on a much-used towel as he spoke.

"Lobsters. I'd like several." Mr. Pearson looked around. He had no idea which lobsters he was to choose from, and he glanced at the various crates piled all around the dock. They were everywhere.

"Here." The man leaned down and opened a trap door at his feet. "Got plenty of bugs, a few wicked big. Pick the ones you want. Got some steamers, too, if you want."

Mr. Pearson laughed. "Just lobsters. Any are fine. Four, please. No, six."

The man pulled five from the water, dropped one back in, and pulled out two more. He set them into a cardboard box lined with newspaper and stood. "Finest kind on the wharf, if I say so myself. Eighty dollars."

Mr. Pearson reached into his pocket and pulled out his wallet. He reached in and found a fifty and two twenties. He handed it over and said, "Keep it." Then, he bent to pick up the box.

The man looked at him and at the bills. Then he reached out his hand. "John Traynham. I'm here most afternoons. Stop by if you need more." Then he looked around at the cloud-covered sky and back to the water out beyond the harbor where it was starting to whitecap. "Weather's picking up. Don't wait too long before heading back to the mainland. Might get rough in a few days."

Mr. Pearson shifted the box to one side and shook the

proffered hand. "I will. Er, I won't. Thanks, John."

As he toted his lobsters to his car, he heard John call out, "In the fridge. Bottom drawer 'til you cook 'em. They'll be fine. Ch'out for those pinchers."

At the car, he checked the bottom of the box to see that it wasn't leaking, then he set it in the front seat. "Keep out, Tee," he ordered.

Climbing in the driver's seat, he headed through town. He drove down Main Street where he remembered watching the parade during several long-ago summers. He'd even played his clarinet in it one time. He drove past Carver's Pond and the gazebo, before he realized he'd gone too far. He wasn't here to tour the residential part of town. He pulled into a drive, put the small car in reverse, and turned around. At the Tidewater Motel, he recalled he was supposed to turn right. Downshifting, he crawled up the hill, accelerating faster once he reached the top.

Following the road past the cemetery, he turned right on North Haven Road and headed out to Mags'. She'd said to follow this one all the way past Round Pond to the hawk's nest, then take a left on Crockett River Road. Just take the road on the left after the cove, she'd said. It would be a gravel one, though, so don't look for asphalt.

"Hawk's nest?" he'd asked her. "That's my landmark?"

She'd laughed. "You'll see."

He did, too. It was atop a utility tower and massive. He laughed and turned at the road that matched her directions, catching just a glimpse of water as he swung onto Crockett River Road. Even though the water of the cove itself was mostly obscured, he found the view through the trees just as spectacular as he'd been led to believe. As the lobsters shifted and clattered next to him, the rubber banding keeping their claws closed, Tee constantly adjusted his position in the back seat. Without warning, the full cove appeared in its glory outside the car's window. It was lined with the tallest spruce trees, the kind that grew in abundance all over the island, and in one or two places, houses could be seen with steps that led down to varying kinds of docks. A few had ramps leading to floats bobbing peacefully on the water.

The cove was long and narrow, and Mags had said he would follow it for a mile or so to her place. The road twisted and turned, taking him under the overhanging branches of enormous spruce, some hanging quite low. Once, he drove away from the cove for a bit, and dropped through the most picturesque, vertical-sided, granite-walled gorge he'd ever seen. Wild ferns landscaped the sides of the road, and moss and lichens etched the sheer walls. Small trees grew from clefts in the stone, and dappled sunlight littered the entire scene. It took his breath away, but whether from the fairy-tale beauty or from the fact that it barely left enough room on either side of his car for him to get through, he couldn't have said. Emerging on the other end, he breathed a sigh of relief.

Finally, the road ended, and he reached a forbidding wall of untamed greenery. He looked around, and there were two simple gates, one on the left, and another on the right, both open. Each had signs that said private property. He stopped to think. Mags had said hers faced the cove, and that meant left. Taking his cue from that, Mr. Pearson drove ahead.

Chapter 18

PETER'S HOTEL room door opened, and he turned from the window. He hadn't been able to see much, anyway. Rain had blown in, and all of New York was awash. The glass was fogged, too. Reports said it would soon blow north, but it hadn't done so, yet.

"Man, you should be happy, excited, even." Frank, the publisher's rep, threw some paperwork on the bed. "You write a book, and the company is dancing like they're on needles to get it out. I've never known them to hop so fast."

"And expecting me to hop right along." Peter said it bitterly, and even as the words left his mouth, he knew it was unfair.

"Of course they want you to dance by their rules, and I have to shake them at you, but still. All in all. Everybody makes money. Most people would beg to be in your position." Frank dropped into a chair and reached for a piece of fruit in a bowl.

Peter laughed sourly. "You people have been begging for a year and a half." He pointed to his companion. "*You've* been begging for this book." He tried to find the city outside the window, but the moisture on the glass fought him, and it was winning. "It was my recent hospital stay that gave me time to finish it." He paused, and when Frank cleared his throat, he turned, and he saw the rep frown.

"Not dying, are you? The high-ups might like to know."

Peter laughed again at that. "Not according to my doctor. The thing is, I lost touch with my editing mentor after I got out."

"Thank God for publishing companies. We have editors out the kazoo." Frank laughed. "We do your heart good. Get it, Cassel? We do your heart good."

"Yeah, I get it." Peter wiped his hand across a pane of glass, leaving a watery smear. Then, he took his palm and placed it in a spot that was still fogged. He held it there a moment and was pleased to find that when he removed it, the warmth from his skin had cleared the glass, letting him see outside.

"Hey!" Frank jumped up. "You cleared a spot. Can you make out anything out there?" When he got beside Peter, he peered at the handprint. He turned to the rookie author with a grin, then ducked and looked through the opening. "Look. Flashing lights. I hope no one died." He stood and drew a heart beside Peter's handprint. "That's you, buddy.

Live a long time. You're at the top of your game."

Peter looked at the handprint and the outline of a heart. It reminded him of the heart he thought he'd found, and it hadn't been the one in his body. It had stood at the front of a classroom, and it had shared a picnic in the park with him. Then, without warning, he'd fallen into that two weeks that had allowed him to finish his book, and when he crawled out, she'd disappeared. He reached and wiped the window with his hand. He turned back to the room, his patience with being in a hotel worn thin.

"Is it time to leave?" He needed to be someplace else. He guessed today's planned events were as good a redoubt as any. Being busy might keep his mind off Jessica. It might, but he didn't feel it.

Still. Still.

When Frank gave him a thumbs up and dropped the remains of his fruit in the waste bin, Peter followed him out the door. He reached back in, and just before he pulled the door to, he glanced to the window where he had wiped the heart away. He felt his eyes burn for a moment, and then Frank called. With a sigh, Peter stepped into the corridor, and the door slowly clicked shut behind him.

TRENT'S MOTHER stacked the plates in her plastic tub, and she set it in a chair. The weather was getting rough outside, and she was grateful the crowds had slowed inside the cafeteria. She had hated making all those trips to Boston to work in the hospital, but it had been less busy there. Here by the campus, it was a mad rush at mealtimes. Maybe she could catch up now. After wiping the table, she lifted the tub and balanced it on her hip.

As she walked into the kitchen, she glanced up at the TV that was always running. Pushing her tub up on the counter by the dishwasher, she paused to rest her arms, and she listened to the narrator's words.

"The tropical storm seems to have skimmed New York with minor wind and showers, although Boston will see heavy rain for the next few days. Forecasters have predicted the storm will upgrade to hurricane force by the time it impacts Maine's Mid-Coast region. Those directly on the coast are warned to prepare. Tides will run high, and there will be wind damage. Expect branches to come down, and on the coastal islands, entire trees may topple.

For those of you in the Midwest, expect sunshine over the next few days as this storm moves on up into Canada . . ."

"Sorry, Trent," she whispered. "I guess we don't get to go to the park on Saturday." Then, she turned to her tub and began pulling dishes out and stacking them in the washer. When she had a load, she pushed the tray inside and powered it up. After a minute or so, the high-pressure spray cut off and she pulled the tray back out. With a cloth, she transferred the clean dishes to a drying rack, and she began to reload the washer.

Her mood unaccountably lifted, and she began to whistle softly. She only had this one shift, and the dining room was empty. She might even get to go home on time today. Thank God for the storm. If it kept the crowds away for a change, it would be the best thing that could happen to her weekend.

MR. PEARSON beeped his horn to get someone's attention. This was some place. After passing the private property sign, he had driven past several buildings, what appeared to be an old basement, and then he'd seen the house. It was grand, in the fashion of something from the 19th century. It was white and two-storied, and the front was wrapped with a porch on two sides. Additions at the ends rambled out, with exposed granite piers holding them aloft. Lattice filled in the openings around the foundation, and there were native flowers growing all around. As the drive circled through the front yard, he could see the path to the dock wending far down the treed slope to the water, and tucked in the trees, there was another house wrapped in gray shingles. He parked his car off to the side by one just like his own. Dr. Johansen's, he recognized.

Preparing to climb out, he reached to leash Tee. Opening the car door to let the animal jump out, he paused to look at the box of lobsters in the front seat. He'd have to come back for those.

Standing for a moment, he breathed in the smell of the spruce trees, and he could taste the acridness of wood smoke in the air. He was surprised, though, that no one had come to greet him. He had honked his horn.

Then he heard the sound of a motor on the water. He looked to see a boat pulling up just off the dock. He smiled as an arm reached out and waved. Turning to the dog, he called, "Come, Tee." Then he started off down the path, holding on as the big animal strained at the leash.

"Let him go," wafted up to him. When he continued to lead the dog beside him, he heard the words again. "Let him loose. He can't run away. It's an island!" It was Mags' voice, one he had grown accustomed to, and it felt good to hear it.

Mr. Pearson looked at the dog at his side. He hadn't thought about it, but she was right. They were twelve miles out in the ocean. Where could the dog go to get lost? He knelt and unclipped the leash. When Tee just looked at him, he said, "Go, boy." With that, the dog was off and running toward the dock.

It was when Mr. Pearson rounded the path just where it approached the dock that the wind hit him. He shivered. He looked out the mouth of the cove to the open ocean. The water was really kicking up out there. A pang of concern hit him, then he pushed it away. He wasn't the expert, and he supposed the ocean looked as it should. After all, the ferry had made it just fine, and they should know.

As he walked out along the dock, he saw Tee already at the big wooden box at the end, wagging his tail. Reaching the ramp, he saw Mags and Dr. Johansen rowing up in a small skiff, leaving the motorboat tied up to a buoy.

"Greeting, ladies! This is beautiful!"

They waved, and Mags yelled at him, "We were just in town. We must have missed you."

Obviously, he thought with a grin. However, he simply waved and watched as they pulled the skiff up on the float. The water in the cove was somewhat smoother than that in the open ocean, but it was growing rough, too. The women wrapped their light jackets tighter and ran up the ramp to greet him.

They looked askance at the dog wagging his tail, watching them expectantly. Mags spoke first.

"He's a horse, Michael."

Jessica looked at her with a bemused expression. "It's Michael, now?" When she saw Mr. Pearson drop his head in embarrassment, she laughed and placed her hand on his arm. "I'm sorry. Call me Jessica, Michael. This isn't the university. Thank God for that."

He brightened. Then he looked at the dog and gave them a warning. "He's had onions. I fed him a hot dog on the way up, and when he passes . . . well, anyway, just stand back."

Mags cackled in hilarity. "Then we'll all four eat onions tonight, and no one will notice." She looked at the dog, reaching a hand to touch his nose. "He has a name?" She knelt and rubbed his fur around his ears. "He's beautiful."

"Tee." Michael reached to brush his hand along the animal's head. "He answers better to Transplant, though."

JESSICA LOOKED at him sharply. The name jarred her, stirring memories of Jeffrey, but she put it aside. It didn't matter. It was just a goofy dog's name, and the animal would be gone in a month. It was just as well, too. She shivered in the rising breeze.

"I'm cold," she said. "You two can visit, but I'm heading in." She noticed she had company following directly on her heels. The temperatures *were* dropping, and when they looked up, the tips of the trees were whipping in the wind.

"Is a storm coming, Michael? Did you hear on the radio?" Mags reached to his arm as they walked to the house.

"I don't know. The dog was sleeping most of the way,

so we rode in silence. The ferry ride was rough, though."
He walked along for a moment, his shoulder sometimes touching Mags', occasionally grinning in a very pleased fashion, then he called out brightly, "Lobster. I bought lobster. From a man named John. They're in the car."

Mags called, "Did you hear, Jess? Michael brought lobster. He bought them from John, *my* John who takes care of my house here. That's wonderful. We'll fix them tonight."

"Whatever you say." She'd noticed the shoulders, and it made her lonely. She drew in a breath and let it out in a heavy sigh, as she stepped heavily up the incline.

Mags laughed, "I'm glad Michael's come up to be with us. When you decide to be in the dumps, Michael and I can entertain each other."

"Witch!" Jessica said it with a laugh. She hoped it didn't sound forced. It wouldn't do for her to bring down everyone's mood because she was melancholy. She watched the cinnamon retriever leap after something in the tall grass crowding the path, and she realized she was having a good time. Maybe today would turn out to be a good one after all.

Transplant clearly *was* having a good time. He ran through the open areas close to the house, and for a time, the island was his. He liked people, though, and when they went inside, at Transplant's insistence, there were four to enjoy the first two of Michael's lobsters. The bites the big dog stole didn't give him gas, either, and everyone was very glad of that.

MAGS ENJOYED her opportunity to run Michael all over

the island the next day. The wind whipped through the trees, and the clouds made it cool, but that was as familiar to Vinalhaven in summer as brilliant, sunny days of calm winds and balmy temperatures. Jessica took Tee and drove her car around the cove to share the afternoon with Auntie. After a lazy lunch, the two women curled up in front of Auntie's fireplace with the big retriever, and they dozed the afternoon away. After throwing her summer school classes to the wind in her desperate attempt to run from her breaking heart, it was the most peaceful and relaxing day Jessica had known.

The rain started that night. It was gentle at first, splattering the windows, and was wonderful for sleeping. The day after, however, it was windy, and the rain repeatedly came in sheets before occasionally letting off for an hour or so. It was on Saturday night that it lashed the house with a fury that could easily tip toward unnerving. The farmstead was sturdy, though, constructed of the toughest of materials. It was also on the lee side of the Point, giving some measure of protection during the island's most violent storms. Over one hundred years of weather had tried to take it down, but it still stood.

It wasn't until the phones rang early on Sunday morning that the people inside were aware of anything seriously amiss. Jessica heard the ringing, but this wasn't her home, and the rain on the windows was a sound she found comforting. She remembered hating the rain after Jeffrey's death. Now, for some reason, she didn't mind it. When the ringing stopped, she smiled and turned over in bed, letting the warmth of her comforter tease her eyes closed once again.

The second time the phones rang, she threw the bedclothes back and plodded to the door. She had on flannel, now. Mags had told her there were always extras stored away. Feel free to use whatever she found. She learned that in a summer home on a Maine island, flannel was always better. Now, she stepped into the hall and knocked on Mag's door.

"Yes," the groggy voice called.

"The phone, Mags." She knocked again. "It's ringing." She opened the door and turned on the light. "Sorry, Mags. It's rung more than once. It might be important."

When Mags answered, she learned her aunt was taking the first ferry out. She was simply being cautious. Reports said a storm was rolling it. It might be bad.

Still groggy, Mags asked, "Auntie, you didn't ring the bell. How did you know the phone would work?" She glanced up at Jessica as she asked.

Her aunt gave an answer that showed her practical side. "I always call first, Magenta. If it doesn't go through, I ring the bell."

"For three years, Auntie? You've been doing this for three years?"

Ever practical, she answered, "It had to be fixed sometime, dear. You see? It finally is. I'm heading out now. No one will be here. Call John if you need anything. When the storm passes, I'll be back."

"Is it going to be that bad?"

Auntie answered, "They might close the ferry, or so Beth in town told me when I called her this morning. Can't take a chance. Think about joining me, Magenta, you and your friend. You don't want to be stuck out here in a big one. Whole town's closing down." An alarm clock could be heard ringing in the background. "That's for me, dear. Have to leave now, or the ferry'll go without me. Bye, dear."

When she hung up, Mags looked at Jessica, her eyes wide. "It's a storm."

Jessica laughed. "You think? Listen."

Mags' voice was ominously shaky. "Jess, Auntie weathers everything up here. Nothing drives her off the island. *Nothing.* She's leaving, says the town's shutting down. She says she'll come back when it blows over. What do you think?"

Jessica sat beside her. She put her arm around her and hugged her. "I don't know, Mags. We can ask Mr. Pearson. Michael, sorry. He's in the other house, but I bet he's still asleep. I do know this, though. If your aunt is leaving now, we've already missed this ferry. The next leaves in how long?" She looked at Mags for her answer.

"Several hours. Two and a quarter, two and a half. Depends."

"Then we have that long to sleep. We can wake Mr. Pearson then." When Mags fell back in bed, Jessica took time to tuck her in. Then, with a weary sigh, she trudged back to her own room, and the driving of the rain quickly allowed her to drift off once more.

JOHN TRAYNHAM sat and tapped his list. The words were written in his rough, blocky letters, and several of them were scratched out. The storm reports had been coming in for days, and he'd been working to prepare. He had several houses he took care of on the island, summer places, and he got good money for it, too. He'd built a reputation. He also had lobster pots all over the island in coves and bays. So did others, but it was his he worried about. He had to get his pots up and summer people's floats ashore, and he had his own boat to think of, too.

What really worried him was seeing Mrs. Brier-Abercrombie on her way out early this morning. He'd been walking along the road by the ferry, on his way to check on yesterday's catch, and he'd seen her car. She'd rolled her window down and waved him over.

"Be in Rockland; might even drive up to Bangor. Be back when it's over. Watch the place."

He'd been watching her place since he was a teen, and she'd never gone for a storm. Lots of people did, but never Mrs. Brier-Abercrombie. Now he was wondering if he should go ahead and pull all his pots in. Then, he still had his list, and there was only so much time. Plus, if the storm skipped them, what he did had to be undone.

He scratched his head and made checks by five of the items. These were the ones he'd do first, and he might as well get started now. They wouldn't get done yesterday, that was for certain. He'd have to run to Rockland for one of them, but his boat was fast, and it could take heavy weather.

He reached into his locker and pulled out his newest and best slicker. He would get wet today. There was no way around that. No way at all.

THE AIRPORT windows were wet, but the rain had let up. Several of the airlines had resumed their flights already, and the backlog of passengers seemed glad for that. Gusts

298

occasionally blasted the windows, but it wasn't the fero-cious lashing of several hours ago.

Peter and Frank sat side by side. They were stranded. All they'd had to do since early that morning was watch the news reports on the monitors strewn throughout the building, and all of them had shown the same thing. The storm was hitting Maine. The rest of New England was taking a beating, but it should survive. God help Maine.

"I'm headed to use the phone," Peter said, standing. He looked over to where there were pay units across the wide corridor just outside their waiting area.

The rep stopped him. He reached into a pocket and pulled out a cell phone. "Here," he said. "Don't wander too far. If we get a green light, I want you here. Chicago needs us."

Peter chuckled humorlessly as he took the phone. He knew he didn't need Chicago. He needed something a little more personal. He needed a woman he'd let slip through his fingers, and she was lost. Perhaps he was lost, too.

No, there was no perhaps when it came to his own con-dition. He knew he was lost. Why else would he be in a New York airport terminal waiting to fly out of the edges of a hurricane to go to a Chicago terminal, when he didn't want to be in either place?

When he first decided to write his story, he'd thought of it as something he would sell, and it would go off and make him money, leaving him to his little life in his house with his dog. Now his story was demanding everything. People had told him this was how it would be, and some-how, he still thought he would be left to his own devices, in peace, and alone.

Now, stranded in this airport, he had time on his hands, and he felt the need to check on Tee. Central Mass was reported to be unaffected except for localized flooding, but he needed to be certain. Tee was important to him, and he didn't want to take any chances.

Peter looked at the phone and back to Frank. "Directory assistance? How do I get it on this phone?" The rep explained, and Peter keyed it in. "Worcester, Mass," he spoke in response to the operator's question. "Business. Restaurant. Scortio's." He waited a moment, and then he heard the phone ringing at the other end. When it picked up, without waiting, he quickly thrust his words over the line, "Is this Paul? Is he in?"

The voice on the other end chuckled. "Thank you for calling Scortio's. This is Paul. How may I assist you?" Paul's voice was very friendly and helpful.

"Paul, thank you. It's Peter. You know, with Tee. I'm glad I got in touch with you. I know it's only been a couple of days, but with the storm that's blown in, I want to check on my dog. I'm in New York, and it's been pretty bad here. I'm flying out to Chicago as soon as the airport opens flights back up. What's it like there?"

There was silence for a time, then Paul coughed uncomfortably. "Sir, er, Mr. Cassel," and he paused before continuing, "I have a confession to make. When I first spoke with you, I explained my work and school schedule, and, er, well, Ms. Brier-Sheldon, Dr. Johansen's friend, is helping me out. She has your dog with her."

"Ms. Brier-Sheldon?" Peter had to think for a moment. "Dr. Johansen's friend?" He didn't know people by their hyphenated last names. Then he remembered. "Oh, the one named Mags?"

"Yes, sir. That's correct. She's sitting with your dog for me while I'm at work."

Peter breathed more easily. "He's there in Worcester?"

"No, sir. I haven't been completely upfront with you, and I apologize. Ms. Brier-Sheldon is at her place in Maine. She's been there the past week, maybe two."

"Paul, please tell me her place is in western Maine."

"I don't know, sir. I can give you the name of someone who would. A Mr. Pearson. He works here at the university."

"Mags' friend. I remember him. He teaches at the school." Then it hit him. He was the man who had picked up Tee. He had been somewhat vague and rather nervous sounding. Peter had written it off as insecurity due to dealing with a large dog. Now he thought differently. "Yes, I would like that, Paul. Will I be able to reach him now?"

"Perhaps. Mr. Cassel, thank you in advance for your understanding. You'll be calling his cell phone. However, I'll need to contact him on a landline and have him prepare to receive your call. Then, you should be able to get right through. The signal. You know how it is."

Peter was awash with concern for his dog, and he had no way to vent his frustration. He now wished he'd left him with Lennie. She wouldn't have complained. Now he was under pressure to get to Chicago, and Tee was heaven knew where, somewhere up in Maine. Exasperated with things that were not being said clearly, and more importantly, not being done the way he had expected, he sighed.

"What's the number?"

PAUL GAVE him the cell number, and as soon as he was off the line with Peter, he called it himself from his personal phone. When Peter had first called, he'd cut off Paul's usual greeting, and Paul had taken it in stride, even found it amusing. People did that sometimes, and being early, Peter was the first for the day. As the conversation continued, he'd felt his dog-sitting bonus crumbling around his ears. Even so, lying hadn't been an option, no matter how much he needed the money for school. He hoped Mr. Pearson might be able to pull his tuition out of the fire yet, if he could get him on the line before Peter spoke with him. The part about the cell phone signal? He supposed there could be poor reception farther north.

As it was ringing, he reassured himself he hadn't really lied. He did have a landline number he could call if he needed. It just wasn't to Mr. Pearson, and it wasn't the one he was presently calling. The landline was to Ms. Brier-Sheldon, although he thought it rang to an aunt's house. Now, he was calling Ms. Brier-Sheldon's personal cell phone.

"The number you are trying to reach is either turned off or out of service range. Please leave a message or try again. Thank you."

Paul spoke a few words into the phone, and then he disconnected and tried the landline. If he couldn't get through to Mr. Pearson, then neither would Mr. Cassel, and he would be right back on the phone to Paul. Maybe Ms. Brier-Sheldon could help him out.

The phone began to ring in a distinctive pattern. Party line, Paul remembered. He knew how it worked, from visiting his grandmother in Western Pennsylvania as a boy. She'd shared with her sister who lived down the road. Listen for your pattern of rings and pick up. The good thing about a party line was that more than one household *could* pick up, meaning someone, at least, might get the message to Mr. Pearson.

What Paul didn't know was that there was no one at the aunt's house on the other end of the line, and just like he thought, the ring pattern was specific to her residence. He let the phone ring a good twenty times before giving up.

He pulled out a tissue and patted his forehead. He wasn't quite sure what he'd do, but he'd better do it fast.

He punched in the number and tried one more time, hoping *someone,* no matter where, answered his call.

Chapter 19

MICHAEL PEARSON struggled out of the sleep that had buried him for the night. Lobster three nights in a row always did that to him. It was better than a sleeping pill.

He reached beside him to feel a warm body. He smiled. The hair was soft as silk. Just then a long tongue licked his face. His awareness sharpened, and with that, he jerked into a sitting position. The dog had stayed with him. Now it was *sleeping* with him.

His head throbbed, continual banging noises thumping in his brain, and he reached to press against his temples. Lobster usually didn't do *that* to him. Alcohol did, and he hadn't had any the night before. Then he realized his head didn't hurt. The noise wasn't in his brain. It was coming from outside.

He leaped from the bed, and he pulled the blinds. It was nearly dark on the other side of the glass, and if it was morning, even early morning in Maine, it should be light, already. Instead, rain pelted the window, and wind lashed what trees he could see against the cloud-shrouded sky. The storm howled in its ferocity.

He reached to the nightstand and grabbed his cell phone. He flipped it open. Nothing. The time was displayed, but there was no signal. Mags had said there wouldn't be, so that didn't surprise him. However, with the storm, it did disgruntle his thoughts, making him growl.

Then the loud banging started up again, and he realized it was at the door. He ran through the living room and to the kitchen. Stepping onto the enclosed service porch, he saw a person through the glass wearing a yellow slicker. Water poured off the yellow form, and then Mags' face was revealed as she raised the front of the hood. He yanked the door open. The wind and rain blasted in with her.

As soon as she was inside, he pressed the door shut, shutting off the worst howling of the storm. She panted with her run from the big house, laughing as she pushed her hood all the way back. She pointed at him.

"Mr. Pearson! Michael, I mean. Your boxers. You couldn't get dressed for a lady?"

He looked down, embarrassed. Just then, Transplant heard her voice, and he barreled onto the porch, jumping in between them. Michael stumbled and fell, and Mags roared with laughter. Transplant began to lick the water from her slicker.

Pushing the animal away, there was a change in the tone of Mags' voice as she spoke. A new level of urgency punctuated her words.

"Michael, I've called town. John is holding two spots in the ferry line for us. This is to be the last ferry for the duration of the storm, and it leaves in twenty-five minutes. The only reason they're running this one is for an ambulance that has to get across. If we want off the island, we must go now. Grab your clothes." She glanced at him still sprawled at Transplant's side and laughed. "Or just go like this. I wouldn't mind."

"Storm?" he asked from his position on the floor. He knew the weather was blowing hard, but he'd just gotten up, and his mind was still groggy. Transplant turned to lick his face, and he pushed him away.

Mags jerked her thumb to the door where the rain could be seen whipping the trees in the near darkness. "I don't know where you grew up, but in Maine, we call this a storm. A hurricane is about to hit, and we can get off the island now. We must leave immediately, though. As in right this minute."

Michael grabbed the front of the utility sink, and he pulled himself erect. He grunted, adjusting his internal assessment of the situation. "Five minutes, Mags."

She retorted, "Two. Where are your keys? Tee goes in Jess's car. Put him there. I'll be in your car waiting."

He stepped into the kitchen and grabbed them from the table, his heart pounding. He tossed them to Mags, and she was gone, yanking the door shut behind her.

As he stumbled up the three steps to the bedroom and yanked on his pants, he wasn't sure if his racing heart was from the sudden adrenalin rush caused by the impending storm, or from Mags having seen him partially undressed.

Either way, he had no doubt she'd leave him if he wasn't there. He suspected that was why she had taken his keys.

He stumbled over Transplant as he reached for his shoes. "Sorry, Tee," he said, as he reached under the animal. When he heard the beeping of the horn, he grabbed his wallet and the leash. "Let's go, boy." He snapped the dog down, and they raced to the door, flipping out the lights as they went.

JESSICA GRABBED her most vital things. She looked around, evaluating what to leave behind. She had more clothes at home, and they could leave the dog's case. They could pick up more dog food. What they left would still be here if, no, *when* they returned. Mags had said the house would be fine, or *should be fine* was the phrase she'd used. With a sigh, she grabbed her keys.

Tee would be with her, and she would follow the other two. As soon as Michael put Tee in her car, the two of them would head out. Of course, Mags would drive, because she knew the roads. As long as they were at the ferry landing, John could give them the spots. If the ferry was loading, and they hadn't arrived, he'd have to let their places go. "Just catch up, Jessica," Mags had pleaded in a near-hysterical tone. "Just catch up as quickly as you can. They'll hold the ferry a few minutes, if I'm already there."

Just as Mags ran out the door to get Mr. Pearson's keys, the phone rang. "Mags!" Jessica stepped across the room to call out the door. "Mags! The phone!" Then she turned to see it still ringing in an unusual three two pattern that she remembered from earlier. "Mags," she said, although she didn't say it loudly this time. Just then the lights flickered. Jessica froze and held her breath. When they stayed on, she stepped to the phone and picked it up.

"Crockett Point." She had no idea who would be calling, but she knew it wasn't for her, and she had to get to the ferry. She looked out the door into the blackness to see the interior lights in her car flicker on momentarily, as Mr. Pearson put Tee inside. As soon as he returned to his own, the brake lights on his car flashed, and the car drove off.

The voice was bright and cheerful. "This is Paul with Scortio's. I need to speak with Ms. Brier-Sheldon, please."

Jessica's response to him was much more intense. "Paul, she's not here, and I have to go." She paused and put one hand to her throat, suddenly afraid of being left behind. "I've got Mr. Cassel's dog, and I have to make the next ferry off the island. The hurricane's here. All Vinalhaven Island's closing. Everyone's leaving me. I'll have her call, Paul—"

Just then the lights went out, and when Jessica pressed the phone to her ear, she realized it was dead as well.

THE PHONE in front of him rang. Paul's heart sank. He looked at the display, and it showed the same number it had when he had spoken with Mr. Cassel. He took a deep breath.

"Scortio's. This is Paul speaking. Mr. Cassel?" He held his breath in the hope Mr. Cassel had been able to reach Mr. Pearson. He hoped they'd been able to get things sorted out. However, he thought not. Otherwise, he wouldn't be back on the line.

"Paul, were you able to reach Mr. Pearson? I cannot get through on that number you gave me. My flight to

308

Chicago will probably be reinstated soon, and I must be on board when it is. I really need to find out something about my dog."

Paul stepped up to the plate, his voice tense, and told him the news. "I was able to find your dog, Mr. Cassel." He paused, clearing his throat. "However, despite the promising tenor in those words, I can only wish I were more positive in my results."

Peter interrupted, "He's not injured, is he?"

"I don't know, sir. I wasn't able to find out that."

"Paul!" Peter pressed him. "I've got my publisher's rep waving our tickets at me. Our flight's being called, and I have to board. Sum this up. What do you mean you don't know?"

Paul put his very best professional tone in his voice as he spoke. He felt it would come across better that way. "I've spoken with someone who has Tee, and your dog is on Vinalhaven Island in Maine."

"Who, Paul? Who has him? Where's Vinalhaven Island?" Peter's voice rang with desperation.

"That I don't know, sir." He thought it had sounded somewhat like Dr. Johansen, but the caller had been frantic, and he hadn't really been sure. If he claimed it was Dr. Johansen who was on the line, it might not be the truth. "The caller just identified the location as Crockett Point, Vinalhaven Island. It seems as though the hurricane was about to hit." Paul hated saying the next part. If the dog were lost, he would feel responsible. However, he didn't dare hide this. "Before I could find out anything clsc, sir, the line abruptly went dead."

THERE WAS nothing else to say. Peter vibrated with anxiety as he disconnected the call. He was also furious. He was furious at that Pearson fellow, at Paul, at Mags, and probably at Jessica, as well. All of them. He had no idea just what they had done to get Tee to Maine and on an island. He just hoped the place didn't lie directly in the path of this storm.

As he returned to his things, Frank stepped in his way. "Mr. Cassel, our flight's boarding."

Peter turned and snapped to him, "Then board. I'm not." His eyes flashed, and there was iron in his voice. He held out Frank's phone, and when he refused to take it, Peter dropped it into the man's coat pocket. Then he turned to find a place to exchange his ticket.

"Mr. Cassel, Chicago is waiting. Your book. This is your chance. You cannot be serious."

The pleading words rolled off Peter's new determination, and he didn't even look back. As Frank followed him, Peter carried his things to the nearest airline counter and stepped up to an agent, Frank on his heels the entire time.

"Vinalhaven Island. I need the nearest airport." The agent's fingers immediately began to tap an inquiry on her keyboard.

Frank grabbed his shoulder and whispered loudly, "Chicago, Cassel. We're going to Chicago." His eyes jumped to the agent's and back to Peter.

The agent paused, unsure. Then, she asked, "Maine?" She looked at Peter for confirmation. When he nodded, she typed in her information. "Bangor is the closest airport accepting incoming flights. You do realize there's a hurricane moving that direction. Even Bangor will probably close by noon. Do you wish to purchase a ticket?"

"Yes," he said. "How soon can I leave?" He glanced to the publisher's rep at his side, his eyes narrowing, knowing this man was not about to stop him from this new course of action. He had been misled—lied to, in fact—and his best friend, Tee, was now in mortal danger. There was no book promotion opportunity that could compete with this sudden and overwhelming need for action on his part.

The agent looked at her display, and then her fingers flew over the keys. "We've had a number of flight cancellations throughout the system. If you'll let me search for a moment, I'm sure I can find something." She glanced up at him and smiled. "I see nothing coming up that will leave directly for Bangor before the airport there is expected to close. However, it seems we are currently boarding a flight for Toronto that's scheduled for a brief stopover in Bangor. It's not full, but the doors are closing as I speak. It's boarding just behind you."

"Can I make it?" His eyes pleaded with her. His window of opportunity couldn't be allowed to slip by when it had just opened. "Please!"

She looked at him, and she picked up a phone. She spoke into it for a minute, then she looked at him with her eyebrows raised. "Do you have a credit card?"

"Will cash do?" He reached into his pocket for his wallet.

She smiled. "Certainly. You will have a seat, sir. However, we must hurry." She began taking his information as Frank looked down the airport concourse to where his own flight was boarding the final few passengers. He looked at

Peter with venom in his eyes and cursed under his breath.

"Cassel, I need you, and I need you in Chicago. This is idiotic. Don't throw this opportunity away."

Without looking, Peter muttered his reply, "Letting my dog die would be idiotic. Going to rescue him is the best thing I've ever done."

Frank gave a snort of disgust, and he began to run toward his own gate. Peter did glance after him, and he was glad to see him gone. He hadn't wanted to go to Chicago, anyway.

"MAGS, I CAN'T see them. You must slow down." Water and wind-borne debris beat the windows, making the car vibrate with noise. The tires slipped at a corner taken too fast, and after a heart-rending moment of doubt, they caught, jerking the automobile back under Mags' control.

Michael was frantic. At the university, Jessica had been no more than Mags' friend, one he would have felt distressed to leave behind. However, it would have been a sacrifice he would have let go as a decision not under his control. Now, he didn't want her left here. He also felt responsible for the dog. He had played a part in bringing it, and with deception, even.

Tears were in Mags' eyes. "I can't, Michael. There's a time-honored method for boarding the ferry, and not even a storm changes that. We might as well ask the islanders to change the course of the sun and the moon. When the ferry leaves, it leaves. I can't slow down, or we're left here. There's a second reason I haven't mentioned. If the landings are damaged, we're stranded for a very long time. Days. Weeks."

"You have a boat." He remembered it floating just off the dock back in the cove. Anyone with a boat wouldn't have to depend on the ferry. He understood he would have to leave his car, but he would be able to retrieve it eventually. "When this is over . . ."

She looked at him, and tears ran down her face. "If the ferry landing doesn't survive, do you actually think my boat will still be afloat?"

He sat back in his seat. He hadn't thought of that. He turned to look out the window at his side. The rain continued to beat at the glass, and in the near-darkness, bits of tree branches suspended by the wind blew angrily around, slamming against the side of the car. He didn't see how the ferry could make the crossing in this. He guessed there was a chance they would get there, and it would already be closed.

He turned to Mags. "The ferry," he began. He watched her face. He hated to even mention this, but certainly she would know. This was her home. "It was rough when I came over three days ago. Surely they've already closed it in this weather. This would be impossible. The cars, they'd just wash over the side."

She smiled, but there was little humor in it. It was a look that spoke instead of the bad things of life that people must endure, and the hard decisions that often had to be made. "You're correct. However, for an ambulance, they'll brave even this. John told me an islander is due for triplets, and a C-section is probable. She's in labor. When her ambulance arrives, the ferry leaves, and we're either on, or we're not."

"Falling off, though? That's a very real possibility,

isn't it?" That frightened him.

Mags patted his knee. "They'll strap the wheels down. The ferry will have to go under before we do." She chuckled. "Pray that doesn't happen." She glanced at him and winked.

He sat quietly as she tore around corners only she knew were coming. He didn't see how Jessica would be able to make the same time they did. In his heart, he knew she would be left, and he didn't want that to happen. However, he also knew storms had hit here before, and the island wasn't gone. He tried to find comfort in that.

As they arrived in town, activity was frantic. Fishermen were hastily preparing the docks for the worst, strapping down what they must, moving inside what they could, and leaving for the storm all that was expendable. John was by the side of the road. He slapped the glass and had Mags roll her window down.

"I've been waiting," he said from under his slicker. The water poured off in rivulets. "My truck is there, and the cars at the front have already loaded. The ambulance is due any minute. You said there would be two cars." He looked to see if another was following.

"Another just like this one, John. My friend and a dog are behind us." She glanced at the moving line. "They're coming. Should I wait before pulling into line?"

He patted the door of the car, looking in the window at Mags and her passenger. Mr. Pearson waved, but the roar of the storm had grown so violent he knew there was no point in speaking. The noise forced John to lean down to talk to Mags as if not wanting the rest of the town to hear.

"No, I'll watch for them. When the ferry leaves,

though." He left the rest unsaid as he handed her a card with her line number on it. It told the order in which she would load the ferry. He looked around, the frenetic pace of the town's preparations taking precedence over everything, and then his eyes turned to lock onto hers.

Mags drew a breath and let it out. "I understand. I'll pull into the line. Thank you, John. No one could have been more helpful." She put a quick hand on his, then drew it back into the car.

He pursed his lips, looking up as a wailing sound found its way through the fury of the storm. "Go. I need to move my truck. Watch for my blinker and pull your car in. I hear the ambulance on its way already. Five minutes, maybe. Your friend has that before the final cars load." He tapped a second card with an additional line number on it with one finger before noticing it had gotten wet, and he slipped it inside a pocket.

Grimly, Mags rolled up her window and pulled ahead. As they made their way onto the car deck, Mr. Pearson breathed a sigh of relief. One car loaded and one down. They were halfway there, at least.

JESSICA HAD no options. She placed the phone on the table, and she squeezed the key in her hand. Tee was in the car, already. She could do this.

She felt her way to the door, and she stepped through into the blinding rain. *My umbrella,* she thought. In an instant, she knew she couldn't find it if she went back through that door. The house was black inside. Outside, she could barely see shapes in the near darkness.

Stumbling in the torrent, she struggled to the car.

315

Opening the door, she saw the light flicker on, and she was relieved. Tee was in the back, and he leaned his head between the seats in an effort to get to her.

"Tee," she soothed. She reached to his head, realizing he must be as frightened as she was. With her fingers, she rubbed behind his ears, then she turned to her task. It was at that moment she remembered her purse was in the house. She couldn't go for it now.

She put the key in the ignition, and the car stirred to life. She triggered the lights and saw the wall of greenery just in front of the car. Water poured from where the promontory reared up to defy the storm. She reached to turn the wipers to high. Putting the transmission in reverse, she carefully maneuvered it onto the driveway.

Speaking to Tee, describing her actions and the things she was driving around, she knew she was really trying to calm herself as much as calm the dog. However, she felt it was doing both. Her confidence was strong as she approached the rock-walled gorge that she had to drive through. Mags had driven it on the way in, and the sides had been close. Jessica had braved it, but only in daylight. However, if she took it slowly, she felt it would be something manageable.

It was when the lights of her car shined into the gorge's flat-bottomed crevasse that she knew she wasn't going home. She wouldn't make the ferry, and no one would ever know why. The hurricane would sweep her into the sea, and she would be lost forever.

She also understood why the lights and the phone had gone dead. In the middle of the gorge was a tree. It had toppled over, and it was held just above the bottom by the power lines that led to the house.

Jessica reached to Tee. She pulled him into the front seat beside her and wrapped her arms around him. The car's wipers valiantly thrust the water from the windshield as the storm beat down. As the rain came in ever-increasing sheets, the headlights of her car illuminated the thrashing torrent, and she began to cry.

THE WHEELS of the airplane let out a whistling screech as they touched the pavement. It wasn't yet raining in Bangor. However, the sky was dark, and the wind was brisk. The storm was coming, they said, and it wouldn't be long before the airport here was closed, as were so many others.

The rental agency was loaded with cars to rent. The agent laughed when Peter asked if there were any left. He said they were *all* left. No one wanted to come *into* a hurricane zone. People were returning their cars and flying *away* from the coming storm.

Now, he barreled toward the coast under darkening skies. Something large, the agent had said. If Peter must do this, he must have something large. The agent had given him a map and the biggest SUV on the lot, and he had warned him that he couldn't insure the vehicle if Peter chose to drive it into the town closest to Vinalhaven. Rockland was where he would find the Vinalhaven ferry, and Rockland would take a brutal hit by this hurricane.

Peter hadn't cared. His heart was too deeply bruised by a woman's love, one that he had found and then lost. Now, this stranger's heart that he carried in his body was being torn from him by this impending danger to his best friend.

As he drove down the roads highlighted on the map, he knew this wasn't all about Tee. He had said it was, and in the airport in New York, he'd reacted violently to the news about the oversized animal. However, he knew his feelings of frustration and lost love went deeper than that.

This was about the woman he had met on that college campus. She'd fallen on him, and he'd held her in his arms. He hadn't forgotten that for one moment. He might have put it aside during those two weeks he was lost in the hospital, but forgotten? Never. That had been his desperate need to get his story out, and his very real fear he wouldn't survive. Once that faded, the truth had flooded over him once again. He had sat in her class, and her beauty and her enthusiasm for life had pulled him in. She had drawn his heart around her, and then she had disappeared, leaving him hollow inside. He didn't know where she was, and he hadn't been able to find her.

However, he could find his dog. If he couldn't rescue his relationship with this woman, he had no choice but to save his dog.

Soon, he began to hit spattering rain, and the sky darkened further. He knew it was early, yet the world was turning black. The rain pelted his windshield. Despite the storm, he barreled on. How he would do what he needed to do, he had no idea. That it would get done, he was certain. Tee needed him, and Peter would be there.

JESSICA WIPED her tears and pushed Tee away, slipping her car into reverse. Working it slowly, she managed to get it turned around, and she carefully drove back to the grandmother's house. Pulling up as close to the door as possible, she grabbed Tee's leash.

"Ready, boy? It's going to be wet." With a quick motion, she threw the door open and pulled Tee from the car. Entering the house, she shook herself off as the dog did the same. In the darkness, she knelt and put her hands on his face. "It's just you and me, boy. Let's see if we can survive this storm."

She remembered the purse she had left on the counter. Feeling for it, she thought how she would be glad to do without it, if she could at least be on that ferry with Mags and Mr. Pearson. Reaching inside, she pulled out her cell phone.

Turning it on, she was relieved. She had light. She could see there was no signal, but she could look for matches. Mags said oil lamps were used in the house until she was a teenager, and none of them had been thrown away. Mags had also said they were still used for emergency backup lighting. They had to be in the house somewhere, hopefully filled with oil. If she couldn't find them, at least locating matches would enable her to start a fire in the Franklin stove. That would give her some light. Warmth, too.

In the living room by the Franklin, she found not only matches but also a propane fire-starter wand. "Bless you, Mags," she said aloud. Turning to see that Tee had followed her through the house, she held the wand up. "I am woman. I have fire." She laughed at herself, but she did feel better. She flicked the wand and watched the flame flare forth.

That was when she saw the lamp. It was high on a bookshelf. Reaching for it, she was relieved to see it had a glass reservoir, and even in the dim light of her flame, she could tell it was indeed full of oil. She knew how to do this. She had regularly used tiki torches around her pool when Jeffrey was alive. She could trim wicks and keep them burning cleanly.

Rolling the dial at the side, she adjusted the wick and touched it with the wand. She breathed a sigh of relief when it flared into brightness. Placing the globe on the lamp, she saw the dust on it and realized it would give off more light if it were clean, but she also knew that any light on this day was better than no light at all.

It was cold in the room, though, and that she did not have to live with. There was wood by the stove, and she would have heat. She knew how to do that, also.

Chapter 20

"MUMMY, LOOK." Trent stared at the television.

"What, baby?" Yesterday had been long and hard. The rain had pelted Central Massachusetts, and they hadn't been able to go out. Then, Trent's mother had been scheduled to work the evening shift. She'd struggled with whether to go. She had hated to leave Trent as bad as the weather was, but she'd bundled up in her waterproof gear and fought her way to the cafeteria. It was closed. The weather had decimated business, and the higher-ups decided they didn't want to pay the help. They hadn't called her.

Now, they were stuck inside again. The rain had lessened, but not enough to be outside. She was tired of this storm.

She walked into the room so she could see the television. "I'm here. What do you want me to see?" He usually had cartoons on, or sometimes he would watch a comedy show. Now, it seemed the channel he had chosen was the news.

"*Reports are rolling in. As we all know, airports from Down East Maine to the Cape are closed. The closest airport to the coast still open is Bangor . . . wait . . . we can also add Bangor to that list of closures. Anyone wanting out now needs to plan to ride out this storm.*

"*While still rated only a strong Category 1, the damage will be compounded by the timing of landfall at the highest tide of the month. It's feared that the islands just off Mid-Coast Maine will be the hardest hit.*

"*If you know anyone from that area, please do not attempt to contact them. A search and rescue plan will be implemented as soon as the storm subsides. The full brunt of the storm will hit this evening at about eleven O'clock.*

"*Rob Risinger, your CBS affiliate reporter on location in Maine.*"

"Oh, my word, Trent," his mother said as she sat beside him. Pictures were flashing across the screen showing places that had already taken damage. "This will get worse?" She reached her arm around him and gave him a hug.

His little face looked up at his mother's. "Can we pray for them?"

She smiled at him. "Of course, baby. I think they would like that." She got up and knelt beside him. Looking in his eyes, she began hesitantly, "Dear God—"

Before she could go any further, Trent stopped her by

grabbing her wrist. "Mummy, let me. I know how." He bowed his head and closed his eyes. "Dear Jesus. Keep Transplant safe. Don't let him get hurt, and if the storm comes near him, give him good people to love him. Jesus, keep his master safe, too. Thank you, Jesus." Trent raised his head and smiled. "Like that, Mummy."

She put her hand to the side of his face. He was so sweet. "Honey, Tee . . . Transplant, that is," she amended, stroking his small cheek with her thumb, "is right here in town with us. He'll be fine. His master is off on a book tour, probably in Denver or Dallas. Do you want to pray for some of the other people in the storm?"

He smiled and hopped up, satisfied. He ran to the table and grabbed a crayon, and then he turned to look at her. "You don't know, Mummy. They might be there. Jesus will keep them safe."

She walked up to him and tousled his hair. After a moment, she bent down and put her arm around him. "What are you drawing, Trent?"

He paused and looked at her. "It's a hurricane, Mummy. I'm going to draw Transplant and that man. Then I'm going to draw Jesus taking care of them."

She stood and touched his hair again. She could feel the moisture of tears in her eyes. "Then they'll be very safe. You can be sure of that."

Without looking up, he replied, "I am, Mummy. I am sure."

THE WHEELS of Michael's car were strapped down. Mags assured him it was nothing to be worried about. However, she *was* worried. While driving in, she had satisfied him by saying this would keep their car safe. However, if they were indeed strapping the wheels down, she knew it would be very bad, indeed.

They sat in the darkness with the storm raging around them. Then, flashing lights appeared. Mags reached to grab Michael's arm.

"It's the ambulance, Michael. Jessica isn't here, yet."

He reached to her to take her hand. "Be patient, Mags. The ambulance hasn't loaded. She still has time."

As the ambulance rolled on, a knock came at their window. When Mags rolled it down a fraction, it was John.

"The ferry has to go, Mags. I must tidy up some things. Your friend will be safe. This is a good island." He tapped the window and was gone, running off the ferry. Just then, the ferry's horn blast sounded.

Mags began to panic. "No, Michael. It cannot go without her." She attempted to struggle out the door. Before she could get it open, they could feel the ferry surge as its powerful engines thrust forward into the maelstrom.

Michael grabbed her arms, and he pulled her to him. He brushed her hair as he whispered in her ear, "It's too late to do anything. Trust, Mags. Have trust. In God, if you will. In that big, white house. In Tee. Just trust that she'll make it through."

She began to sob. "What if she dies, Michael? How will I ever live with that?"

He looked out the car window at the homes lining the rocky shore around the harbor. As the lighted buildings moved past, giving way to the ferry's frantic push to the sea, he could tell that this town had been built in a good location. The shore formed a pincher that kept the worst fury of the storm at bay. These people had to be tough, he knew. In the summers he had spent here, he saw some of that. Now it was becoming clear just how much fortitude they really had.

Michael lifted Mags' head to look in her tear-filled eyes. "What if she lives?" He smiled. "How will she ever be able to survive without you? You must be safe, also."

That brought a smile to her face, and she reached a hand in the near-darkness to wipe her tears. "Thank you, Michael. I'm just frightened."

He pulled her tight again. "So am I, Mags. So am I."

PETER'S VEHICLE was large, and still, the wind buffeted it back and forth. He didn't know this area, and he was having trouble reading the street signs. Some of them were vibrating violently in the wind, and others were too far away to be read easily in the driving rain. There were a few that were lighted, but most were dark.

Several times, he turned off on a street that seemed like the correct direction only to drive five or ten miles before he realized nothing was matching what was on his map. He would turn around and retrace his steps to try to find the place he'd made his mistake.

Once, he just stopped the truck he was driving. It was warm and dry inside, despite the way the wind buffeted the windows. As he sat there, the vehicle shook with the force of the coming storm. He reached up and turned the radio off. Then he bowed his head, thinking of those long-ago years in divinity school.

"God, I'm lost. I admit that. I never wear my collar, but You know who I am. I know that unreservedly. Yet, I've lost my faith in You, and I don't know what to do. I can't even love You with my heart, because the one inside of me isn't mine. It belongs to Jeffrey Jay, and he was a better man than me. I need help to find my dog, God. If You won't do this for me, then do it for Jeffrey. Do it for whoever loved Jeffrey. God, please help."

He sat for a moment more, and when he lifted his head, he undeniably felt his calm restored. He reached an arm, shifted into gear and drove on. He did seem to make better decisions after that, and he didn't have nearly as much trouble seeing the signs. He didn't know if it was God, or if his focus had somehow improved on its own, but he was doing better. He'd let God have the credit, if He wanted it.

Then he saw the sign he needed to find. It jumped out of the darkness. Rockland. He knew that just past this town, an island named Vinalhaven was out there somewhere, and if Paul was correct, on it he would find Tee.

However, as he drove into town and up to the waterfront, he began to have doubts that he would find anything. Even against the blackness of the afternoon, he could see what the water was like. Occasional lightning lit the surface of the sea. It surprised him that this close to shore, the water was roiling. No ferry was going out in this. His eyes searched for boats he could hopefully hire—or borrow, if he must—to find his way to the island. He looked for anyone out on the street who could help him. Water rolled across the pavement, and the buildings were dark. Everyone seemed to have run from this storm.

Following the signs for the ferry, he turned into a sloping lot that led to a terminal and the ferry landing just beside it. There were no cars. All around him, the town was a shrouded backdrop to the fury of the storm, and only in the frequent flashes of lightning could he see the white-capped water beyond. Even the sailing yachts anchored just beyond the ferry terminal danced wildly to the hurricane's demanding choreography as they strained at their moorings.

Then, as he sat there, he got the surprise of his life. Through the rain and the wind, from the middle of the harbor, came the blinking lights of a car ferry. Cracking his window a bit, he heard the bleating thrum of the ship's horn, and he knew it was coming home.

That's when he knew he might have a chance to save his dog after all.

JESSICA FELT the walls shiver. Needle-sharp blasts of rain made the glass in the windows sing. A ghostly hand reached and grabbed the house, shaking it violently. She wondered if the old building would survive. She could no longer tell. However, the living room was warm. The rest of the house wasn't, but she didn't care about that.

She looked out at the blackness of the storm. There were no blinds of any kind on the windows. She had liked that when they came up back in college. Even last week, it had been a treat. The views were always there, and when the sun streamed in the windows, the warmth of its rays was a welcome treat.

Now, the reflections were unnerving. Lightning sometimes flashed, and in the distance, she could see the thrashing of the sea. She didn't enjoy that one bit.

Tee hovered next to her and brushed against her leg. She knew he was frightened, also. She didn't blame him, either.

"Boy, I bet you're hungry. You've not eaten today. Let me check that case with all your things. I seem to remember you had food there."

She stood and took the lamp, and she walked toward the kitchen. She smiled when she saw the big, golden dog at her heels. She located the case, and she knelt on the floor to open it.

"Hey, boy. Let me get you a treat out." She set the lamp on the floor and reached with one hand to rub his ears. At least he was warm, and she didn't have to be alone.

Without warning, a violent gust of wind whipped past the house with a keening sound, and the floorboards vibrated underneath her feet. Jessica shivered as she flipped open the case and moved a thick, bound stack of papers to look for food. Finding a small bag, she sighed with relief.

"Boy, you do get to eat tonight. Lucky you." She set it down and rummaged in a cabinet to find a bowl. Then, with the dish in her hand, she reached for the food bag.

That was when she noticed the cover on the papers. She read it and looked over at the dog. She remembered Mr. Pearson saying something about him answering to Transplant. She had thought it very unusual, but that name certainly matched the title on the papers.

"Okay, Transplant." He stood and wagged his tail at the mention of his name. Jessica smiled at that. "I guess that *is* your name. Let's read about you. I see your picture is even on the cover." She gathered the book with all her other paraphernalia, and she headed back to the warmest spot in the house.

She intended to have a good read, no matter what was in the book. There was nothing else to do. If the storm took her out, then it would do so. If she survived, then that was fine. Either way, death by boredom was not her cup of tea. She patted the sofa beside her.

"Come on, Transplant. Keep me company. At least you can do that while I read your story."

He wagged his tail, and then he jumped up beside her.

She adjusted the oil lamp's wick for the best brightness, and she opened the book. She laughed when she read the first words aloud.

"I am a man who died twice."

She closed her eyes and remembered his words that day in class. He said this, and the class laughed. Later, he refused to explain it to her, telling her she would have to read the story to understand. She never thought it would be during a hurricane on an island out in the middle of the ocean, and with no electricity and no way to get out. However, he had promised, in a manner of speaking, and this was her chance.

She turned her eyes back to the book and read on, speaking the words on the paper aloud to comfort the dog, so she pretended, but as much to comfort herself. Despite her bravado, she was very frightened, indeed.

"As a divinity student at Harvard, I was taught that to become part of God's perfect plan, I had to give my heart to Him. Years later, I learned I had to face a new obstacle to become part of God's perfect plan. What if I no longer carried my own heart inside of me? Could I give Him someone else's heart? For, you see, I'm not one hundred percent Peter Cassel. I'm part another man. In fact, I carry two men around in my body. One day two years ago, I died when my diseased heart was taken from me. Another man died and his healthy heart was given to me. Each of us died once, and now we share this body. Together, we've died twice. So, you see, I can truly claim that I am a man who died twice, once for each of us."

Jessica closed the book. She had read no more than the first paragraph, and she knew Peter had done everything she had taught and more. From the first sentence she was hooked, and from the first paragraph, she knew no one who picked up this book would be able to put it down.

She reached a hand to wipe the tears from her face, and she moved her arm to work her hands into the dog's fur. She looked up to see the fire crackling merrily in front of her and back to the book in her hand. She opened it once again, and reading aloud, soon, the storm no longer raged around her. All she was aware of was the story of one man's life and the events that had led him to what he had become.

As her spoken words slowly faded into silence, the story moving ahead once riveting scene at a time, the shadows shifted in the room. The dog at Jessica's side adjusted his position and placed his head in her lap. As he drifted off to sleep in the security of her presence, she turned page after page, unaware that she would read about herself, and that the other man Peter had spoken of was none other than Jeffrey "Jay" Johansen, the much-loved sportscaster who had given his life to save Peter not once, but twice on the very same day. She had borne the loss, and Peter had garnered the gain. Now it was time to move on, but she would get to that, if she read far enough, and she intended to read it all.

JOHN TUCKED his slicker tightly around him, and he ran along the road towards his boat. It was about to get bad. He'd been out in plenty of nor'easters, but this was putting those to shame. Here in the harbor, the water was rough, but out there? He could hardly see it, but it frightened him.

This was number three on his list. Number one had been that girl with the triplets. Number two had been Mags. Now Old Man Lee up on the hill had to have his medicine. Diabetes. He'd die without it. Waited too long to order it, he had, and now Equinox Island Transit, the delivery boat that normally transported his medicines in an emergency, wouldn't risk it. John would, though.

He thought of four and five. Four was the Brier family's floats, one on each side of the cove. Five brought tears to his eyes. His lobster pots. He was saving that to last, though. He could replace the pots, that was for certain. Friends, family, and lives. Those were things that once lost were lost forever. He had lost the important things before, and he wasn't losing any more.

He ran down the dock and jumped past the ramp onto the float. The tide was wicked high, and he knew the docks might be awash before he returned. He knelt, and with expertise born of doing this a thousand times a year, he tossed the lines aside, setting his craft free.

Throwing himself into his boat, he fired the engine and threw the throttle forward. The boat leaped away from the dock, and the bow bit into the waves. This was just the beginning, he knew. Once he was out of the protection of the harbor, he had twelve miles of open sea. He could stay in the relative safety of the smaller islands as long as he was close to Vinalhaven, but he also knew that's when his knowledge of the sea floor would be put to the test. Just one wrong move, and he could hole his boat. If that happened, he was already dead, and so was Lee. That couldn't be allowed to happen, so he had to be at his best on this run. It was the most important trip of his life, and that was as certain as a lobster already in a pot.

PETER WATCHED the ferry rock with the waves, and he didn't see how it would be able to pull to the landing. He held his breath as the crashing surges that tried to force it down into the sea tore at its sides in the darkness. Then, with a final, thrumming roar of horsepower, the ship slammed into the landing and was captured.

Peter watched as men furiously unstrapped the wheels on the cars, sending them off one at a time. One of the first was an ambulance that roared into the darkness of the city streets without a second glance to see who was coming. They were safe in doing so. The town was empty. He had just been there.

Then, car after car came off, the rain whistling around them as if they were being pushed onto land by the storm. One of the last was a small car that looked familiar to Peter. The tags were from his own state. He blinked his lights and jumped from his truck as it passed, trusting they had news, hoping beyond hope that the car held his dog.

He ran to catch it as it skidded to a stop. He placed his hand on the window, and when he removed it, in the cleared imprint of his hand, he could see eyes peering back at him. Then the car's door burst open, and arms were flung around his neck, catching him by surprise.

"You came!" The unexpected person hugging him, clearly a woman, sobbed, yelling her words over the roar of the storm. "I'm so sorry!"

"Mags?" Jessica's friend? Surely this must be her. She was the only person he knew from this place. He felt her body shake as he held her. "Mags, is this you?"

The rain beat at them. She stepped back, and in the glare of the lights from his truck, he could see her face. Whether covered with tears or rain, he couldn't tell, but from her expression, it was obvious this woman was distraught.

"You must get back there." She yelled the words at him, and over the storm, he could barely hear her. She raised her hand to point to sea. "She's still out there. Find a way." The final car pulling from the ferry honked and blinked its lights, and Peter pushed Mags back to her car.

"Go! I will!" As she turned, he ran back to his truck and climbed inside. He glanced over, and in the darkness of the blinding rain, her car was gone.

She had said to find a way, and in the press of the moment, he hadn't thought to ask any questions. He also knew he must have misunderstood her. *She?* Tee wasn't female, not by a long shot. *He's still out there.* That must be what she meant.

Now, he didn't know what to do. He saw a light come on in the building by the landing, and he pulled ahead. He threw his door open against the bluster of the storm and ran inside. Inside was quieter, and he could hear the throbbing hum of a generator providing energy, lighting the premises for as long as needed. Somewhere in the back of his mind, he knew it would shut itself down when the lights went off once again.

"Pardon me," he called out, when he saw a man moving in the back. "Is the ferry going back out?"

The man, soaked and obviously just in from outside, looked at him as if he'd lost his mind. He just shook his head and turned to continue what he'd been doing.

"I need to know." Peter made his way to the counter that separated them. "I have to get to the island. Can you help me?"

The man stopped and faced him. "I just came in on that ferry, and that boat's not moving again. If this storm gets worse, it may go down where it sits. Only a fool would go out in this." He shook his head.

Peter persisted. "I'm a fool, then. How can I get there?" His look of pleading finally touched some chord of sympathy in the man.

"Then there's two of you out tonight." He reached under the counter and brought out a box. "Here's why I opened up the building. This goes with John. He's on his way. Perhaps he'll let you ride back with him."

"With John?" Peter didn't know who John was, but he was ecstatic. "Thank you. What's in it?"

The man paused and looked at him as he headed to the door. Then he walked on. At the exit, he turned to Peter. "Your ticket's in that box. Your ticket to a fool's hell. Tell John to turn out the lights and lock up." He opened the door, and he disappeared into the storm.

TRENT'S MOTHER stirred as something moved against her in the dark. She was dreaming of flowers in her hair and ice skating on a frozen pond in the moonlight. The cold of the air was brisk against her face, and the moon made the world glow like it was on fire. She breathed deeply and didn't want to wake.

A hand touched her face. She smiled and kissed the fingers, and her face became warm. Her breathing coming faster and faster, she began to rouse, and she realized she could barely catch her breath in the heat of the room. She jerked as she realized her son had climbed in bed with her.

"Trent, it's hot in here. Have you done anything to the air conditioner?" She threw back the covers to get up, and she glanced at the clock. It was dark. She could still hear the spatter of rain on the glass next to the bed. Looking out, she could see the near darkness of the black clouds overhead. Sunday was her day for sleeping in, but it must be afternoon by now.

"There's no electric, Mummy. I was scared." He was huddled into a ball next to her.

She lay back down and pulled him to her. "Baby, don't be scared. Here. Mummy's got you." She started to hum a tune that she knew he liked to hear. After a few minutes, he began to talk to her. He told her stories of the dog he used to own and the boys he had played with before school let out in June. He told her of what he did when she was at work, and he described his hurricane picture. He told her he hadn't drawn Jesus, yet.

He paused a long time before asking, "Mummy, do you think Jesus will still take care of Transplant during the storm, even though I didn't draw Him, yet?"

His mother lay beside him and rubbed her fingers over his shoulder and down his arm. His skin was so soft, and his arm was so thin. She didn't know how he managed to draw the things he did.

She whispered softly, "Jesus always takes care of dogs, especially when we ask him to."

Trent was quiet after that, and soon he had fallen asleep. Trent's mother finally laid her head back in the heat and murmured, "Anyway, the storm's very far away, Trent. It's very far away." Then, she, too, drifted off to join him.

Chapter 21

JESSICA SNUGGLED deeper into the cushions, and she turned another page. Reaching the end of a chapter, she looked up, realizing the room was getting chilly. It was summer, she knew, but summer on an island in these cold Atlantic waters was not the same as summer in Massachusetts. It was especially not the same when a storm, no, make that a *hurricane*, was beating against the land.

She looked at the dog next to her to see he was supremely comfortable as he slept. He had turned around without her being aware of it, and his head was propped on the far arm. Glancing at the oil lamp, she was relieved to see there was no shortage of fuel in the reservoir, and she reached to adjust the wick.

Just as she did, something crashed into the house, and

she jumped. Tee's head jerked up, and his body caused the cushions to shift. Jessica's heart pounded as fear drove her pulse hard. She looked at the dog next to her to see him looking around, his ears twitching for further sounds.

She hadn't heard anything break, and the noise of the storm wasn't any louder. After a few minutes, her pulse slowed, and she began to relax. Standing, she reached to put another log on the fire, and she watched the flames begin to lick around the dry wood. It would soon warm back up in the room. She rubbed her arms and looked for a throw, for something to drape over her as she waited for the room to become comfortable once again.

Looking in an old chest underneath one of the windows, she realized there were stacks of afghans and shawls, and others of scarves and gloves. She dug for a moment and discovered blankets and throws, also. She smiled, realizing she wasn't the first person who had felt the chill of Maine's summer weather. Reaching inside, she pulled out several. Turning to the sofa, she saw Tee's head resting on the arm once again, but his eyes were following her. The skin around his mouth quivered from time to time as something adjusted itself in his mind.

Before she sat, Jessica took one of the throws and covered the dog. If they had to be here together, at least they could both be warm. She turned to look at the chest she had forgotten to close and decided it didn't matter. Reaching, she finished adjusting the lamp when she felt moisture on her arm.

Looking up, she ran her eyes across the ceiling, but there was nothing there that she could see. Turning, she stepped to the window. Running her open hand over the century-old glass, she could feel the wind squeezing through the joints where glass met wood. Suddenly, the skin across the entire back of her hand felt wet. She touched the glass with her nail, rubbing it across the surface, and was surprised to find a hairline crack. Standing very still, she was aware of a new vibration of the floor under her feet, and at the same time, another small spray of water burst through the crack in the glass.

"Tee," she murmured, really talking to herself. "How is this house still standing?" She glanced at him to see his head up, and his eyes once again following her. "Shush," she soothed. "Everything's fine. Lay down." At the sound of her voice, his head dropped to the sofa. She pressed her palm to the glass to feel the vibration brought on by the force of the storm.

Standing at the window, with the world wrapped in the blackness of the blistering winds outside, and the occasional flash of light revealing the cleared concourse that stretched down to Flat Rocks, Jessica remembered what seemed like a lifetime ago. She had stood in the school's library, and it was raining outside. It had rained for her every day back then. She hadn't realized it, but she'd been drowning in her grief, and she would have, too, if a man hadn't come along to jerk her out of that.

That day she'd pressed her hand to the glass, and in that motion, she she'd felt a connection with Jeffrey. She had wanted to cry, and then one of her students had drawn a heart next to her handprint. "Love," the girl had said. "It makes me think of love." It hadn't made Jessica think of love, not the way the girl meant it. Jessica had known the sorrow she bore then, but she hadn't seen the full picture, either. At the time, she thought the heart on the window made her think of Jeffrey, and to her, it was the same thing, just with sadness coating the love. She knew better, now.

She pulled her hand away. The glass was still clear, as clear as glass can be when it stares out into the darkness of a hurricane. She didn't know if the full force of the storm had hit yet, but this was a hurricane, certainly. The glass remained clear, but the warmth of her skin had caused a ghost of an outline to appear, the condensed moisture revealing where her hand had been.

That day in the library, she hadn't felt love. She felt grief, and she felt longing. She knew that now. She also felt sorrow and self-pity and hate. She had buried the hate deep, but it was there.

She knew the story of the day Jeffrey died, not all the details, but enough. She had hated that man who had taken his heart. Oh, she wasn't *cruel.* She hadn't refused when asked. Besides, Jeffrey had signed up as an organ donor, and she knew he would want that. She wasn't certain if she would have been allowed to refuse the hospital's use of her husband's heart, but she hadn't. Another man could live, and Jeffrey was already gone. However, if that man had just died in that crash, her Jeffrey would still be alive. If that explosion that had engulfed the ambulance had happened just minutes earlier, he would have seen the flames. He would have been horrified, but he would have driven on.

No, that man had lived, and Jeffrey had died. *Her* Jeffrey had died, except for his heart, and now it beat in the chest of some other man. This book she was reading was opening her eyes, though, to how it must feel to be on the opposite side of the equation. As she read on, at one point, she thought it might even be her Jeffrey's heart that this man had, but she laughed at herself. That would be too much, too convenient. Peter would have told her, or she would have guessed. If he had Jeffrey's heart, there would be *something* there she would have felt, that would have pulled her toward him. She would have recognized *something.*

No, this man didn't have Jeffrey's heart. Jeffrey had given his heart in a hospital in Worcester. Jessica knew of the doctor Peter had mentioned. She was renowned, but she was in Boston. Boston and Worcester were not the same.

Jessica took a deep breath and looked around the room. She was dry, and she was becoming warm once more. The storm was outside, and there was no way out even if she wished to try again. She could still read, though, and this story had her addicted. She was finding that when a man was given a heart, it wasn't a casual thing to him. She had warmed to that. It made her feel as if Jeffrey really did go on somewhere, in someone's body, that he had found a life that continued to be lived, and she was finding, to her surprise, or perhaps to her relief, that she was letting him go, that the man she had loved so desperately was becoming a treasured part of her past, but just that. He wasn't her present, and he couldn't be her future.

She was also finding forgiveness, real forgiveness at last. The man who had taken her husband's heart hadn't stolen Jeffrey from her. She had seen that in Peter's story. Instead, she saw that giving up his heart had kept Jeffrey's death from being a senseless tragedy. It was a tragedy, still, but now one with a higher meaning. She hadn't forgotten all those verses she'd learned in her father's church. She just didn't use them much anymore. There was one that she'd always liked. "All things work together for the good of them that love the Lord." Maybe that's the way a transplant patient had to view life. It wasn't his or her fault that someone died. Instead, part of that person was allowed to live on, providing the gift of life to someone who desperately needed it.

She also knew one other thing. She had been attracted to Peter, but she had been afraid, too. She'd blamed it on student-teacher propriety, but she knew better. Now, if she had another chance, if another man walked into her life, she wouldn't let him slip away. She would grab him and hold on. She glanced out the window at the storm beating in fury against the land. She knew that not even a storm such as this would keep them apart. She wouldn't let it. Not again.

Sitting, she laughed, reaching to pat Tee as he looked up. "He's gone, Tee. Your master's gone from me, out chasing his literary dreams. I've started reading his book, and I know he'll be a success. I suppose I can feel that I've been a small part of that, but I must let him go. He might have been mine if I'd let him, but he's not mine now. I wasn't sure enough, and I didn't move fast enough. You're the lucky one." She put her elbow on the arm of the sofa, and she looked at the glass where she'd earlier placed her hand. As the sky flashed brightly in a series of sudden bursts, she saw the print was still there.

Come for me, Peter. Come for your dog.

Her heart called, but that wouldn't happen. She knew

it was impossible. He didn't even know they were here.

THE DARKNESS of the day had reached its silent fingers into the room, and as she sat at the table, Lennie's heart was lifeless. Oh, it was beating away inside of her body, and it was pumping her blood through her veins. It was performing admirably, but it was lifeless all the same.

She blinked and looked out the window. Peter's house sat there, and it was silent and still. She'd grown to love this man, this charming man and the dog he treasured. She knew he was gone, and he'd found a place to board his dog. She wished he had asked her, though. She would have taken the dog in.

For forty years she had moved her hands in that factory, and for forty years it had been the same. Pick this up. Put that there. Pick this up. Put that there. She hadn't cared. Nothing around her had been important.

She flattened the papers in front of her. They were from the Department of the Army. Three of them. All three were the same. *Your son . . . Your son . . . Your husband* . . . and they had never come home. All within weeks of each other. Her life had become a cardboard world that was tasteless and flat.

Lennie pushed her chair back and stood in the near darkness, then she stepped to the counter. Taking a knife from a drawer, she slowly cut a slice of the cake she had made the day before. At nearly eighty, her joints didn't work the way they once had. She pulled a plate from a shelf, and she laid the slice there. With a sigh of resignation, she carried it to the table and resumed her vigil.

Peter's house. He wasn't home, but she had enjoyed

making the cakes once again. She had made them for her sons, and they had eaten them before they could cool. After all the years, she would have thought she'd forgotten how. She hadn't, though. It was all there just like before. She might throw most of this one out, but she would make another. Not today. Tomorrow, perhaps, when the power was back on.

With her fingers, she broke off a piece of the slice of cake, and she slipped it into her mouth. As she chewed, she imagined that the young man she had grown to love as her own was there with her, and she smiled. He was enjoying his own piece of cake, and the room was warm. A big dog was at their feet, and the animal would get a share when they had finished theirs. Then, she would wrap the remains of the cake, and she would send it home with the man she had made it for.

She reached for her plate, and she leaned down to set it on the floor for the dog that wasn't there. Her back hurt as she pulled herself back up, but the pain would go away. What wouldn't go away was the loss of two sons and a husband. What wouldn't go away was an empty house next door, and the longing for a man she had come to love as much as she had ever loved her own sons.

Lennie stood and closed the blinds. In the darkness, she walked the familiar steps to her living room, and she sat. She looked into the darkness, and she was alone. She was always alone.

JOHN SPUN the wheel and threw the throttle forward. Rain flung itself up under the wheelhouse and splattered his slicker with a hollow sound. A white-capped wave tore past the boat as the sea reached and tried to take his storm-fighting craft for a prize.

"Ha!" he exulted. "Huck at me what you will, you can't take down a Maine lobsterman's boat, can you?" He spun the wheel again as another wave came at him from a different direction. The wave rushed past, and the back of his boat was quickly underwater. John surged the engine forward, and the strong craft he had depended on for years jumped ahead, leaping into the air.

He turned the wipers to their highest speed. He had his GPS on, and he knew Penobscot Bay. He also knew if he watched his readouts too closely, something might come at him out of the waves, and his boat would become a rock in the storm, falling straight to the floor of the sea. He had to do this by feel.

As he drew closer to the mainland, he watched for those boats still tied to their moorings. This could be the tricky part. The moorings were heavy, either granite or concrete, but in weather like this, they could be dragged around the seafloor and into the open channels. He knew he couldn't predict just what he might find. In the darkness of the storm, he might be upon something before he could turn away. Even the lights on his own boat were little more than a match flame for him. They lighted the flooding rain and not much else.

Just as he was beginning to wonder if his compass was off, if he was heading out to open sea, he breathed easier. There, between the rising swells, was the Breakwater Light. He would be able to navigate once again. The water might still be rough, and there might be boats moored where boats shouldn't be; John was good, however, and he spun his wheel, throwing his throttle forward and pulling it back again, working his craft like the fine-tuned machine it was. Squinting, he was relieved to see a light still shining by the ferry landing.

"Left John the light on. Good job, Ben." He liked Ben Cutshal, and Ben was a good man, but he'd told John this was a death run. *"Fool. Pull your boat in. Live to see tomorrow."* John hadn't listened, and he wasn't listening, still. Lee needed him.

As he approached the ferry landing, he gunned his engine and then pulled it back. The side of his boat slapped the piers. He was surprised to see the water was nearly to the top of the wharf. Much higher and the town's waterfront would be awash.

Jumping to throw lines around waiting cleats, he tugged them securely. Then, dashing to the building, he threw open the door.

"Ben!" He wanted to get back out as soon as he could. He was surprised to see someone he didn't know sitting across the room. He called to him, "You seen Ben?"

"Are you John?" The man looked at him anxiously. "With the boat?"

"Could be. Why're you asking?" He didn't know this man, and he hoped he wasn't bringing bad news. He'd fought the storm all the way in to get Old Lee's medicines, and he'd be upset if they weren't here. This storm would get worse, he thought, and he wanted home before it did. That or out rescuing his lobster pots.

Peter called, "If you are, I have a package for you." He held up a box. "A man, your Ben, I guess, said it was my ticket to the island." He smiled hopefully.

For a moment, John stood and looked at Peter, evaluating. He didn't know what this man needed, but help should be provided when help was available. John's boat was sitting outside, and it was headed back to Vinalhaven. He pressed his lips tight, and then he cautioned, "It's bad out there, bad as I've ever seen. Can't promise to make it back to the island, and I'm not coming back here. Are you sure you want aboard?" When he saw Peter nod, he broke into action. This man wasn't dressed for the sea, and he ran to a hallway, emerging with a slicker and waterproof boots. He threw them at Peter. "Get dressed while I visit the men's. Be ready when I come out."

Peter did stand ready when he returned. "Ben said to turn out the lights and lock up."

John laughed. "He did? Better do it, then." He reached to the wall, and the building was suddenly dark. In the background, the sound of the generator ceased, and the roar of the storm took over. He looked to the front. "Your truck? Lights are still on."

Peter groaned. He couldn't believe he'd forgotten that. "Running, too, I think." He looked at John, pleading for him to wait just one minute. He couldn't miss this chance to get to Tee.

John slapped his shoulder. "Go fix it. Got that much time. Gives me the chance to lock the door."

Peter stumbled through the building, the only light inside coming from the headlights of his truck. Throwing the door open, he felt John's hand on his arm.

"Come around back." He pointed down the outside of the building. "I'm locking this."

Peter nodded and headed into the maelstrom. Over-

347

joyed at his good luck, he was glad for the slicker. He had just begun to dry out, and maybe he could stay that way.

As he put the keys in his pocket, he slammed the truck door and ran around the building. He saw John waving at him from a boat next to the wharf, and he leaped in.

"Hold on. Rough ride coming up." John pointed to hand grips Peter could use. "You can take purchase there."

Peter leaned in to be heard. "Peter. Name's Peter."

John nodded. "Know where you're going?"

"Crockett Point." The name was torn from his mouth by a blast of wind as the lobster boat leaped from the wharf. "Know where that is?"

"Yup. What do you need there?" John suddenly spun the wheel and hit the throttle hard. Crockett Point was his home turf. It wasn't his, of course, but it had been like his since he was a teen. As a boy, when the family was off island, he'd stayed in one of the sleeping cabins, working during the day to clear brush or paint the houses. It felt like home. He didn't know this man, though, and he didn't understand why he would want to go there in the middle of a hurricane. He glanced over to see his passenger jerk sideways as the boat caught a rogue wave. He was pleased to see he was holding on tight. He'd hate to lose him.

"My dog's there. There was a call from Crockett Point, and the line went dead." The words had to be yelled to be heard.

That sparked John's memories of earlier. *"Another one just like this one, John. My friend and a dog are following."* He immediately thought of a hundred things that could have kept that friend and that dog from making the ferry. There was the road that ran along the edge of

Crockett Cove, and there was the sharp bend to navigate by the pond. In the rain, a wrong turn anywhere could be a nosedive into the cold ocean currents. Someone unfamiliar with the island might not be alive any longer. However, he was a pragmatist, and in his mind, he mentally scratched off number four on his list. In his head, he penciled in new words. *Save the dog.*

He turned to the man at his side, and with confidence he called out, "We'll find your dog. Just hold on."

Peter leaned in, "You know where Crockett Point is?"

John barked out a laugh. "Oh, I know it. It's home."

"I STUMBLED to my bed and lay there, almost unable to breathe."

Jessica was reading aloud again. The storm had grown stronger, and things could be heard hitting the house regularly. Earlier, lightning had flashed, and it had seemed to strike a huge tree she could see through the window. The sound of the thunder had thrown Tee into her lap. She thought she heard the tree fall, but with the other sounds of the storm, she hadn't been for sure. Then, with the next flash of lightning, she could tell. The tree was gone.

She sniffed. The wind was causing the stove to occasionally belch smoke back into the house. It wasn't bad, yet, but she knew she had to keep an eye on it. She returned to the book.

"Rachel was gone. I was a man with three university degrees, one in divinity, for God's sake, and my heart was failing. My wife couldn't take it, and she had chosen to leave. I was alone."

Jessica closed the book, holding her place with her finger, and turned to Tee, rubbing his fur. She blinked away her tears as she looked at him. Laughing softly, she whispered, "At some point he got you, Tee. I would've been there for him. I wouldn't have left him alone." Yet, she knew that was a lie. She *had* left him alone. Mags had said that to her. That first day he hadn't shown up in class, she'd gone into the hallway, and she had wailed her distress to her friend. After two weeks, she hadn't even tried to find him. She had simply run away.

If only he'd tried to contact her, just to leave a message. Mags had suggested the flashing light on her phone might have been a message from him, but then they'd gone to her parents' for the weekend; and when she'd returned, she'd cleared her messages without listening to a one, finally stacking some papers on the phone. If the message were important, they'd try again. Anyway, that wouldn't have been him. He'd have come by to see her. She knew he would. He'd been in class that morning. He could have talked to her then.

She took a deep breath and sighed. She jumped as a branch hit the window beside her, but it held. She heard the tinkling of glass somewhere else in the house, but she ignored that. She couldn't do anything about it, anyway.

She opened the book again. She looked at how far she'd read, and on an impulse, she turned toward the end, rifling the pages until she located the final chapter. Pausing, she let her eyes find the lamp's flame, and she watched it for a moment. She glanced at the dog lying at her side before reading again. He was watching her. She put aside a twinge of guilt at her actions.

"I'm sorry, Tee. I want to know the final part of the

story. I promise I'll come back and read what I've skipped." She smiled at him and ran her fingers over the fur between his eyes. Then her focus drifted back to the pages she held in her hands.

The storm wasn't letting up, and neither was Peter's tale.

MAGS' FINGERS struggled as she tapped the keys on her cell phone. She could barely control her hands. When she was finished, she held it to her ear.

"Yes?" The voice that answered sounded old and tired.

"Auntie, I was so scared." Mags could barely speak, and she stopped to catch her breath.

"Magenta, is that you? Did you get off?" Her aunt was suddenly brighter, as if she had been worried for this favorite niece of hers.

"He came, Auntie. I didn't tell him where to go, though. He doesn't know, and there's no way back." Mags was distraught, emotions flashing through her head in a kaleidoscope of images, and she could barely get her words out. She had held on as the ferry had battled the waves, and she didn't see how anyone could have made it back to help her friend. Anyone who tried would now be lost against the rising storm, buried at the bottom of the sea.

"Who, dear? You did all get away?"

"No, Auntie. Jessica's still there, with his dog."

"Whose dog? Magenta, think. Who came? Whose dog is with your friend?"

Mags sniffed. "Peter's dog, the man she loves." Then she wailed, "He might die, and she doesn't even know he came to find her."

THE PUBLISHER'S rep sat on the plane and brooded. He was in a pickle. He had been following this story for two years, and he had begged for it. It would be his rising star, his personal ticket to more wealth and prestige than he'd conjured up with any other author he'd ever signed. He remembered the day he had seen the reports in the papers. From the first headline, he knew this story needed to be in print. If he could chase this down, he could ride it with the profits it would bring in. Now, his story had gone to Vinalhaven Island, of all places. He pressed his lips tightly together, forming a line that turned the skin around his mouth white. This man was under contract, and this was Frank's opportunity, the opportunity most authors clamored for and never got. How could Cassel walk away from Chicago, after New York had been such a resounding success?

Vinalhaven. At least he'd managed to hear that before he'd been forced to run for his flight.

He'd googled it just to find out where the island was. That had made him sick to his stomach. In the Atlantic, off the Maine coast, and more importantly, it was directly in the path of that early-season hurricane.

Once the plane had gotten in the air, he'd called the main office. They'd been sore, telling him all the acrid things he'd hated hearing others in his company endure for years. He'd gotten cocky, he knew, over the past decade. He was the man with the golden touch. Now, he was eating crow. His gold had just turned to lead, that was for certain. He had to figure out how to get this man back, to get him here safely. Chicago, if possible. Anywhere, if necessary.

He snapped his fingers with a flash of brilliance, as he remembered he'd done a book for a Coast Guard commodore a few years back, maybe eight or ten. Nobody'd wanted to publish it. Wouldn't touch it. Frank had liked it, though. His dad had been Coast Guard years before and had even served under the old man. Frank had desperately wanted it published for his dad's sake.

He'd gone to bat for the book, even when the big bosses had tried to knock him down. "Irascible," they'd said. "Nobody'll read it. We'll be crucified." Frank hadn't bought that. He'd known who would read the book. Anyone military. Those in boating. People who lived on storm-ravaged coasts. They had, too. From an initial printing of 57,500 copies, the numbers had grown and grown. The last time he'd checked, there were a total of 787,000 copies in print.

Maybe the old buzzard could still pull a few strings out of gratitude. Frank slid down in his seat and pulled his cell phone out. He wasn't supposed to do this during the flight, but he didn't see how a cell signal could affect the plane's guidance system. He didn't want the airline tracking his calls, either. Plus, his contact numbers were all in his personal phone, and people might not pick up if they didn't see his caller ID on the display. He scrolled through his phone book, then he clicked on one number in particular. It started to ring. "Pick up, pick up, pick up." Frank glanced around to see if anyone was noticing he wasn't using the airline's phone. He was glad to see everyone else sleeping or otherwise occupied. Even the attendants were visiting at the front.

"Good morning! Goodbody Publishing House. We open the world to you. How may I direct your call?"

Frank was relieved. Gwen was at the switchboard. She had worked with him on the Coast Guard project.

"Gwen, this is Frank." He glanced at his watch. "Morning?"

"Hey, golden fingers." There was a pause, then she giggled in an embarrassed way, sounding as though she was more interested in Frank than whatever he'd called about. "Do you want me to start over? The clock is just about to change, but you must be on Central Time, already. How's this: Good afternoon! Goodbody Publishing House—"

"Gwen," he interrupted. "It was just a question. I don't need you to start over, but my watch says three." His words had grown terse, and he made an effort to relax. He needed Gwen's help. "Are you busy?"

"You know," she breathed, "I'm never too busy for you, Frank." She was off again, though, her words filled with enthusiasm. "So, it's two here?" She laughed lightly. "Look at the clock on my desk. Batteries. They never work when you need them to. Oh, my!" She giggled. "There on my phone it does say two. Oh, hold on, Frank." Bright pop music filled the line for a minute, and then Gwen was back. "Sorry. I had to take that. How's our heart transplant? I hear New York was a major success. Are you on the flight to Chicago, yet? The lines are buzzing. Everyone wants this guy in person. Lucky you, Frank." Her voice sounded pleasant and charming. She was, too. Frank knew that.

"Listen, Gwen. I *am* on that plane to Chicago—"

She was suddenly breathless, breaking in, "Can I talk

354

with him, Frank? I saw the mockup of the book. That cover was so cute, the one with the kid's drawing of the dog. Please, Frank?"

"Gwen, you didn't hear everything. *I* am on that plane to Chicago. However, he isn't—"

She interrupted again, and she sounded appalled, "Oh, my God, Frank! He died, didn't he? God, Frank, that is the most awful thing!"

"Gwen! Chill your panties! He's alive. That's part of it. He's too much alive, and that's the problem. He's gone off on his own to a place you couldn't guess." He paused for effect. "Try, Gwen."

"Um," she said. "Tahiti?"

"Gwen," Frank hissed. "Why Tahiti?"

"That's where I'd go," she burbled, quite happy now that she knew this new author wasn't dead.

"He's gone to Vinalhaven Island, Gwen." He expected her to exclaim in dismay. However, she saw it very differently.

"An island. Like Tahiti! How romantic! I'm pleased for him." Then she paused, and he could hear a beeping in the background. "Frank, I have another call."

"Let it go, Gwen. Vinalhaven Island is off the Maine coast, and that hurricane is about to hit." He paused to see if she was finally catching on.

"Hurricane, Frank? That big one?"

He sighed in relief. "Yes, Gwen. That big one."

"Oh, Frank. We have to do something."

He smiled. He could hear the anguish in her voice, and he knew if he could see her face, her eyes would already be turning red. Gwen was a miracle worker. She knew everyone and had all the phone numbers. He liked to claim success for the commodore's book, but there were times he allowed himself to admit it had been as much Gwen as him.

"Gwen, that's why I called you. Remember that Coast Guard commodore about a decade back? You helped me with his book. It seems he had a nephew or a cousin or something who had some sort of transplant. Kidney or liver. We'll see if he still has the big guns to pull our writer out of the fire. Are you seeing the picture I'm trying to paint?"

Gwen was once again breathless. "You're a scoundrel. You know that? I see where you're going. The Coast Guard will rescue anyone. However, this man might be able to pull the strings to get them out specially to rescue *our* guy. Our *transplant* guy."

Frank chortled. "Gwen, you're my girl."

"But, exactly where is he on this island?"

Frank was silent for a moment. "I'm not sure. I'm working on that. You just get that commodore and get back with me."

"Sure. I'll do that."

Frank wasn't completely sure Peter would even *be* on the island. However, he'd never be able to rescue him if he didn't get the ball rolling now.

That's why he was brooding once again.

Chapter 22

JESSICA TURNED to the last page in Peter's book. The fire had burned low, and the storm continued to batter the house, now more ferociously than ever. She hadn't paid attention to any of it. All she could see were the events in the story she held in her hands. He'd told of things she hadn't known, and he told of things she did. Several times, she knew beyond a doubt he was telling the story of her own Jeffrey, and then she would convince herself he wasn't.

When she read the part that told of the woman he'd met, she'd known this was a man in love. Then she'd turned the page and read of Mags and herself. That was when she realized she was the woman in the tale. The final page was what tore her sobs from her and convinced her she had to find this man again, no matter the cost. It was in the final line that the truth of Peter's story bared itself to her.

"Now you know who I share my body with. If you sit and speak with me, you're holding a conversation with two men. If you reach to hug me close, you're also holding Jeffrey Jay."

When her sobs had ceased, she opened the book one last time. At the bottom of that final page was the tagline she knew so well. *"Play by Play."* Underneath that were the words, *"For Jeffrey Jay."*

She turned as Tee raised his head. She smiled when his ears perked up, and then he began to howl. She turned to look around as she heard an increasingly high-pitched wail from the wind outside. Then, through the windows, as a bolt of lightning flashed across the sky, she could see what had gotten the dog's attention. A section of one of the huge spruce trees had torn loose. It was tumbling through the air and coming directly at the house.

DOCTOR ROSSI took the call. She was at home, and it surprised her when the hospital operator asked if he could transfer a personal call to her number. It wasn't unusual to be called on her days off, but to have a personal call transferred in? That was very unusual, indeed.

"Gwen with Goodbody Publishing? You say this concerns Peter Cassel?" Doctor Rossi quizzed the caller. This was the only reason she'd agreed to this. This young man was a concern that she held dear to her heart, and if it concerned him, then she owed it to herself to at least check it out. "I thought he was on a tour with your publishing company."

"Yes, Doctor Rossi. However, we seem to have misplaced Mr. Cassel."

The doctor cleared her throat. "Misplaced? Can you please explain that?"

Gwen laughed with her most disarming phrase, "Of course I can do that for you." Then she laughed one more time. "He's gone to Vinalhaven Island."

The doctor breathed easily again. "So, he's not misplaced. He's on vacation, right? It will probably do him good."

Gwen cautioned her, "Doctor, you don't understand. This is Vinalhaven Island, Maine."

With those words, the doctor did understand, and very quickly. She had been following the reports. Her hospital was teamed with others across the New England coast, and they were preparing for a massive injection of aid as soon as the storms cleared. She just didn't know the names of each one of the hundreds of islands off the New England seaboard.

"Maine. Do you know why he's there?"

Gwen paused. "The real question we would like you to help us with is where. Can you give us any suggestions?"

Doctor Rossi paused, thinking. "I can only point you in a new direction, and I don't know if it's the right one. At one time he mentioned two names. Both were in connection with a class he was taking at Clark University to help with his book. When he had his latest setback, he spoke of these people as if he knew them quite well, or at least one of them. I only jotted down their first names, but the university might be able to give you more information."

"Doctor, that's better than what we've learned anywhere else. Thank you. If you could give me those names?"

"Let me see," she said. "I take notes on everything, you understand. Ah, here it is. Ask about a Jessica and a Mags. Yes. Those are the names, Jessica and Mags."

"I'm sorry, Doctor. Are you sure there's no chance you happen to know the last names of these two people?"

She chuckled. "I'm lucky to have the first names. I'm not a detective, Gwen."

The voice on the phone pressed her with one more question. "Is it possible either of these women work at the university?"

Doctor Rossi shook her head. She knew it couldn't be seen over the line, but she did it anyway. Habit, she supposed. "I don't know, Gwen. I assumed Jessica did, but in honesty, I don't know. Perhaps if you call the university."

"Do you have that number?"

"No, I'm afraid. It's just Clark University, Worcester. That's Massachusetts."

"Thank you, Doctor Rossi. I'll try to make that call."

After she hung up, the doctor looked at her phone. That was a most unusual call. Hadn't Peter mentioned his professor's last name? She knew she should have written it down. However, she could help, perhaps. She had other resources. After all, she and the provost had attended university together decades before. She had her home number, too. If anyone could help, then she would be the one to pull into play.

"ROOSTER, ARE you in there?" A knock came at the glass-infused door. When there was no answer, the voice tried again. "Rooster Argyle! Don't you try to hide from me. This is important."

An old, gnarled hand reached to the knob, and through the glass, it could be seen twisting it open. A face haloed by thick, white hair with full, bushy brows appeared from behind the massive slab.

"Babs, you're interrupting my private time. What do you need?"

Babs gave a *harrumph* of a sound, and she backed away. "I don't need anything from you, sir. Someone else does. If you want to know what it is, you can come to the phone." She turned and waddled down the hall. She was as wide as she was tall, and her knees tended to bend poorly. She muttered to herself as she strode away, "I should have listened to Mother. Marrying into the service was a bad idea."

"Babs, wait! Someone needs me? Who?" Rooster threw the door wide, and he shuffled down the hall after her as fast as he could. "Babs!"

When he got to the living room, he glanced out through the wall of glass to the shore. The lawn was perfectly cut, and the trees were lined up in an orderly fashion, each one trimmed at least eight feet from the ground. There were no dead branches, either. If a storm came through Rooster's property, it would have to take an entire tree to have anything to blow around.

His and Babs' grandkids were playing on the dock. The children were in their trunks, and two of his grandsons were picking up their sister and preparing to toss her into the water. "No life jackets," Rooster muttered, as he walked along. "They can probably swim, though. The older boy must be in college, and surely the younger's about to go." He muttered that he wasn't certain about the girl, as these were his youngest's kids, and he hadn't been able to keep up with their ages.

"The phone, Babs. Where's the phone?" he called into the emptiness of the room.

She waddled forward to poke her head in the door. "It's on the desk where it always is. Rooster, are you thinking clearly today?" When she saw him pick it up, she turned to go back to her business. However, when she was out of sight, she stopped to listen.

"Yes? Yes? Oh, I see. I know Vinalhaven. A hurricane, you say? New England? Heart transplant? He wrote about it? My God! We must save him. My nephew had a transplant one time. Jerry. That's my nephew. A leg or an eye or something. We must save this boy." He slammed down the phone. "Babs! They need me. The Coast Guard needs to save someone, and I have to help. God, this feels good. Someone needs me."

In the hallway, so low he couldn't hear, Babs muttered, "I'm glad someone does, Rooster Argyle."

"SCORTIO'S. This is Paul speaking. Our special of the day is sautéed onion in bisque sauce. How may I schedule your reservation?"

The voice on the line was very bright. "Paul? Paul Rizzo?"

"Yes, this is Paul. How may I assist you this morning?"

"This is Provost Binghamton. I have a question about Dr. Jessica Johansen and a friend of hers named Mags. I understand you know them."

Paul's blood froze, and the phone slipped out of his hands. He grabbed for it as it skittered across the floor. On his knees when he finally caught it, he put it to his ear, his voice shaking. "Yes, Provost Binghamton. They come in and eat here regularly. Am I in tr . . . what have I . . . how can I help you?" He knew he was in dire straits now, and he couldn't help stumbling over his words.

When another employee looked in to see what the disturbance was, Paul grinned weakly and gave him a thumbs up from his kneeling position on the floor. The other employee just raised his hands in front of him as if he didn't want to know what it was all about, and he backed out the door. Paul turned his attention back to the phone.

The provost chuckled. "Are you all right, young man? I understand you're a student at our school. Is that so?"

He cleared his throat. "Yes, ma'am, I am."

"None of that Southern foolery. Just yes or no will do. I'm attempting to locate either Dr. Johansen or her friend, Mags. I'm told you may be able to help me."

Paul's heart began to settle. Apparently, she wasn't calling to attack him, and he fell easily back into his cordial waiter mode. "Mags' surname is Brier-Sheldon, Provost. I believe they went together to Ms. Brier-Sheldon's family home on Vinalhaven Island, Maine."

"I know that much, Paul. Can you tell me anything more specific? I understand Vinalhaven is quite large, and the Coast Guard could get lost out there."

He cleared his throat, leaning his head back against a cabinet that held the menus. "Provost, you might have them try Crockett Point. They were there this morning."

"Ah, thank you. You've been most helpful. By the way, Paul. I understand you work quite a few hours at Scortio's each week and still pull down outstanding grades. This fall, I believe you should have the opportunity to apply yourself fully to your studies. Please see me tomorrow. I believe I can access some scholarship funds that need to be spent."

Butterflies tripped through Paul's stomach. He took a deep breath. "Thank you, Provost. I'll certainly do that." After he hung up, he pulled himself to his feet. His knees were weak, and he held to the counter as he stood immobile for a moment. Scholarship. He smiled. Then the phone rang, and he picked it up.

"Scortio's. This is Paul speaking. Our special of the day is sautéed onion in bisque sauce. How may I schedule your reservation?"

Tomorrow he might have a scholarship, but today he had to work. Not many people had come in with so much of the city blacked out, but he was still getting paid, and that was what counted.

JESSICA SCREAMED and threw herself over Tee. The tree slammed into the house, and the structure vibrated under the onslaught. The very network of branches that softened the blow of the tree as it crashed against the building, keeping it from breaking through the century-old structure, was the same one that shattered the windows and flung shards of glass across the room.

When Jessica looked up, the house still stood around her, but water blasted in through the broken window openings. She looked at the fire as it continued to burn, sputtering as the water swept over it in repeated bursts of wind-driven fury. Within moments, she could see its life fading away.

The lamp was still lighted, and she grabbed it in her hand. Looking at the damage, she stood, considering. Locating the fire-starter wand, she grabbed it, knowing there was wood in the kitchen. It was on the front side of the house, and perhaps she could take refuge there.

Shaking the glass from her clothes, she moved to the dining room door, calling Tee. She stepped through, and when Tee was beside her, she closed it, shutting off the intruding storm. She was truly frightened, now. If this house were taken, there was no way for her to survive. She could go to the smaller house, perhaps. However, if this house went, what would keep the other from the same fate?

She looked to see Tee's eyes on her. He was shivering. She knelt and put the lamp on the floor, then she wrapped her arms around him.

"I bet you wish you had your Peter here to protect you now." She put her face against his fur, and she could smell the frightened dog smell of him. She raised her head and let out a quavering laugh. "I want Peter here, too. However, it's just you and me. Let's go find us a warm room."

She walked him into the kitchen, which was at least dry, and she knelt to fill the stove with kindling, topping it off with wood. She held the starter wand close and pulled the trigger until the fire caught. With the flames blazing, there was soon heat rising into the room. She laughed when she saw another starter wand beside the stove. It was the one she had used to cook the pie. She'd forgotten all about it.

Jessica placed the lamp on the kitchen table, and she sat on the floor beside Tee. As the room continued to warm, she lay down next to him and draped her arm over the softness of his fur. After the events of the day, her exhaustion was both mental as well as physical, and with the comfort of Tee's body, her mind began to relax. Soon, in the relative safety of the kitchen, she slept.

"I THOUGHT it was bad going in." John's voice jerked as the lobster boat slammed into another wave. He yanked the wheel as a rising wall of water reared its dark fist over them. Then he slammed the throttle hard as the boat plowed its bow through the unforgiving darkness. Water surged around the wheelhouse, and it flooded the deck at their feet.

"How much farther?" Peter yelled. He had no experience with this island, and it seemed to be in the middle of nowhere. Surely they hadn't missed it. The battering of the waves against the boat was taking a toll on his body as well as his nerves. In the flashes of lightning that tore the sky, all he could see was the thrashing sea. He didn't know how anyone could tell their way in this. He would hate to find they had bypassed their destination and were tackling the open ocean. Back at the ferry landing, John's boat had seemed large and ready for the raging waves. Now, it felt tiny and very insecure.

"See? The lighthouse there? Brown's Head. It's on the back side of the Point." John pointed and then immediately grabbed the wheel to steady the boat. "We just keep right. Watch the shoals just near. Tides's running high, so it's probably not a problem. Hit, though, and we're gone."

With his free hand, Peter grabbed John's shoulder and leaned in to his ear. "Let's not hit, then."

John laughed. "Sure, that is! I'm with you on that!"

THE COAST GUARD vessel moored at Coast Guard Station Rockland shuddered. The Keeper Class Tender was firmly lashed down, and barring a tidal wave, it would be there for rescue as soon as the storm lessened. The commanding officer grabbed his coffee as the ship heeled to port. He held it a minute, then the ship settled, and he dared to set it down. He glanced at his pants to see a stain from earlier that he hadn't been able to remove with the damp cloth he'd had available. He hadn't grabbed his coffee fast enough last hour, and now he had that to show for it.

Behind him on a shallow console were a number of mementos of his life, ones he enjoyed keeping on view. There were several military ribbons, and an antique gun given him by his father. One of his most treasured items was a framed bullet he'd had removed from his leg after a teenage hunting accident gone awry. Off to one side was his picture taken just after that accident. His face was the unlined and unshaven innocence of youth. He had on old-fashioned swimming trunks, and one leg sported a rather large and cumbersome bandage. He was leaning on a pair of crutches, standing on a float that looked very much like the one at the end of the Crockett Point dock. A cinnamon-haired girl of about ten stood off to one side holding a live lobster. She had a broad smile on her face. The sun in the picture was bright, and her eyes seemed to rest on the older boy. It was clear she worshipped him.

The CO looked up as a face appeared in his view. A hand shot out, and a paper was on his desk. Just as quickly, the face was gone. Good. That's the way he'd told them. Until the storm's over, don't talk to me. Don't salute or please or thank you. Keep it simple. His crew was doing it, too.

"Crockett Point. Vinalhaven Island." He read the words just to hear them aloud. There was a rescue to attempt. He glanced at the coordinates. He didn't need that, though. He'd grown up there during summer vacations. His distant cousin by marriage, Mags Brier-Sheldon, still owned the Point. He could find Crockett Cove and the Point in the darkest hour of any storm. He hoped his cousin and her aunt across the cove had been smart enough to get out before the storm. However, obviously, someone hadn't.

He glanced at the bottom of the paper. He smiled. He liked what he saw there. *By special request, Commodore Rooster Argyle, USCG (Retired).* Good for him. He missed the old man, and he was glad to see him back in action.

He leaned his head back and closed his eyes. Now if the storm would just ease, they'd get there. They couldn't go out now, though. It just wouldn't do for the Coast Guard to go down. Then, who'd rescue everyone else?

"IT'S THERE, man. Do you see it?" John grinned, pointing. "Crockett Cove."

However, Peter had no idea what he was looking for. He could see rain-washed rocks, and he could see waves that looked like rain-washed rocks. How this man told the difference, he didn't know.

"I trust you," he called back. He had to. He had no control here. At this point, even if Tee was here on Crockett Point, he had no idea what he'd do once he found him. This man piloting this boat wasn't prepared to return him to Rockland. If anyone would like to know the truth, Peter wasn't prepared to return to Rockland, not through this storm. Surely this island wouldn't blow away no matter how bad the weather. Whatever happened next, he expected they'd be stranded here together.

"Water'll be calmer in the cove. Wait and see." John nodded as he rounded an outcrop of rock.

The water wasn't calm, but it was less violent, and Peter called out, "At least we don't have water around our feet. Think the storm's letting up?"

"Not likely. The Point blocks the wind. The lee side'll give us a bit of a breather." He pushed the throttle forward, and the lobster boat surged forward in the darkness. In the lights of the boat, the end of a dock appeared. It didn't seem to be attached to the shore, though, almost as if it were moored in the middle of the cove.

Peter asked, "Is that thing supposed to be floating out here?" He pointed. It was the large box at the end of Mags' dock. It had sides, and there were handrails that led off into the water.

"Can't believe this," John said to himself. "Float's gone. Ramp, too. Never made it out to pull them in. Dock's still there, at least. Just never saw it underwater before. Might be tricky to tie up." He pointed up the hill to where a white house could be seen in the occasional flashes of lightning, and he yelled, "Crockett House."

Peter grinned. "My dog."

John nodded his head in a quick jerk of assent. His next words were for himself, though. "Maybe," he muttered. "Hope so, anyway." Then he turned his head as he worked the controls on his boat.

"Looks home free, to me." Peter was ecstatic.

They weren't to the dock yet, John cautioned, and while the water was better here than it had been out in Penobscot's open water, it was still rough enough. If he couldn't do this, it wouldn't matter if the dog were here or not. The men who had come to rescue it would both be dead. That wouldn't do. Plus, John still had the medicine to deliver. He had to do this, and he had to do it well.

FRANK WAS chomping at the bit. The plane was finally down in Chicago, and he'd had the best idea he'd ever come up with. It was brilliant, in fact. However, he needed into the airport to call Gwen. She had one more job to do.

Finally finished disembarking, he found the first seat he could, and he pulled out his phone. He dialed the number to the main office.

"Good afternoon! Goodbody Publishing House. We open the world—"

Frank interrupted, "Crystal, is that you?"

"Frank? Golden Fingers Frank? Yes, this is Crystal. What can I do for *you?*" She purred the words into the phone.

"Crystal, transfer me to Gwen. Pronto." He had no time to waste.

Crystal wasn't so fast. "Frank," she whined. "You owe

me a date."

He thought fast on his feet, and there was only one way to get this done. "Great, Crystal. You've got it if you get me to Gwen in thirty seconds."

She laughed, charmed. "Sure, Frank. It's a deal." Then she was gone.

Another voice came on the line. "Frank? I'm surprised to hear from you again so soon."

"Yeah, thanks for the help you've given." She'd already done everything he'd asked, and he knew it hadn't been easy. She did still have switchboard duties, and had told him she'd been forced to fit in his special requests between her own work.

"What is it, Frank?"

"Gwen . . ." He paused for a moment, chuckling.

"Yes, Frank?" She nearly giggled on her end of the line, and it came through as an aborted hiccup.

"Gwen, I have the best idea for this rescue." He'd done some calling of his own back on the plane, and he knew a few things, now.

"Is this about that transplant man on that island?"

He laughed. "Sure. That transplant man. See, it's all here, the perfect promo for this book he's written. It'll appeal to everyone. See it this way. A man gets a heart transplant. At the same time, he gets a puppy and names it Transplant."

Gwen interrupted, "He did that? How sweet!"

Frank laughed at her response. "He really did that. I didn't make that one up. Now, listen. The dog gets lost on a remote island in a hurricane."

Gwen interrupted again, "The dog did *that*? Really?"

Frank coughed. "I'm not sure about the lost part, but he's going after the dog. Now, we've got the Coast Guard picking them up, that is if this Peter actually made it out there and found the dog. How perfect is this? It can go on the book jacket."

"That's sweet, Frank. But what proof will you have? Like Jack Kennedy's WWII exploits, he had witnesses. You need proof to put it in print."

Frank's voice got low and serious. "That's gotta be your part, Gwen, the other thing I need you to do. We need a photographer on that Coast Guard ship, and as soon as possible. Picture the ship pulling up after the hurricane. The island is wrecked, and there's Cassel, holding his dog. It'll kill the show, Gwen."

She paused. "But, what if he's not holding the dog, Frank? We won't get the picture, then."

Frank laughed. "Who'll we send that can get there in time? Trevor Rice . . . no, he's in Upstate New York, running from the storm. Hmm, Gwen?"

"There's Stefanie Tremont. She lives in Mid-Coast Maine. Camden, I think. On my map, it shows that's right by the Coast Guard station in Rockland." A faint, repetitive, staccato sound bled through over the line.

Even though he couldn't see her, Frank knew Gwen was tapping her pencil eraser on her desk, her mind thinking. Suddenly, he realized just what she was suggesting. He hooted, "Gwen, you're brilliant! Stefanie Tremont on a ship full of men? She'll have them eating out of her hand. Get on the phone, Gwen. Call Argyle back, if you have to. Let's get some pictures."

"Yes, sir," she barked. She was laughing, though.

Frank's enthusiasm always got her worked up, even though she often wound up doing most of the work.

Chapter 23

JESSICA WOKE up cold. Tee was snoring quietly despite the rain pelting the house. The fire in the stove had burned low, and she drew herself up on her elbow. The wind still beat against the windows, and the floor vibrated continuously with a low-pitched hum. That puzzled her until she remembered this part of the house had been a later addition, and it rested on granite blocks rather than the foundation that girded the rest of the structure. Somehow, that didn't make her feel any more secure than she'd felt five minutes before. She was certain it had gotten darker outside until she caught sight of the lamp. The flame was sputtering, and it was clear that the wick needed to be trimmed. She reached to adjust the dial, causing the light to leap into the room.

Working quickly, Jessica opened the stove and dropped several small logs of wood inside. Rubbing her hands for warmth, she felt the heat rise with the stirring of the coals. After a minute, she replaced the cover and sat back by Tee. She noticed his eyes looking at her, and then she remembered the book in the other room.

"Tee," she cried, dismayed she hadn't brought it with her. "I have to get Peter's book. The chapters I skipped. What if it's his only copy? It'll be ruined."

She stood and picked up the lamp. Moving quickly, she stepped into the dining room and reached to open the living room door. When she grabbed the knob, the door rattled in its frame. Wind whistled around the edges, and Jessica's heart throbbed in response. After a minute, it quieted, and she twisted the knob.

However, the winds had lessened only by comparison. The strength of the hurricane force winds whipping through the broken windows blew it back at her, throwing her to the wall. The sudden thrust of the door flung the lamp from her hand, and the glass oil reservoir shattered on the floor, flinging the liquid across the room.

Tee jumped back into the kitchen and began barking ferociously as the burning wick ignited the oil, and the flames whipped across the spreading fuel.

"Tee!" yelled Jessica, horrified. This was a disaster worse than the storm. The house was at least still here, even with the attempts of the hurricane to tear it from its foundations. Even the tree hadn't been able to do more than break a few windows, and the storm would have to end sometime. If she could just hold on, it would soon be over. It had been hours, already. However, if she didn't stop this fire, this century-old structure would burn to the ground with her inside.

As the flames continued to spread across the floor, the room flared into brightness, and Jessica remembered the throws from the living room. There had been a trunk of them under one of the windows. If she could get them, she could use them to smother the fire.

With Tee barking furiously at the flames, as if his very enthusiasm could beat them back, Jessica threw herself into the blinding sprays of water that blasted repeatedly through the living room's broken windows. Struggling with the branches protruding through the jagged shards of glass remaining in the window frames, she felt past the flickering shadows cast by the burning oil, and she struggled to grasp the throws, only to find that they were soaked. Crying out as unexpected glass fragments dug into her palms, she slipped on the water-soaked floor, and she dropped the sodden cloth. With a desperate cry, she pushed a dripping chair aside and dragged the pile of waterlogged fabric across the wooden floor.

Smoke had begun to fill the air as she threw the first blanket onto the dining room floor. She gasped as she watched the water-filled fabric hit the burning oil, only to splatter it up the wall, creating even more sources of flame. She knew there had to be a different way to put out the fire. She stood, and she struggled to unfold the second blanket as she felt additional pain shoot through her hands. Slivers of glass from the broken windows had become embedded throughout the cloth. Stepping inside to place the wet blanket more carefully on the oil, she realized she could no longer breathe through the smoke that filled the room.

Choking, she dropped the blanket and retreated to the living room. She was separated from Tee, smoke was filling the house, and she knew the wooden structure would soon be an inferno.

At the top of her lungs, she screamed out, "Tee! I need you to come to me. I need you." When he didn't appear, she looked across the room, seeing dancing shadows filling the space, wondering just how things could have gone so wrong. In desperation, she pictured the man she had been reading about, and despair swept through her. In anguish, she cried out, "I need you, Peter." She sank to the floor in exhaustion, tears filling her eyes, knowing the foolishness of her desperate plea. He was nowhere near. She was alone, and there was no one else. She felt all hope leave her, and quietly, to herself, she whispered, "I need anyone."

"JO-JEEZLY, THE wind's justa wailing. We've taken the long way round Robin Hood's barn, but we're there. We'll tie her here," John shouted. He pulled up to the box. The lights from the boat showed the dock was still there, just buried under a foot of water. "It's built on granite pilings. If anything holds, it will."

Peter looked to see how far the dock ran to the shore, and then his eyes caught the house. Brightly flickering light could clearly be seen in the windows of one room in the center of the building. It was the red and yellow of raw flames. He was sure it hadn't been there moments before. He grabbed John's arm.

"The house is burning." He pointed. "We must get there."

John assessed the situation. "It's from the dining room. Help me tie the boat." He looked up at the lights shining across the dock. "Those can stay on. Without them, we're lost. Then, we must take care of that fire."

With quick, sure motions, he stretched lines and wrapped them around posts that extended out of the water, thrusting into the air several feet above the half walls of the box. When he was satisfied his boat was secure, he grabbed a flashlight.

"Let's go. Follow me. We might yet save the house."

The water was cold on the dock, and Peter found that the walkway sloped down as it approached shore. They were quickly chest deep. With John flashing his light to illuminate the way as they approached the shore, Peter noticed one small building that was half under water. Off to the right was a large boathouse, and the doors swung back and forth as the waters surged in and out. He was surprised both hadn't washed away already.

The climb to the house soon took them out of the water, and in brilliant flashes of lightning, they could see branches from the towering spruce trees that had been broken and flung across the walkway, forcing them to go around. Ahead, the light from the fire grew brighter, and the windows in the house stood out in the darkness. The faster they moved, the more they slipped and struggled on the flooded grass and the mud that oozed from underneath their feet.

John stopped and listened. "A dog! Do you hear it?" Against the fury of the storm, the sharp bark of an animal fought for supremacy.

"It's Tee!" Peter surged ahead, knowing that if he

didn't get there in time, his beloved pet might die as the fire spread. He couldn't watch the house collapse in flames with Tee inside. Reaching the building, he rushed to the uncovered windows to see a room filled with flames. As he stood there, he heard a woman's voice yell over the barking of the dog.

"I need you." There was a short pause, and the voice called out once again. "I need you, Peter."

TRENT'S MOTHER stirred in the mugginess of the Massachusetts heat. The lights were still out, but she could see a bit. At least the room wasn't in total darkness, anymore. She reached beside her to touch her son only to find the bedding empty.

"Trent?" She listened. "Trent, are you there?" She shifted to sit on the bed. Just then a small form walked through the door. She called softly to him, "Trent, what have you been doing?"

He walked to her and grabbed her hand. "Come and see, Mummy." He pulled her until she stood and followed him to the next room. There on the table was a small, thin candle, and it was burning softly, fighting back the darkness.

"Baby, where did you find a candle? We were out." She walked with him to the table to see a plate with the remains of several burned birthday candles. "Baby, you should have asked."

"I was careful, Mummy. I saved my birthday candles. I burned one at a time."

His mother knelt to hug him. "Why, Trent? Why did you burn them?"

He reached to the table. "Didn't you look, Mummy? I did it for Transplant. I wanted him to be safe."

"How, Trent, baby? What did you do?" She stood to look at the paper in the center of the table, shifting it to catch the light of the candle. It was his picture of the hurricane.

"I drew Jesus, Mummy. I drew Jesus, and now Transplant will be safe."

Trent's mother grabbed her son with both arms. She picked him up and hugged him tightly. "I love you, baby. I love you very much."

He whispered back, "I know. Do you love Transplant?"

"Yes, Trent, I do." She chuckled, but she could feel tears in her eyes for this boy who would get up in the dark to draw a picture to protect someone else's dog.

Trent leaned his head in real close. "And Transplant's master, and Jesus?"

She swung him around. "All of them. I love all of them, Trent."

He whispered, "I love you most of all, Mummy."

Just then the lights flickered once, and after a moment of continued darkness, they came on and stayed. In the silence of the moment, they could hear the small window unit in the bedroom click on and begin to hum.

Trent's mother whispered to him, "It looks like Jesus loves us, too."

With his face pressed tightly to hers, she could feel him smile. "I know Mummy. I thought you knew, too."

"I did, baby. I just guess it took you to remind me."

JOHN CLUTCHED Peter by the arm and pulled him away from the window. He pointed with his hand toward the front porch and the shadow of a doorway just visible in the darkness.

"The front door is just there. Follow me. We must get inside."

Together they stumbled up the steps to the wide, covered porch. Finally out of the worst of the driving rain, John pulled Peter to the entrance, and he flung open the front door. The entry hall and staircase were free of flames. The smell of smoke was strong, though. Just to the left was the closed door to the dining room. They could see light flickering underneath. However, straight ahead, the living room danced with shadows, and in flashes of lightning, they could see the shattered windows across the back of the house. Wind-driven water blasted the room.

John stopped Peter. "I could see no flames in the kitchen windows. I know this house. There's an extinguisher in there. I'm dripping wet. I can run through and get it. It'll put this fire out, but I must go now before the flames get worse. Close the door after me." Without waiting for a reply, he threw open the door, and in one long stride, he was across the room. Peter slammed the door after him.

Peter knew he'd heard a woman's voice. Had it called his name? It seemed impossible. Searching, he stepped to the storm-shattered living room. He glanced to the right to see an old Franklin stove with the charred remains of a fire still inside. Ahead, tree branches dangled through shattered windows.

As he looked left, huddled beside a door that led into the burning room was the crumpled shape of a person illuminated by the flickering light of the fire. Peter rushed to see if he could help. Kneeling, he reached and raised the bowed head to find a familiar face looking back at him.

With an incredulous look on her features, Jessica whispered, "You came. I called for you, and you came."

"Jessica?" Peter's thoughts were fogged, and he could get nothing else out.

In a rush, she reached for him, and throwing her arms around him, she hugged him tightly. "I wanted you from the day I met you, and I let you get away. I love you, Peter. I love you so much." She kissed his face. Laughing in the sudden euphoria of his unexpected presence, she chided, "You never called. I didn't know where you were. I missed you and love you so much."

In that moment, Peter's emotions did a somersault in his chest. He now understood Mags' words at the ferry landing. She had been telling him about Jessica. He let his arms wrap themselves around her, and he pulled her close, pressing his face into her hair. "I thought you were lost to me. I know now how much I loved you, and I will love you always. I was stupid, that's all. Nothing will ever come between us again."

Just then, a loud hissing came from the dining room, and a bit at a time the light died away. They heard John call, "I found your dog. Did you find the friend?"

Peter called out, "I found her, John." As soon as his words were out, a big, tawny dog crashed into the darkness of the living room, toppling Peter and Jessica. He stood in the middle of them, and he reached to lick Peter's face.

"I thought nothing would ever come between us again." Jessica laughed, giddy as she brushed tears of joy from her cheeks.

"I may have to make allowances for my dog. He doesn't seem to understand." In the darkness, as the rain from the windows blew across his slicker, Peter pushed Transplant's tongue from his face. He put his arm around the big animal, shaking his fur roughly, and he glanced at Jessica. "I did call, you know. I left you a message on your machine at the college."

"My machine?" Jessica froze.

Peter reached in the darkness to put his hand to her face. "It doesn't matter, as long as you're here now."

John stomped into the room, the extinguisher still in his hand. He flashed his light around, pausing for a moment at the tree branches extending through the windows, and then at the three on the floor.

"My boat's gone. I guess we're all stranded, now." He turned and walked heavily to the front porch.

Peter jumped up and took Jessica's hand. She yanked it back with a yelp. He dropped on one knee to her side. "What's wrong?"

"The window glass. I've cut my hands. I can walk, though." In the darkness, he took her elbow and helped her stand.

"Your hands," Peter began. "How badly . . ."

She whispered, "I'll be fine. Check on your friend."

Together they followed the glow of John's flashlight to the porch. As they stepped outside, Peter looked in Jessica's eyes for a moment, then he kissed her on the cheek and smiled. Even in her pain and injury, she'd shown the depth of character to care about other people before herself. He'd known she would. He'd just known it.

He stepped to where the other man was standing, looking out into the storm.

"John," he began. "Your boat?"

John pointed with the flashlight. "The dock." A flash of lightning threw illumination across the scene as if to support his words. "It's gone. It's taken my boat with it. Old Man Lee's medicine." He looked at Peter. "The box that was your ticket was in that boat."

"I'm sorry about that."

His attention was diverted by Tee walking quietly to his side. Wind-driven rain peeled off the top of the house, sweeping toward the cove, yet leaving the porch relatively calm and untouched. Then a gust hit the men, and their clothes whipped around them. John knelt to put one arm around the animal's neck. He rubbed his fur roughly as the beam from the flashlight bobbed in the darkness. "Good old Number Four. That's what I'll call you. Four. You were the last one I got marked off my list, do you know that?" Looking back out into the storm, he murmured, "Can't do anything about the boat now, can I? Does no good to worry about what I can't control."

Peter looked at Tee and smiled. He didn't know just what John meant by the new name he'd given the animal, but he was pleased to hear it. John had returned Peter both to his dog and the woman he loved. The man could call his dog anything he wanted, just so he called him home if he were ever lost again.

Jessica stepped up to peer through the door, quickly moving aside as the men slipped out of the storm back into the protection of the house. The darkness overhead was a black blanket of terror, and the lashing rain and wind made it dangerous to be exposed to the elements. However, this house was near uninhabitable. The odor of smoke was overpowering.

"What will we do?" She'd wrapped cloth around her hands, and she placed one of them on Peter's arm.

"Live." He glanced at her, grinning. "That's not what you mean, is it?"

"It works for me." She looked at the dog glued to his side. With amusement, she questioned the new name the animal just been given. "Four, Peter?"

He looked down at the dog and back to Jessica and shrugged. "I don't know, but I like it." He smiled and rubbed the animal roughly along the back of his neck.

"Not Tee, anymore?"

"Not by John's reckoning, probably." He grasped her forearms in his hand, looking directly into her eyes. "I tried to tell you something about me at one point, and you didn't understand."

"Is this about your book? I remember your hook. You wouldn't explain what it meant."

"My hook. Yeah, there's that." His fiasco that first day in her class, and his lunch date that had come from it. He'd started to tell her then, and she had misunderstood. She had thought it a conversion experience. She might be repulsed by the truth. However, he couldn't let this go. It needed to be faced head on. "I have someone else's heart inside of me. A transplant from another man." He turned his eyes to the darkness that screamed outside, afraid to see her response. "Can you love me with that?"

He cared deeply about this woman, but he had to have that reassurance for their relationship to go any further. He had distanced himself from people for too long for that very reason. He didn't want to have to do so any longer.

He wanted this to be real.

JESSICA LEANED her head against his arm, and she reached a bandaged hand to him. She pressed her hand to his chest, unable to feel anything underneath his yellow slicker. She knew now what was there, though, and this was the man to whom her Jeffrey had given back life. Her Jeffrey's heart beat in this chest. She'd read his book. She knew his story and just whose heart beat inside him. She slipped her hand inside his slicker, and inside his shirt, her fingertips found the scars on his chest. She stood silently for a time. Then, with a deep sigh, she removed her hand.

"I'd like to try. There's something about me that you don't know." She rarely spoke about this with anyone except Mags, and she felt exposed to share it with Peter. Despite her joy at being reunited with this man, they'd by no means built an unshakable granite foundation. It could still all fall apart. She drew a deep breath. "My husband was lost to me in a terrible accident, and I've missed him for two years. I still grieve for him. I know I'm not completely through with my grieving, either. It still comes back to haunt me. Can you love me with that?"

COULD HE love this woman, even with the flaws she claimed? Of course. He remembered when she'd called out Jesus as just a character in The Bible. Yet, without reservation, she'd admitted the rest of the book would fall apart without him. She had become that to him. He knew now that the rest of his life would fall apart without her.

He wanted to have the chance to love this woman.

He looked at her and smiled. It seemed two wrongs *could* make a right. Wrongs *had* happened to them, and now maybe all that was being put right. He pulled her close and said over the roar of the storm, "It seems God does have a point in everything He does." Peter knew that, now. God had brought Jessica back to him, and he had used a dog and a hurricane to do it.

"Is that another hook, cryptic until the story is finally revealed?" Jessica brushed a hand across his chest. "If so, I wouldn't mind reading the rest of the book, even if it takes all of our lives." She chuckled. "I realize how silly that sounds. I mean it, though, and I'm not sorry to have said it."

Peter's response came with no hesitation. "We'll write it together. How about that?" He laughed.

At a rustling from behind them, they turned.

"Um, I don't think we can stay the night here." John had a sheepish look on his face. "If the mush stuff is finished, I'd like to try to get to Murphy's."

Peter looked puzzled. "Murphy's?"

Jessica pulled his arm close. "There's another house. I didn't try to burn that one down, I promise. If the storm left it standing, it's still there."

No matter which house they sheltered in, or what ordeals they had to face as this storm wound itself down, Peter was satisfied for the moment knowing this woman was at his side. He could touch her, and for now that was enough. He smiled as she reached her arm around him, pulling him close. In that moment, he felt comforted, held in the arms of a women he loved.

Chapter 24

PETER OPENED his eyes to see blinding sunlight filling the room. He was momentarily disoriented. Next to him slept the most beautiful woman in the world. At their feet was a large, yellow dog.

He looked across the room. John was draped across the sofa, and he was snoring quietly. Then, Peter remembered: the fire and moving to the smaller house down the hill; picking the glass from Jessica's hands.

Before settling on the floor to sleep the previous night, Jessica had explained Mags' story behind the name of the house. Murphy's, it was called now. Originally, the house had been a simple sleeping cabin, affectionately named Amorpheus, supposedly after the god of love. Over the generations, lazy translations had become the simpler

Murphy's.

When they had taken up refuge in the undamaged shingled residence, John had built a fire in the red, porcelain stove used to keep the living room warm. Jessica's eyes had twinkled in the flickering light as she told Peter the story. "Amor," she'd laughed. "Get it? Amorpheus? I think it's the pretend god of love. Mags says it's a family joke."

She had reached and touched his face with her freshly bandaged hands, letting the tips of her fingers stroke his skin. She had laid her head on his shoulder, and she'd reached her arm across his chest, falling asleep against him.

Now, the sun poured in through the window, and it was blinding. The sudden blaring of a ship's horn jerked him from the floor. He stood to see John struggling to pull himself awake. Jessica reached to rub her eyes, momentarily surprised to see her hands wrapped in gauze.

Stepping to the window, Peter called to the other two, "Come see this. Quick!" He laughed. There in the cove was a Coast Guard ship, and there were people on board waving frantically. One of them had long, flowing hair with a camera in one hand. She was quite striking, too.

John moved to stand beside him, remarking, "The summer visitors have come to pay a call. That-them-there's a whole 'nother kind of rescue. Someone important must be somewhere close."

Jessica laughed. "They're here for us. I know it. Let's go see." She grabbed Peter's arm and led him outside as Tee crowded through the door with them.

As soon as they stepped through the door, a rousing

round of cheers erupted from the people on board the big vessel. A voice rang from the ship's loudspeaker system.

"Peter Cassel. Are you one of the three onshore?" When he raised his hands and waved, the loudspeaker responded, "Welcome aboard with your dog. Your friends are welcome, too."

"Of course, they are," he whispered, as Tee leaned against his leg, and Jessica held him tightly around the waist. Peter reached to grab John's shoulder, glancing that way, and he repeated, laughing, "Of course, you are." Then he called out, pointing for John to see. There was his boat on the far side of the cove, and it was floating, still tied to the box. The storm had simply moved it to a protected spot on the far shore. Its light bar was missing, though. It must have been ripped off when the box was torn loose.

They smiled as the tender coming ashore disgorged the striking woman with the camera first. She introduced herself as Stefanie Tremont, telling them she wanted photos of the big house and the damage they'd survived. She insisted Peter pick up the dog for a series of shots. Several snaps were taken of Peter holding Jessica in his arms.

Stefanie seemed to want lots of photographs, and it also seemed that the men on the Coast Guard ship were content to let her take as many as she wanted. They said they could use the time to deliver John to his lobster boat.

It was good they were in no hurry, because the commanding officer wanted word that his cousin Mags was safe and sound. It didn't take long for John to assure him that she was.

Before he left, John stepped up to Peter. "Thank you. If we hadn't come, this house that's stood for a century would now be gone. You did us all a good turn." He held his slicker in his hand, and he looked at the one Peter carried under his arm. "I'll take that for you. Ben'll be glad to get it back. Might have another bit of weather one day."

"You just might at that." Peter grinned as he looked around at the damage inflicted by the hurricane. A bit of weather. That was an understatement.

As John roared away in his boat to deliver his medicine, Jessica walked up to him and put her arm around his waist.

"John's a good man. Mags seems to think so, anyway. She trusts him. I can see why."

Peter gave her a squeeze and laughed. "So can I." He looked down at Tee at his side. "Don't we, Four?"

THE COPY editor studied the headline. "Heart Transplant Recipient Braves Hurricane to Rescue Lost Dog and Finds Lost Love Instead." He reached with his black Sharpie and marked out the word "instead." Over it he wrote in the word "also." He handed it back to the copy boy.

"There. That's what it should say. Finds lost love *also*."

With pounding feet, the boy took off down the hall. The editor put his feet on his desk and smiled. This edition was going to sell a million copies. At least. Maybe even a million and one.

Epilogue

THE WIND lashed Jessica's hair, wrapping it around her face. With a practiced hand, she reached to pull it out of the way, tucking it behind her ear. She turned to the man at her side, and her eyes misted at the small form he held in the carrier snuggled next to his chest. Spray from the ferry's bow turned her attention back to the scene around her.

This week was to be a celebration. Two years had brought another checkup, and Dr. Rossi had been determined to do this one on her own. The heart pump replacement had gone smoothly and efficiently, and Peter had been in and out in a day. A new method of testing the components had eliminated the risk of unexpected flaws like the one that had nearly bested Peter's endurance two short summers before.

Mags was already at the Point. Jessica smiled at that. It was Mags Pearson, now, and although Mr. Pearson was busy with his summer school classes, he had encouraged his new wife to spend time at her grandmother's newly renovated summer home.

This was also little Pete's first visit to the island. It wouldn't be his last, though. Jessica was glad his godmother Lennie was along with them. Her attentions would allow his parents time to relax on their trip to the island.

She smiled, remembering how the last time out had been a bit of an adventure for both Peter and herself. This time they hoped to be able to find some time to enjoy the scenery and the company of friends. Little Pete's Auntie Mags had promised him she would let him visit her own children as they played at Flat Rocks and Mussel Beach for years to come, until he was as old as she was, if he could imagine that.

Of course, he just cooed. He hadn't been able to understand her words, but he understood her love. That was what counted. Now they just had to wait until Mags delivered. It was in the oven, as Mr. Pearson described it. It just wasn't quite done.

Jessica entwined her arm into Peter's, and she could feel her child's small limbs pressed against hers. Sometimes at night, she would trace her hand over Peter's scars, and she would thank Jeffrey for what he had done. In his sacrifice, he had given her the opportunity to continue to live. She knew Jeffrey had loved her, and she had learned to live with her loss. Now, when she held this man next to her, she knew how lucky she was. She had felt the love of two men, and they were both at her side.

"Look!" As the ferry carried them by, she pointed to a distant house on the island. From a clothesline fluttered enormous banners of sheets. A person could be seen wrestling them off the line. "It's Mags. She's there and getting the house ready. I'm so excited to see her again."

Peter patted her arm. "I know you are. So am I." As Little Pete reached his arms up to his daddy, Peter laughed. "I guess the little guy is, too."

Jessica leaned her head against her husband's shoulder and murmured, "All things do indeed work together for the good of them that love the Lord." She glanced up to Peter's face. "I love you, Peter, both of you."

He smiled, his eyes still watching the island as it slipped by. "Romans 8:28, King James Version, paraphrased." He chuckled and put his arm around her shoulder. "I love you, too."

She didn't need to say anything else. This day was perfect, and there was no way to improve on it at all.

Did you enjoy this book?

Find more by this author at:

 THREE SKILLET

www.ThreeSkilletPublishing.com